KU-078-704

Acknowledgement

This book was mostly written during the Lockdown of 2020. Thank you to all the NHS and keyworkers in the UK and also medical professionals throughout the world for keeping us safe during this extraordinary time.

The Fifteen

MICHELLE KIDD

The Fifteen

Tell No One. Trust No One.

23-11-20

First edition

This book was professionally typeset on Reedsy.
Find out more at reedsy.com

Chapter One

Time: 4.45pm
Date: Friday 8th February 2013
Location: The Laurels Nursing Home, London

It didn't take much effort to hold him down; his frail body could offer little resistance. The rough, vice-like grip easily enclosed his brittle wrists, and caused the paper-thin skin to tear and break. Pin-prick droplets of blood spotted the bedsheets beneath.

The old man's breathing rate increased, sharply; the harsh wheeze audible from the end of his bed. Years of cigarettes and cigars had taken their toll on his now shrivelled and scarred lungs; the oxygen tank propped up by his bedside lay disconnected and out of reach.

Wide-eyed, he searched frantically for someone to help; for anyone to come to his rescue. But all he saw was those eyes. Eyes that bore into him with every twist of the wrist, peering out from an otherwise obscured and masked face.

But they were eyes that he recognised.

And eyes that he would never forget.

Silently, the flimsy bedsheet was ripped from his body, leaving his frail, skeletal figure exposed. Thin nylon pyjamas hung loosely from his emaciated frame. A leather-gloved hand appeared in front of his eyes and pressed down over his nose and mouth. He tried in vain to wrench his head from side to side, but the clamped hand was too strong.

As his oxygen levels began to plummet, he could do nothing but make feeble attempts to wriggle his arms and legs, none of which would dislodge the suffocating glove. His eyes bulged in their sockets as the strain on his already weakened lungs increased.

But just when he thought the end was coming, when his suffering would be at a merciful end, the gloved hand receded. His body sucked in painful gasps of air, the sound whistling through his cracked and broken teeth.

As the figure took a step back and moved silently towards the end of the bed, Eddie Wakefield turned his head towards the door. He willed the evening drug-round to begin early, or maybe the WRVS ladies, with their trolley laden with tea, biscuits, and other goodies that he was unable to swallow, would take a look through his window as they passed by.

But there was nothing.

And no one.

No one but the figure in the mask.

He felt the pain before he heard the man speak. Glancing away from the door, the glint of the blade in the light that seeped through the blinds caught his eye. Flicking his startled gaze down to his exposed thigh, he watched as the penknife cut through the thin fabric of his nylon pyjamas.

Blood began to trickle from his mottled skin and seep beneath into the bedclothes.

"This is for the Fifteen," the man grunted, once again taking hold of the bed-bound man's frail wrists in one gloved hand. With the other, he continued to slice into the transparent skin.

Muffled cries lodged in Eddie Wakefield's throat, but none escaped his lips. Oxygen dependent, he was weakened to the point of incapacitation; he could do nothing but watch in silent horror. Pain engulfed him with every stroke of the blade.

He sank back into his sweat-stained pillows, his mouth open and gasping for air. The pain coursed through his carbon-dioxide laden veins, fighting for space. No more than gurgles, akin to a new-born baby, escaped his mouth.

Eddie Wakefield knew the end was coming. He had been told that numerous times by countless doctors and other specialists in recent years.

But not like this.

This was not how it was meant to end.

The last thing he saw was the gloved hand back in front of his face once again. His frail body could offer no resistance, and neither did it want to. The time had come. With a mere twitch from his toes and one last lungful of air, Eddie Wakefield's life was extinguished.

* * *

Time: 6.45pm

Date: Friday 8th February 2013

Location: Isabel's Café, King's Road, London

"I can't believe how amazing it looks!" Isabel Faraday stepped back to admire the freshly painted walls of what used to be the art studio at the rear of her café. "It looks completely different."

Sacha Greene smiled. "That was the idea. Dominic did most of the painting – he's been brilliant."

Sacha's son, Dominic, hovered in the archway between the café and the old art studio, his cheeks tinged with a pale pink. "I used thirty-five litres of paint and four paint brushes," he announced, shyly, reading from his notebook.

Isabel beamed and pulled the awkward twenty-two-year-old towards her, enveloping him into a hug. "It's wonderful, Dom. Really wonderful."

The walls were covered in a soft creamy-caramel, with one feature wall in a darker, rich-chocolate tone. Gone were the many canvas paintings and other artwork that had adorned the walls. Instead, recessed lights gave a warming hue, bringing to life the only painting left hanging. The one remaining canvas had pride of place in the centre of the feature wall above an antique pine sideboard.

Isabel's tree.

Isabel gazed at the treasured canvas, painted by her mother in the summer of 1985 when Isabel was five years old. She stepped forwards and ran a finger over the name "*E. Faraday*" which was nestled in the corner. She felt a shiver wash over her as she did so; as if touching her mother's name was a direct link to her soul.

Sacha saw the haunted expression fluttering over her best friend's face, and stepped forwards to guide Isabel away from the painting. They stepped backwards onto a plush oatmeal rug that took up most of the floor space, a rustic pine table at its centre. An elegant vase with an abundance of dried flower stems and wooden foliage completed the look.

Tears began to prick at the corners of Isabel's eyes.

"It's your own space now, to do with as you wish." Sacha squeezed Isabel's arm and gave her a warm smile. Stepping back into the art studio, after what had happened only six months before, was always going to be a daunting prospect. Sacha had been worried about Isabel returning to the café and that was the main reason, while Isabel was away overseas, she and Dominic had taken it upon themselves to renovate the art studio. Gone were the paintings that had hung from every available space on the walls; gone also were the artists' easels, paintbrushes and chalks. And gone, hopefully, were the memories attached to them. Although Sacha doubted a mere lick of paint and a few soft furnishings would be able to rid Isabel of the horror that had unfolded last summer.

But it was a start.

"And Livi has already made herself at home on the new leather armchair." Sacha nodded towards the leather-backed chair that nestled in the corner by the patio doors. Isabel gave a chuckle as she saw the cat-hair strewn soft cushion, with its unmistakable Livi-shaped indentation in the centre.

"I bet she has," smiled Isabel. "I can't wait to see her."

As if on cue, the door leading to the stairs and Isabel's flat above was nudged open by a wet, pink nose, and Isabel's tabby cat padded into the room. Scooping Livi up into her arms, Isabel buried her face into the soft fur.

"While you two get re-acquainted, I'll take the bags up." While Isabel and Sacha has been looking around the newly furnished studio, Mac had emerged from the café, dragging Isabel's wheeled suitcase behind him. "Give us a hand, Dom?" Stuart MacIntosh, whom everyone called Mac except his brother, nodded at the extra flight bag and duty free carrier bag by his feet. The Italian sun had lightened his hair and given his unshaven face a bronze-tinged glow.

Sacha smiled at him, gratefully. Dominic hastily closed his notebook and slipped it into the back pocket of his jeans. Nodding enthusiastically, he grabbed hold of the two bags and followed Mac up the stairs towards the flat.

"So, how have you been?" asked Sacha, as soon as Dominic and Mac had disappeared out of sight. "And I mean *really*." She raised her eyebrows, giving Isabel a knowing look, and led her friend back out into the main café. Livi jumped down from Isabel's arms and went to curl up on her new favourite armchair.

The sign on the front door had already been flipped over to CLOSED, and it didn't take Sacha long to whip up two mugs of strong coffee. Isabel gratefully took hold of a mug and settled herself into one of the soft leather sofas that filled the café. She looked around, familiarity flooding her senses. Everything looked exactly the same as the day she had left. Bookcases groaned under the weight of the many paperbacks stacked on their shelves; newspapers and magazines were arranged in neat rows on the racking. A mis-match of comfortably worn sofas and chairs were arranged haphazardly around the café floor.

Taking a sip of the hot coffee, and wincing slightly as it scalded her lips, she gave a small shrug. "I've been fine. We've both been fine."

Sacha slipped herself into one of the armchairs opposite Isabel. "*Really?*"

Isabel gave another shrug and forced out a weak smile. "Most of the time," she admitted, softly. "The last couple of weeks haven't been great – knowing that the case is coming up for trial soon. And that we have to give evidence."

Sacha thought she could detect a slight shudder as Isabel spoke. "I can imagine," she replied, giving Isabel what she hoped was a reassuring smile. "You did the right thing. Getting away. Just the two of you. And staying away until you really needed to come back."

Isabel took another comforting sip of her drink. "I'm so grateful to you and Dominic for holding the fort here. I hadn't intended to be away for this long."

Sacha shook her head. "It's been no problem, really. And to be honest – it's done Dominic the world of good. He's loved the routine of coming in every day and really took to renovating your studio space. He has it all documented for you in his notebook, day by day." Sacha gave a chuckle as she recalled how her son would document his movements each day, including how many coats of paint each wall took, how much paint he used, and probably even how many brush strokes were involved.

"He's a good lad," nodded Isabel. "I'll sit down with him and go through it all when I'm a little less tired."

Isabel loved Dominic as if he were her own family. And, in a way, she felt that he and Sacha were just that; family. Having dropped in for a milkshake not long after Isabel had opened her café, Dominic was hired as an extra pair of hands. And with his mother, Sacha, being an expert home-baker, Isabel's café soon had a plentiful supply of cakes, biscuits and pastries to tempt the passing public.

On the autistic spectrum, Dominic lived his life by way of routine, and was never seen without his trusty notebook where he noted down important aspects of his day-to-day life. Dates and times, names and addresses. Anything and everything was duly noted. And the fact that he did this unquestionably saved Isabel's life last summer.

Something she would never forget.

So both Sacha and Dominic had earned a very special place in her life - and in her heart.

"Italy was wonderful." Isabel sipped again at her coffee, briefly closing her eyes as she cast her mind back to happier times. "I could have stayed there forever. Even Mac enjoyed himself and you know how set in his ways he can be."

Sacha laughed as she placed her half-finished coffee mug on the table between them. "I thought you were going to try and get to America? How come you ended up in Italy?"

"It was easier - there were too many hurdles in getting a visa for the USA." Isabel smiled and drained her mug. "So I thought about Italy – I loved it the last time I was there. It inspired me to open the café."

"And how are things between you?" A small glint entered Sacha's eyes. "Still love's young dream?"

"Hardly!" laughed Isabel, wiping coffee froth from her lips. "Neither of us are exactly young anymore!" She paused, and let a smile twitch at the corner of her mouth. "We've spent the last few days at his flat in Islington, after we landed on Tuesday. We just needed some space to adjust to being back, without having to see anyone. It's not long until the trial, so..." Isabel let her words peter out.

"Well I'm glad, for the both of you." Sacha collected up the coffee mugs and headed towards the kitchen. "You both staying here tonight?"

Isabel shook her head. "No, just me. Mac has to work early in the morning. And I think he's going to head over to Jack's a little later, just to say hello. How is Jack, by the way?"

Sacha paused by the door to the kitchen. "He's good, I think. You know he's been away too?"

Isabel nodded. "Yes, Mac mentioned it. Scotland I heard."

With Sacha finishing up in the kitchen, Isabel pushed herself up from the sofa and went upstairs to her flat. Livi, having leapt off her favourite armchair, followed in her wake.

* * *

Time: 6.50pm
Date: Friday 8th February 2013
Location: Metropolitan Police HQ, London

DI Jack MacIntosh slipped into the chair opposite Chief Superintendent Dougie King, shaking his head at the proffered whisky tumbler.

"I'm trying to stay off the hard stuff, Sir. For the moment."

Chief Superintendent King nodded, placing the two glasses back inside his desk drawer. "Probably wise, Jack. Probably wise. I'll make some coffee instead."

Jack was about to decline the offer of a hot drink too, but the Chief Superintendent had already pushed his more than ample frame out of his chair and turned to the sideboard behind that housed the expensive looking coffee maker. Whilst two mugs were being poured full of piping hot, caffeine laced, Arabica bean coffee, Jack took the opportunity to glance around the room.

Six months.

Six months since Jack had last been inside these four walls. Six months since he had last set foot inside the station. He remembered it well - the night of the Opening Ceremony of the London Olympic Games.

Jack's gaze flickered to the window, noting the flurry of tiny snowflakes being whipped up and around in the freshening breeze – in stark contrast to that July evening when the longest heatwave to hit the UK was only just coming to an end.

Chief Superintendent King sat back down, passing a mug of fresh coffee towards Jack. "So, how are you settling back in? First day?"

The question Jack knew had been coming hung in the air while they both took sips from their too-hot drinks. His six-month sabbatical, to finally try and extinguish the demons that plagued both his sleeping and waking hours, had gone well. As far as he knew.

Dr Evelyn Riches, Consultant Psychotherapist, had been pleased with his progress; she had said as much. But Jack knew that completing a ten week course of hypnotherapy was not a cure – it was just the start.

Had he faced his demons? Had he beaten them? Only time would tell was Dr Riches' non-committal answer. He certainly hadn't had as many vivid dreams as before; his sleep no longer plagued by nightmares each and every time he closed his eyes. No more visions of his mother's dead body swinging from a light fitting after taking her own life. For now, at least, such memories were gone – or maybe, more accurately, they were hidden in remote parts of his subconscious; safely locked away, only occasionally rising to the surface to haunt him.

After the ten-week course had finished, Jack took extra time off and checked into a remote bed and breakfast in the Scottish countryside – filling his days walking alongside misty lochs and scrambling up steep hillsides, tripping over rough clumps of heather as he went.

December was an odd time of year to go hill-walking in Scotland, as the raised eyebrows of the landlord of the Tannochside Bed and Breakfast had confirmed. As soon as the ill-prepared Englishman crossed the threshold of the stone-walled former farmhouse, complete with just the one bag and dressed in jeans and a thin jumper, Willie McArthur suppressed a smile and dutifully checked him into a twin room for one.

Jack had lasted a day before enquiring where the nearest outdoor clothing shop could be found. Willie McArthur's eyes twinkled when he saw Jack step back into the reception area later that afternoon, kitted out in a thick, waterproof jacket, soft fleece sweatshirt, thermal undershirt, hat, gloves and sturdy walking boots. Jack had noted the appreciative nod from his host as he walked past the front desk in the direction of his room, reassuring him that he was now equipped for anything.

"Jack?" prompted the Chief Superintendent, his enquiring gaze peering above the rim of his coffee mug. "Your first day?"

Jack tore his thoughts away from the Scottish lochs and hillsides and sipped at his cooling coffee.

"All good, Sir. It's like I've never been away."

"Hmmm." Chief Superintendent King nodded, slowly, not taking his eyes off Jack. "Well, you take things slowly. We're pleased to have you back – but don't go overdoing things."

Jack took a larger gulp of coffee, feeling the caffeine enter his bloodstream. "I'm fine, Sir. Really."

"I know you are, Jack. Just offering some friendly advice." Chief Superintendent King placed his own coffee mug back down onto his desk and rummaged amongst the paperwork in front of him. "Back to business then. How are things progressing in the Holloway case – are we all ready for trial?"

Jack's last case before he went on his six-month sabbatical had involved Peter Holloway, a serial killer now facing six counts of murder and one of kidnapping and false imprisonment. Jack felt a shiver course through his veins, despite the warming coffee in his hands.

"We're good to go, Sir. All witnesses are fully prepared." Although Holloway had admitted the killings, even putting forward a signed confession via his solicitor, he had pleaded not guilty at his plea hearing on the grounds of insanity. It was not a defence that the Crown Prosecution Service were prepared to accept, looking for nothing short of a murder conviction. So, to trial they must go.

Which meant putting witnesses on the stand, and making them re-live the horrors of the previous summer; horrors that they had been working hard to put to rest.

"Good, good," replied Chief Superintendent King. "Well, keep me in the loop. We need to make sure this one sticks and there are no surprises once we get to court. What are the chances of a not guilty verdict?"

"No chance in my opinion, but I'm no lawyer" replied Jack, sipping more of his coffee. "He knew what he was doing – but he's clever."

"And your brother?" Chief Superintendent King raised his eyebrows, questioningly. "How is he doing after his chat with DS Carmichael? I heard that St Bartholomew's had cropped up in his Operation Evergreen investigation?"

Jack paused before replying. How was Stuart? If he were being honest, Jack didn't really know. During his time in Italy with Isabel, and Jack's hibernation in Scotland, they hadn't really spoken. A couple of brief text messages here and there, that was it. Even Jack's birthday had gone by unacknowledged. Jack knew that DS Carmichael had gone out to Italy to ask him about his time at the former foster home, but beyond that? The last message Jack had received from his brother told him that everything was fine.

That word.

Fine.

Everyone said it.

"He's fine, Sir." Jack gave a small shrug. "I'm catching up with him later this evening."

Chief Superintendent King gave a slow nod. "Well, you keep an eye on him. In fact, keep an eye on each other. With the Holloway trial coming up and DS Carmichael's Operation Evergreen – it could be a tricky time." After a slight pause, the Chief Superintendent continued. "And yourself? How are you...after everything?"

Jack found himself shifting awkwardly in his seat. As much as he liked and respected the Chief Superintendent, Jack wasn't a touchy-feely type of officer, and knew the man sitting opposite him was even less so. He gave another nod in response.

"I'm fine, too, Sir."

Chief Superintendent Dougie King cleared his throat and broke the awkwardness by rising from his chair. He reached across his desk with an outstretched hand.

"Then it's good to have you back, Jack."

* * *

Time: 7.50pm

Date: Friday 8ᵗʰ February 2013

Location: The Laurels Nursing Home, London

Natalie Evans silently cursed as the front wheels of the drug trolley caught, once again, on the edge of the thick, rubber mat. Brought in to protect the carpet from the muddy, wet footprints caused by the February slush outside, it was a constant hindrance to the nursing staff when performing their drug rounds.

Giving the trolley an additional heave, it rattled over the edge of the mat and Natalie continued her journey along the east wing. She glanced down at the fob watch attached to the breast of her starched uniform – she was running behind schedule and would be lucky to be finished in time to catch her bus home. Anticipating a long wait at a cold bus stop, Natalie tutted under her breath and quickened her step.

Eunice had been her downfall. She had kept Natalie chatting for twenty-five minutes while dispensing her evening Parkinson's medication. But Natalie didn't begrudge spending a little time with Eunice – she was a sweet old lady, pleasantly confused most of the time, with short interludes of surprising lucidity. She was having one of these rare moments of clarity when Natalie had tapped on her door and arrived with the drug trolley – so Natalie had taken advantage of the warmth of the room and perched herself on the end of the bed.

Eunice took a hold of Natalie's hand, and proceeded to tell her all about her life as a teenager during the Second World War. How she used to have to take shelter in a coal shed at the bottom of next door's garden in Tottenham when the air raid sirens blared. And how she had met her childhood sweetheart, Tommy, during one such trip to the makeshift shelter.

Natalie had heard the story many times before, but continued to lean up against the slightly-built eighty-nine-year-old and squeeze her fragile hand whilst listening to her re-live her youth. With only sporadic visits from what was left of her family, Natalie often felt sorry for Eunice and liked to try and spare her a few extra minutes on her rounds – even if it did mean she would miss her bus home.

Eunice had been especially lucid tonight, so it had put her a good half an hour behind schedule, with six residents still to see with their evening medication before she could clock off. Natalie gave the drugs trolley another shove and turned the corner towards rooms E15-E19, consulting her medication planner as she did so.

Eddie Wakefield was due his usual steroids and also antibiotics for the current chest infection that was exacerbating his known chronic obstructive pulmonary disease. With the disease now in its end stages, Eddie's lungs were less receptive to treatment, but they were doing all they could to make his final months as comfortable as possible. The recent cold weather had sparked a wave of chest infections to sweep through the nursing home, meaning that already poor and frail residents were quickly struck down and incapacitated. The resident GP could barely keep up with the demand for fresh prescriptions.

Natalie stopped outside room E16 and paused. The first thing that struck her as odd was that the blinds were drawn over the window next to the door. It was a policy in the home that blinds were always left open, so that passing staff could easily see into a resident's room and ensure that all was well. The only time the blinds would be closed would be during the end of life days – when privacy for the resident and their family was a priority.

The second thing that struck her as odd was that the small whiteboard attached to the door already indicated that the evening drug round had been completed and drugs dispensed. A small tick sat in the box next to 'Friday'.

Natalie hesitated outside the closed door, an unnerving feeling creeping into the pit of her stomach. All pleasant thoughts of the last twenty-five minutes spent with Eunice, smiling at her stories and sharing mint humbugs from her handbag, instantly evaporated.

Biting her bottom lip, nervously, she reached forwards and twisted the handle, pushing the door open with her trolley.

"Mr Wakefield," she called out, entering the darkened room with a rattle from the trolley's wheels. She squinted through the dimness of the room, noting that the blinds were also drawn across the window opposite, and the bedside lamp had been switched off. "Mr Wakefield? Eddie?" she repeated, turning her gaze to the shrouded mound on the bed. "Is everything all right?"

* * *

Chapter Two

Time: 9.25pm
   Date: Friday 8th February 2013
   Location: The Laurels Nursing Home, London

The call had come in just after 8.30pm – just as Jack was about to crack open the first two bottles of San Miguel. But instead of a quiet night in catching up on his brother's adventures overseas, it had taken him less than a minute to bid Stuart MacIntosh a hasty farewell and leave him with an Indian takeaway and the password to his Netflix account.

Although it looked as if the time away in Italy had done his brother some good – his usually pasty complexion now tinged with a sun-kissed hue, and his hair lightened at the temples - Jack could see the faint shadows beneath his brother's eyes. And although he greeted Jack with a back slap and a wide smile, Jack saw the smile didn't quite reach those eyes.

Unable to call him by the name-tag he had been given in his youth by the street gangs that had lured him onto a dark path towards youth detention and a criminal record, Stuart MacIntosh would always be Stu in Jack's eyes. Although he would quietly admit to himself that the name Mac did somewhat suit him. Following the death of their mother, both had been swallowed up by the foster care system and spat out the other end. Jack had fared well – his brother not so.

But the brotherly catch up would have to wait. On his first day back at work, and having signed himself up for the on-call rota that evening, Jack

14

knew he wasn't exactly taking it as easy as Chief Superintendent King had asked.

I've missed this, Jack thought to himself as he sat for a moment outside the front entrance to The Laurels Nursing Home. The adrenaline rush of receiving that first call; the inexplicable buzz of never quite knowing where you were going and what you were going to find. Although he had enjoyed his recent escape to the Scottish countryside, with his days filled with nothing more than heather, whisky and his own solitude, it was here that he needed to be. Here, sat in a frozen car with an empty stomach and the prospect of a long night ahead with little sleep.

Just how Jack liked it.

He cranked open the door to his Mondeo, the chilled air having already frozen it solid on the journey over. With his breath billowing out in front of him, Jack knew that he would be scraping the ice off the windscreen for the return journey. Snow was already in the air; tiny flakes being whipped around on an unseen breeze.

The Laurels Nursing Home stretched up into the leaden night sky before him. It was usually a quiet place during the night, with residents tucked up safely in their beds, and nursing staff quietly patrolling the corridors in soft-soled shoes, with just the hushed rustle from their starched uniforms.

But tonight wasn't an ordinary night.

Jack could tell that by the number of vehicles parked haphazardly near the entrance, and in particular a well-maintained Volvo that he knew well. He headed across to the front steps, nodding at the police constable on guard duty and flashed his ID while he signed the attendance log.

With a protective suit and overshoes handed to him as he entered, Jack headed towards the main huddle of bodies and commotion coming from one of the corridors. As he approached, the bodies parted to reveal the blue and white crime scene tape stretched across the corridor leading to room E16.

Slipping on the white protective suit and overshoes, Jack ducked underneath the tape and went in search of the owner of the Volvo.

* * *

Time: 9.30pm
  Date: Friday 8th February 2013
  Location: Metropolitan Police HQ, London

DS Robert Carmichael rubbed his eyes, feeling their grittiness beneath his touch. He needed to finish up and go home; the beginning of a headache was throbbing painfully at his temples. He sighed at the volume of paperwork strewn across the top of his desk, and reached for the remnants of the energy drink he had started not long before. The promised energy contained within had failed to materialise. Now he just felt wide awake and tired at the same time.

Reaching for a fresh buff-coloured folder, he began inserting the freshly typed set of witness statements that were decorating his desk. As he scooped them up and slotted them away, his gaze fell on the final statement hot off the printer – and the one most recently taken. He felt his eyes drawn to the name printed at the top.

Stuart MacIntosh.

DS Carmichael had sensed an initial reluctance of Jack's brother to engage in any form of conversation about his life at St Bartholomew's Home for Boys, which was understandable. Who would want to resurrect the painful memories they had so carefully packaged up and locked away?

Hidden away, out of sight.

Until DS Robert Carmichael came calling.

Operation Evergreen was starting to gather pace at an alarming speed. DS Carmichael had been allocated a whole room to himself, housing wall to wall filing cabinets that were quickly filling up. A printer in the corner on a makeshift table constantly churned out evidence and supporting documentation in a seemingly never-ending cycle.

A paperless investigation this was not.

Primarily investigating reports of physical and sexual abuse of children in local authority care, DS Carmichael's investigations were going hand in hand with the much wider, and more publicised, Operation Yewtree.

Exploding onto the scene late last year, Operation Yewtree was continuing to saturate the media with almost daily reports of investigations and arrests involving high profile celebrities from the entertainment and broadcasting industry. It had started with Jimmy Savile, but where it would end was anybody's guess. The public's insatiable desire for information meant the press were knocking at his door on a daily basis.

Originally concentrating on allegations arising from ten local authority children's homes across the south-east, it was when his investigations led to St Bartholomew's Home for Boys near Christchurch that DS Carmichael felt a chill enter his bloodstream.

St Bartholomew's Home for Boys.

The children's home which Jack's brother had spent the best part of five years in, from the tender age of eight until his eventual diversion into crime. The final destination of an approved school and youth detention waiting for him not much further down the line.

DS Carmichael gathered Stuart MacIntosh's witness statement together and slotted it into the new buff folder. He couldn't face working any more tonight. His head was thumping and his stomach was in knots.

St Bartholomew's Home for Boys had been a bad place, that was becoming increasingly clear.

And DS Carmichael was not relishing having to disclose to Jack just how bad it had been.

* * *

Time: 9.45pm
Date: Friday 8th February 2013
Location: The Laurels Nursing Home, London

The police pathologist towered a clear head and shoulders above everyone else, so it was easy for Jack to spot him in the sea of bodies now filling the area outside room E16. Shuffling along the carpet in his plastic overshoes, he caught the eye of Dr Phillip Matthews as he exited the room.

"Evening, Jack," greeted Dr Matthews. He retreated to a safe distance, stepping out of his protective overshoes to reveal a highly polished set of brogues. "Not a great night to be out and about."

"Doc." Jack returned the greeting and gestured over his shoulder towards the commotion. "So, what can you tell me?"

Room E16 was still buzzing with the white-suited bodies of the crime scene investigators, several huddled around the bed and one snapping away with an impressive-looking, and no doubt expensive, camera.

Dr Matthews straightened his tall, wiry frame and took a glance back towards the resident's room he had just vacated. He shook his head, briefly, as a cloud crossed his vision not unlike the swirling snow flurries accumulating outside.

"It's not good, Jack. It's not good at all." The aged pathologist paused before taking a step away from the rest of the bustling bodies. "Walk with me."

Jack dutifully followed Dr Matthews along the corridor, back the way he had come, leaving the sound of clicking cameras and low, murmuring voices behind them. As they entered the foyer by the front reception desk, the pathologist came to a halt. He looked troubled.

"Male. Aged eighty-one years, so I am told. Goes by the name of Edward Wakefield. Known as Eddie. Approaching end of life care with end stage COPD. On continuous oxygen. Bed-bound." Dr Matthews paused, collecting his thoughts. "Cause of death undetermined at present, possible signs of asphyxiation. I'll know more after the post mortem."

"Asphyxiation?" Jack raised his eyebrows. "Suffocated?"

Dr Matthews shrugged and nodded at the same time. "Very possibly. I can't commit at the moment. I've only had a very rudimentary look at the body so far. He wasn't in the best of health and death wouldn't have been unexpected. To be honest, by the looks of him, he's done well to last this long."

"But definitely not natural causes?"

Dr Matthews gave Jack a rueful smile. "You know the procedure, Jack. Let me get him back to the mortuary and I'll update you as soon as I can." With another nod of the head, he turned to retreat back out into the wildness of the winter's night.

"But what about the blood?"

Dr Matthews stopped in his tracks and hesitated before turning himself around.

"I saw blood...on the bedsheets," continued Jack. "I'm sure I did." Jack cast his mind back to only moments earlier, standing outside room E16. When one of the crime scene officers had moved away from the bedside, Jack was sure he caught a glimpse of the rumpled bedsheets.

And the unmistakable stain of blood. Fresh blood.

Dr Matthews' gaze faltered, and for a moment he avoided catching Jack's eye. But he knew he wouldn't be able to fool the experienced Detective Inspector for long – they knew each other too well for that.

"I'll fast track the post-mortem, Jack. Let you have my preliminary findings as soon as I can." Again, the pathologist took a step towards the door, slipping on his overcoat that he had discarded on his way in. "You're more than welcome to attend – but it'll be an early one. I have a full list tomorrow, but I can squeeze this one in first."

Jack waved the offer away. "But the blood, Doc," he persisted. "I did see blood, didn't I?"

This time Dr Matthews didn't break his stride and carried on out of the front door. "In my report Jack. It'll be in my report." With a wave of the hand, the pathologist let the doors swing shut behind him and he was gone.

* * *

Time: 9.55pm

Date: Friday 8th February 2013
Location: Farnborough Street, London

He pulled the woollen hat further down onto his head, covering his ears, and took a step backwards into the shadows. The Farnborough Street bus stop was conveniently located directly across from the entrance to The Laurels Nursing Home, so he could watch the comings and goings unfold under the guise of waiting for a bus. As far as he could tell, no one seemed interested in him, or had even noticed his presence. In particular, no one noticed that despite several number seven buses stopping in front of him, he had failed to board any of them.

He had made the spur of the moment decision to return to the scene of his crime, and had already found the police cordon set up upon arriving at the bus stop. A small flicker of excitement teased his senses.

He leant against the back of the bus stop, hands thrust deep inside his pockets. One hand closed comfortingly around the pen knife, the other hand around his ski-mask. Why he still had these items in his pocket, he wasn't quite sure, but their presence gave him a thrill.

Someone was leaving the nursing home, so he dipped his head down as if consulting the bus timetable at the side of the Perspex bus stop. A tall man jogged down the front steps and headed towards a Volvo parked in the car park. Glancing out of the corner of his eye, he noted the bald-headed, wiry-framed man pulling out his mobile phone as he unlocked his car and slipped inside.

Just as the Volvo swung out of the entrance, another vehicle crossed its path, approaching from the street outside – a black transit van with 'Private Ambulance' printed discreetly on the side.

Eddie Wakefield's final transport had arrived.

With the beginnings of a satisfied smile crossing his chilled lips, he decided he had seen enough and pushed himself away from the bus stop and headed for home.

* * *

Time: 9.55pm
   Date: Friday 8th February 2013
   Location: The Laurels Nursing Home, London

Jack returned to room E16 to observe the flurry of activity that still continued
under the watchful command of the crime scene manager, but there was
little that he would be able to achieve tonight. He would hang on for a short
while to get the general feel of the scene, and gather together the bodies he
would need to start the interviews with staff members, but he would only
be getting in everyone's way the longer he stayed. He stepped back into the
room to take another brief look, noting that photographs were still being
taken from every possible angle.

His gaze rested on the lifeless body still in situ on the hospital bed. A
frail-looking old man, no more than a bag of bones judging by the way his
pyjamas were hanging off his frame. He had sunken cheeks and waxy skin
that stretched thinly across his face. Jack noticed the drip stand and oxygen
tanks lined up next to the bed, and although there was a window to the
side, Jack felt saddened that this was what the final weeks, months and
sometimes years of someone's life looked like. Bedridden with nothing but
four magnolia coloured walls to stare at.

Shoot me, thought Jack. Shoot me before I need something like this.

He stepped back outside into the corridor and glanced at his watch. Ten
o'clock. Pulling out his phone, he dialled his brother's number. The
phone rang emptily without connecting and eventually the voicemail service
clicked in. Jack ended the call and instead dialled his own home phone
number. Again, the phone rang out without being answered. He glanced
down at his watch one more time and frowned. Maybe Stu had sunk the beer
and crashed out on the sofa.

Instead, he tapped out a brief message to both DS Cooper and DC Cassidy
to advise them they had a new case and to be ready for a briefing at eight

o'clock tomorrow morning. Satisfied there was nothing productive that he could achieve by staying, Jack nodded at the crime scene manager and disappeared back along the corridor. Stepping out of his protective clothing, he made his way to the entrance and pushed open the doors, striding out into the chill air outside. The cold wind almost took his breath away, and small flakes of snow brushed his cheeks.

His heart was thumping.

The thrill of a new case rippled through his veins.

Detective Inspector Jack MacIntosh was back.

* * *

Chapter Three

Time: 5.00am
   Date: Saturday 9th February 2013
   Location: Westminster Mortuary, London

Dr Phillip Matthews adjusted the overhead light while one of the assistant mortuary technicians wheeled away the steel gurney that had transported Edward Wakefield's chilled body into the post mortem room. Nodding his thanks, he waited for the same technician to return and drag a second trolley to his side, this one housing an array of sterilised equipment and utensils.

It wasn't unusual for the pathologist to start work this early, even on a weekend. He had been known to be performing post mortems at one or two o'clock in the morning, such was his desire to untangle the secrets of the dead. And this one particularly troubled him.

Switching on the overhead microphone and setting it to 'record', Dr Matthews reached out with a latex-gloved hand and selected a glistening scalpel.

"Let's begin."

The harsh overhead lights bounced off Eddie Wakefield's already ice-white skin. Years of self-neglect with tobacco and alcohol had taken their toll and reduced the once heavily-built northerner to almost skeletal proportions. His original five foot eleven-inch frame seemed to shrink in front of Dr Matthew's eyes.

Lying there on the cold metal table, Eddie Wakefield's ribs and hips stood

23

proudly from beneath paper-thin waxy skin. Sunken cheeks and prominent eye sockets completed his emaciated look. Having been bed-ridden for much of the preceding eight years, any musculature that had been attached to his bones had long since melted away.

Dr Matthews paused before making his first incision. He half knew what to expect from the body of a self-confessed former tobacco addict, but the other half of him remained open to persuasion. Whatever had brought Eddie Wakefield to his mortuary slab on this cold, dreary February morning, it was not entirely due to his smoking habit.

His brief look at the recently deceased's body last night at The Laurels Nursing Home had told him that much.

Eddie Wakefield he was sure, before even raising a scalpel to his skin, had been murdered.

* * *

Time: 6.45am
   Date: Saturday 9th February 2013
   Location: Kettle's Yard Mews, London

Jack had had a restless night's sleep, even by his own standards. The buzz of the new investigation had coursed non-stop around his head, cluttering his mind, and forcing sleep into the shadows. As he stepped out of the shower, he rubbed the water and soap from his eyes and wrapped a towel around his waist.

When he had arrived home late last night, Stuart was nowhere to be seen. Jack had half expected to find him sprawled across the sofa, head back and mouth open, snoring contentedly. But, instead, the flat had been empty. The Indian takeaway lay uneaten exactly where Jack had left it, and the beer bottles were still chilling in the fridge.

No doubt the lure of a night with Isabel had proved more enticing than an evening alone in Jack's bachelor flat. Netflix or no Netflix.

Jack dressed hurriedly, having forgotten to set the timer for the heating to come on. He pushed the thought of his disappearing brother from his mind, and swigged down some orange juice straight from the carton. He didn't have time for breakfast – and didn't have anything in, apart from last night's takeaway. The thought of re-heated chicken biryani made his nose wrinkle.

Grabbing his keys, he resolved to pick up something from the canteen – or with any luck, DS Cooper might have brought in a couple of his favourite greasy bacon sandwiches.

With his stomach grumbling, he headed out into the crisp morning air. The sun had not yet risen, so the hard frost of the night before still lingered. He unlocked the Mondeo and turned his attention to the task of unravelling the mystery of Edward Wakefield's death.

* * *

Time: 7.30am
Date: Saturday 9th February 2013
Location: Westminster Mortuary, London

The lungs had given up no great surprises.

Dr Matthews took the steel bowl that housed both the left and right lung, and watched while the assistant mortuary technician recorded their weight in the post mortem log. Both lungs were a charcoal-black, with a wizened appearance. Cutting into the tissue, even with a sharp scalpel, had been like cutting into toughened rubber. The effects of tar and tobacco had done their worst, and Eddie Wakefield's lungs were barely functioning at all at the time of his death.

Initial examinations had also thrown up some well-established tumour-like masses in both upper lobes, which Dr Matthews had removed for histological analysis by the pathology lab. His own expert eye, however, together with the emaciated and cachexic appearance of the rest of the body, had already diagnosed advanced lung cancer.

Dr Matthews' initial suspicion as to asphyxiation being the cause of death was supported by signs of contusions and abrasions around the nose and mouth – consistent with a degree of force being applied and held over the face. Due to the nature and colouration of the bruising, Dr Matthews estimated that death occurred very soon after the initial smothering. Petechial haemorrhaging in both eyes and signs of cyanosis also pointed in the direction of asphyxiation.

Picking up Eddie Wakefield's scrawny arms, Dr Matthews leant in to take close-up photographs of several areas of contusions and broken skin around both wrists, suggestive of some kind of forced restraint. Had the man been held down by his wrists while being suffocated? It was a theory at least.

Dr Matthews knew that such speculation was beyond his remit, but knew that such a question would be the first escaping the lips of Detective Inspector Jack MacIntosh as soon as he read the post mortem report. Putting on his detective's hat, Dr Matthews would have to agree that restraint looked likely. However, in a bed-bound patient, and one with such limited physical reserves as Eddie Wakefield, only minimal restraint was probably required.

Although no one was seen entering or leaving Eddie Wakefield's room that evening, Dr Matthews could be sure, beyond any reasonable doubt asked by judge and jury, that *someone* had been there at the time of Eddie Wakefield's demise. He had not died of the final effects of his end stage COPD; his lungs had not given up and taken their last breath due to the build-up of tar or other toxins, or even from the cancerous growths rapidly multiplying within their blackened tissue.

No.

Someone else had been there.

Dr Matthews knew that for certain.

Because whoever had been there at the end, had also left their mark.

* * *

Time: 7.55am
   Date: Saturday 9th February 2013
   Location: Metropolitan Police HQ, London

Jack pulled the blinds closed at the one and only window in the investigation room, shutting out the bleakness of the freezing February air outside. The sun had now struggled into the sky, banishing the darkness of the night, but the heavy grey clouds were already threatening to disgorge a blanket of snow before the day was through.

He checked the lone radiator with a brief touch of his hand. Tepid at best. Bending down, he twisted the thermostat up to its highest setting, feeling its resistance as he did so. The surrounding pipes clunked and gurgled in protest.

DS Chris Cooper had already positioned two computers at the far end of the room, close to the interactive whiteboard. The paperwork, such as it was, into the as-yet unexplained death of nursing home resident Edward Wakefield, was spread out on the table in front of them.

DC Amanda Cassidy had managed to commandeer a hot water urn from the canteen upstairs, which was a plus. Quite how she had done so was being kept a closely guarded secret, but DS Cooper suspected she had used her pixie-like, fresh-faced charms on the unsuspecting new food services manager upstairs. Trying hard to suppress a smile, she hummed quietly to herself as she unpacked a packet of tea bags and jar of instant coffee from her shoulder bag.

Jack took a seat next to the whiteboard, not due to any close affinity to the newly acquired technology, but more to do with the inevitable deterioration in eyesight as you passed the magical forty years of age.

"How much has been uploaded since last night?" he enquired, squinting up at the screen.

"Not much, boss," replied DS Cooper, taking the seat opposite. "A brief,

27

initial report from the crime scene manager, but we should find more added as the day goes on. I think they're finishing up at the scene later this morning."

Jack nodded. "I've assembled a small team to interview the nursing home staff. They should be there now and hopefully be concluded before too long. So, what background, if any, have we managed to find out about the victim?" He reached out and accepted the mug of hot coffee from DC Cassidy, watching the steam spiral as it hit the still-chilly air of the investigation room. DS Cooper had, indeed, picked up some breakfast on his way in – not the greasy bacon sandwich that Jack had been hoping for, but warm croissants, which were a decent substitute. Jack bit into one and let the buttery, flaky pastry melt in his mouth.

"The victim has been named as Edward Wakefield," confirmed DC Cassidy, returning to the other side of the room and leaning up against the still-tepid radiator. Next to her was a pin board on wheels. As she brandished a drawing pin to stab the photograph of the elderly nursing home resident onto the board, she noticed the faint flicker of a smile tease the corners of Jack's mouth. A faint nod of his head confirmed his appreciation and approval of the use of the pin-board over the flickering whiteboard to their side. "Photos and details of the victim have yet to be uploaded onto the system," she explained, with a grin. "Glitches to the system overnight or something." Both she and DS Cooper knew how much Jack detested technology, and so she took great delight in pinning several more sheets of paper to the good, old-fashioned cork board.

"Age eighty-one. Date of birth January 31st 1932. Has resided at The Laurels Nursing Home since 2005. Diagnosed with end-stage COPD and has been effectively bed-ridden for the majority of the last eight years." DC Cassidy paused, turning back towards Jack and DS Cooper. "Last home address before that was in Finsbury. From what I can gather from the nursing home file, his wife died in 1992, and his only next of kin is a son. The nursing home are trying to contact him now. Initial reports are that Edward Wakefield didn't receive many visitors."

"We'll need to check that out," interrupted Jack, taking a long sip of his coffee to wash down the flakes of croissant. "If they keep a visitor log or record book, we need to see it. Find out if anyone visited him in the last, say, three to six months, and in particular yesterday afternoon."

"Boss." DS Cooper nodded and made a note in his notebook.

Jack nodded for DC Cassidy to continue. Tucking a wayward strand of her jet-black hair behind her ear, she turned back towards the pin-board.

"Work history. This is still very sketchy; we only have the nursing home files to go on at the moment. They have him as previously being a bit of an odd-job man, and also some form of caretaker in the past. But that's about it. They don't have any firm records as to names of previous employers though, probably due to his age and not feeling it to be relevant."

"Check it out anyway. Get onto HMRC and see if that shows up anything." Jack took another long gulp of coffee. "We need to flesh out his background; find out what kind of man he was."

DS Cooper added another action to his notebook. "I've already put in a request for any CCTV recordings both inside and outside the home. They confirmed they do have some cameras and will get back to us about a time to go and view them."

"Good work, Cooper." Jack drained the rest of his coffee and stood up. "I'm going to shoot back to my office. There's a few calls I need to make on the Peter Holloway case. Give the nursing home another nudge about the cameras. Arrange a time for us to go over later today – and mention the visitor log books as well. Call me when you have anything."

Both DS Cooper and DC Cassidy gave nods in Jack's direction as he walked towards the door.

"And welcome back!" added DC Cassidy, giving him a grin and a mock salute. "We've missed you!"

Jack hesitated in the doorway and flashed an amused expression at his team. "Glad to hear it – I've missed you too, guys."

And he meant every word.

* * *

Time: 8.00am

Date: Saturday 9th February 2013

Location: Westminster Mortuary, London

A frown deepened across the brow of Dr Phillip Matthews as he leant in closer towards the pale skin on Edward Wakefield's right thigh. The sound of the camera's shutter stuttered through the otherwise still and chilled air of the post mortem room. The pathologist held the lens steady and clicked several more close-up shots.

Standing up, Dr Matthews paused briefly before handing the camera to the waiting technician by his side.

"Can we get these uploaded as soon as possible?"

The technician nodded and turned towards the door.

"And then maybe give Detective Inspector Jack MacIntosh a call," added Dr Matthews. "Tell him he might want to pop over."

Another nod from the technician as he departed, and Dr Matthews was left alone with Eddie Wakefield. The chest cavity lay open – the tobacco-scarred lungs and stilled heart had already been removed for analysis. The folds of skin and subcutaneous tissue draped outwards, revealing the space that had once been the epicentre of the old man's life. The abdominal cavity was similarly exposed – initial examinations revealing nothing more sinister than evidence of cirrhosis of the liver, likely alcohol-induced, and a degree of diverticular disease in the intestines. A minimal amount of blood had collected underneath Eddie Wakefield's frail body, draining away into the stainless steel channels at the side of the table.

Dr Matthews turned once again towards the deceased's right thigh, the same frown plastered across his forehead. Leaning closer, he placed a gloved hand at one side of the bruised flesh and carefully explored the wound, noting the deep, jagged edges that had been cut into the skin. At this stage, his best guess was a semi-sharp small blade or pen-knife had been responsible. And although crude, Dr Matthews could instantly see that the injury to Eddie Wakefield's thigh was no random wound.

An attempt had been made to ink the gaping flesh; the bloodied tissue had been tainted with the deepest, darkest shade of blue-black ink.

Dr Matthews straightened up. Judging by the bruising that had formed around the wound and the now-dried blood that clung to the man's otherwise pallid skin, he could be confident that the injury had been inflicted ante-mortem.

Before death.

Before Eddie Wakefield's heart stopped beating.

Before his life had been snuffed out.

And although the carving was crude, the message it portrayed was clear to the naked eye.

Fifteen.

The number fifteen.

* * *

Time: 8.15am
Date: Saturday 9th February 2013
Location: Metropolitan Police HQ, London

Jack eased himself into his chair and surveyed his desk. While on his six-month sabbatical, his caseload had been allocated to other officers, much to the various recipients' dismay. But as soon as word hit the street that Jack was coming back, it seemed that all unsolved cases somehow made their way back to him. And his desk.

He gave a rueful smile and a brief shake of the head as he slowly edged a teetering pile of files marked "urgent" to the side. There was only one case that Jack truly regarded as urgent at this moment in time, and that particular file sat squarely in the centre of the otherwise over-crowded desk.

Peter Holloway.

His trial was due to start at the Old Bailey on 4th March and the department was getting its usual pre-trial jitters. Such a high profile case could make or break the reputation of a number of officers housed in the building around him – Jack being one of them. He had a meeting with the senior prosecutor from the Crown Prosecution Service lined up in the next fortnight, plus a conference with the prosecution QC and his junior.

Insanity.

That was the defence Holloway was trying to pull.

Jack gave a snort and shook his head. Peter Holloway was no more insane than he was. So now they had the added task of preparing the case to disprove any claims that he didn't know what he was doing. Yet another unnecessary hurdle in the legal race for justice.

Jack felt his stomach rumble again. The croissant had been good, but had barely touched the sides.

He was about to push himself up out of his chair and head up to the canteen, the thought of a bacon sandwich calling him, when the phone on his desk began to chirp. Contemplating ignoring the incessant ringing and slipping out of the door, Jack sighed and leant forwards to pick up the receiver.

"DI MacIntosh," he spoke, somewhat gruffly.

"Ah, just the person," returned the voice on the other end of the line. "Dr Matthews has asked that I give you a call. I'm his assistant technician here at the Westminster Mortuary."

"Yes?" Jack's tone lost its gruffness. "What's up?"

"Dr Matthews has almost completed his preliminary post mortem on your deceased from last night. A Mr Edward Wakefield." The technician paused before adding. "There are some photographs Dr Matthews would like you to see, before he dictates his report. He would like to discuss them with you in person."

Jack paused just long enough to grab his car keys and jacket from the back of his chair, all thoughts of breakfast now instantly forgotten.

"I'm on my way."

* * *

Time: 9.00am

Date: Saturday 9th February 2013

Location: 5 Charlotte Street, Finsbury

Terence Wakefield replaced the telephone receiver and steadied himself against the kitchen worktop. He had noted the six missed calls from last night that were blinking away on the handset, but he had no memory of hearing the telephone ringing.

That being said, he had no memory of a lot about the previous night – which was not unusual. He ran a shaking hand over the prickles on his unshaven and unwashed chin, and rubbed the crusts from the corners of his blood-shot eyes.

The empty bottle of cheap vodka on the draining board told him all he needed to know about last night's events. Whether the shakes and tremors were from the news he had just received, or from his body's cravings for more alcohol, he wasn't sure. He bypassed the bread-bin, which housed a two-week old, green-tinged half loaf of white bread, and reached for the fresh bottle by its side.

A liquid breakfast. Like most of his breakfasts these days. And his lunches. And often his dinners too, if he was still conscious. He twisted the cap with trembling, nicotine-stained fingers, and brought the bottle to his lips. The glass clunked against his broken teeth as he wrapped his chapped lips around the bottle's neck. He took a long swig and shuddered as the alcohol hit his stomach.

Soon the shakes would stop.

Another swig and he stepped backwards on unsteady feet towards the small, square table behind him. Covered with empty cigarette packets, spent stubs and yet more empty bottles, he lowered himself down into the one solitary plastic chair by its side.

He replayed the telephone conversation in his head.

He was dead.

His father was dead.

* * *

Time: 9.20am
  Date: Saturday 9ᵗʰ February 2013
  Location: Westminster Mortuary, London

Jack felt the blast of cold air hit him as he stepped into the corridor leading to the post mortem room. Although it was barely above freezing outside, the mortuary still managed to feel at least ten degrees lower. He quickly made his way to the small office tucked away to the side of the examination room, not wanting to linger any longer than necessary. Raising his hand to knock, the door swung open and Jack found the doorway filled with the towering, lean frame of Dr Phillip Matthews.

"Jack, glad you could come." Dr Matthews made space to allow Jack to step inside. "Sorry it was such short notice."

"No problem, Doc," replied Jack, noting the slight increase in warmth as he edged inside. He spied a small electric heater positioned close to a very neat and organised desk. "What can you tell me?"

Dr Matthews gestured for Jack to take a seat whilst he slipped into his own leather-bound chair. Jack duly sat, noting a large stack of files, precisely arranged, next to a blot-free notepad and pen. He shook his head to rid himself of the image of the carnage of his own desk waiting for him back at the station, and raised his gaze to meet the pathologist's. The troubled expression that was returned to him made his heart sink.

Although the post mortem room itself was across the corridor behind a set of sturdy doors, Jack could still sense the aroma of that glorious mix of formaldehyde, antiseptic and decay wafting around his nostrils. His stomach churned once again, and not this time due to hunger. He was grateful he hadn't had time for that bacon sandwich.

"This will all be in my report, Jack," began Dr Matthews, his voice almost as heavy as the air around them. "But I just wanted to show you something first."

34

Jack nodded, finding himself holding his breath – which wasn't a bad idea bearing in mind the odour of death that surrounded them. "Of course."

Dr Matthews reached for a thin file from the centre of his desk, pulling out a series of four colour photographs. Without saying anything further, he lay the six inch by nine inch pictures in front of Jack.

Jack's eyes darted from picture to picture and it didn't take long for him to see exactly why Dr Matthews had called.

"What...?" began Jack, a frown creasing his brow. "Are these...?"

Dr Matthews nodded, gravely. "These photographs were taken from Mr Wakefield's right thigh." The pathologist tapped the first picture with a well-manicured finger. "This one shows quite clearly its location – the upper thigh, on the lateral aspect."

Jack reached forwards and took the first photograph in his hand. "And the other three are close ups of the same.... wound?"

Dr Matthews nodded, clearing his throat. "All four images show the same injury to the thigh. The close-ups detail the incision into the subcutaneous tissue."

"They look deep," commented Jack, his eyes still flicking from one photograph to another. "What weapon would have been used to make such cuts?"

Dr Matthews gave a slight shrug. "A pen-knife, potentially. Sharp, but not razor-sharp. You can tell from the ragged edges – the blade was blunted to some degree."

Jack followed the pathologist's gaze to one of the other photographs that showed a close-up of the wound; the uneven and craggy edges of the flesh looking raw and inexpertly inflicted.

"Before death?" questioned Jack. "Or after?"

"Before." Dr Matthews shifted back in his leather chair and Jack thought he could hear a faint sigh escape the man's lips. "Definitely before death. The wound bled – that was the blood you saw on the sheets - and bruising can be seen around the edges. Blood was still circulating at the time the injury was inflicted. But it obviously was not the cause of death."

Silence followed Dr Matthews' statement.

An inflicted wound.

Before death.

"That would have hurt, right?" Jack asked the question he already felt he knew the answer to.

"Undoubtedly," agreed Dr Matthews. "The wound is very deep, going through both epidermis and dermis, and down into the subcutaneous tissue. Almost as far as the bone. This would have hurt a great deal."

"And in a bed-bound patient?"

"As I understand it, Mr Wakefield was unable to mobilise, and had been for some time. His body shows severe muscle wastage consistent with that. He would not have been able to put up any sort of fight."

Jack's eyes rested again on the photograph in his hand. "So the purpose of this wound?"

Dr Matthews shrugged again. "That's your forte, Jack. But if you want my unprofessional opinion, they were inflicted to cause pain. A great deal of pain."

"And a message," mused Jack, tapping the image in his hand. "It's been inked in – a message never to be erased."

Dr Matthews nodded. "Looks like normal pen cartridge ink to me – but we'll analyse it just in case. The staining around the exposed flesh suggests it was hurriedly poured into the open wound as it bled."

"Can I take this?" Jack waved the first photograph in the air.

Dr Matthews smiled and nodded. "Of course. I'll be writing up my report this afternoon – and I'll attach a full set of photographs. It'll be emailed and biked across to you when it's ready."

Jack thanked Dr Matthews and got to his feet. The churning sensation in his stomach persisted, and wasn't going to subside without some fresh air. As he stepped out into the corridor and headed towards the main entrance, he longed to feel the icy wind and snowflakes outside. Still gripped in his hand was the photograph. He didn't need to look at it again – the message it portrayed, the message carved into Eddie Wakefield's flesh, was burned into his brain already.

Fifteen.

The number fifteen.

* * *

Chapter Four

Time: 12.15pm
Date: Saturday 9th February 2013
Location: The Laurels Nursing Home, London

The tyres crunched on a mixture of gravel and freshly laid snow. The Laurels Nursing Home looked almost picturesque – a dusting of icing-sugar like snowflakes across the roof and gable ends gave it a postcard, chocolate-box type appearance. Any passers-by would be forgiven for not realising the horror that had taken place within its walls less than twenty-four hours before.

Jack swung the driver's door open and stepped out into a bitingly cold wind. The churning sensation in his stomach had not been quelled since his earlier visit to see Dr Matthews, and the lukewarm coffee he had gulped on his return had not helped.

"Guv?" DS Cooper had exited the passenger-side door and was nodding up at the CCTV camera that was hanging over the main entrance. Jack returned the nod and gestured for DS Cooper to follow him inside.

As they pulled open the main door, they were greeted by a body of warmth and light. The horrors that had been discovered the night before were not apparent on stepping through into the entrance hall. Soft light emanated from recessed wall lights, the air was cosy and warm. All that hinted at the previous night's terrible events was the remnants of the blue and white police tape lying curled up on the floor by the entrance to the corridor leading to room E16.

Jack flashed his ID badge to the receptionist, who greeted him with a warm smile. "Of course, Detective Inspector," she breezed. "We've been expecting you. Please follow me."

Janine, as it stated on her name badge, led Jack and DS Cooper along one of the opposite corridors and into a room bearing the nameplate "main office".

Inside, the office was partitioned in the middle with one desk on each side. On the right hand side sat a rosy-cheeked woman with short, tightly curled hair, a pair of spectacles on a chain perched on the end of her nose. She looked up and smiled as Janine and her visitors entered.

"Ah, thank you, Janine," spoke the woman, rising up out of her chair and thrusting a sturdy hand across the desk towards Jack. "I'm Rosemary Ward – the manager here at The Laurels."

Janine bid them goodbye and closed the door behind her.

"Thank you for seeing us, Ms Ward," replied Jack, stepping forwards and taking hold of the proffered hand, surprised by the fierceness of the grip.

"Not at all. Not at all." Rosemary Ward gestured towards two chairs opposite, and deposited herself back down into her own swivel chair. At a little over five feet tall, she almost disappeared behind the two computer monitors housed on her desk. "I have the visitor log book you asked for," she continued, patting the front cover of a hard-backed A4 notepad sitting on the desk in front of her. "This one goes back to November last year. If you need anything further back, I can ask Janine to find them for you."

Jack nodded his thanks. "November should be fine, thank you. And the CCTV?"

Rosemary Ward leant forwards and swivelled one of the monitors so that it faced Jack and DS Cooper. "All on here. It starts from the beginning of the day yesterday right through to..." She broke off, her rosy cheeks paling somewhat and her bright blue eyes clouding over. "Well, until yesterday's discovery." She paused and cleared her throat. "If you need any other time frames, just let me know."

Jack gave what he hoped was a reassuring smile. "Thanks, we will."

"Well, I'll get out of your way, gentlemen." Rosemary Ward pushed herself out of her chair and headed towards the door. "I'll be at the front desk if you need me."

"Much obliged," replied Jack, already reaching for the visitor log book. "Just one more thing before you go."

"Yes?" Rosemary Ward hovered by the door.

"Mr Wakefield's next of kin. I believe he had a son?"

"Yes, yes. That's correct." Rosemary Ward nodded once again, the chain from her glasses swinging and giving off a faint tinkle. "Terence."

"Do you have an address for him?"

"I'll get Janine to sort that out for you. We have already informed him of his father's death. I rang him myself earlier this morning. We had tried to get hold of him last night, but he wasn't answering his telephone."

Jack nodded. "Great. Thanks. If you could phone it through to the station, we'll get a family liaison officer out to see him as soon as we can."

With that, Rosemary Ward left them to it and closed the door behind her.

"Right, Cooper," said Jack, pulling the visitor log towards them. "Let's see if we can't find ourselves a killer."

* * *

Time: 12.20pm
Date: Saturday 9th February 2013
Location: 5 Charlotte Street, Finsbury

The vodka bottle was three-quarters empty – or a quarter full, depending on your perspective. To Terence Wakefield, it was almost certainly the former. He sat, silently, in his darkened and musty front room, the faded and worn-out armchair sagging beneath him. He hadn't moved for some time, still dressed in his pyjama bottoms and an old stained vest.

The three-quarters empty vodka bottle sat on the floor beside him, and an ashtray, full to overflowing, rested on his leg. Moth-eaten curtains were pulled across the only dirt-encrusted window in the room – plunging the room into an ever-deepening darkness.

But that was fine by Terence.

He liked the dark.

He could hide in the dark.

He stubbed out yet another butt into the crammed ashtray, his opposite leg jigging up and down in a repetitive fashion. His fingers trembled as he reached for another cigarette, taking several attempts to light it.

Whether the tremors were due to his alcohol or nicotine addiction, he didn't know. And he didn't particularly care. All he could think about was the voice he had heard on the other end of the telephone.

I'm so sorry, Mr Wakefield.

I'm so very, very sorry.

It's your father.

He's dead.

Terence Wakefield took in another long drag on his cigarette, letting the vapour escape his nose and mouth, rising up towards the already nicotine-stained ceiling above.

The police will come to see you.

Terence Wakefield shuddered. The room was cold, and his breath misted out in front of him. He couldn't afford to put anything more on the electricity, not until his benefits were paid at the end of next week. Then he could maybe afford to put a tenner onto the electricity card and maybe switch the battered heater on. After he had bought his cigarettes, of course. And his alcohol.

Reaching down to the floor beside him, he grabbed the vodka bottle and brought the neck towards his lips. The liquid momentarily warmed him as it slid down his throat. He felt the comfortable and familiar burn as it made its way down into his empty stomach; the dormant ulcer that he knew was there would begin to twinge before too long.

The police.

Terence shuddered again, this time at the thought of the police turning

41

up on his doorstep.

He took another swig of the bottle, noting that the vodka was now verging on empty. He tried to remember what other alcohol he had in the house. But his attention soon returned to the problem in hand.

The police.

He could always recognise their tell-tale rap at the door. It was unmistakeable.

The police made him nervous.

But what was making him more nervous was the thought that whoever killed his father would also be coming for him.

* * *

Time: 1.40pm

Date: Saturday 9th February 2013

Location: The Laurels Nursing Home. London

The visitor log book wasn't giving up many secrets, and even less answers. Eddie Wakefield had received virtually no visitors from November through to February. The only recorded visitor had been his son, just before Christmas. The obligatory festive visit had lasted less than thirty minutes. Other than that, Eddie Wakefield saw no one, other than a weekly visit by the registered on-site GP.

Jack sighed and closed the hard-backed A4 notebook. "We'll take a copy of the visits from November onwards," commented Jack. "Keep it on file."

DS Cooper nodded and placed the visitor log book to one side. He was sure that the lovely Janine would be more than happy to copy it for them on their way out.

The CCTV hadn't helped much either. Jack and DS Cooper had run through the images on all three of the nursing home's cameras, but nothing looked like it would be turning up any new leads. The inclement weather had kept visitors down to a zero for yesterday – the only comings and goings had been the daily laundry delivery and a chaplain who had been requested to visit a terminally ill resident.

The only cameras the nursing home had were focused on the front entrance, the rear delivery entrance and a side-door fire exit. Rosemary Ward had admitted that there were two other doors in and out of the home that were not covered by any cameras at all.

"Let's go, Cooper. I don't think we're going to find much else." Jack rose from his chair and turned towards the door. "We'll get that visitor book copied and then head back to the station."

DS Cooper scooped up the visitor log book and followed Jack back out into the corridor. As they made their way to the reception area, where the smiling face of Janine greeted them from behind the main desk, DS Cooper's phone buzzed.

"Message from Amanda." DS Cooper paused as he read the brief message. "Family liaison officer is heading over to the son's address this afternoon."

Jack nodded. "Good. We'll see if they can get any more background on the poor and unfortunate Eddie Wakefield. In particular, why no one seemed to want to visit him – including his own son."

* * *

Time: 2.30pm
 Date: Saturday 9th February 2013
 Location: 5 Charlotte Street, Finsbury

Terence didn't know how long he had been sitting in the worn-out armchair, but the rapping on the front door jolted him back to his senses. He glanced at the aged clock on the mantelpiece, above the un-lit fire. He was still none the wiser, unable to recall exactly when he had stirred from his alcohol-infused stupor, or when he had received the ill-fated phone call. But the ashtray full of cold cigarette butts still perched on his leg confirmed that time had, indeed, passed him by.

The rapping continued and Terence slowly made to ease himself out of his chair. Although only sixty years of age he looked, and no doubt felt, twenty years older; years of alcohol abuse had ravaged him to the point of no return. His clothes hung off his thin frame as if hanging from a clothes rack; his pyjama bottoms hitched up around his waist and held with a piece of string.

The police.

He knew their door-knocking anywhere.

It was most likely the family liaison officer that had been promised or whatever it was that they called themselves. Someone to sit with him, to be with him during his time of grief. Terence would have chuckled to himself if he had had the strength. Instead he gave a throaty cough that rattled his lungs.

Grief.

He wasn't grieving for his father.

Good riddance to the man was his first thought when he had received the news.

No. It wasn't grief that he was feeling now. It was something far more concerning than that.

It was fear.

Terence shuffled as quickly as his calloused feet would allow, crossing the cold linoleum floor towards the darkened hallway. As he made his way along the narrow corridor towards the front door, he looked up at the small, square pane of frosted glass in the centre. He squinted through the dim light, but was unable to see anything but a fuzzy outline of whoever was outside.

The knocking continued as Terence approached the door.

"OK, OK," he muttered under his breath, "no need to break the bloody door down." He reached forwards and unlocked the door, pulling it open to be immediately met with a gust of chilled air. Blanching at the icy wind, he squinted and looked up into the face of his visitor.

The figure standing on the doorstep smiled. "Terence Wakefield? Terry?"

Terence hesitated before nodding. "Yes?"

"Can we go inside?"

* * *

Time: 2.45pm

Date: Saturday 9th February 2013

Location: Isabel's Café, King's Road, London

Isabel wiped her warm brow with the back of her hand and fanned herself with a tea towel. The lunchtime rush was over and they now had a brief, and very welcome, lull. She stepped through to the rear of the café and sat down on Livi's favourite armchair with an exhausted sigh. Sacha followed with two cups of camomile tea.

"That was a busy one," remarked Isabel, accepting her cup, gratefully. "Is it normally like that on a Saturday?" She closed her eyes and rested her head back against the armchair.

Sacha nodded and settled down on a soft leather pouffe by the patio doors. "It is now. Dom designed some flyers and spent three days trawling along the streets handing them in to each and every business premises he could find. We've got a lot of lunchtime trade now during the week, and now at weekends too – we've had to expand the sandwich selection just to accommodate them all."

Isabel drank deeply from her soothing tea. "I'd noticed the menu board had changed – lots more sandwiches and wraps. You'll have Dom going out on an old fashioned bicycle delivering them next!"

"Don't think he hasn't already thought of that!" laughed Sacha. "The extra responsibility while you've been away has done wonders for him. He's really getting into the business side of things."

"Then he should consider doing a business course or something." Isabel turned her head towards the café where they could both hear the subtle sounds of Dominic hard at work in the kitchens, loading the dishwasher and manning the ovens. "I mean it. He's a clever lad. I hate the business side with a passion, so I would be happy to hand over the reins."

Sacha smiled and nodded. "Maybe. Anyway, how was your first night back in your own bed? I bet Livi was cuddled up by your side!"

Isabel grinned. "She was. We both slept like babies."

"Mac was quiet yesterday," remarked Sacha, wrapping her hands around her cup. "He didn't have much to say for himself. Is he all right?"

Isabel sipped her tea and gave a small shrug, accompanied by a sigh. "I don't really know to be honest. He's struggling a bit, I know that. We both are, I guess – what with the trial coming up in a few weeks. It's not a great time."

"I can imagine. I can't understand why that monster is pleading not guilty and putting you all through a trial." Sacha drank another mouthful of tea and smiled across at Isabel. "But you do know you don't have to worry about this place, don't you? Dom and I are more than happy to help you with that. You take as much time out as you need."

Isabel smiled, gratefully. "Thanks, it's much appreciated. But I am worried about him, you know? Mac, I mean."

"In what way?"

Isabel sighed and nursed the cup of camomile tea in her lap. "I don't know – nothing specific really. He's just not...he's just not himself. Ever since DS Carmichael came out to see him, he's been different. Distant."

"That's to be expected, I guess. Dragging up the past like that. That St Bartholomew's place sounded horrific."

Isabel nodded, slowly. "Maybe. Mac hated that place so much. He won't even talk about it with me. I called him a few times last night but he didn't answer."

"I'm sure he'll work it out. And the trial looming must be having an effect on both of you." Sacha gave her friend a reassuring smile. "You'll both come out of it OK. I know you will."

"I hope so," mused Isabel, finishing off her tea. "The few days we spent at his flat after landing, I barely saw him. He disappeared during the day, and sometimes in the evenings, too. He wouldn't answer his phone or reply to any messages. Wouldn't even tell me where he'd been."

"Try not to let it get to you," finished Sacha, pushing herself off the pouffe. She reached out and took Isabel's empty tea cup. "Leave him to it. He'll come around when he's good and ready. Anyway, we have a Chinese evening to prepare for! Have you had any ideas?"

Isabel shook her head and followed Sacha back out into the café, the sound of the bell above the door signalling that their brief interlude of peace and quiet was at an end. "I'll leave that in your capable hands, Sacha. You've done wonders while I've been away."

Sacha beamed and went to serve the customer hovering by the counter, while Isabel tried to put her worries about Mac out of her mind.

* * *

Time: 5.15pm
  Date: Saturday 9th February 2013
  Location: Metropolitan Police HQ, London

DS Cooper clicked on "print" and the machine behind him whirred into action. Jack hovered nearby until all twelve pages had been spewed out before heading back to the investigation table.

"Dr Matthews has emailed across his initial findings on the post mortem of Eddie Wakefield." Jack held up the pieces of paper in his hand before depositing them on the table, in between an empty pizza box and several discarded soft drink cans from the vending machine. "From the brief look we had on screen," Jack nodded at the whiteboard where the pathologist's report had been loaded, "we can conclude that Mr Wakefield died of asphyxiation."

DS Cooper and DC Cassidy both had their eyes trained to the whiteboard, while DS Cooper manoeuvred the mouse to select the conclusions at the end of page eight. Jack had preferred a physical copy. He liked to feel paper underneath his fingers. There was only so much screen work he could put up with. He liked paper. And he liked pens.

Flicking through the pages, Jack also arrived at the conclusions section. "Asphyxiation. Contusions and abrasions around the mouth, consistent with the deceased having been smothered. Further abrasions to the wrists, indicating some degree of restraint." Jack paused and looked up to find both DS Cooper and DC Cassidy training their eyes on him. He briefly lowered his gaze back to the post mortem report, turning over the last four pages and spreading them out on the table. "And these are the photographs showing the wound carved into the deceased's right thigh."

Jack let silence fill the room as DS Cooper flooded the screen with the blown-up images at the end of the report. They had all seen the photograph Jack had brought back with him from Dr Matthews' office, and it remained pinned to the cork board at the side of the room. But somehow, seeing all four in quick succession enlarged on the screen caused the temperature in the room to drop a degree or two.

"What does the number fifteen mean?" mused Jack out loud. "It can't be random. It has to mean something – either to the victim or to his killer."

"Fifteen victims?" suggested DS Cooper, instantly horrified by his own words. "That there are more?"

"I sure as hell hope not, Cooper," grimaced Jack, rubbing his tired eyes. "Someone entered that nursing home yesterday, with the sole intent to end Mr Wakefield's life. We need to find out why."

"We know that nothing unusual showed up in the visitor log book for yesterday," added DS Cooper, flicking the screen to show an uploaded copy of various pages kindly provided by the lovely Janine. "It confirms no one visited the victim at all that day, or anyone else for that matter. Zero visitors all day."

"Well somebody visited him," interrupted DC Cassidy. "What's to say they just didn't sign the log book? If I was going to kill someone, I'd sure as hell not sign my name in the visitor book. Killers are usually cleverer than that."

"True," conceded Jack. "We don't know if it's obligatory to sign in at reception when visiting, or if people can just come and go as they please. We'll get Ms Ward to clarify."

DS Cooper reached for his note book. "With two entrances not covered by CCTV, anyone could slip in and out undetected. I'm not sure the visitor log book is going to be worth the paper it's written on, boss."

"You're right, Cooper," nodded Jack. "The killer almost certainly slipped in one of the unmonitored doors, and then out again, without being seen. Or if he was seen, he did so without raising suspicion. Let's get some uniforms back out there – I want everyone who was on duty that day to be re-interviewed. Who did they see, and when?"

"Boss." DS Cooper added the action to the list.

"And for what it's worth, research the number fifteen. Does it have any hidden meaning or represent anything? Amanda, I'll leave that one with you."

DC Cassidy nodded. "Will do, boss."

Jack nodded his thanks. "It's probably another blind alley but let's tick that box. So, what else do we have? I know it's early days, but what evidence has gone to the lab?"

DS Cooper rummaged amongst the paperwork on the table. "No results uploaded yet, obviously, but there is a log of what has been sent. Mr Wakefield's pyjamas and bedclothes have both gone. The room itself didn't have a great deal in it – but it's all been dusted for fingerprints and luminol for any blood not visible to the naked eye. There was a scarf though..."

"A scarf?" Jack frowned, looking up at the screen as DS Cooper brought up images of the evidence bags that had been sent away to the lab. He clicked through several thumbnails of standard issue plastic evidence bags containing what looked like a pair of pyjamas and hospital issue bed sheets. The final image filled the screen.

"It was found in Edward Wakefield's room – the staff aren't sure if it belonged to him or not." DS Cooper clicked the mouse and enlarged the image, filling the screen with a picture of a plastic bag with a multi-coloured scarf folded up inside. "They don't seem to remember seeing it before. It's been bagged up and sent to the lab along with everything else."

Jack stared at the scarf and frowned. There was something familiar about the multi-coloured stripes that stirred something in the back of his mind, but he just couldn't place it.

Interrupting his thoughts, Jack's phone began to ring. "DI MacIntosh," he answered, motioning for DS Cooper to close down the whiteboard screen. "Yes?" After several seconds silence, Jack rose from his seat and froze. "What did you say?"

DS Cooper and DC Cassidy watched as colour started to drain from Jack's face.

"When?" Jack nodded, slowly, as he listened, then reached for his jacket. "OK, we'll be right over. Text me the address."

Jack hung up and turned towards his team.

"Shit," he breathed.

* * *

Time: 6.15pm

Date: Saturday 9th February 2013

Location: 5 Charlotte Street, Finsbury

Terence Wakefield looked as though he was asleep. Still sitting in his favourite armchair, facing the empty grate in the empty fireplace. By his feet was still the empty bottle of cheap vodka, and an opened packet of cigarettes lay balanced on his lap. His eyes were closed and his unshaven chin rested against his chest.

The only visible indication that all was not well was the scarlet red staining on his grease-marked and grubby vest.

Jack hovered in the doorway, clad in regulation protective suit and overshoes. He watched from a distance as Dr Phillip Matthews knelt down by the side of the armchair and conducted his initial cursory examination to confirm that life, had indeed, been extinguished.

Three other crime scene bodies silently danced their way around each other, moving in respectful synchronicity. Jack caught Dr Matthews' gaze and raised his eyebrows. No words were needed, just a simple nod of the pathologist's bald head was sufficient.

Dr Matthews got to his feet and back-tracked out of the living room, shuffling over towards Jack in his own plastic overshoes. "Different cause of death, Jack." He nodded back over his shoulder towards the deceased form of Terence Wakefield. "As you can no doubt see."

Jack nodded. It was impossible not to see the gaping wound in Terence Wakefield's neck and the resultant torrential blood loss. Splatter patterns were also visible on the walls surrounding the body, some reaching as high as the ceiling. His pyjama bottoms had been pulled down around his ankles.

"No asphyxiation?" Jack asked, stepping aside as yet another protective-clad crime scene officer entered the room with a high specification camera.

Dr Matthews shook his head. "Can't say for sure, Jack, not until the full post mortem but it doesn't look likely. There's a deep cut to the neck, likely severed the carotid artery. Plus, a single stab wound to the chest. I'm unsure as yet which one came first."

"Father one day, son the next," mused Jack, glancing back towards the body.

Dr Matthews edged out into the hallway, his presence no longer required. "Different kill method it may be, Jack, but – off the record – apart from the obvious family tie, your number fifteen is still your link between them."

Jack tore his head away from watching photographs being snapped of Terence Wakefield's body, and found himself trailing after the pathologist towards the front door. "The number fifteen? You're sure?"

Dr Matthews hesitated briefly and turned, locking eyes with Jack. He gave a brief nod. "Top of the right thigh, Jack. The number fifteen."

* * *

Time: 9.30pm
 Date: Saturday 9th February 2013
 Location: Kettle's Yard Mews, London

Jack scraped the rest of the chicken biryani and pilau rice into the bin, and added his dirty plate to those already in the sink. The takeaway he was meant to have shared with Stu the previous evening had still tasted pretty good, but as usual his eyes were bigger than his belly.

Bypassing the temptation to open another can of beer, Jack switched on the kettle and reached for the coffee jar. He had left the crime scene at Terence Wakefield's at a little after eight o'clock and badly needed sleep, but he doubted it would come easily

After sloshing hot water into his mug, and adding a splash of milk, Jack headed back to the sofa and the letter from the Department of Social Services that had landed on his doorstep that morning. He picked it up once again and studied its rather brief and perfunctory contents.

Boxes.

They had boxes that belonged to the MacIntosh family, formerly of Old Mill Road, Christchurch. But due to a department restructure, the aforementioned boxes could no longer be stored free of charge. Please make arrangements for collection or delivery at your earliest convenience.

Boxes.

Jack frowned.

He wasn't aware there had been any boxes of belongings from their days at the Old Mill Road flat. He had assumed that everything had moved with them to their successive foster care placements.

Not that they had very much. Jack couldn't remember much beyond a few sets of clothes.

Picking up his mobile, he scrolled through to his brother's number. The boxes were as much his property as they were Jack's. He tapped the screen and brought the phone to his ear, while sipping at his coffee and reading through the letter one more time.

The call went unanswered.

He left a brief message for a call back and placed the phone back down on the coffee table. It niggled him that Stu hadn't stuck around last night – it wasn't like him to turn down food and alcohol. Taking a drink from his mug, he noticed from the phone screen that he had three missed calls since yesterday – all from the same number.

Dr Riches.

Although he knew he would need to talk to her at some point, Jack pushed himself up from the sofa and decided on an early night.

Dr Riches could wait.

* * *

Chapter Five

Time: 7.30am
  Date: Sunday 10th February 2013
  Location: Metropolitan Police HQ, London

"We now have two murders." Jack nodded at the whiteboard as DS Cooper activated the screen. "Father and son."

Jack reached for the greaseproof paper bag that DS Cooper had placed in front of him. "Cheers, Cooper," he winked, as the aroma of freshly grilled bacon filled his nostrils. "Terence Wakefield was found by a friend who dropped by to give him his betting shop winnings – some five pounds and twenty pence. The door was unlocked, so he walked in to find Mr Wakefield Jnr already dead in his armchair." He paused to take a mouthful of bacon sandwich. "That was at approximately 4.30pm. And as you can see from the crime scene photos uploaded so far, Terence was stabbed in the chest and the neck."

DS Cooper clicked the screen to enlarge a photograph of Terence Wakefield's head and upper body.

Jack continued. "A police liaison officer called round at the property at approximately 3.15pm, but received no answer. They placed a card through the door and left. It is thought that Mr Wakefield would already have been dead at this point."

"And then we have the tattoo," added DC Cassidy, suppressing a smile as she watched both Jack and DS Cooper devouring their bacon sandwiches while she sipped her skinny chai latte. "It's very similar to the one found on his father."

"Exactly," agreed Jack, wiping tomato sauce from his mouth. "Dr Matthews is planning on completing the post mortem at some point today, and no doubt he will send through some close-up photographs. But for the moment, we have the scene of crime images that clearly show a very similar wound on Terence Wakefield's right upper thigh. Off the record, Dr Matthews confirms both are so similar they had to have been made by the same hand."

"I've started researching the number fifteen, guv," said DC Cassidy, flipping over her notebook. "There's not much to go on. Most references are to healing and harmony. Its biblical significance points to a symbol of restoration. And it's often thought to be a lucky number."

"Not for the Wakefields," mused Jack, reaching for his mug of strong coffee. "OK. Officers should be concluding the house-to-house in Terence Wakefield's street later today. I want to see those statements as soon as they're in. I want to know who has been coming and going from that property. I'm assuming the area doesn't have CCTV?"

DS Cooper shook his head. "Nothing even remotely near, boss."

"We're waiting for results on the items taken from Eddie Wakefield's room at the nursing home," continued DC Cassidy. "The lab is going to rush them through for us – hopefully they'll have some initial results for us tomorrow. Other tests might take a bit longer. Obviously, there are now samples from the son's house, too. And DNA samples have been taken from the nursing home staff to rule them out."

"Or in," commented DS Cooper, his voice muffled behind his own sandwich. "There's nothing to say it can't be a member of staff."

"Nothing is ruled out yet," agreed Jack, nodding. "For the rest of this morning – Amanda, get yourself over to the mortuary and sit in on Terence Wakefield's post mortem. Cooper, I want more background on both our victims. There has to be a connection between them, and not just because of their surname. While you're both busy, I'm going to take another trip back to The Laurels to have a look at the entrances and exits - see how easy it would have been for our killer to get in and out unseen."

Both DS Cooper and DC Cassidy nodded.

"Keep digging, guys."

* * *

Time: 8.30am

Date: Sunday 10th February 2013

Location: Westminster Mortuary, London

Dr Matthews pulled the overhead light down, closer to the steel examination table, and switched on the tape recorder.

"We have the body of a Caucasian male, known to be sixty years of age. Pre-post mortem weight is given at sixty-one kilos. Visible injuries – one deep laceration to the left side of the neck, five centimetres in length. And one single penetrating wound to the left upper chest, diameter one centimetre."

Dr Matthews paused, reaching for one of the sharpened scalpels from the metal tray held by his technician. "The rest of the body appears free from external injury – save for a wound to the right thigh, which I will come to in a moment."

Nodding to the technician, Dr Matthews watched as the slightly built assistant set down the scalpel tray and picked up the Nikon camera. The taut silence of the post mortem room was interrupted by a series of clicking noises from the camera's shutter, as the technician proceeded to photograph Terence Wakefield's body from every angle. The macabre photo shoot lasted only minutes; the flash of the Nikon blanching the deceased's pale body to an even whiter shade.

Satisfied there were enough pictures, Dr Matthews stepped forwards with the gleaming scalpel in his steady right hand to begin his first incision.

"Everything all right over there, DC Cassidy?" Scalpel poised, Dr Matthews peered across Terence Wakefield's body towards the far side of the room where DC Cassidy was leaning up against a metal counter. She gave a weak smile and even weaker nod, hoping her complexion didn't look as green as she was feeling.

Post mortems were not her favourite, if, indeed, it could ever be anyone's. She didn't have a great track record in Dr Matthews' post mortem room, having fainted twice before. She gripped the cold steel counter and plastered another smile to her face.

Dr Matthews gave her a wink. "Well, if you need to step outside no one needs to know." He turned his attention back towards Terence Wakefield. As he worked, he began his running commentary directed towards the tape recorder above. The words escaping his lips were soft and respectful in the cold starkness of the examination room. Other than his own voice, there was not a single sound in the room save for the subtle clinking of instruments.

A brief interlude of noise disturbed the peace, as Dr Matthews used the rib cutters to expose Terence Wakefield's chest cavity. DC Cassidy turned her head away at the sound of snapping human bone, trying to ignore the churning feeling in her stomach.

Once complete, the pathologist's low tones filtered once again through the air as he made quick work of examining the upper body. The chest cavity itself had thrown up no surprises – visible chronic lung disease due to smoking was evident, although the pathologist acknowledged Terence's lungs were not in quite so bad a shape as his father's - organs that had been removed in this very room just twenty-four hours before. But they were heading in that direction.

Moving down into the abdomen, the grossly enlarged liver was leathery in texture – confirming the history of chronic alcoholism. The outer surface of the liver, instead of being soft and pliable, was tough and cirrhotic. Further evidence of Terence Wakefield's unhappy relationship with alcohol was seen in the abdominal cavity – a build-up of ascitic fluid filled the area, evidence of the liver being unable to perform its most basic of functions.

Dr Matthews took tissue samples from several lobes of the liver and also some of the ascitic fluid.

With the preliminaries out of the way, Dr Matthews returned to the chest cavity to explore the wound that had ended Terence Wakefield's life. A single entry wound had punctured the aortic arch. It was a clean wound, made by a sharp instrument; most likely a knife. There was no evidence of any bruising from the hilt around the entry point, so Dr Matthews concluded the blade was at least eight centimetres in length and had entered Terence Wakefield's chest from above, most likely whilst he was still sitting in his armchair.

Dr Matthews stepped back while more photographs were taken by the technician. Once the snapping had ceased, the pathologist leant forwards and explored the neck wound. The wide gaping hole was almost deep enough to see the cervical vertebrae beneath.

"A sharp, bladed instrument has penetrated deeply into the subcutaneous tissue of the neck, completely severing the carotid artery. Together with the single stab wound to the aortic arch, both injuries would have caused death in a matter of minutes." He glanced up and caught DC Cassidy's eye. "If not sooner." He turned his attention back to the table.

"Due to the nature of the injuries, the stab wound to the aorta is likely to have been the first injury the deceased sustained, causing the blood spatter patterns visible at the scene. The blood would have exited the body at high velocity. The carotid artery laceration is likely to have occurred very soon after – the blood loss from both wounds would have been catastrophic and not compatible with life."

Dr Matthews took swabs from around both wound sites. "The person responsible either has a very intricate knowledge of human anatomy, targeting the blood vessels that would do the most damage, or he was extremely lucky."

Unlike Terence Wakefield.

Terence Wakefield had not been lucky at all.

"No visible signs of any defensive wounds." Dr Matthews examined both of Terence Wakefield's hands – and, apart from nails that had been bitten to the quick, they provided nothing of consequence. No evidence that the deceased had had time to defend himself from such a ferocious, yet precise, attack. Dr Matthews took swabs anyway, and gently dug beneath the badly bitten nails to scrape a sample of tissue.

Moving on down towards the lower half of the body, Dr Matthews beckoned to take the camera from the technician still standing attentively by his side. The click of the camera lens once again cut through the chilled air. Dr Matthews leant in for a series of close-up shots from Terence Wakefield's right upper thigh, focusing on the crudely created jagged wound that mirrored the wound found on his father. Again, the roughened edges of soft tissue suggested a somewhat blunt instrument. Not the sharp, murderous weapon that had sliced through Terence Wakefield's neck and punctured his heart.

"No significant bruising or bleeding around the wound would suggest the injury to the upper thigh was inflicted post mortem," continued Dr Matthews, handing the camera back to his technician. "There are crude edges to the wound, penetrating deep into the subcutaneous tissue." With a gloved hand, he gently explored the area and proceeded to take a swab of the blue-black ink that had been hurriedly poured into the flesh and stained the surrounding skin.

Dr Matthews looked up and beckoned DC Cassidy to move closer. Hesitantly, she let go of the metal counter and tentatively stepped towards the table, her legs feeling like rubber. He nodded towards Terence's right thigh. "See how the inking has occurred, with some splashback over the inner thigh."

DC Cassidy swallowed past the bile that was rising up within her throat. She kept her gaze trained on the wound, forcing herself not to let her eyes wander towards the exposed chest and abdominal cavities above.

Dr Matthews stepped back and looked down at Terence Wakefield's body. A father and son murdered within a day of each other, in itself, made the presenting situation unusual. But the crude tattoo carved into their dead or dying bodies only served to feed the sense of morbid disquiet that was circulating unchecked around the chilled mortuary.

The killer had left their mark once again.

The number fifteen.

* * *

Time: 9.30am
   Date: Sunday 10th February 2013
   Location: Abbotts Road Park, Finsbury, London

He hadn't been able to return to the scene of Terence Wakefield's demise. The whole road was very quickly swarming with police, and with no convenient bus stop opposite within which to conceal himself this time, he decided to walk on by and head for a quiet bench in a deserted section of a nearby park.

They would have made the link by now – that the victims were father and son. It didn't take a genius to work that one out and the police were not generally stupid. But whether they made the other link between Edward and Terence Wakefield remained to be seen.

He had felt strangely calm after leaving Terence's house. Apart from a nosy neighbour twitching her curtains across the street, he was sure that he hadn't been seen. Or if he was, he believed he was inconspicuous enough not to have warranted any further attention.

The feeling of calmness remained.

The job was nearly done.

Nearly, but not quite.

He had called in sick at work, claiming to have the flu that had been doing the rounds lately. It would buy him some time. He could self-certificate for seven days before eyebrows would be raised as to his absence.

Seven days would be enough to finish it.

He had been careful.

Everything was back to normal.

Until the next one.

* * *

Time: 10.35am
   Date: Sunday 10th February 2013
   Location: Westminster Mortuary, London

The rest of the post mortem examination was concluded in silence – the only sound being the occasional comment by Dr Matthews into his tape recorder. Once finished, the pathologist nodded to his trusted technician to take the bloodied scalpel from his hand.

DC Cassidy had exited the post mortem room a few minutes earlier, looking grey around the gills and in desperate need of fresh air. She smiled, gratefully, at Dr Matthews as she made her way towards the door on rubbery legs.

With one last look at the deceased, Dr Matthews sighed and stepped away from the table. Bowing his head momentarily at the lifeless body of Terence Wakefield, a respectful gesture he had begun as a trainee technician himself, he stepped away and headed for the door. Two further technicians were hovering in the doorway, ready to take on the task of the clear-up. Although it was unlikely there would be anybody wishing to view the body, Dr Matthews always insisted that the dead arriving on his table were treated with respect and dignity. They would be cleaned and made presentable, even if they never saw another human face.

Pushing open the swing door, Dr Matthews took in a deep breath and filled his lungs with the slightly less pungent air of the corridor and made his way towards his office. Stepping first of all into his private changing room, he peeled off his protective apron, gown and rubber boots. He then reached for the freshly laundered shirt that was hanging up in front of his locker, courtesy of the ever-organised Mrs Matthews. Slipping his feet into his waiting brogues, he made a mental note to slip into the shower before heading home – another stipulation laid down by Mrs Matthews. Freshly laundered shirts every day, and a shower before coming home.

But first, he needed to call Jack.

Heading back out into the corridor, he opened his office door and was greeted by a pleasant waft of warm air. The small electric heater was doing its job nicely. Plus, the air fresheners he had lined up on the shelving helped to mask the penetrating aroma of death – a heady mix of blood, bodily fluids and formaldehyde that clung to your nostrils once you had breathed it in.

Dr Matthews didn't bother to sit down before reaching for the telephone. He stabbed at the speed dial for the Metropolitan Police, drumming his elegant, piano-playing fingers on the desk as he waited.

The disquiet in his stomach hadn't left him even though the air around him was sweeter. In fact, the feeling was intensifying. He had only seen it once before – a long time ago, not long after he had qualified. And the vision had remained with him ever since.

Branding.

This wasn't about the act of killing, or death. Not for this killer. This was about leaving a message.

This was about leaving a mark.

* * *

Time: 11.00am
  Date: Sunday 10th February 2013
  Location: The Laurels Nursing Home, London

Jack nodded at Janine as he made his way past the reception desk, heading in the direction of room E16. All evidence of the commotion from two nights ago had melted into the background, even the crime scene tape that had still been present on Jack's visit yesterday had now been cleared away. Room E16 was, however, still unoccupied.

Jack peered around the open doorway, noticing that the mattress had been replaced, together with a set of fresh, plump pillows. Any remnants of fingerprint dusting powder had been carefully brushed away. The rest of the room looked stark and empty, no evidence of the life that had been extinguished within its walls. Jack frowned as his eyes swept around the room once more - there was still something that bothered him about the scene, something tugging at the back of his mind. He just couldn't place it.

Stepping back out into the corridor, he continued his journey around a sharp bend which ended in a regulation fire exit door. Jack had counted his steps from Edward Wakefield's room. Fourteen steps between room E16 and the fire exit.

Fourteen steps.

It had taken him less than ten seconds.

Jack hovered by the fire exit, noting that it had been fingerprinted by the dust residue still evident on the metal bar. He held out little hope of it yielding a result. Whoever the killer was, they had been clever enough to enter and leave The Laurels undetected; it was unlikely they would be so careless as to leave behind something as basic as a fingerprint.

But stranger things had happened and Jack made a mental note to check the lab results.

From their initial enquiries with the nursing home, this fire exit was one of two which were not covered by CCTV. The other was on the opposite side of the building, next to the kitchens. Fourteen steps to Edward Wakefield's room – Jack was convinced this was the one selected by the killer.

Pushing the metal bar emblazoned with 'Emergency Use Only' in bold green letters, Jack stepped out into a narrow alley that hugged the side of the nursing home. One way seemed to disappear around the rear of the building, the other led to the front car park; opposite was a low wall and an area of dense trees and bushes.

Perfect for disappearing, thought Jack, noting the wall could easily be scaled. An escape route under cover of thick greenery, away from the CCTV of the front car park. It was perfect. He glanced back at the fire door which he had wedged open with the heel of his shoe. Like most fire doors, it could only be opened from the inside, so how had the killer got in?

Jack scoured the immediate area for anything that could have been used to keep the door from closing. There were various stones and pieces of discarded wood, but Jack dismissed the idea almost as soon as he had thought of it. The killer would have had to enter the nursing home via another door and make his way to this fire exit. It was too risky, and this killer was cleverer than that.

Stepping back into the building, Jack let the fire door swing shut behind him.

Except it didn't.

Frowning, Jack pushed the metal bar again, opening the door out into the alleyway. He then released his grip and let the door swing back. It closed, but not completely – the lock not quite catching. Nudging the door without using the metal bar, Jack found that the door opened perfectly.

* * *

Time: 11.15am
Date: Sunday 10th February 2013
Location: Isabel's Café, King's Road, London

Isabel bit her bottom lip and ended the call. There was still no answer from Mac and she had now called him at least half a dozen times since yesterday, including leaving two voicemail messages. Nothing.

No reply.

She hadn't seen him since Friday evening when he had dropped off her suitcase; and even then he didn't stay long. Pushing herself off her stool, she started pulling decorations out of several boxes Dominic had left on the counter. It was Chinese New Year and Sacha had organised one of her themed events for later that day.

Isabel felt exhausted but could see her best friend was excited, so she put on a brave face. "Sacha? Do you want to help me put up some of these decorations?"

Sacha appeared from the kitchen, her face flushed with a sheen of perspiration. "Sure. I've put some of the snacks in the oven already – the ones that can be eaten cold. We'll start cooking the others a bit later."

She joined Isabel at the counter. "Has Dom left already?"

Isabel nodded and handed Sacha some Chinese lanterns. "I've sent him out to get the fortune cookies. He should be back soon."

Sacha clambered up onto a chair and began to hang up a succession of lanterns above the counter. With it being the year of the snake, Isabel had managed to get hold of some snake-themed decorations and started placing them in the window.

"Is Mac coming tonight?" Sacha stepped down from the chair and dragged one of the boxes over to Isabel, handing her more snake decorations. "We might need an extra pair of hands if it gets busy."

Isabel pinned a concertina snake above the door and gave a small shrug. "I'm not sure. He said he was, but..." She broke off, finding the words catching at the back of her throat. "We'll see." She felt the familiar sensation of tears starting to prick at her eyes so she turned her back to Sacha and began rooting through the box for more decorations.

Sacha placed a hand on her friend's shoulder. "Well if he does, we'll put him to work in the kitchen. He can keep Dom company."

Isabel nodded and flashed her friend what she hoped would pass for a smile.

"Speak of the devil." Sacha looked up as the door swung open and Dominic backed into the café carrying a teetering pile of boxes in his hands. "Wow, are those all fortune cookies?"

Dominic nodded, his head hidden behind the towering cardboard boxes, managing to dump them onto the counter before they fell from his arms.

"They gave us extra, just in case." He pulled his notebook out from the back pocket of his jeans. "Eight boxes of fortune cookies, plus one extra."

Isabel watched as Sacha and Dominic carried the boxes through to the kitchen, unable to stop herself from glancing back down at her phone.

Still nothing.

She pushed the worried thoughts out of her mind the best she could.

She had a Chinese night to prepare for.

With or without Mac.

* * *

Time: 11.30am
   Date: Sunday 10th February 2013
   Location: The Laurels Nursing Home, London

Jack headed back towards room E16. He noticed that the short section of corridor that had been home to Edward Wakefield for the last eight years, also had four other rooms. All were empty, except for one - Room E18 sat directly next to Eddie's. As Jack passed by, he took a quick glance in the window to see an elderly gentleman sleeping soundly with his mouth open; a newspaper lay open on his lap.

Jack continued on towards room E16 noticing that it was no longer unoccupied. A young woman, dressed in a nurse's uniform, was pulling a trolley laden with sheets and blankets to the side of the bed.

"Need a hand?" Jack flashed his ID badge and stepped into the room.

Natalie Evans looked up and caught Jack's gaze, her face flushed from dragging the heavy trolley. "Thanks, but I'm just leaving them here for the night staff. We have a new resident coming tomorrow." She leant into the trolley and pulled out a bundle of sheets and blankets, placing them on top of the new mattress.

"I'm DI Jack MacIntosh. I'm investigating the death of Mr Wakefield." Jack nodded towards the mattress; Eddie Wakefield's last resting place before the cold mortuary slab. "Did you know him well?"

Natalie nodded, pushing away a strand of hair that had plastered itself to her brow. "It was so awful. I'll never get over seeing him like that."

"You were the one that found him?" Jack remembered reading a statement from a nurse who had discovered the body.

Natalie nodded again. "It was awful," she repeated. "I was doing my drug round. I was a little late – Eunice had kept me chatting, bless her. So I..." She stopped, the words catching in her throat. "So I was late getting to Eddie. Maybe if I had been on time, arrived a little earlier, he wouldn't have..."

Jack shook his head. "From what I can gather from the pathologist, Mr Wakefield died several hours before you found him."

A faint look of relief crossed Natalie's pale face as she began to push the trolley back towards the door. "That's something I suppose."

"Do you mind if I hang on in here for a while? I'm still trying to piece together what happened."

Natalie nodded and gave a tired smile. Jack noted the dark circles beneath her eyes. "Of course. Take as long as you need. The room isn't being made up until tonight."

"You didn't see anything odd that night, when you walked into the room?"

Natalie paused in the doorway, leaning up against the trolley. "No, not really. As I said, I was running a little late with my rounds. I should have been with Eddie over half an hour earlier, but..." Natalie stopped and her eyes darted towards the door. "Actually, there was something, now I think of it. The board on the door."

"What board on the door?"

"Here." Natalie gestured towards the small whiteboard on the outside of the door to room E16. "It's the drug round board. Each room has one. Once the drug round had been completed, the box gets ticked."

Jack stepped towards the door to see where Natalie was pointing.

"I thought it was strange at the time...but I forgot all about it, after I saw him..." Natalie gave a shudder at the memory.

"What was strange about it?" pressed Jack.

"The board had been ticked, as if I had already been and gone. Except I hadn't." Natalie turned towards Jack, her glassy eyes wide. "Do you think that's important?"

Jack gave a small shrug, "I'm not sure, but thanks anyway." He filed the additional piece of information away inside his head. "Was there anything else that looked out of place or unusual?"

Natalie bit her bottom lip and shook her head. "No. I don't think so. Mr Wakefield never had much in the way of belongings. He didn't have any photographs or personal items that some of the other residents bring from home. It was quite sad really. I felt sorry for him as he didn't have many visitors. I think he was lonely." Natalie paused as she looked around the empty room. "I think he spent most of his time asleep or listening to the radio."

Jack nodded towards the small set of drawers next to the bed, each one pulled out and empty of any contents. "Have all his personal effects been bagged up?"

It was Natalie's turn to shrug. "I'm not sure. But as I said, he didn't really have much in the way of personal possessions. The only clothes I saw were his pyjamas and dressing gown. He didn't have any outdoor wear."

Jack nodded his thanks and watched as Natalie resumed pushing her trolley back along the corridor towards the reception area.

No personal possessions.

No outdoor wear.

And then it hit him; what had been niggling at the back of his mind all this time.

The scarf.

* * *

Time: 8.40am

Date: Thursday 10th September 1981

Location: West Road Comprehensive School, Christchurch

Jack ran as fast as he could towards the school gates, glancing hurriedly at his watch. Registration was in five minutes – he would make it; just. The bus had been late – again. Something about traffic lights on the high street, and a burst water main. Jack had managed to leap off the bus while it had stopped in traffic, and ran the entire length of West Road, his rucksack bouncing painfully up and down between his shoulder blades. There had been no sign of Stuart – but that was nothing new. Sometimes he was there, sometimes he wasn't. Mostly he wasn't.

Jack slowed down as he ran through the gates, clutching at his sides as they began to ache with a stitch. As he did so, he glanced over his shoulder to see the usual congregation of youths huddled on the street corner by the newsagent's. Jack recognised them immediately as the gang that Stuart had taken to hanging around with on the streets of Christchurch. He suspected that they must all live at the same foster home – St Bartholomew's – and it didn't take him long to spot his brother's unruly mop of hair in amongst the melee.

Stuart was sporting an imitation leather jacket and faded jeans – no school uniform, Jack noted, so he clearly wasn't intending to join Jack in classes today. Jack sighed and started to turn back towards the school building. He had three and a half minutes to get himself to Mrs Beasley's form room before she shut the door.

"Hey, Jack." The voice rang out from across the road. "Have a nice day at school!"

Jack turned his head to spot his brother stepping into the gutter, a spindly cigarette dangling from his lips and a bottle of something in his hand.

Good God, not alcohol already, thought Jack. It's not even nine o'clock. But he wouldn't put it past Stuart. He wouldn't put anything past him. Not anymore.

"Better hurry up; you don't want to be late!" Stuart MacIntosh collapsed in peals of laughter, in between drags on his hand-rolled cigarette.

Jack gave one last glance across the road before jogging across the playground towards the main entrance of the school. Out of the corner of his eye he saw Stuart giving him a wave; his multi-coloured Swap Shop scarf draped around his neck.

* * *

Time: 11.45am
Date: Sunday 10th February 2013

Location: The Laurels Nursing Home, London

The Swap Shop scarf. Jack's heart thumped wildly in his chest as he strode as quickly as he could across the car park. He could remember it vividly now. Stuart had somehow managed to get hold of one – winning some competition or other on the Saturday morning TV show, so he said. He wore it everywhere.

Jack swallowed, suddenly feeling an overwhelming sense of nausea. He wrenched open the door to the Mondeo and slipped inside, regretting DS Cooper's greasy bacon sandwich from earlier. Multi-coloured stripes swam in front of his eyes.

The same scarf being at the scene of Edward Wakefield's murder; surely that was a coincidence? Jack felt his heartbeat racing as he fumbled with the keys in the ignition. It had to be. Otherwise… Jack pushed the unwanted thoughts from his mind and switched on the engine. As he did so, he felt his phone vibrate in his pocket with an incoming message. Pulling it out and glancing at the screen, he automatically hit redial.

Dr Matthews answered almost immediately. "Jack. Thanks for returning my call."

"No problem, Doc," replied Jack, turning up the heaters as the engine idled. "What can I do for you?"

"Your second victim. The younger Wakefield. I've completed my examination."

"And?" Jack almost dreaded to ask.

"It's as we thought, Jack. DC Cassidy will no doubt fill you in, but I'll be sending my report over this afternoon. It was a single stab wound to the heart followed by a severing of the carotid artery, just to make sure."

Jack nodded, gazing back out of the window towards The Laurels. "Not suffocated this time, then?"

"No, not this one, Jack. No need. Death would have been very quick."

"And the tattoo?"

"The same. Upper right thigh. Same size, and I would be so bold to say inflicted by the same knife." Dr Matthews paused. "Whoever your killer is,

Jack, they're leaving their mark."

Jack briefly closed his eyes. "Thanks, Doc."

He ended the call and took one last look back towards the closed doors of The Laurels. An image of the number fifteen swirled around inside his head, intertwined with the unmistakeable stripes of the Swap Shop scarf.

* * *

Chapter Six

Time: 1.30pm

Date: Sunday 10th February 2013

Location: Metropolitan Police HQ, London

Jack switched on the overhead lights, the overcast skies outside already casting shadows over the investigation room. "How was the PM?"

DC Cassidy looked up, her face still pale but having lost the pale green tinge from earlier. She nodded and took a sip of water. "It was fine." It was all she could manage.

Jack nodded. "Well, thanks for attending. It's not the easiest of tasks. I've spoken to Dr Matthews and he's sending his report over later today. It was as we thought — stab wounds to the heart and neck. And the same number fifteen tattooed to the right thigh. While we wait for the report, what else is new?"

DC Cassidy took another sip of water, taking control of the whiteboard screen. "Updated statements from the staff at The Laurels are in — just one or two are still being processed and uploaded. Nothing too striking from the first read through though. The nurse on drug round duty that day, Natalie Evans, confirms that she didn't see anybody who wasn't a member of staff in the building throughout the day. It was very quiet. Both Rosemary Ward and Janine Carter were working that day, too. Neither saw anything unusual — although Ms Ward had been in her office for the majority of the time. Janine says she is sure that there were no visitors at all, but did admit to not always being at her desk. So your guess is as good as mine on that one. All staff re-interviewed report not seeing anything out of place."

"I spoke with Natalie Evans earlier today," replied Jack, taking a seat next to DC Cassidy. "Someone filled in the whiteboard outside Edward Wakefield's room." Jack then filled both DC Cassidy and DS Cooper in on the faulty fire exit door just fourteen steps from room E16. "So, I think we can conclude this is someone who has been inside The Laurels before. Either as a visitor or a member of staff. They knew about the faulty fire exit door, and the drug round boards. We'll need to go through the visitor log book again."

"No statements in yet on the door-to-door along Terence Wakefield's street," added DC Cassidy. "They're finishing up as we speak."

"Give it a chase tomorrow, along with the lab; see if they have any preliminary results from The Laurels." Jack grabbed a couple of chocolate digestives from an open pack on the table. His stomach was telling him he hadn't eaten in a while; the bacon sandwich from earlier seemed a lifetime ago and his nausea from before had subsided during the drive back from The Laurels. "Cooper? What about any background on the victims?"

DS Cooper flipped over his notebook. "This may or may not be relevant boss. I haven't had a chance to get it typed up onto the system, but I've compiled a list of where the Wakefields have been living over the last twenty years or so, and their employment histories. Such as they are. Details are pretty sketchy. Neighbours seem to confirm that they both worked cash in hand, doing handyman kind of jobs, but I've managed to get a general time line."

Jack crammed another digestive into his mouth. He nodded at DS Cooper to continue.

"As we know, Edward Wakefield spent the last eight years at The Laurels Nursing Home, moving there in 2005. Before that, he lived with his son at Charlotte Street, Finsbury. – the address where Terence was killed. However, they only moved there in 1992, around the same time that Mrs Wakefield passed away. Before that, housing records show that between 1987 and 1992 they were in receipt of housing benefit at an address in Bethnal

Green. During that time, it seems they set up a father and son gardening and general handyman service. Before living at Bethnal Green, the Wakefield family lived together down towards the South coast. This seems to have been their family home for some time. While living there, both Edward and Terence worked at a local boys' home near Christchurch." DS Cooper paused and slipped a piece of paper out from his notebook. It showed an image of a Victorian-style mansion set amongst mature trees and fields. "I've printed a copy of the only photograph I could find online. I'm told its pretty derelict now."

Jack almost choked on the remnants of his digestive biscuit. His eyes widened as DS Cooper pushed the photograph towards him. As his eyes flickered over the image, he felt his heart quicken once more and the familiar feeling of dread clench at his insides.

"St Bartholomew's Home for Boys," chimed Jack and DS Cooper in unison.

* * *

Time: 3.15pm
Date: Sunday 10th February 2013
Location: Metropolitan Police HQ, London

Jack quietly shut the door and sat down behind his desk. He avoided looking at the ever-growing in-tray that appeared to be swelling in size by the second. Back at work for three days and people had already heard that Jack MacIntosh was in the building.

But that wasn't what was on his mind.

With a few moments to himself, having sent DS Cooper on an errand to replenish the dwindling stocks of tea and coffee for the investigation room, a ten-pound note pressed into his palm, and DC Cassidy collating witness statements, Jack reached for the stack of phone messages pinned underneath a paperweight. Glancing through them, he picked out the one he needed and snatched up his desk phone, punching in the number. It was answered on the third ring.

"Jennifer Davies, how can I help?" The voice was light and melodious, a faint Welsh accent discernible on the fringes.

"Jennifer. Hi. It's DI MacIntosh."

"Hello, Inspector. What can I do for you?"

"The samples from the Edward Wakefield crime scene, the one at the nursing home," began Jack. "You have a scarf that was found with the victim's body?"

There was a slight pause before Jennifer's Welsh tones filled the receiver once more. "Yes, indeed we do. We still have quite a few samples still to process from that scene, Inspector. And your second crime scene now, too. It will take some time." She paused. "DS Cooper has already requested that they be done ASAP. We're doing our best."

"Yes, yes, I know. I appreciate it." Jack nodded, his eyes trained on the closed office door. The last thing he needed right now was an interruption. "Just as fast as you can, that's all I can ask. But in relation to the scarf..."

"Yes?" Jack imagined Jennifer Davies' eyebrows raising. "What about it?"

"It's quite old...probably the late 1970s, I think. It's an original from the Swap Shop Saturday morning TV show."

"OK. Well, it's not a show that I'm familiar with, Inspector. Long before my time!"

Jack suddenly felt very old. "Well, it was pretty popular back in the day." He couldn't help the memories flooding his brain of sitting watching TV on a Saturday morning, dressed in his pyjamas, eating his breakfast on his lap. He shook his head to dislodge the visions. "I just wondered...we're obviously interested in any samples on the scarf in relation to the deceased and his killer, or killers. But I wondered if any tests would show up samples that were already on the scarf prior to the offence." Jack paused. "As in decades ago?"

"I'm not sure I follow, Inspector?"

Jack sighed. "When running your tests for DNA traces, will it pick up any DNA that may have been there for, say, thirty years? From the original owner of the scarf?"

Jack heard rustling at the other end of the line and some muffled voices in the background.

"DNA can take many millions of years to decompose, Inspector, as you probably already know. But it will depend on how the object, in this case the scarf, was kept or stored. DNA will degenerate over time, just like anything else. It's a question I cannot really answer, I'm sorry." Jennifer paused. "Everything will be tested in accordance with our established protocols. If there is DNA there to be found, Inspector, we will find it."

That's what I'm afraid of, thought Jack, rubbing his eyes. "Thanks, Jennifer. Let me know when you have any results in."

"I will. And call me Jenny. Jennifer makes me sound old." She gave a faint laugh at the other end of the phone. "I must go now – we still have lots to do. I'll try and get something out to you tomorrow, but no promises."

The call ended and Jack replaced the receiver.

Jennifer's words echoed around inside his head.

If there is DNA there to be found, Inspector, we will find it.

Jack's stomach churned.

Putting aside his growing disquiet at the discovery of the Swap Shop scarf, he now had another concern competing for space.

St Bartholomew's.

The name echoed emptily inside his head.

Shaking the mouse to re-activate his desk-top computer, Jack brought up Google and typed in 'St Bartholomew's Home for Boys Christchurch'.

The page was instantly filled with thumbnails of various images of the same building – most giving the exact same view of a dilapidated Victorian mansion house covered in rampant ivy and hidden behind a wire-mesh fence. Jack clicked on one of the images and brought up an accompanying newspaper report from July 1992.

'DEMOLITION ORDER HALTED FOR FORMER FOSTER HOME'

Jack scrolled through the report – an article that had made it to page seven of the Christchurch Weekly News. English Heritage had blocked a demolition order imposed by the local Council which would have seen the former Victorian foster home razed to the ground to make way for a housing development. Citing that the building was of national importance, a year-long legal wrangle resulted in a stay of execution.

Jack scrolled down through the later and more recent thumbnail images on the screen – noting how run-down and abandoned the home now looked. He recalled visiting the site some nine months ago with Stuart – the first time either had visited for over thirty years. Now an empty shell, all that seemed to hold it together was the creeping ivy entwined amongst the reddened brickwork. The roof had partially collapsed, leaving the internal structure exposed to the weather. Every window was either broken or boarded up.

Jack clicked on another image. This was the only image he could see of the Victorian mansion in its heyday – if that could ever be the correct term for a place with such a grim past. A tiny box in the corner stated the photograph had been taken in June 1840. It was a black and white image of an imposing, yet impressive, three storey building with a grand double-fronted door. Jack noticed two large Greek-style urns, one each side of the entrance, filled with flowers – giving the impression of Victorian grandeur. The woodwork around each window looked clean and freshly painted, the windows themselves shiny and new. The sweeping gravel drive that led up to the entrance was lined with flowers and shrubs.

Jack turned his attention to the collection of beaming smiles on the faces of ten people lining the front steps. Peering closer and enlarging the screen, Jack identified whom he guessed to be the owners, or at least the managers, standing in the centre. A tall man in a well-fitting three-piece suit, complete with monocle and moustache, stood stiffly by the side of a slightly shorter woman. She was dressed in a full length regal-like gown, with her hair scraped harshly away from her porcelain face in a bun sitting firmly atop her head.

To each side of them were two women, whom Jack presumed were staff members. They wore neat matron-like uniforms with crisply starched white aprons and each sported mirror-like beaming smiles. At their feet, sitting on the bottom step, were four boys who could be no more than six or seven years of age. They were dressed smartly in their Sunday best, with their hair combed back away from their freshly scrubbed faces.

Jack noticed the headline for the 1990 article that contained the image.

'150-YEAR ANNIVERSARY OF ABANDONED LOCAL FOSTER HOME'

He quickly printed off a couple of the thumbnail images and folded everything up inside his jacket pocket. The churning sensation inside his stomach continued, unabated.

Both Edward and Terence Wakefield had once worked at St Bartholomew's Home for Boys.

It was too much of a coincidence.

And Jack didn't believe in coincidences.

Checking his watch, Jack knew there was somebody he needed to go and see.

* * *

Time: 4.00pm

Date: Sunday 10th February 2013

Location: Metropolitan Police HQ, London

DS Robert Carmichael nodded at Jack to take a seat.

"I wasn't sure if you would still be here," commented Jack, moving a case file from the only vacant chair. "As it's Sunday."

"I'm always here, Jack," mused DS Carmichael, rubbing his eyes. "This investigation is never ending."

"That's kind of what I wanted to talk to you about."

"Operation Yewtree?" DS Carmichael raised his eyebrows above an intense, beady stare. When Jack and Robert Carmichael had first crossed paths in the summer of 2012, Jack would freely admit that he got the hard-working, dogged detective sergeant wrong. Initially labelling him as obstructive, lazy and secretive, Jack hadn't been enthused with the latest addition to his investigative team.

But Jack had been wrong about DS Robert Carmichael.

Jack had been very wrong indeed.

"Not Yewtree as such," replied Jack. "More your own investigation – Operation Evergreen?"

DS Carmichael nodded, slowly, and reached for the mug of coffee that was now stagnant and cold. He had a feeling he knew where this conversation was heading. "And what do you need to know exactly?"

Jack paused, all of a sudden unsure of how to put his thoughts into words. He could be making a mountain out of a molehill, diving down a rabbit hole head-first never to resurface. Or he could be right.

He decided to trust his instincts.

"I need to know what you have on St Bartholomew's – the foster home in Christchurch."

DS Carmichael nodded. "Of course. There's been a lot of work done already – hundreds of witness statements taken from all manner of institutions, including St Bartholomew's. This investigation has gone off in a multitude of directions."

"The two murders my team are investigating – Edward and Terence Wakefield. Father and son. It seems both worked at St Bartholomew's in the 1970s and 1980s. It might be nothing, but..."

"You think that's the link to the killer – St Bartholomew's?"

Jack shrugged. "I don't know. Maybe. Maybe not. But something's telling me it's not a coincidence."

DS Carmichael replaced the cold mug of coffee and pushed his lean frame up out of his chair. Turning towards the bank of filing cabinets that lined the wall to the rear, he quickly found what he was looking for. Pulling open the drawer marked S-V, he retrieved a thin buff-coloured folder and returned to his seat.

"There's not much I can tell you at the moment, Jack. Not because of any operational restrictions – nothing like that. You know I'd always help you where I can. It's just that we don't have a lot to go on right now. Investigations into St Bartholomew's are at an early stage. It's been difficult to track down former workers at the home – it was closed in the mid-eighties. Most of them could very well be dead by now. And it's been even harder to trace the boys that were housed there. People change their names. Move away. People don't want to be found."

Jack sighed and nodded. He had thought as much. He pulled out the images and articles he had printed off earlier. "I only have a few basic facts about the place so far. A couple of newspaper articles about the anniversary and demolition order."

DS Carmichael glanced over at the images while opening the folder in front of him. Taking a few seconds to leaf through the pages, he looked up at Jack with his beady eyes. Where once Jack had thought the jet-black eyes were cold and callous, he now saw that they had hidden depths of compassion and empathy. "I've got a bit more about the history of the place here. I'll copy it for you, in case there's anything in there that's helpful. You may want to talk to the manger we managed to trace –Albert Dawson. He ran the place in the 1970s until it closed. There's a statement and contact details in here. He's still alive. Just."

"Thanks, Rob," replied Jack, nodding his appreciation and watching as the detective sergeant again rose from his chair and began feeding sheets of paper into the photocopier. Jack took the opportunity to clear his throat and ask the question that had really brought him to DS Carmichael's door. "I heard that you managed to catch up with my brother – that you went out to Italy to take his statement?"

Jack saw DS Carmichael's back stiffen slightly as he continued to feed the photocopier. Stuart hadn't spoken much about Carmichael's visit. Only confirming that a visit had, indeed, taken place and that he had given a statement about his time at St Bartholomew's. Nothing more, nothing less. Clearly a sensitive subject, Jack had not felt able to press his brother any further.

"I did," confirmed DS Carmichael, scooping up the photocopied paper and turning back round to face Jack. He reached for an A4 sized brown envelope and slotted the paperwork inside. "I think you need to speak to your brother, Jack. I have his witness statement in here, plus whatever else we've managed to get so far." He tapped the envelope and handed it across the table. "But I think you need to speak to him first, before you read it. For his sake, as well as your own. You don't want to find out about this stuff from words on a sheet of paper." DS Carmichael paused again. "Talk to your brother, Jack. And quick."

* * *

Chapter Seven

Time: 8.45pm
Date: Sunday 10th February 2013
Location: Kettle's Yard Mews, London

Jack pulled two cans of Budweiser from the fridge and brought them back to the coffee table, placing them next to the Chinese takeaway that had just been delivered from the China Garden restaurant around the corner. He had ordered a New Year banquet, but had no idea what he would find inside. Although Jack had barely eaten all day, he still didn't feel hungry. With an ever growing and spreading sense of disquiet, he took a swig from one of the cans and glanced nervously at the door.

Stuart was late.

His brother had eventually returned his call and agreed to come over. Jack had noticed the usual lightness and humour in his voice was missing, a dullness to his replies. He didn't mention the letter from Social Services about the boxes – unsure if his brother was ready for more ghosts of the past to be revealed.

Jack glanced at his watch for what seemed like the thousandth time. He felt nervous. He had left DS Carmichael's office earlier armed with more information on St Bartholomew's, and also the contact number for the former manager; but Jack knew deep down that the only way to get the information he needed would be to get it from Stuart himself. He needed to know about the home, and he needed to know about the Wakefields.

Taking another mouthful of Budweiser, Jack felt the alcohol hit his empty stomach and start to enter his bloodstream. He had some single malt somewhere, but something told him he might need to keep the hard stuff for another time.

The buzzer for the outside door startled him back to his senses, and he padded over to the internal phone immediately pressing the door release.

He knew it would be Stuart, without even needing to ask. He received little or no visitors these days, being the eternal bachelor that he was. Taking a deep breath, Jack buried the thought of how sad that sounded, and pulled open the door.

* * *

Time: 9.30pm

Date: Sunday 10th February 2013

Location: Isabel's Café, King's Road, London

Isabel flipped the sign over to closed and sank, gratefully, back against the door, her eyes closed.

"Thank goodness for that!" she sighed, letting her shoulders sag. "What a night!"

Sacha took a hold of Isabel's arm and pulled her across to the comfortable leather sofa by the window, gently pushing her down amongst the cushions. "Sit yourself down here. Let me and Dom clear up. That's an order!"

Isabel smiled and watched as Sacha began collecting up the large platters of Chinese New Year delicacies from each of the tables; platters which were now, thankfully, empty. The Chinese themed evening had gone down a storm, just as Sacha had predicted. While Isabel had been away in Italy with Mac, she and Dominic had put on several themed events and each one had caused the café to be packed with customers. With Spanish, German and

Swedish under her belt, she had chosen Chinese to coincide with the New Year celebrations.

Although Isabel had only just returned from her travels, she insisted that she wanted to help – so, despite her tiredness, she had mingled with her customers and marvelled at the Chinese creations that were on offer. Sacha really had done her proud.

But now, feeling utterly exhausted, all Isabel could do was watch her best friend tidying up around her. She could hear Dominic in the kitchen busily loading up the dishwasher and no doubt preparing the kitchen for the following morning. Isabel couldn't bring herself to think about tomorrow – all she could think about was sleep.

"That was amazing, Sacha. Really. The whole evening was spectacular. Thank you." Isabel accepted the hastily brewed cup of raspberry tea that Sacha brought to her side. "It was such a wonderful idea!"

Sacha beamed, happily. "Pubs and restaurants do it – so I thought, why not us? Our first one, Spanish night, was so successful I just felt that we needed to keep doing it!"

Isabel nodded, gratefully, and took a long sip of the relaxing tea. "I couldn't have left the café in safer hands. Really, thank you. You've been amazing. Both of you."

"You're more than welcome." Sacha busied herself brushing crumbs from the table tops and sweeping them up with a dustpan and brush. Although it was late, and she was really tired, she was buzzing with excitement. "I thought maybe the next one should be Polish, or maybe Italian – after your recent travels?"

"Maybe," nodded Isabel, her eyelids closing as the warmth from the soothing tea washed over her. "I'll leave that up to you – it looks like you've got it all in hand." She stifled a yawn behind her hand.

"You go on up. You look exhausted." Sacha placed her dustpan and brush down and reached for Isabel's arm, gently pulling her to her feet. "Dom and I can lock up." Isabel opened her mouth to protest but Sacha pulled her towards the stairs. "Go on, up you go! There's not much to do down here – everything's been eaten, so it's a question of a quick sweep and wipe down.

It won't take long."

Isabel found herself yawning once again. Tiredness was seeping into her bones, and all she could think about was tumbling into bed. She nodded, gratefully. "Ok, thank you. I am tired."

Sacha smiled and nudged Isabel further towards the stairs. "Off you go, then. We'll see you tomorrow."

Isabel willed herself to put one foot in front of the other. She reached the bottom of the stairs, and was about to grab hold of the handrail to pull herself up when Sacha called out.

"Oh, before you go, someone left this for you." Sacha scurried over to the counter and picked up a small fortune cookie. They had sold hundreds during the course of the evening, but this one had been left by a customer, specifically for Isabel.

Isabel frowned and took hold of the small hollow biscuit. "For me?"

Sacha nodded. "Can't remember who gave it to me now. But I was to make sure you got it."

Isabel continued to frown as she broke open the fortune cookie and pulled out the tightly curled up piece of paper inside. She flattened the paper out and read the proverb, a shiver rippling up her spine as she did so.

"The best way to get rid of an enemy is to make them a friend."

* * *

Time: 9.35pm
Date: Sunday 10th February 2013
Location: Kettle's Yard Mews, London

"I made a statement to your mate DS Carmichael." Mac drained his second can and crumpled it inside his fist. "I don't want to go over it all again."

"I'm not asking you to, Stu." Jack kept his voice low and steady. A full-on row with his brother was not what he had intended. "I just need you to talk to me. I haven't read your statement, so I don't know what you may have told Rob." Jack paused while he watched Mac grab another can from the six pack he had brought with him, and rip it open.

"Why don't you just read it then?" Mac gulped at his beer and avoided Jack's gaze. "I didn't come here for it all to be dragged up again."

Jack could detect the all too familiar barriers starting to form before his very eyes.

"Just read my statement if you want to know what I said. I'm not repeating it."

Jack shook his head. "Rob said it would be best coming from you. I could read it, yes, but I'd rather you told me."

There was a strained silence for a while as Jack finished his beer and placed the empty can on the coffee table next to the takeaway that had, so far, remained untouched.

"Do you remember Betty and John?" The question came out of the blue and took Jack by surprise.

"Betty and John?" replied Jack. "The Garners?"

Mac nodded. "Yes. The Garners. You remember them? I remember them more than I remember mum."

Jack reached for his second can of Budweiser and let his mind wander, casting his mind back to when he was four years old. Betty and John Garner – the first proper foster family that had taken them both in after their mother's death. "They were good times, Stu."

Mac shrugged, still avoiding his brother's gaze. "Maybe for you. Didn't quite work out like that for me."

Jack sighed. Here we go again, he thought. "You didn't make life easy for them, Stu. They were good people. They were good to us."

Mac flashed a hot look at Jack. "I know it was all my fault, Jack. You don't need to rub it in. My life went down the toilet and it was all my doing – I get it."

Jack flinched. He hadn't heard his brother quite so animated or hostile for quite some time. Since they had crashed back into each other's lives last summer, after spending years without contact, Jack had felt Stuart had relaxed a little; lost the famous hot-headedness that had landed him in trouble for much of his teenage years...and beyond. Finally, he had felt that his brother had matured, and somehow come to terms with his past.

But something had changed.

Something had rattled his cage again.

"No one's saying that, Stu," replied Jack, trying to keep his voice steady. "What's in the past is in the past. We've been through this."

Mac paused, swallowing past a lump in his throat that had materialised, unbidden and unwanted. "I can't help thinking that if we had stayed with the Garners – if Betty and John had kept us – then none of this would have happened." Mac's words hung in the air alongside the aroma of chicken chow mein. The only sound that could be heard was the faint feathery snowflakes tapping against the kitchen window pane.

"None of what would have happened?"

"They could have kept us, Jack." Mac's voice was no more than a whisper. "If they had, I might not have ended up where I did; doing the things I did. Things could have been different. *I* could have been different. They could have kept us together, couldn't they, Jack?"

Jack looked up and saw, not a forty-four-year-old grown man across the table, but a frightened and bewildered four-year-old about to be separated from the comfort and safety of his older brother. He found himself shaking his head, and watching a range of emotions fighting for space on Mac's face. "They couldn't keep us, Stu. You know that."

"I didn't mean to keep setting fire to things, Jack." The four-year-old Stuart MacIntosh was still very much evident and Jack could only watch helplessly from across the other side of the coffee table. "I don't know why I did it. Even after hours and hours of therapy while I was inside, I never really knew why I did it."

"None of that matters now, Stu." Jack reached for the bag of prawn crackers; somebody had to start eating something. Alcohol on an empty stomach whilst reminiscing about misspent childhoods was not the best mix. "Betty and John couldn't keep us anyway. You know Betty had cancer?"

Mac looked up and nodded. "Yeah, I found out a while later."

"She died not long after we were taken away." Jack nudged the prawn crackers across the table. "I doubt John would have been allowed to keep us on his own. It was the seventies. Rules were different about foster carers back then."

"I liked Betty." Mac paused and a hint of a smile ghosted his lips. "You remember the scones she used to make? And how she would let us eat left-over cake mix from the bowl while John wasn't looking?"

Jack felt himself smiling. He didn't think about his foster care days very much anymore; whether by choice or circumstance, he wasn't sure. Thinking back to those days would undoubtedly unleash more of the nightmares that he had been struggling to control in recent years. His recent sabbatical and hypnotherapy course with Dr Riches confirmed it wasn't something he wished to re-open. He shook his head to rid himself of the thoughts. "She was a wonderful woman, Stu. But don't beat yourself up about what came after. You're not that person anymore."

Mac shrugged and leant forwards towards the coffee table. He raised one of the plastic lids on the now cooled Chinese takeaway. "Maybe we should heat some of this up?"

Jack felt his smile widen and twitch at the corners of his mouth. The barriers were coming down – slowly. He picked up the plastic trays and headed over to the microwave, rummaging in the cupboards for two plates while their dinner re-heated. Out of the corner of his eye he saw his brother reach for another can of Budweiser and handful of prawn crackers, a faraway look in his eye, lost in his own thoughts.

It's now or never, thought Jack.

Bringing the re-heated chicken chow mein and chop suey back to the table, Jack took in a deep breath.

"Tell me about St Bartholomew's, Stu. I don't want to read it. I want to hear you tell me – in your own words."

* * *

88

Chapter Eight

Time: 10.15pm

Date: Sunday 10th February 2013

Location: Kettle's Yard Mews, London

Most of the chow mein and chop suey lay congealed and uneaten on their plates; their initial alcohol-fuelled hunger quickly evaporating as Mac began to recount life at St Bartholomew's Home for Boys.

Jack felt increasingly sick to the stomach.

"You never said anything." It was all Jack could think to say. "You never once said *anything.*"

Mac shook his head. "Who would I tell?"

"Me?" Jack looked up and locked eyes with his brother. "You could have told *me.*"

Another shake of the head. "No I couldn't, Jack. Until last summer, we hadn't spoken in years. The only time I ever got in contact with you was when I needed money. I was a leech, Jack. You know that. You didn't need me to burden you with this as well."

"Well, someone then. You should have told *someone.*"

Mac gave a small laugh that caught in his throat. "Yeah, I tried that. It didn't work. I tried talking about it during one of my so-called therapy sessions while I was in juvenile detention. I had a really nice case-worker at the time; someone who I thought was really listening to me, and really wanted to help."

"And?"

Mac's chuckle deepened. "Waste of time, Jack. I hinted to her about what had been going on at St Bartholomew's. I really trusted her; thought that I could at last tell someone who could help. Get it off my chest."

"What did she say?" Jack asked the question, but felt he already knew the answer by his brother's tone of voice.

"She cut me loose, Jack. Assigned me to someone else. I never saw her again." Mac paused and took another sip of beer. "I learned very quickly after that to keep my mouth shut."

Jack sighed. "Well, it might not feel like it right now, but it's good that you've decided to talk."

"That DS Carmichael," nodded Mac. "I like him. He's a good bloke."

Jack smiled. "Yes, he is."

Mac fiddled with the ring pull on his beer. "I was one of the lucky ones. I saw a lot of stuff there – stuff I never want to see again. And yes, I got beaten black and blue some days – but there were boys in there who got it far worse than me."

Jack nodded. He had got the general gist from the statements DS Carmichael had handed to him, including the statement of Stuart MacIntosh. And although Jack had promised he wouldn't look at it before speaking to his brother, he had ripped open the sealed envelope as soon as he had returned to the quiet sanctity of his own office.

And he hadn't even read through to the end; halfway through he had to give up before his sanity gave way.

But he had still needed to hear the words from his brother's mouth – without that they were just words on a piece of paper. They weren't real. They weren't true.

From what he had managed to read, Jack saw that violence, neglect and abuse was widespread at St Bartholomew's Home for Boys; that was plainly evident. Physical beatings and whippings with all manner of bats, belts and canes were commonplace. Never to the head or face, though. Never where it was visible.

Attendance at school appeared to be sporadic at best; suspensions and expulsions were rife, neither of which seemed to raise concerns with the local education authority. The boys were out of sight, and out of mind. Locked in their rooms or put to work around the foster home, their days were filled with mindless chores. Cleaning. Scrubbing. Polishing. A few chosen ones had the luxury of working in the gardens and tending to the flowerbeds and vegetable patches – the rest were kept inside, waiting for the scraps of food that would come from the kitchens at the end of the day and pass itself off as a meal.

Only when visitors came were the boys allowed out of their rooms, cleaned up and made presentable. Clothes covered the bruises and scars; plastic smiles adorned their carbolic-soap scrubbed faces. The older boys would take visitors on a tour of the home; stopping by the recreation room where boys could be seen holding books they were never allowed to read, and sitting in front of a television they were rarely allowed to watch.

If that were not grim enough reading, the other statements DS Carmichael had managed to obtain also suggested that physical abuse was not the only abuse that occurred within the thick Victorian walls of St Bartholomew's. Jack felt physically sick as he read his brother's account of life at the home – where he described witnessing occasions of sexual mistreatment and abuse on a disturbingly regular pattern.

Although relieved to hear his brother had not been subject to the abuse itself, he felt sickened that he had had to witness it first-hand. Anyone reading Stuart MacIntosh's statement would feel a shiver run up their spine as he described being lucky to have been beaten. Lucky to have had his forearm broken; twice. Lucky to have required stitches to a gash on his scalp. Lucky to have scars on his back and legs from the belts that whipped them black and blue.

Lucky.

Lucky because that was as far as it went.

Jack went on to read how his brother would see boys taken from their rooms, late at night, to attend parties that were held somewhere within the grounds. Statements from former residents, now grown men, described how these parties occurred once or twice a month, with a handful of boys picked especially for each occasion.

And although he may not have known exactly what went on at these parties, Stuart MacIntosh prayed to God every night that he would be spared.

And God seemed to have listened.

"What about the Wakefields?" Jack's voice cut through the uncomfortable silence that had now descended into the room. "You remember them?"

Mac gave another quiet laugh. "Oh yes, I remember them all right. Edward Wakefield was the first person I met on the day I arrived at St Bartholomew's. And the last person I saw when I left. I'll never forget that face, not in a million years."

* * *

Time: 1.30pm

Date: Saturday 10th September 1977

Location: St Bartholomew's Home for Boys, Christchurch

"Stand up boy!" growled Edward Wakefield, caretaker of St Bartholomew's Home for Boys. "And don't start with any of that crying. I can't bear children who cry."

Stuart MacIntosh looked up into the leathery skin that was now inches from his own, recoiling slightly from the stale cabbage and cigarette breath that wafted towards his face. The vice-like grip the man had on his wrist tightened as Stuart was forcibly dragged across the cold tiles of the entrance hall towards an oak door at the rear. Stuart clenched his eyes tightly shut in a bid to halt the tears that threatened to spill from his eyes. The slap the caretaker had given him only seconds before still stung on his cheek.

The journey up the three flights of stairs seemed to take forever, with Stuart stumbling behind Edward Wakefield's large, lumbering frame. But within a minute they came to a halt outside another wooden door, and Stuart found himself pushed roughly up against the crumbling brickwork of the darkened corridor.

"Don't get any funny ideas about running away, boy," snarled Edward Wakefield, his chipped and uneven teeth showing beneath his sneer. More stale, watery cabbage and cigarettes wafted towards Stuart's face. "You stay right where you are and don't move an inch. *Don't even breathe.*"

Stuart watched, petrified, as the wooden door was pushed open and he was dragged once again by the wrist and shoved inside.

"Meet your new room-mates," chuckled Edward Wakefield, to no one in particular, his gravelly laugh turning into a throaty cough as he started to pull the door shut again. "And I don't want to hear a peep out of any of you. If I so much as hear a whisper, I'll take my belt to the lot of you."

Stuart MacIntosh shivered at the sound of the key turning in the lock, while the rattling cough disappeared down the corridor away from his new home.

* * *

Time: 10.35pm
Date: Sunday 10th February 2013
Location: Kettle's Yard Mews, London

"He was the caretaker for the whole time I was there," continued Mac, gazing down at the beer can in his lap. "He took it upon himself to be the one who dished out most of the beatings, too." Jack saw his brother give an involuntary shudder at the recollection. "He was cruel, just because he could be. He hated children, I'm sure of it. He never showed one ounce of kindness towards anyone." Mac paused. "I heard that he was the chap killed in that care home a couple of days ago. I'm glad he's dead. I hope he suffered."

Jack continued to watch as Mac's face contorted with hidden anger and frustration; his hands starting to crush the can in his lap.

"And the one yesterday; that was his son, right? Terry?"

Jack nodded. "Yes. Terence Wakefield was found dead at his home late yesterday afternoon."

Mac nodded, his mouth set in a firm line. "Good. Another one that won't be missed. He was no better. Made in his father's image, that one."

"What did Terence do at St Bartholomew's?"

Mac shrugged. "He was a kind of handyman and gardener. He basically did what his dad told him and followed in his shadow. He would dish out a fair number of the beatings himself, too – or at least help. I remember one time; Edward Wakefield was laying into me because I hadn't mopped the stairs properly. He was beating me with his belt across my back. When he'd finished, Terry stepped up and poured bleach into my wounds and just laughed. It hurt like hell and all I could see was this look of glee on his face."

Jack shivered, despite the warmth of the room. "I had no idea, Stu. I'm sorry."

Mac merely shrugged again and avoided Jack's eyes. "Yeah well, the pair of them can rot in hell as far as I'm concerned. The world is a better place without them. Are we done now?"

Jack thought about the Swap Shop scarf and the burning questions he wanted to ask – *needed* to ask. But at the same time, felt as though he might not want to hear the answers. The barriers were coming back up and Jack knew that he wasn't going to get any further with Stu tonight.

"Yes, we're done. Eat your chicken."

* * *

Time: 11.50pm
Date: Sunday 10th February 2013
Location: Kettle's Yard Mews, London

Jack sighed and leant back against the door, hearing the communal front door below slam shut behind his departing brother. As much as he didn't want them to, the Wakefields and the Swap Shop scarf seemed to be inextricably linked to Stu. The thought churned the remnants of the chop suey in his stomach.

He picked up the dirty plates and ran hot water over them in the sink. Although he knew it was a bad idea, he reached for the bottle of Glenfiddich and poured a couple of inches into a clean glass. Leaving the plates to soak, he sat back down on the sofa and glanced at the letter from Social Services buried underneath empty beer cans. More secrets, he mused, taking a sip of the whisky and instantly feeling its warmth. He resolved to ring first thing in the morning and arrange for the boxes to be delivered. Although they surely couldn't contain much, certainly nothing he had missed over the last forty years, he was intrigued.

With the whisky taking effect, Jack relaxed back on the sofa and closed his eyes, pushing all thoughts of the Wakefields and the damned Swap Shop scarf from his mind. What he wouldn't give to be back at the Tannochside B&B, sharing a fireside whisky with Willie McArthur – with no cares in the world, save for where he planned to walk early the next day.

* * *

Time: 3.35pm
  Date: Friday 14th December 2012
  Location: Tannochside, Scotland

Clad in his brand new waterproof trousers and hiking boots, Jack stepped out onto the deserted road and headed back in the direction of the Tannochside B&B. He glanced back over his shoulder at the bleak, grassy mountain ridge that he had just scaled, and gave himself a self-satisfied smile. His fingernails were ripped and torn, and he had scratches across the back of each hand, but he proudly displayed his war wounds as he forced his weary legs to trek the two miles back to his temporary home.

He had forgotten his gloves, hence the scratches and ripped fingernails, but was glad of the thermals underneath his waterproof outer clothing. Although the day had dawned bright and clear without a cloud in the sky, the temperature had hovered only a touch above freezing all day. The sun was now sinking quickly, taking with it whatever warmth there had been, leaving the air sharp and crisp in its wake. Jack felt it burn his throat with every laboured breath he took.

The rustling of his waterproof trousers rubbing against each other was the only sound he could hear as he trudged along the narrow road. His legs and shoulders ached; the climb up the mountainside exercising muscles that had lain dormant for far too long.

He began to think about the roaring fire and tantalising smell of Mrs McArthur's cooking wafting in from the kitchen - a thought that helped him ignore the stabbing pain from the newly formed blisters on his heels. Although the boots had been a godsend across the rough terrain, they were unforgiving to his naïve feet, unaccustomed as they were to climbing mountains.

Jack covered the two miles more quickly than he had anticipated, and could soon see the neat stone-walled B&B nestling into the hillside, just across a small bridge that spanned the River Tannoch. He stepped onto the bridge and noticed that although the water level was low, it still tumbled and frothed over the rocks and pebbles in its path. The water was so clear, the rapidly sinking sun glistening on the surface as the water cascaded past, faster and faster until it was out of sight.

Jack could see a plume of smoke snaking up from the chimney at the centre of the B&B's roof. Thoughts of a fireside whisky began to warm his heart, and he quickened his step. Pushing open the outer door, he stamped his feet on the doormat and used the hardy cast-iron boot scraper to remove the mountainside from his boots. Satisfied he wasn't traipsing in mud and dirt, Jack nudged open the inner door and stepped down into the first reception room.

It was a welcoming wood panelled room with a small reception desk that doubled as a bar. A selection of comfortable sofas and armchairs sat in a haphazard fashion surrounding several small oak tables. The room was empty except for a lone hiker sat by the window, reading intently from a battered paperback; a black Labrador napping contentedly at his feet.

Although Mrs McArthur had sent him on his way earlier that day with a large, door-step wedge of a sandwich, filled with ham, cheese and pickle, Jack's stomach rumbled as the enticing aroma of home cooked food wafted towards him. He followed his nose and continued on through to the second reception room, a much larger room with more tables and comfortable chairs and a much larger, and well-stocked bar. Pride of place, however, had to be the open inglenook fireplace that hugged one wall, and Jack was pleased to note that the table in front of it was empty.

He hobbled over to the table, noticing how his muscles were already starting to seize up, and shrugged himself out of his jacket. Hanging the heavy waterproof across the back of a large wing backed armchair, he wondered if he dared take off his boots. His blisters were crying out to be released from their uncomfortable prison, but before he could make up his mind, a man appeared from the door next to the bar and headed towards him.

"Afternoon, Jack," spoke Mr McArthur, in his low, lilting tone. "How was your wee walk?"

Mr McArthur stood over six feet tall, often having to duck beneath the exposed beams of the stone walled bed and breakfast. Dressed in a comfortable woollen cardigan over the top of a tartan jumper, he looked as cosy as the fire roaring by Jack's side. His weather beaten rosy cheeks sported a large grin as he approached Jack's table.

"Good, thanks, Mr McArthur." Jack nodded towards his host, and let himself sink back into the high backed armchair.

"Ach, I've told you before – it's Willie, to you." Mr McArthur laughed heartily and perched on a neighbouring stool. "No more Mr McArthur...makes me sound like a headmaster."

Jack returned the smile. "OK, Willie. I'm glad to be back though – these boots need breaking in a bit more." He nodded down towards his walking boots, still itching to remove them.

Willie McArthur laughed again, holding his ample belly as he did so. "Give them a few more weeks and they'll be the most comfortable boots you've ever worn."

Jack groaned inwardly. He wasn't sure he could stand a few more weeks of throbbing pain.

"Anyway, where did you get to?" Willie McArthur inched his stool closer to the fire.

Jack pulled the sweater he was wearing over his head, suddenly starting to feel the heat of the flames; his newly-acquired thermal long-sleeved top beneath would be ample. "I headed out over the bridge, and then past that ruined farmhouse...then I turned down the lane just opposite and carried on up to the mountain that you can see in the distance over there." Jack turned his head and nodded out of the window behind him. "Got all the way to the top and back down again without breaking my neck."

Willie McArthur gave another chuckle. "Good man. Although I'll let you into a wee secret." He leant in closer to Jack, lowering his voice. "That there is no mountain." He nodded back out of the window and a broad grin crossed his face. "That'll be just a wee hill, laddie. *That*, is a mountain."

Willie McArthur turned to the side and pointed to a watercolour painting on the wall opposite the fireplace – a huge canvas depicting a snow-capped mountain stretching skywards.

Jack felt his cheeks colour, and not just from the heat of the fire, but he knew that Willie's jests were good humoured. The host of the Tannochside B&B enjoyed making a little fun of his English guest from time to time, and Jack found it somewhat endearing.

"Well, it's a mountain from where I come from," smiled Jack, reaching forwards and picking up the bar menu from the table. "What do you recommend tonight?"

Willie McArthur glanced down at the menu, pushing himself up off the stool. "You can't go far wrong with Margaret's venison stew and dumplings. Something to warm you from the inside. Or else the fish supper is always good - fresh fish caught this morning."

Jack let his eyes sweep the menu once again – it all looked and sounded so good, and so did the smells that were constantly teasing his nostrils. So long as it was hot and freshly made, his stomach was telling him that he could eat almost anything.

Almost anything.

Willie McArthur had tried to get Jack to eat haggis a few nights ago, but that had been a step too far in Jack's book. Despite being plied with a few stiff glasses of whisky beforehand, it wasn't a taste he particularly liked, or intended to indulge in again any time soon. Jack had, however, enjoyed the square sausage that Margaret McArthur served up for breakfast, sometimes with black pudding, but he would need much more acclimatising before he would let haggis pass his lips again.

"The venison sounds good," replied Jack, returning the menu to the table. "That'll suit me just fine."

Willie McArthur nodded, and started to make his way back towards the kitchen. "A wee dram while you wait?" He turned back towards Jack and raised his eyebrows, nodding towards the bar. It wasn't really a question that needed an answer. "A day's mountain climbing deserves a few glasses of the good stuff." He emphasised the word 'mountain' and gave Jack a good humoured wink.

Jack nodded and smiled. "That'd be grand, Willie."

"Good man." Willie McArthur slipped behind the bar. "I've got some Macleod's here that you should try." He pulled a bottle out from beneath the bar and grabbed a heavy crystal tumbler. "All the way from the Isle of Skye. Let me know what you think."

After pouring Jack a more than generous measure, and placing it on the fireside table in front of him, Willie McArthur disappeared into the kitchen to emerge a few minutes later with a basket of warm bread rolls and a small bowl of pea and ham broth.

"That should warm you up nicely in the meantime," he nodded. "One of Margaret's best, that is."

Jack settled back in his seat and sipped at the warming amber liquid in his glass, letting the heat of the whisky seep into his bloodstream. The aroma from the steaming bowl of broth made his stomach give a satisfying grumble.

All was good with the world.

All was good with Jack MacIntosh.

* * *

Time: 1.15am

Date: Monday 11th February 2013

Location: Kettle's Yard Mews, London

"Isabel?" Jack glanced at the time as he scrambled for the phone. "It's late. What's up?"

"I'm sorry, Jack – I shouldn't have called. I've woken you up." Isabel's voice sounded faint and distant.

"No, no – you're fine." Jack stretched his neck from side to side. He'd fallen asleep on the sofa again. "I'm still up. What's on your mind?"

"I...um...it's hard to say," began Isabel, stumbling over her words. Now that she had summoned up the courage to make the call, she wasn't quite sure what to say. It all sounded too silly when spoken out loud. "I don't know where to start..."

"Try the beginning," replied Jack, softly, getting to his feet and padding over to the kitchen to switch on the kettle. "I often find that helps."

"I..." repeated Isabel once again. "Tonight, we had a Chinese themed evening at the café. As it's Chinese New Year. An idea of Sacha's. It went really well."

"I'm glad to hear it." Jack heaped a teaspoon of coffee into a mug and waited for the kettle to boil. Caffeine at this time of night probably wasn't the best idea, but he wasn't expecting to sleep much anyway.

"Yes...well..." Isabel broke off. "It all sounds so silly now I've had time to think about it. You'll think I'm imagining things."

"Try me." Jack poured boiling water into the mug and slopped in a dash of milk.

"It was really busy. Lots of customers all night." Isabel's voice was still quiet and shaky around the edges. "At the end of the night, just as I was going up to the flat, Sacha passed me a fortune cookie." She paused for a moment. "One that a customer had left for me."

"OK." Jack stirred his coffee.

"Just an ordinary looking fortune cookie, so I broke it open." Isabel's voice faltered.

"And?"

"And I looked at the message inside. It was just so...weird."

"Weird in what way?" Jack didn't like weird; especially not in the early hours of the morning. There was silence from Isabel's end of the phone, but Jack knew she was still there as he could hear the faint rasp of her breath. He rubbed his eyes and brought his coffee back to the sofa. "Weird in what way, Isabel?" he repeated.

"The message – it was for me."

"Yes, you said." Jack frowned, taking a sip from his mug. "It was left for you by a customer. Maybe as a thank you?"

"No...no...I mean the message *inside* was for me, Jack."

Jack again rubbed his eyes and tried to shift the fog of tiredness that he felt creeping over him. "Isabel, I'm not following. The message inside the fortune cookie – what did it say?"

"It said 'the best way to get rid of an enemy is to make them a friend'."

"That was the message?"

Isabel nodded at her end of the phone. "Yes. That was the message. Don't you see what it means?"

"See what *what* means?"

"It's from him. The message. It's from *him*."

Jack paused. "Him?" He started to frown before realisation suddenly swept in. "You think...?"

"It's from him, Jack. Kreshniov. It's a message from him, I *know* it is."

"But...why?"

"Look, I don't know, Jack. But I know it's him. That message was meant for me."

"But Kreshniov..."

"It's the *words*, Jack. Don't you see? He was our enemy and now he wants to be our friend. It's him, I'm telling you. It's *him*."

After several more minutes of Jack placating an increasingly agitated Isabel, he managed to end the call by promising to stop by sometime in the morning and take a look at it for himself. In the meantime, he urged her not to worry. Kreshniov, if it was indeed him, was unlikely to mean her any harm. He wasn't sure if she believed him, but it was the best he could do.

Taking his cooling mug of coffee into the bedroom, he stood by the window and looked out over the frost covered rooftops as far as the eye could see. The whole of London was encased in a crisp, frozen shell.

Kreshniov.

Jack added the elusive Russian to the other worries that would be keeping him awake until morning.

* * *

Chapter Nine

Time: 7.55am
   Date: Monday 11th February 2013
   Location: Metropolitan Police HQ, London

Chief Superintendent Dougie King noted the gathering crowd and sighed. He had chosen an extra early press conference on a Monday morning in the vain hope that the majority of the capital's reporters might still be in their beds – but his hopes were dashed when he saw Pippa Reynolds, head of PR, organising extra chairs to be dragged into the conference room. She raised her eyebrows at him as he passed and gave an apologetic smile.

Gripping the brief notes that he had managed to scribble over an even earlier morning bowl of cornflakes, he made his way over to the raised platform and the table with two chairs positioned behind. He took his seat and nodded a greeting at DS Cooper who was already seated and pouring them both a glass of water.

"Jack happy to sit this one out?" Chief Superintendent King accepted the glass, taking a mouthful of water to loosen his dry throat.

DS Cooper nodded. "More than happy, Sir."

The Chief Superintendent forced a smile. "Wise choice. I'm not intending to let this lot keep us any longer than necessary, but needs must."

Press conferences were not usually joyous occasions at the best of times, but in today's information hungry world, they were unavoidable. There was an insatiable desire for news; media outlets constantly looking to feed their twenty-four hour rolling news platforms with a revolving diet of facts and opinions – some accurate, others not so.

Chief Superintendent King cast his eyes over the rows of reporters that were now beginning to fill the room; some he recognised, most he did not. Most had digital recorders in their hands, others opting for the traditional pen and paper; all had a look of quiet expectation on their faces. Taking another mouthful of water and gripping his page of notes, he nodded at Pippa to let the circus begin.

* * *

Time: 7.55am
　　Date: Monday 11ᵗʰ February 2013
　　Location: Metropolitan Police HQ, London

Jack glanced at his watch. The press conference would be just about to start – and if he knew the Chief Superintendent as well as he thought he did, it wouldn't last long. Jack had been more than happy to hand the reins over to DS Cooper on this one; having his unshaven and crumpled face on the early morning news was not part of Jack's plans for the day.

The Chief Superintendent had tactfully suggested that Jack needed to settle in after his extended leave before jumping into a press conference; and Jack had acquiesced without any argument. But they both knew the real reason the Chief Superintendent had suggested Jack sit this one out; Jack and the media were often a toxic combination. And another showdown with the press was not something Chief Superintendent King particularly welcomed.

Jack stifled a yawn and rubbed his eyes. Sleep had been evasive once again last night. After he had managed to calm Isabel down, promising to call by and take a look at the fortune cookie, he had tossed and turned for the rest of the night. Pictures of St Bartholomew's flooded in and out of his brain, together with an image of the multi-coloured Swap Shop scarf wrapped around Kreshniov's neck. Jack almost reached for the bottle of Glenfiddich again, anything to numb his brain, but had managed to resist.

It was the scarf that bothered him the most.

Once again, Jack brought up the image of the plastic evidence bag on his computer screen; the multi-coloured stripes clearly visible through the transparent cover. He told himself the likelihood of it being Stu's scarf was minute; minuscule even. There must have been hundreds, if not thousands, of them back in the heady days of Saturday morning kids' TV.

But there was equally a chance that it might be.

And as remote a possibility as that might be, it was still a possibility.

And that bothered Jack.

A vibration from his pocket interrupted his thoughts and he pulled out his phone to see that it was a message from Isabel. Thinking it might be another plea to call round about the fortune cookie, Jack opened the message, but he was surprised to see that it was a series of pictures. With the press conference no doubt underway, he reached for his coffee and opened the first image.

It was a picture of a beach with a wide expanse of golden sand; Isabel was standing on the edges of the shore, shielding her eyes from the sun.

Holiday snaps.

Jack inwardly groaned. Ordinarily, he could think of nothing worse than sitting through someone's reels of holiday photos, and as a rule usually made a point of not being subjected to them – but as he had time to kill, he continued scrolling.

Several more showed the inside and balcony area of an apartment, some atmospheric shots of cobbled Italian streets and the obligatory pictures of food at a variety of cafes and restaurants. Jack stifled another yawn and sipped at his coffee. The final few pictures made him smile – his brother trying his best to avoid the camera, but Isabel finally getting her way on one or two. His face looked different – and it wasn't just the hint of a golden tan on his skin. His eyes sparkled and reflected what could only be described as happiness.

Jack was about to close the message when the last photograph caught his eye. Stu was sitting on a rock at the edge of the water, the sun beating down overhead. He was wearing a pair of cut-off shorts and a cap on his head, wrap-around sunglasses shrouded his eyes. But that wasn't what had piqued Jack's interest.

It dawned on Jack that he couldn't remember ever seeing his brother without a top on. Not that he could recall anyway; not since they were kids living with Betty and John. He took in his brother's toned and tanned upper body, subconsciously pulling in his own belly as he did so. But it wasn't the muscles or six-pack that had caught his attention.

Jack's gaze was drawn to Stu's upper arm, which was facing the camera. Stu had a tattoo.

A tattoo of the number fifteen.

* * *

Time: 8.10am
Date: Monday 11th February 2013
Location: Metropolitan Police HQ, London

"As soon as we have any further information on either of these murders, an update will be placed on our website. Thank you. No questions."

Chief Superintendent King placed his sheet of notes back down and made to rise from his chair. His statement had been short and sweet; his favourite type. Yes, the murders of both Edward and Terence Wakefield were being linked but beyond that no further information could be divulged at this time. Several lines of enquiry were active. Standard police speak.

"Why isn't Detective Inspector MacIntosh here, Chief Superintendent?" The voice rang out from the back of the conference room. "It's his investigation, right?" Dougie King searched the sea of faces in front of him, hesitating behind his chair and finally locking eyes with Jonathan Spearing. The senior crime correspondent for the Daily Mail was leaning up against the rear wall, digital recording device held in his hand. The reporter nudged his wire-rimmed spectacles further up onto the bridge of his nose, raising his eyebrows beneath a mop of hair masquerading as a fringe.

"Well, Jonathan, you are correct, yes. This investigation is being led by Detective Inspector MacIntosh."

"So why isn't he here?" Jonathan Spearing stepped further into the room, his eyes trained on the Chief Superintendent. "Isn't it true that he's had treatment for psychological issues?"

Those reporters that had begun to drift towards the exit, already scribbling their headlines down for their next bulletins and dictating into their hand-held devices, stopped and turned back, eager not to miss a useful sound-bite.

Chief Superintendent King moved away from his chair, his face hardening. "DI MacIntosh has had a period of leave; it is no business of mine how my officers choose to spend their time. That is all. No more questions." He flashed a look at Pippa who was hovering at the door.

"If you could all now make your way outside please..." Pippa once again stepped forward to shepherd the reporters at the front towards the exit. "Any updates will be on the website."

"Is he competent to lead this investigation?" Jonathan Spearing pressed on, his voice carrying above the noise of scraping chairs and general murmurings from the departing media.

"Are you suggesting he isn't?" countered the Chief Superintendent, his eyes darkening and an irritated edge entering his tone.

"I'm merely asking if you are confident in his abilities, after such a long period of time on leave." Jonathan Spearing emphasised the words *on leave*. "It looks to me as though this killer could end up running rings around you...like Peter Holloway did last year."

Chief Superintendent King bristled. "I tell you what, Mr Spearing; you stop playing armchair detective and I might just resist the urge to write a feature on my wife's excellent Jamaican hot pot for your Sunday supplement. How does that sound?"

With a curt nod in Pippa's direction, Chief Superintendent King swept out of the conference room, his frown deepening. You owe me, Jack MacIntosh, he grumbled to himself. You owe me.

* * *

Time: 8.10am
Date: Monday 11th February 2013
Location: Metropolitan Police HQ, London

The phone rang out and eventually clicked onto voicemail.

"Stu, I need you to call me back. Now."

Jack tossed his phone back onto his desk and rubbed his eyes. This could not be happening. This could seriously not be happening. First the scarf, then the Wakefields. And now the tattoo.

Jack closed his eyes and tried to push the unwanted thoughts out of his mind. He could maybe try and explain away the scarf, but the tattoo? The sickness he felt in his stomach began to spread. He picked up his phone once more and stabbed wearily at the screen. In contrast to the half dozen calls he had made to his brother that morning, this one was answered on the second ring.

"Isabel?" Jack looked up and nodded as DS Cooper entered the office, arriving back from the press conference. "Have you heard from my brother this morning?" Jack paused, listening to Isabel's response at the other end. He nodded, slowly. "OK, I'll pop by later. We can talk about that fortune cookie. I need to talk to Stu, too. But..." Jack hesitated, the image of the tattoo on his brother's upper arm flooding his brain. "Don't tell him I'm coming. I'd like it to be a surprise."

Jack snapped his phone shut and faced DS Cooper.

"How do you fancy lunch at your favourite coffee shop?"

* * *

Time: 9.00am
   Date: Monday 11th February 2013
   Location: Green Park, London

His phone hadn't stopped ringing all morning. Each time he watched the phone icon flash up on the screen, and each time he waited for the caller to give up. Deciding he needed some fresh air, he headed into the park and selected a quiet bench. Once the call he was waiting for came in, he would switch the damned thing off.

The park was empty, not surprising for a cold and dreary Monday morning in February. There had been a couple of trusty, or maybe foolhardy, joggers out for their morning exercise, kitted out in thermals and woollen hats, but beyond that he had a secluded corner of the park to himself. Work still thought he was at home, in bed, with the flu. As he slipped onto the cold, damp bench the thought of being wrapped up under a duvet suddenly sounded appealing.

But he needed to think. And to plan. And for that he needed fresh air and solitude. The cool, crisp air sharpened the senses and focused the mind. The final stages of the plan were coming together, and nothing else mattered.

Someone said that revenge was a dish best served cold – he couldn't remember who right now, but they had been right. The Wakefields were testament to that. They hadn't seen him coming; not until it was too late.

And revenge had tasted so sweet.

And what was even better - there was still one serving left.

* * *

Time: 9.45am

Date: Monday 11th February 2013

Location: Metropolitan Police HQ, London

"Come in, Jack." Chief Superintendent King waved at Jack to step in and close the door. "Take a seat. I don't have long but I thought I'd fill you in on this morning's press conference."

Jack nodded and slipped into the vacant chair. "How did it go?"

Chief Superintendent King puffed out his cheeks and shook his head, settling himself back behind his desk. "They're like a baptism of fire sometimes, these press conferences. I gave them the facts, Jack. Such as they are. But nothing more. Just like you asked."

"I hear you had a run in with Jonathan Spearing." Jack tried to mask the smile ghosting his lips.

Chief Superintendent King raised his bushy eyebrows and gave Jack a withered look. "You heard about that?"

"News travels fast around here, Sir," smiled Jack. "I wouldn't worry about it. His bark is worse than his bite."

"Yes, well, he was starting to rub me up the wrong way. It's a good job Pippa was there to take control at the end. They can be a rowdy bunch."

"Indeed they can, Sir."

"Anyway, how much further are we on with the investigation? I was suitably vague with the press, as you requested, but do you have anything else you wish to share with me?"

Jack paused, flicking his eyes away from the Chief Superintendent's gaze. "It's still early days, Sir. I'm expecting some lab results in today."

"I kept the tattoo out of the press conference," confirmed Chief Superintendent King. "As you asked. Anything further on the meaning of it?"

Jack hesitated momentarily before shaking his head. "Not at this stage, Sir."

"Well, in that case, I won't keep you. I have a department budget meeting to attend – although I'd almost prefer another run in with our Mr Spearing than have to sit through another one of those." The Chief Superintendent's eyes twinkled and he nodded at Jack to take his leave. "Keep me up to speed,

Jack."

Jack rose from his chair and headed towards the door. "Of course, Sir."

As he slipped out into the corridor, Jack felt a pang of guilt. He didn't like lying to the Chief Superintendent; keeping him in the dark about his brother's link to the scarf and also the tattoos. He knew it wasn't the greatest career move he could make, but what else could he do? Skating on the proverbial thin ice was a pastime he was becoming increasingly good at.

* * *

Time: 10.15am

Date: Monday 11th February 2013

Location: Metropolitan Police HQ, London

"The lab has got back to us with some preliminary results." DC Cassidy waved a piece of paper in Jack's direction as he entered the investigation room. "Fingerprints at The Laurels haven't shown up anything unusual. And nothing on the fire exit door; that came back as clean. Also, no fingerprints in Edward Wakefield's room other than staff members."

Jack nodded, perching on the end of the table and taking a hold of the lab report. "Anything else? What about DNA?"

"Some partial results in for The Laurels. Edward Wakefield's pyjamas and bedclothes haven't revealed anything. The blood on his sheets belonged to him."

"As expected," agreed Jack. "I don't think our killer is that daft."

"But it's the scarf that's the interesting one," continued DC Cassidy.

Jack felt his heart begin to thump. "The scarf?"

"Yes. Jenny from the lab managed to get the scarf analysed. She said she spoke to you about it yesterday?"

Jack nodded but no words escaped his mouth.

"Well, she's managed to identify three full separate DNA profiles. One is

Edward Wakefield's, as we might have expected. There was a bloodstain on the scarf belonging to him. The other two are still going through the database at the moment – no results as yet."

Jack cast his eyes down at the lab report in his hand. As he did so, his vision started to blur, the words swimming in and out of focus. He rubbed his eyes and saw the words jump out of the page at the bottom.

Three DNA profiles. One identified, two currently unknown. All male.

'If there's DNA there to be found, Inspector, we will find it.'

Jenny's words echoed around Jack's head.

* * *

Chapter Ten

Time: 12.15pm
  Date: Monday 11th February 2013
  Location: Isabel's Café, King's Road, London

"You haven't been answering your phone all morning, Stu." Jack and DS Cooper breezed through the café and into the room at the rear. "I needed to talk to you. Where have you been? I rang your work – they said you'd rung in sick."

Mac was sitting in the armchair by the patio doors, staring outside at the heavy, overcast skies that threatened snow at any moment. "I'm allowed to take time off, Jack," he muttered, avoiding eye contact. "It's not against the law."

Jack sighed. "I know, I know. It's just..."

"Is everything all right?" Jack turned round to see Isabel hovering in the archway that led back into the café. She had a tea towel in her hands and seemed to be twisting it, anxiously. Jack raised his gaze to her eyes and noticed the concern that lay beneath them. He gave her what he hoped was a reassuring smile.

"Everything's fine, Isabel. Thanks. Sorry for barging in..."

Isabel's face broke out into a smile. "You're not barging in, Jack. It's a café. Can I get you anything?"

Jack was about to open his mouth and decline when he caught sight of DS Cooper's expression out of the corner of his eye.

"I'm fine, but I'm guessing Cooper, here, wouldn't say no to one of your coffees - and, unless I'm very much mistaken, some of your chocolate chip cookies."

DS Cooper's head nodded enthusiastically and he quickly followed Isabel back out into the café. When they were gone, Jack turned his attention back towards his brother.

"What's going on, Stu?" Jack walked over to where Mac was sitting. "Talk to me."

"Jesus, Jack. You saw me last night; we talked. Stop harassing me." Mac continued staring out into the rear courtyard. "I just want to be left alone."

"No can do, Stu. I've got a murder investigation and I need your help."

"I can't help you."

"Can't or won't?" An edge of irritation entered Jack's voice.

Mac tore his eyes away from the patio and flashed a hot look in Jack's direction. "Just leave me alone," he repeated.

Jack saw the familiar barriers standing firm. "As I said, Stu. I'm investigating two murders. I don't have time to leave you alone."

"No one cares about the Wakefields," grunted Mac, resuming his staring out of the window. "Leave them to rot. They've had it coming for years. Whoever did it, good on them. I hope they suffered."

Jack sighed and ran a hand through his hair. Exasperation was about to hit. He saw DS Cooper returning through the archway from the café, armed with a tall latte and a plate of cookies. Jack silently signalled for him to turn around. What was coming next, Jack needed it to be for his brother's ears only.

When he was sure DS Cooper had slunk back into the café, Jack turned back towards his brother. "Look, I get what happened to you, Stu. I do. *Really.* What you told me last night. But I don't have much time here. If you have information, then you need to give it to me – *now.* What happened to your Swap Shop scarf?"

"My what?" Mac turned towards Jack and frowned.

"Your Swap Shop scarf. Remember it? You said you'd won it, some competition on the telly."

114

"What about it?" Mac turned his face back to the window.

"You never used to take it off. Whenever I saw you, you had it on. Where is it now?"

"Jesus, Jack. I don't know. That was years ago."

"That's as maybe. Do you still have it?"

"I don't know, maybe. I went to prison, Jack, unless you've forgotten. I don't remember."

Jack nodded; the barriers weren't moving. "So, what about the number fifteen?"

"The what?" Mac whipped his head round and fixed Jack with a piercing look. "What do you mean the number fifteen?"

"Come on, Stu," Jack repeated. "It's an easy enough question. What does it mean?"

"Nothing." Mac flicked his eyes away from Jack's. "It means nothing."

"I know about the tattoo. *Your* tattoo." Jack nodded at his brother's arm. "Show me."

Mac drew in a deep breath and eventually turned his head away from the window. "My what?"

"Your tattoo, Stu. I know you have one. I saw the photo."

The barriers grew taller and multiplied. Jack could sense he was getting nowhere fast. "Look, Stu. I'm giving you one last chance to help me here – before this has to become more formal. If I need to take you into the station, I will. Believe me, I will. One last time, just answer the question – why have you got a tattoo of the number fifteen?"

Mac's eyes darkened. He turned to Jack and gritted his teeth. "The number fifteen - you really want to know what it means?"

* * *

Time: 11.15pm

Date: Thursday 10th April 1980

Location: St Bartholomew's Home for Boys, Christchurch

Edward Wakefield took great pleasure in threading his belt back through his belt-loops, a sickly sneer on his unshaven face. His pale eyes twinkled as they peered out from beneath heavy eyelids, his craggy face creasing as his smile widened. "You see, Terence, my boy? *That's* how you discipline boys properly."

Edward Wakefield began to laugh, the tell-tale odour of rotten cabbage once again escaping from between his broken teeth. One step behind him, Terence Wakefield let out a cackle to mirror his father's; a look of exhilaration on his thin, pasty face. Greasy strands of hair fell down across his acne-ridden forehead as he eyed the four boys cowering by the wall opposite.

"Yes, dad. You're the best." Terence followed his father out of the room, taking the oil lamp and only light source with him, and pulled the heavy door shut behind them. The sound of the rusty iron key scraping in the lock echoed off the damp brickwork.

Darkness instantly descended over room fifteen. The tiny window set high up, close to the ceiling, afforded them little or no light – just a pale strip of moonlight giving the room a ghostly sheen.

Four blotchy, tear-streaked faces were lined up against the far wall; the bodies they belonged to huddled close together on a thin mattress. One moth-eaten blanket stretched across the four pairs of scrawny legs, tucked in tightly to retain what warmth there was.

"I hate that man." Jason Alcock wiped his eyes with the back of his hand. The oldest of the four, and by far the stockiest and strongest, he sat at the edge of the worn mattress and let his friends take up most of the blanket. He turned his head away and stared out into the darkness of the room. He didn't want anyone to see him cry. The fresh welts on his bare legs were beginning to sting in the cool night air. The fifteen lashes from Edward Wakefield's belt still felt raw to his skin.

And he wasn't the only one.

Stephen Byers, the tallest in the group by a clear head, sat next to Jason, and rested back against the damp wall behind them. He hid his own bruises beneath the blanket and tried the best he could to stop his legs from trembling. Whether they were trembling with fear or anger, he couldn't quite decide. "He'll get what's coming to him one day," murmured Stephen. "Don't you worry about that."

Both Jason and Stephen heard a faint whimpering coming from beside them. The smallest boy of the four, with a head of dark, unruly curls, was shuddering underneath the blanket. The curls flopped over his forehead and shielded his eyes, so no one could see what expression they held – but they could all guess.

"Don't worry, Kyle," said Jason, his voice low, not much more than a whisper. They had to be careful – talking after lights out was forbidden and was punishable by more whippings. The four of them had had enough of that for one night. "You'll be all right. Just stick with us."

Kyle Williams buried his face in the scratchy blanket and sobbed.

"You all right over there, Mac?" Jason turned his head to the boy on the far side of the mattress. The newest resident of room fifteen was ordinarily quiet, not usually having a great deal to say for himself. He had arrived at St Bartholomew's some three years ago, as a quiet and nervous eight-year-old; thrust into the dungeon-like room fifteen like a gladiator to the slaughter. But room fifteen had instead been his saviour – Jason, Stephen and Kyle had been there since early primary school age and wasted no time in welcoming the new recruit. With MacIntosh being a bit of a mouthful, the nickname "Mac" quickly stuck.

Mac's silence was often mistaken by Edward Wakefield, and his son, as insolence. Jason knew that the boy's back would be covered in fresh wounds, already noticing how he could barely bring himself to lean back against the wall, wincing every time the rough brickwork touched his skin.

"I'm fine, Jase," replied Mac, rubbing his eyes with grimy hands. "They'll need to do better than that to beat me."

Jason Alcock slowly nodded to himself. He cast a glance over the three tear-stained faces lined up next to him, noticing the hardened look in each pair of eyes.

His boys.

They were his boys.

And no one, especially the Wakefields, would get away with hurting them.

* * *

Time: 12.45pm

Date: Monday 11th February 2013

Location: Isabel's Café, King's Road, London

"So – we became The Fifteen." Mac accepted the mug of coffee Isabel had quickly brought through from the café.

"The Fifteen? Like a gang?"

Mac nodded. "Very much like a gang."

"Tell me more about The Fifteen, Stu." Jack nodded at DS Cooper, who had been hovering in the archway, to come back in and take notes. "Everything you know."

"Why?" Mac took a sip of his coffee and again shifted his gaze away from his brother.

"Just tell me, Stu."

Mac shrugged and stared down at the steaming mug in his hands. "The gang was formed to give us some kind of purpose. A feeling of togetherness and strength. We couldn't fight the Wakefields individually – they were too strong. So we formed a unit. We fought them as one."

"Fought?" Jack frowned. "How do you mean fought?"

"Well, not physically, obviously," grimaced Mac. "We couldn't beat them. We were just kids. They'd beat us senseless if we even tried. No...it was more psychological. We knew we would be strong enough to survive the beatings, because we were in it together." Mac paused. "It might sound daft, but just giving ourselves a name – The Fifteen – made us feel stronger. Invincible, even."

Jack nodded. "Doesn't sound daft at all, Stu. And you named yourselves after the number of the room you were in?"

Mac nodded. "Room fifteen. So we became The Fifteen. As we got older, we began staying out later after school. Not coming back to the foster home when we were meant to. Anything to avoid going back there for as long as possible." Mac's eyes began to mist over as recollections flooded his brain, and he diverted his gaze back to the window. "We would hang around street corners, shopping precincts, bus stops, parks – you name it. Anywhere we could make a nuisance of ourselves. We even all got ourselves these tattoos..." Mac broke off and nodded towards his upper arm. "We kept it secret. No one knew we had them. Just us."

"And that led onto..."

"The petty crime, yes. Shop lifting, general thieving, criminal damage..." Mac paused and turned to catch Jack's eye. "I'm not proud of it, Jack. Anyway, you already know all this; it's nothing new."

"I used to see you guys hanging around the school gates," replied Jack, nodding as he remembered. "I just never knew what bound you all together." He broke off, remembering one day in particular. "You were with them, weren't you? On the day of the robbery? That was them opposite the school?"

Mac gave a rueful smile. "That was us, yes – The Fifteen. That day was the last time we all saw each other outside of the nick."

* * *

Time: 1.35pm

Date: 10th May 1982

Location: West Road Comprehensive School, Christchurch

Jack watched from the gates of West Road Comprehensive School and knew that his brother had no intention of following him back into school. Lunch break had ended five minutes ago and Jack knew that another detention was heading his way for being late back to class – again. And it wasn't just any class – it was chemistry with Mr Buckley; the worst teacher you could pick to turn up late to. Jack could already see the elderly science teacher's cheeks reddening and his short-sighted, cataract filled eyes bulging from behind their milk-bottle lensed glasses.

"Stu, come on, don't be daft. Stop hanging around with that lot. They're bad news."

Jack eyed the three teenagers that were skulking around on the pavement opposite. Each one avoided Jack's gaze, whispering and laughing amongst themselves whilst passing around a scrawny hand-rolled cigarette with their equally scrawny fingers. Three motorbike helmets sat by their feet.

"They're my friends," spat back Stuart MacIntosh, thrusting out his thirteen-year old chin in an act of defiance. He moved to stand closer to one of the teenage boys who was leaning up against one of the motorbikes.

"They're not your friends, Stu," replied Jack. "They're using you. They'll get you into all sorts of trouble – and you've been caught enough times by the police already. You know, the next time you get caught they'll take you away? You'll end up in Borstal."

The teenager at Stuart MacIntosh's side began to laugh and turned to face Jack from across the road.

"Run along, goody-goody." Jason Alcock sneered at Jack while taking a long drag from the thinly-rolled cigarette in his hand. "Don't be late for the teacher!" His sing-song mocking tone floated across the tarmac in the warm spring air, and Jack felt the hackles prickling on the back of his neck. "Go on, off you go, teacher's pet!"

"I mean it, Stu." Jack did his best to ignore the insults heading his way. "Come back into school, right now."

"I don't care, Jack." Stuart's words were hot and thick with emotion, his voice catching in his throat. "No one cares about me, so I don't care about them. Just go – leave me alone."

With that, Jason Alcock crushed the cigarette on the pavement beneath a dirty boot, and swung a leg over the motorbike by his side. He pulled on his crash helmet and fired up the engine. Stuart MacIntosh followed suit, jamming a spare helmet onto his head and grabbing hold of the older teenager's waist as he hopped onto the back of the machine.

The two other motorbikes spluttered into action and joined in the collective roar. All Jack could do was step back and watch as the three machines sped off down the road and out of sight.

* * *

Time: 12.55pm

Date: Monday 11th February 2013

Location: Isabel's Café, King's Road, London

"I never saw you again – after that day. Not really." Jack leant up against the patio doors and watched as heavy flakes of snow finally began to descend from the heavily laden skies above. "You were arrested pretty much straight after. I only saw you at the trial."

Mac hung his head. "I know. If I could rewind and re-live that day all over again, Jack, I would. I should've listened to you."

Jack waved the sentiment away. "It's in the past, Stu. But I need to find the rest of The Fifteen. The guys you committed the robbery with. Give me their names again."

Mac hesitated, but then went on to list the names of Jason Alcock, Stephen Byers and Kyle Williams, watching as DS Cooper scribbled them down in his notebook.

"Come on, Cooper." Jack pushed himself away from the patio door and headed for the archway. "We need to trace these names, and fast."

As they made their way to the door, Isabel came through from the kitchen. "Are you off?" Her voice was brittle and Jack could see that she had been crying.

He nodded apologetically. "Sorry, we need to get back. But I haven't forgotten." He paused and held Isabel's watery gaze in his. "About the fortune cookie. I'll ring you later." He tried to give her a reassuring smile. "But don't worry in the meantime. Kreshniov won't be back."

Isabel gave a faltering smile in return and wiped her eyes, while Jack and DS Cooper quickly stepped out onto the pavement and headed for the car.

Right now, Kreshniov was the least of Jack's worries.

"You drive." Jack threw the keys at DS Cooper, who caught them deftly. "I've got some thinking to do."

* * *

Chapter Eleven

Time: 1.35pm
Date: Monday 11th February 2013
Location: Isabel's Café, King's Road, London

Mac continued to stare out of the patio window long after Jack had departed. The cup of coffee in his lap turned as cold as the snow falling outside. Isabel had appeared by his side, offering him a sandwich, but he had waved her away. He knew he wasn't being fair; he just hoped she knew that he didn't mean it.

"I'm sorry," he murmured, under his breath. "I'm so very sorry."

He absent-mindedly rubbed a hand over his upper arm, touching the fabric of his shirt where he knew the tattoo lay beneath. It was as if he could feel it burning through the cotton, feel the energy contained within those two simple digits.

Fifteen.

No one else would understand.

No one else would understand what it felt like to be part of the Fifteen.

Mac glanced down at his phone and noticed the number of missed calls and messages stacking up. And not all of them were from Jack and Isabel. A fair few, but not all. He turned the phone face down, away from his gaze, and continued to stare out of the window.

The Fifteen.

Jack asking about The Fifteen had brought it all flooding back, forcing him to unlock that part of his brain where he had hidden away the memories that caused him the most pain. But now the box was open and the thoughts came rushing out, jumbled and uncontrolled. There was one thought that rose to the surface more than any other – the day when his life changed forever.

* * *

Time: 1.40pm
  Date: 10th May 1982
  Location: West Road, Christchurch

Stuart MacIntosh tightened his grip around Jason Alcock's waist as the motorbike skidded around the corner at the end of West Road, disappearing from his brother's sight. Jason took the corner far too fast, and the tyres slid on the baked asphalt, kicking up a plume of loose road chippings in its wake.

Stuart didn't care. His heart was thumping in his chest, sending the adrenaline coursing through his body with every beat. He pushed the motorbike visor up so that he could feel the wind as they sped through the deserted streets. He wanted to rip the helmet from his head completely and feel the breeze ripple through his hair, blowing away the anger and frustration that was bursting to get out.

Sometimes he hated Jack.

Especially when he had that look on his face; like he did today.

Disappointment. And derision. Even contempt at times. But mostly disappointment.

And today was one of those days.

Jack always thought he knew best. Trying to get him to go to school like a good boy; like a good brother. Like a good *MacIntosh*. Forever telling him to stop hanging around with his friends.

And they *were* his friends, no matter what Jack said. Jack would never understand.

Stuart glanced back over his shoulder as they took yet another corner at speed, heading towards the Wellington Estate. Stephen Byers was right behind them, the hood of his sweatshirt pulled up over the top of his crash helmet, hunched over the handlebars, his eyes focused intently on the rear wheel of Alcock's bike.

Behind Stephen, a few metres distant, was Kyle Williams. Kyle had only just got hold of a second-hand bike, and didn't have that much experience. He took the corners more slowly, putting out his feet to steady himself as they continued their race through the empty side streets.

Everywhere was quiet. The late Spring sunshine and warmth had cast a laziness over the town. People relaxed in their back gardens, soaking up the sun. Others headed to one of the open spaces in the centre of town on their lunch breaks, to sit with their sandwiches and cool drinks, letting the hot rays bake their skin before it was time to return to the office.

On the outskirts of town, where they were headed, the pavements were deserted. The odd pedestrian frowned at the trio of noisy motorbikes as they sped past, the whining engines cutting through the sultry stillness of the air; no doubt muttering something about the 'youth of today' under their breath.

But Stuart didn't care.

He was with his friends, and that was all that mattered. He would do anything for his friends.

Anything.

* * *

Time: 2.15pm

Date: Monday 11th February 2013

Location: Metropolitan Police HQ, London

"If you can handle Stephen Byers and Kyle Williams between you, I'll arrange to go and see Jason Alcock first thing tomorrow." Jack flicked open the file from DS Carmichael that housed all the statements he had so far on St Bartholomew's. "And I'll pass the details onto Rob. He'll no doubt want to interview them for Operation Evergreen."

DC Cassidy nodded and switched on her computer terminal. "I'll start searching for Byers and Williams now. See if we can't track them down."

Jack pulled out one of the statements from the folder; the statement of Albert Dawson. He glanced at his watch. "And I fancy dropping in on the former manager – I want to see what he has to say about the Wakefields. Cooper? Anything more from the lab since this morning?" Jack almost dreaded asking but he knew he had to.

DS Cooper started to nod. "Just received a message from Jenny. Says she's sent over an updated report."

DC Cassidy began loading the forensic evidence onto the whiteboard screen, scrolling through to the most recent additions. "Here it is, guv," she said, clicking the screen and enlarging the lab report.

Jack held his breath and looked away from the screen. He had a sinking feeling in his stomach that it wasn't going to be good news.

"The final two DNA profiles on the scarf..." DC Cassidy paused and scrolled to the bottom of the report. "Remain unidentified. No matches. And they're still processing samples from Terence Wakefield's house."

"One of those profiles could still be our killer," reminded DS Cooper. "He's just lucky enough not to be on the DNA database."

Jack exhaled silently. "Indeed, Cooper. Indeed." Just like my brother, he thought. Stuart had left his wayward days behind him long before the DNA database had been brought in and, right now, Jack wondered whether he should be thankful for that or not. Shaking his head, he grabbed hold of Albert Dawson's statement and headed for the door.

"I'm off to see Albert Dawson. You both keep tracking down Byers and Williams. I'll see you both in the morning after I've caught up with Alcock."

Despite the chilliness of the day, Jack couldn't wait to get outside.

CHAPTER ELEVEN

* * *

Time: 2.20pm
   Date: Monday 11th February 2013
   Location: Isabel's Café. King's Road, London

Mac couldn't ignore the messages on his phone any longer. He scrolled
through the list, reading the latest one, then deleted them all. His heart
was still racing. Thinking back to that day was making him agitated. Every
therapist he had seen during his early years of incarceration had told him
that thinking back and reliving his past behaviour was a good thing. It was
therapeutic. It was beneficial. It gave insight into your own personality
traits and enabled you to learn from your past mistakes.
   Mac had doubted it then, just as he doubted it now.

* * *

Time: 1.55pm
   Date: 10th May 1982
   Location: Wellington Estate, Christchurch

Jason Alcock pulled the crash helmet from his head and used his sleeve to
wipe the sheen of sweat that clung to his forehead. His hair was matted to
his head in damp clumps. "You all right there, Maccy lad?" Alcock's cheeks
were flushed, his eyes bright and shining.
   Stuart MacIntosh nodded, pulling his own helmet off and swinging his
leg from the back of Alcock's bike. His stomach was still churning from the
white-knuckle ride across town. Their breakfast of cheap hamburgers, from
the rusty van by the swimming pool, was threatening to make a comeback.
He swallowed and forced the bile back down, stepping out onto the baked

127

pavement.

"Yeah, cool," he remarked, turning his face away from Jason, not wanting him to notice the green tinge to his cheeks.

"Good lad, Mac." Jason Alcock grinned and turned round to see both Stephen Byers and Kyle Williams parking their bikes next to a rubbish skip, hanging their crash helmets over the handlebars.

The boys were all here.

His boys.

The Fifteen.

"You both ready?" Jason nodded at both Stephen and Kyle, who were making their way towards him, pulling up the hoods of their sweatshirts despite the baking heat of the day.

"You bet." Stephen Byers, the tallest of the group, came to a halt next to Jason and glanced across the pavement to the small parade of shops in front of them. Across some wasteland to the right, on the other side of a graffiti-infused underpass, were the tower blocks of the Wellington Estate – an estate the boys knew well. "Can't wait to shove it to those Wellington boys, right on their own patch."

Jason nodded, his eyes glinting in the sun. "Good man. You OK there, Kyle? You ready?"

Kyle Williams was hovering in Stephen Byers' shadow. He bit his lip, nervously, and thrust his hands into the pockets of his faded jeans to stop them from shaking. "Yeah, ready." Kyle's voice betrayed his nerves. He looked to Stuart for reassurance and got a slow nod in return. Neither of them had done anything quite like this before. A bit of thieving in the town centre; some graffiti on the back of the sports centre; shoplifting from the local supermarket.

But nothing like this.

Kyle warily eyed the rucksack that Jason swung from his back.

"Good." Jason knelt down and unzipped the bag. "Coz you've all got an important role to play here. I need you all to step up and do your bit. So we can show those Wellington boys that they can't mess with us." He thrust his hand into the rucksack and brought out four stunted baseball bats. He handed one to Stephen first, who snatched it up without a second thought. Kyle stepped forwards to get his, hesitating momentarily before accepting the weapon. He wrapped a trembling hand around its base.

"Mac?" Jason held the last bat out towards Stuart, who stepped forwards and grabbed it, all thoughts of bringing up his greasy breakfast now dissipated. He ran his hands along the battered wood, taking a firm grip of the handle and swinging it through the air. "Careful now," joked Jason, standing up and slipping the empty rucksack back onto his back. "You'll have someone's eye out with that!"

Stuart grinned back. The bat felt good in his hands. He felt in control. He felt powerful. He felt strong. He tried to force the image of Jack's disapproving face out of his mind. 'They'll get you into all sorts of trouble.' 'You'll end up in Borstal.' His brother's words echoed around inside his head. He gripped the baseball bat harder and forced himself not to listen.

"So, what's the plan?" Stuart continued to swish the bat by his side, following Stephen Byers' gaze across to the parade of shops.

"We go in the front." Jason nodded towards the small convenience store on the end of the parade. "Maccy – you're on door duty. You stand at the front and don't let anyone in or out. Use your bat if you need to."

Stuart nodded, feeling the adrenaline surge through his body.

"Stevie – you're with me." Jason nodded at Stephen Byers. "We go to the cash desk – it's just inside the door. He's always on his own at this time of day. It'll be a piece of cake."

Stephen Byers returned the nod, and started jiggling from foot to foot, eager to be on his way. He hated those Wellington Estate boys – they looked down on him and everyone else who had the misfortune to be from St Bartholomew's. Called them "scum". Called them "bum-boys". Called them "dirty". Well, today they were going to have to eat their words. Today, The Fifteen were fighting back.

"Kyle?" Jason turned towards Kyle Williams, who was still hovering on the edge of the group. His face was now white, his eyes wide with fear. "You know what you're doing?"

Kyle managed a nod, opening his mouth but no words came out.

"While me and Stevie here are with the guy at the cash desk, you need to grab as much booze and fags as you can get – shove it all in my rucksack. Yeah?"

Kyle nodded again, his mouth clamped shut. He didn't even attempt to speak this time.

"Well, then – let's do this." Jason gripped hold of his own baseball bat and made a move towards the parade of shops.

"No one's going to get hurt, right?" Kyle had managed to find his voice, and was jogging to keep up with Jason as they crossed the litter-strewn pavement towards the Wellington Stores.

Jason turned his head and gave Kyle a wink. "Of course not. We'll be in and out of there in a blink of an eye. No one's gonna get hurt, I promise."

Kyle carried on jogging, hearing his friend's words but maybe not quite believing them. The sight of the four baseball bats had made him nervous. Really nervous. He hadn't known they were going to carry weapons.

The Wellington Stores was a small corner shop, selling everything from toilet rolls to extra strength cheap lager – open from six in the morning until ten at night. Jason had done his research and visited the shop on numerous occasions – so that he knew the layout, and also the comings and goings of its employees. It was essentially a family run affair. Mr McCormack seemed to do the bulk of the shop work himself. Mrs McCormack would make an appearance in the mornings to sort out the paperboys with their deliveries, but she would then disappear and her husband would take over for the rest of the day. Two oafs, that Jason assumed were his sons, would occasionally join him at weekends.

But at just before 2.00pm on a Monday, Mr McCormack would be in the shop alone.

With one last look behind him at his boys, Jason Alcock pushed open the door to the Wellington Stores.

* * *

Time: 2.40pm
  Date: Monday 11th February 2013
  Location: Metropolitan Police HQ, London

Jack pulled out of the rear car park. Albert Dawson lived in West Hampstead, a rather affluent area that Jack rarely had cause to frequent. Traditionally an area reserved for the rich, crime was, as in most areas, on the increase. The gulf between the haves and the have nots was ever widening. Theft was high up in the statistics, whether it be the snatching of mobile phones and handbags from the street or the stealing of cars, bikes and other possessions. West Hampstead was proving to make rich pickings.

Before leaving, he had put in a call to DS Carmichael to give him the names of the Fifteen. He filled the detective sergeant in on the background to the gang's name and the further evidence of cruelty at St Bartholomew's. As soon as they had up to date addresses, Jack promised to pass them on.

His last call had been to arrange to go and visit Jason Alcock first thing in the morning.

But for now, his attention turned to Albert Dawson.

The brief statement in DS Carmichael's file stated that he had begun his managerial role at St Bartholomew's in 1971 and carried on until the home was forced to close in the mid 1980s. The statement was brief; Albert Dawson had not been aware of any wrongdoing within the walls of his Victorian foster home, and had certainly been oblivious to any allegations of abuse.

Of course he had.

Jack had a feeling that Albert Dawson's statement had more holes in it than the proverbial Swiss cheese.

* * *

Time: 2.10pm
  Date: 10th May 1982

Location: Wellington Stores, Wellington Estate, Christchurch

They ran from the shop at full pelt and scrambled back onto their waiting motorbikes. Jason led the way, shrugging the now heavily-laden rucksack onto his back before leaping onto his bike.

"Come on, Mac," he yelled, starting the engine and swinging the bike around. "Get a move on!"

Stuart MacIntosh careered across the pavement and caught the helmet that Jason had thrown at him, pushing it firmly down onto his head while vaulting onto the back of the bike. His heart was thumping so fast he felt it would explode; he felt dizzy with excitement and fear. He was thankful to grab a hold of Jason's waist and feel the bike accelerate at speed from under him.

All three bikes kicked up dirt and gravel from the roadside as they sped out of the deserted street, the sound of the engines screeching through the air. The rucksack bounced painfully into Stuart's face as Jason slung the motorbike around each corner, but he was oblivious to the pain.

They had done it.

They had really done it.

Stuart gripped Jason Alcock's waist tightly as they cornered a bend at speed, his heart in his mouth. He closed his eyes but all he could see was the look of horror on the old man's face as he was confronted with baseball bats and a knife.

Stuart hadn't known about the knife.

All of a sudden he felt sick.

* * *

Time: 2.40pm
Date: Monday 11th February 2013
Location: Isabel's Café, King's Road, London

"Who was that?" Isabel placed a fresh cup of coffee at the side of Mac's armchair and nodded towards his phone. She had heard several tell-tale 'pings' of incoming messages whilst hovering in the doorway. "Is everything all right?" She couldn't help but notice Mac's face had paled, all evidence of the Italian sun tan melting away.

Mac snapped his phone shut and avoided her gaze. He shook his head. "It's nothing. No one important." He pushed himself up out of the chair and reached for his jacket, almost kicking over the fresh coffee cup in the process. "I have to go out."

"But...your coffee." Isabel bent to pick up the freshly made mug. "And you need something to eat. I'll make you a sandwich..."

Mac looked at his watch. "I'll get something later. I need to go."

"But where...?" Isabel watched helplessly as Mac strode out towards the café and headed for the door. Tears started to leak from the corners of her eyes as she watched him disappear onto the frozen pavement outside. Hurriedly wiping the tears away, Isabel headed back towards the kitchen.

"Don't worry too much." Sacha stepped out from behind the counter and gave Isabel's arm a squeeze. "He doesn't mean it."

"Doesn't he?" Isabel's voice quivered and she brushed yet more tears from her cheeks. "He can barely bring himself to look at me now."

"I don't profess to know what's going on but I'm sure it'll work out in the end. I just think you're going to have to give him some space. Let him work it out."

Isabel nodded. "I know." Sacha squeezed her arm once more before heading back into the kitchen to join Dominic. As Isabel turned to follow, her phone vibrated in her pocket.

It was a simple message. Just two words.

Two words that made her heart ache.

"I'm sorry."

* * *

Time: 3.40pm
  Date: Monday 11th February 2013
  Location: 3 Wagtail Drive, West Hampstead, London

Mandy adjusted the pillows behind Albert Dawson's head and gave his shoulder a gentle pat. "You rest up now, Albert, and I'll bring you a nice cup of tea." She turned towards Jack, who was hovering at the entrance to the bedroom. "And a cup of tea for you, Inspector? Come on in, don't be shy. Albert doesn't bite."

Mandy, as the Chiltern Health Care badge proudly stated in bold capital letters, side-stepped past him, her starched blue uniform rustling in the otherwise peaceful silence. She brought a hand up to her mouth and whispered, "he can't – he doesn't have any teeth!"

Jack smiled, glancing at the bedside table that housed a glass of water and what looked like Albert Dawson's upper and lower dentures. "That would be lovely, thank you," he replied, stepping hesitantly across the threshold, casting his eyes around at the medical equipment and other paraphernalia that seemed to take up almost every inch of space in the cramped bedroom.

"Go take a seat by the bed, and I'll be straight back." Mandy shuffled off, leaving Jack alone with the former manager of St Bartholomew's Home for Boys.

Jack edged further into the room, noting that it was a decent size, with a large floor to ceiling window looking out onto the bungalow's small patio and generously sized lawn. The grass was neatly trimmed with a dusting of frost still clinging to its tips. A wooden bird table sat in the centre of the garden, next to a metal stand containing a variety of hanging feeding nets each rammed full of nuts. A small garden shed nestled in the corner.

"Mostly see squirrels these days."

Jack turned his attention back to the direction of the voice, and saw a pair of watery-blue, rheumy eyes staring back out at him from the recently plumped pillow. The face was waxen; the pale and translucent skin stretched thinly across the man's otherwise sharp features. A few wisps of grey hair framed his face. He looked small and frail, dwarfed by his hospital-style pyjamas and the thin blanket that was draped across his skeletal frame.

"Squirrels?" Jack raised his eyebrows.

"Outside," nodded Albert Dawson, his eyes flickering towards the window. "Not so many birds during the winter – the odd sparrow and robin. But more than enough squirrels to keep me entertained." The old man's voice was surprisingly strong, in sharp contrast to his physical state. "Take a seat. Mandy will be through with the tea soon."

Jack spied the only chair in the room, a high-backed armchair nestled next to Albert's bed, close to the window. It was piled high with unopened packets of incontinence sheets and fresh bedding, which Jack picked up and placed on the floor. As he sat, he looked across the bed and noticed a large contraption that he recognised as a hoist to help the old man in and out of bed.

Opposite the bed was an antique-looking sideboard, hosting a variety of bottles, packets and boxes – an array of medication that looked to be keeping Albert Dawson alive.

Just at that moment, Mandy bustled back into the bedroom with a tray housing two mugs of tea and a plate of digestive biscuits. She balanced the tray on the end of the bed and reached across to hand Jack one of the mugs.

"A biscuit, if you fancy one," she breezed, nodding at the plate on the tray. "And before you ask, they are not for you, Albert Dawson. I'll set your feed up for you later." Her kind eyes twinkled as she picked up the other mug and took it over to the sideboard, where she proceeded to stir in several scoops of powder from an open tin. She whisked the liquid vigorously and caught Jack's eye. "Albert has to have his liquids thickened, due to his poor swallow. Otherwise he'll choke, won't you, Albert?"

She gave the old man a good natured wink, continuing to stir the contents of the mug until she was satisfied with its consistency.

Jack nodded, taking a sip of his own tea, and watched as Mandy perched herself on the side of Albert's bed and brought the wide-rimmed mug up towards his lips. "He has most of his food and medications through a feeding tube that goes directly into his stomach," she explained, motioning towards a metal stand next to Jack's chair. It looked just like a hospital IV stand, with a digital display box beneath. "It's the MS, you see. Affects his swallowing. But we do allow a few tastes for pleasure, don't we, Albert?" She supported the back of Albert's head while he took another sip of his thickened tea. "And you do like a nice cup of tea, don't you?"

After a few more sips, Mandy wiped Albert's mouth and chin with a tissue. "I'm not sure what you'll get from him today, Inspector. His memory isn't what it used to be, you see. Dementia on top of his other problems; means that he doesn't talk a great deal, and what you do get from him doesn't always make a lot of sense."

Jack carried on sipping his own tea, eyeing the frail looking man in the bed before him. He glanced over his shoulder, back out through the window to the bird table and hanging nuts. Albert Dawson had seemed quite compos mentis when he had commented about the birds and the squirrels, and his voice had been just fine. Jack tucked a mental note away at the back of his head and returned his gaze to the bed.

"That's OK, I won't keep him long. I just have a few questions about St Bartholomew's – the foster home that he used to manage in the 1970s and 1980s." Jack couldn't be sure but he thought he saw the old man flinch at the name St Bartholomew's. Another mental note, carefully filed away.

"No problem. I'll leave you to it." Mandy helped Albert take a final sip of tea, before laying his head back down against the pillows. She collected up the tray, leaving the plate of biscuits on the end of the bed, and squeezed her ample frame past the hoist and out of the bedroom. "I'll be in the kitchen if you need me."

Jack smiled his thanks and watched Mandy's wide hips disappear through the door and out of sight. It was a few seconds before he turned his gaze back to the old man lying in the bed in front of him.

Albert Dawson.

Manager of St Bartholomew's.

"So, Albert – can I call you Albert?" Jack raised a questioning eyebrow at the frail old man, and leant closer towards the bed. "My name is Detective Inspector MacIntosh; I'm with the Metropolitan Police. I'd like to ask you a few questions about your time at St Bartholomew's Home for Boys. You were the manager there in the 1970s and 1980s, weren't you?"

Jack paused and eyed Albert Dawson. The old man stared straight out across the end of the bed, his eyes fixed and glassy. To anyone watching, it looked like the old man hadn't heard Jack's question – but Jack suspected otherwise, so he pressed on.

"In particular, I'd like to ask you about a group of boys – boys that all shared a dormitory at the home. A room. Room fifteen." Again Jack broke off and paused, looking for a reaction. There was none.

"Maybe their names will jog your memory, Albert. Jason Alcock. Stephen Byers. Kyle Williams." Jack hesitated before continuing. "And Stuart MacIntosh."

Albert Dawson's veined hands lay across his stomach, the bony fingers laced together. Jack thought he saw them twitch.

He can hear me, thought Jack. I know he can.

"And not only that. I also want to ask you about two members of staff at the home. A Mr Edward Wakefield and his son, Terence Wakefield. Do you remember them?"

Another twitch of the fingers.

Jack watched as Albert Dawson's eyelids began blinking, rapidly, his rheumy gaze still focused on the sideboard opposite.

"I think you do remember them, Albert," pressed Jack, continuing to watch as Albert Dawson's pale face seemed to lose even more colour. "I think you remember them very well, and I also think you know what they did to young boys at the home."

More rapid eye movements.

More twitching.

But still Albert Dawson refused to meet Jack's gaze. Music wafted through from the direction of the kitchen, and Jack heard Mandy's faint voice singing along to a song on the radio. The sound of water and clinking glasses suggested that she was busy washing up.

Jack pushed himself up out of the visitor's armchair and walked round to the end of the bed. He stood facing Albert Dawson and leant forwards on the mattress, fixing the old man's watery-blue eyes with his own. "I think you know exactly what was happening at your foster home, Albert. I think you *let* it happen; I think you encouraged it." Jack paused and leant in closer. "You do realise that there is an ongoing police investigation into child cruelty and sexual assault, don't you? And one of the places they are looking at is St Bartholomew's - during the time that you were in charge?"

Jack watched as the rheumy eyes widened.

But still no sound came from Albert Dawson's mouth.

"So, I would expect another visit in the not too distant future, Albert. Aiding and abetting an offence is a crime, as I'm sure you already know. Or maybe you took part in the abuse yourself?"

If Albert Dawson had been wearing a heart rate monitor, Jack would bet money on the old man's pulse going through the roof. He pressed on, noticing that the sound of singing and running water from the kitchen had now stopped. "We won't rest until we get to the truth, Albert. Just you remember that."

Just at that moment, Mandy appeared in the doorway with a small plastic syringe in her hand. She noticed Jack was out of his seat. "Oh, are you off already, Inspector?" She turned towards the sideboard and took a glass medicine bottle from the collection. "I'm just about to give Albert his medication. Don't mind me."

"I've got all I need for now, thank you, Mandy," replied Jack, not taking his eyes off Albert Dawson. "Thank you for the tea and biscuits." He scooped up a digestive biscuit from the plate on the bed, and smiled towards the old man as he did so. "I'm sure I'll see you again, Albert. You enjoy those squirrels."

With that, Jack took a bite out of his biscuit and walked out of Albert Dawson's bedroom.

That man knew things.

The time would come when he would have to start talking.

* * *

Chapter Twelve

Time: 9.30pm
 Date: Monday 11th February 2013

Location: Kettle's Yard Mews, London

Jack glanced at his phone and grimaced. Another missed call from Dr Evelyn Riches. Another one to add to the list. He shook his head and refused to even contemplate counting. He noted that she had left a voicemail this time. His finger hovered over the button to replay the message, but instead he turned the phone off. He already knew what it would say – or, at least, he had a good idea. And it wasn't something he wanted to hear just now.

He wasn't ready.

He cleared away his empty plate – the supermarket lasagne had been somewhat tasteless until he had covered it in extra cheese, but an improvement on his recent diet of takeaways and fast food. It was at times like this that he missed Margaret McArthur's home cooking.

Returning to the sofa with a fresh beer from the fridge, Jack placed the can down onto the coffee table and immediately noticed the coffee-stained 'PTSD – The Facts' leaflet staring back at him – the same leaflet Dr Riches had given him before embarking on his ten-week hypnotherapy course.

His therapy had gone well. Everyone had said so.

Even Dr Riches.

And the nightmares – well, they had lessened to the extent that Jack no longer fought the urge to sleep. No longer did he dread nightfall and the

139

horrors that would await him when he finally succumbed to closing his eyes. Yes, he still had dreams, and some of them could still be termed nightmares. But they didn't consume him in the same way they had before. They were manageable. Acceptable. If he was pushed, he would say that he even had a good night's sleep on rare occasions.

Dr Riches, he knew, had been somewhat surprised by his progress. He knew that she had not expected him to last the full course – hadn't expected him to treat the sessions with the seriousness that was required.

He had surprised everyone.

Even himself.

And when asked how he was feeling, he could now give them the answer 'I'm fine.'"

And he truly did feel 'fine'. Most of the time. People remarked on how well he looked after his six-week retreat to the wilds of Scotland. He looked fitter and trimmer; his skin gave off a healthy glow rather than its usual pallid, tired tone. He even had a glint in his eye, apparently, according to DC Cassidy.

It never ceased to amaze Jack how easy it was to fool people.

What was the famous quote from Abraham Lincoln? 'You can fool some of the people all of the time, and all of the people some of the time. But you can't fool *all* the people *all* of the time.'

Jack eyed the PTSD leaflet once again and then let his eyes dart towards his phone – and towards the message that he knew was burning a hole in it. He sighed and reached for his handset to switch it back on, and then stabbed a finger at the voicemail icon.

Holding the handset to his ear he took a long drink from his can of beer, feeling that he might need the alcohol once he began listening to Dr Riches' message.

"Jack – it's Dr Riches here. Again." There was a brief pause on the tape, and Jack thought he could almost hear her rustling some papers in the background. "We need to talk. And soon." Another pause and some more rustling. "You know what this is about, Jack. You can't go off on your own with this. We need to discuss what happened. I may have found someone who can help you. You can't ignore me forever."

Can't I? thought Jack, jabbing the button to end the message.

You just watch me.

He took another pull on his beer and sank back into the sofa. He knew what Dr Riches wanted to talk about.

Their last session.

And what happened.

* * *

Time: 4.45pm

Date: Tuesday 4th December 2012

Location: Office of Dr Evelyn Riches, Psychotherapist – St James's University, London

"You've made such great progress, Jack." Dr Evelyn Riches beamed at Jack from her side of the coffee table. She settled back in one of the comfy chairs, resting her notepad on her lap.

"You sound surprised." Jack regarded the hypnotherapist from his side of the table, masking the smile that was developing on his lips. "Did you have such little faith in me?"

Dr Riches gave a small laugh, her pale eyes twinkling. "Well, to be honest, Jack – I am surprised. I will be honest; I didn't think we would get to this day."

Jack nodded. She wasn't the only one. They had now completed all ten sessions of his hypnotherapy course, an achievement in itself. "Well, you know me – I like to surprise."

Dr Riches returned the smile that had now grown across Jack's face. She regarded the man that now sat opposite her, and compared him to the one that had sat in the same chair many months ago. "You've done well, Jack. Remarkably well."

Jack nodded again. "So, I'm cured, then." The smile stayed plastered to his lips.

"You know the rules, Jack. No one is ever cured. We just aim to give you the tools and abilities to manage stressful situations in the future – to give you the means to overcome problems, so that they don't become problems anymore."

"Sounds like a cure to me" persisted Jack, enjoying the sight of the pristine and cool-as-cucumber hypnotherapist start to feel uncomfortable.

"Jack..."

"I know, I know, I'm teasing." Jack took a sip from the glass of water he held in his hand. "Sorry. So what are we doing today? I thought our sessions had finished?"

Dr Riches uncrossed her legs and leant forwards slightly. She cast her eyes down at her notepad, where Jack could see she had written a few lines at the top of the page in her neat, uniform handwriting. It was too small to read from a distance, so he took another sip of water.

"We have, but today," began Dr Riches, looking back up at Jack, "I want you to revisit the door – one last time. You made such progress at your final session to step through it – I think we need to repeat that, to finally close that chapter of your life. One last time, Jack. Open the door one last time."

Jack nodded. He had thought as much. During his last few sessions, he had finally managed to reach the door that had haunted him for most of his life. The door that had been the focus of his dreams – and his nightmares. And during his last session he had not only managed to reach it, but actually open it and step through to confront what lay beyond.

He had seen the image of his mother, swinging from the light fitting – something he had seen countless times in his dreams. But this time it seemed not to fill him with the fear that it usually did. During his last session, Dr Riches had told him that his heart rate had remained at a constant sixty-one beats per minute. Positively relaxed.

So, this final time, he needed to see the image of his mother, not through the eyes of a horrified four-year-old, but as a grown man.

And then the door could be closed for good.

"Ready? One last time?" questioned Dr Riches, raising her perfectly shaped eyebrows.

"Ready," confirmed Jack, placing his glass of water back down onto the table and settling back in his chair to close his eyes.

* * *

Time: 4.55pm

Date: Tuesday 4th December 2012

Location: Office of Dr Evelyn Riches, Psychotherapist – St James's University, London

The door stood in front of him as it always did.

It looked the same.

It felt the same.

But Jack looked at the door differently this time - it no longer caused him to feel panic or fear. He knew what was hidden on the other side and it no longer scared him. He had stepped through it once before, and he could do it again. He was no longer afraid.

With a new found tranquillity and confidence, Jack reached out and grasped hold of the handle for the final time. He could feel the coolness of the metal beneath his skin. With his breathing controlled, and his heart beating slowly and rhythmically, he waited...he waited to feel the familiar pull towards the door, the urge to open it one last time.

As if controlled by another force, Jack felt his hand grip the handle more tightly, and rotate it to allow the door to swing open. As he had done on his last visit, Jack took in a slow and controlled breath before stepping over the threshold and entering the kitchen of the flat in Old Mill Road.

In the background he could hear the muffled tone of Dr Riches, encouraging him to move forwards, to do what his body was telling him to do, to trust in his own mind.

He was strong. He was powerful. He no longer felt fear.

Jack tuned out Dr Riches and concentrated instead on his own thoughts. With the door now wide open, he knew it took three steps to bring the vision of his mother into view. Three steps to finally confront what had been the epicentre of his fears for so long.

Jack stepped forwards. One. Two. Three. Opening his eyes, not realising that they had been clamped shut, he prepared himself to see the vision one final time...one final time he would see his mother's lifeless body, swinging just out of reach, beyond his help. One final time to say goodbye.

His eyes focused on the image in front of him. It was just as he had expected, and yet it was not.

Something was different this time.

Something was very different.

Stella MacIntosh was, indeed, still there – dressed in her silky nightdress, swinging in the breeze from the cracked window. Her lifeless body still suspended from the light fitting above, creating the impression of an ethereal figure floating in nothingness.

But that was not all Jack saw this time.

This time he saw someone else.

* * *

Time: 5.35pm

Date: Tuesday 4th December 2012

Location: Office of Dr Evelyn Riches, Psychotherapist – St James's University, London

"I saw him. He was there." Jack gripped the fresh glass of water in his trembling hand, the contents sloshing over his knee. "He was definitely there."

Dr Riches nodded, slowly, not taking her eyes off the notepad she still balanced on her lap. "I hear you, Jack."

"No, you don't. You're not listening. I *saw* him." Jack's eyes were wide, and he didn't need a heart monitor to know that his heart rate was increasing. "I saw a man. There. In the room."

"I said I hear you, Jack." Dr Riches finished making her notes and looked up, resting her pen on the notepad. "It's not unusual. False memories can be quite common – more common that people think."

"That's what you think this is? A false memory?" Jack swigged a mouthful of the cold water, his mouth suddenly feeling like it was full of cotton wool. "Why would it be false? I saw him. He was real."

Dr Riches considered Jack for a moment, fixing him in her pale gaze. "OK. Tell me about him. This man that you saw." She picked up the pen once again and looked expectantly at Jack.

"He was tall. Taller than me. He had dark hair, short hair. And a moustache." Jack felt his body shiver at the memory and took another mouthful of water. "He took hold of the chair, and turned it on its side. He made it look like it had been kicked over, but..." Jack's voice caught in his throat, his airway suddenly feeling constricted. He fought to get the final words out. "He made it look like suicide."

Dr Riches looked up, sharply. "Now, Jack. You need to be very careful here. What you've seen today – what you *think* you've seen today – could be nothing more than a false memory. You've never seen this man before?"

Jack shook his head and drained the rest of the water. "No. Never."

Dr Riches paused and began to add something else to her notes.

"But it looked real – it *has* to be real," continued Jack. "Why else would I have seen him? It makes no sense. I've read about this type of thing; the brain hides traumatic memories in an effort to protect itself – but therapy can bring them out into the open. Recovered memories. I read it in that leaflet you gave me – the PTSD one. It happens – it happens all the time."

"It does," conceded Dr Riches, nodding at Jack. "It does. But you still need to be careful. Not all recovered memories are true."

"I need to go under again...I need to see him again." Jack placed the empty glass back down on the table and settled back in his chair. "Put me under again."

Dr Riches shook her head. "I can't do that, Jack. It wouldn't be right. You're in an agitated state right now and it could do you more harm than good. You need to take a break and we can revisit it again at some other time. You've progressed so well up to this point – we can't risk undoing all that."

Jack gave an exasperated sigh, but accepted that she was probably right. He felt exhausted; his body ached and his head was banging. He felt like he just wanted to sleep.

"You're not due back to work for a while, are you?" Dr Riches closed her notebook and pushed herself up out of her chair, heading over towards her desk.

"No," replied Jack. "Indefinite leave."

"Then I recommend this." Dr Riches returned and handed Jack a business card for Tannochside B&B. "Take some time out, Jack. When you get back, we'll talk."

* * *

Time: 10.15pm
  Date: Monday 11th February 2013
  Location: Kettle's Yard Mews, London

Jack picked up his phone and, without thinking any further in case he talked himself out of it, dialled the familiar number. Despite the hour, the call was answered on the second ring.

"Jack. Good to hear from you, as always. What can I do for you at this late hour?" Dr Phillip Matthews' voice filled Jack's ear.

"Hi, Doc. How are things?"

"In the land of the dead, you mean?" Dr Matthews' dry wit made Jack smile. "It's all quiet here, Jack. Dead bodies don't make a lot of noise."

"And Mrs Matthews? You both keeping well?"

Dr Matthews paused on his end of the line. "As much as I appreciate the sentiment, Jack – I'm sure you didn't call me at this time of night to ask about the health of my good lady wife. Who is, incidentally, in robust health. What is it that you really want?"

Jack tapped his biro against the notepad in front of him. He had tried to write down everything he could remember about his last therapy session with Dr Riches – and every time he thought about it, he always came to the same conclusion. It was no false memory – what he had seen was real. His time away in Scotland had done nothing to change that.

"I need a favour, Doc."

"Of course you do, Jack." The humour in Dr Matthews' tone made Jack smile. "I wouldn't have expected anything less. What can I do for you?"

Jack paused, knowing that what he was about to say could very well go against any one or more professional regulations, and maybe even asking it could put his good friend in an awkward position. But he needed to ask it anyway.

"I need a copy of a post mortem report." Jack could almost hear Dr Matthews raising his eyebrows at the other end.

"A PM report? Is it one I've done for you recently? If so, just give me the name and I can probably access a copy right now."

Jack could now hear what sounded like the esteemed pathologist switching on his desktop computer. He cleared his throat. "Er...no. Not exactly, Doc. It's not one you've done recently. In fact, it's not one that you performed at all. And I'm not sure who did."

If Jack had been in the same room as Dr Matthews right now, he would be sure that the pathologist would be lacing his long, piano-player fingers together and eyeing Jack with an inquisitive stare.

"I'm not quite sure I follow, Jack," replied Dr Matthews. "Just whose post mortem report do you need to see?"

Jack considered his options. He could try and lie his way through, bend the truth a little to protect himself – or he could just tell it as it was.

He decided on the latter.

"I need a copy of the post mortem report on Stella MacIntosh – deceased 5th April 1971."

There was silence for a moment or two on the other end of the line before Dr Matthews responded. "Stella MacIntosh? You mean…"

"My mother, Doc, yes. I need the post mortem report on my mother."

More silence filled Jack's ear, and for a moment he wasn't sure if the pathologist was still there. "Doc?"

"I'm still here, Jack."

Jack let a few more seconds pass. "I know it's a bit unconventional…but I've got good reason for needing to see it."

"I don't doubt it, Jack." Dr Matthews paused, and Jack wondered what was going through his mind. It would have been easier if it had been one of Dr Matthews' own reports – but back in 1971, Jack guessed he was probably still at medical school. To access this one, he would have to delve deeper into the medical records system; no doubt, in this day and age, leaving a digital footprint with every step he took. It was a big ask of such an eminent professional.

"My mother…her death was recorded as a suicide, but…" Jack broke off, not quite sure what else to say. What was he trying to turn this into? A murder enquiry? The very thought sent a shiver down his spine. All he had was one memory – if you could call it that. Dr Riches seemed to doubt it.

"But you don't think it was," finished Dr Matthews, the sound of rustling paper in the background.

"Well I don't know. That's the point." More silence on the other end of the line, and Jack began to feel more and more uneasy about what he had asked Dr Matthews to do for him. He wasn't just a pathologist; he was also a friend. "Look, Doc. Don't worry about it. Ignore me. It's late. Forget I said anything."

"Leave it with me," was Dr Matthews' curt reply, before the line went dead.

* * *

Time: 11.45pm
 Date: Monday 11th February 2013
 Location: Westminster Mortuary, London

It hadn't been hard to find, in all honesty. A few calls here and there; a search of a few databases. There were more than a few people that owed him favours, so the process had been relatively smooth.

Dr Phillip Matthews eased himself back in his chair and studied the freshly printed post mortem report of Stella MacIntosh. He had read it three times so far, and with each reading his brow creased more deeply than before.

The report bothered him.

Even to his expert eye, the post mortem had been a rush job. Not carried out by a pathologist he had heard of before, and not one that he could trace on the system since. Most probably a locum brought in to clear a backlog.

The examination had been scanty to say the least. A cursory initial examination of the body and, in Dr Matthews' opinion, too many assumptions had been made from the very beginning.

He cast his eyes over the beginning of the report one more time.

'A Caucasian female, aged twenty-eight. Obvious self-inflicted stricture marks to the neck, causing compression, and suspected fracture of the C1 and possibly C2 vertebrae."

The words 'obvious self-inflicted' caused Dr Matthews' nerves to grate. Even before the actual post mortem itself had begun, the pathologist was making a massive presumption.

He continued to skip through the body of the report, which was as sparsely populated with facts as the introduction was. The conclusion at the bottom merely stated 'findings consistent with strangulation by hanging. Suicide."

Dr Matthews shook his head. The brief report was swayed fully in favour of supporting the initial police hypothesis of suicide, something that was really for the coroner to decide. The report was so lacking in detail that Dr Matthews could barely believe what he was reading, in particular how it failed to address the more ambiguous areas thrown up by the actual post mortem itself.

The internal organs were unremarkable. This was a fit and healthy twenty-eight-year-old woman, after all. Pelvic examination consistent with having experienced childbirth. Dr Matthews picked up a highlighter pen and highlighted an entire section in the middle of the report which detailed external injuries; details which were not reproduced in the rather scant and brief conclusion at the end.

There was bruising around each wrist, and abrasions to the side of the face. Quite extensive periocular contusions and a small cut to the upper lip.

But what caught Dr Matthews' eye more than the external facial injuries, appeared a little further down the page, tucked away at the bottom; almost as an afterthought, not to be given any further consideration.

"Tissue consistent with skin apparent underneath the deceased's finger-nails on both hands."

There it was.

That one sentence caused Dr Matthews' frown to deepen and a sense of unease to spread within him. Despite the hour, he reached for his phone.

* * *

Chapter Thirteen

Time: 7.45am
   Date: Tuesday 12th February 2013
   Location: Westminster Mortuary, London

"Thanks for coming, Jack." Dr Matthews nodded to the chair opposite his desk. "I thought it best we did this face to face."

Jack felt an uneasy frown cross his forehead and slipped into the vacant chair. He could feel his heartbeat steadily rising. "This is about the post mortem report, isn't it? My mother's?"

Dr Matthews seated himself back in his own chair and held Jack in his own solemn gaze, slowly nodding as he did so. "It is, Jack. It is."

"I take it you must have found it?" Jack knew the pathologist was unlikely to have asked him to trek over to the mortuary just to tell him that the report was lost, or otherwise unavailable.

Dr Matthews didn't reply immediately. Instead he reached for a plain black folder that was sitting at the centre of his uncluttered desk. His long, delicate fingers hovered for a second over the top of the folder, as if he were contemplating something. Satisfied with his own thinking, Dr Matthews nodded to himself and opened the folder.

"I have the report, Jack. It wasn't too hard to find." Dr Matthews slipped out two photocopied sheets of paper from the folder and passed one across to Jack.

Jack took the report and immediately cast his eyes down to the printed details; the name at the top, typed out in black and white, brought a shiver to his spine.

Stella MacIntosh.

He swallowed past the lump that had appeared, unbidden, in his throat and began to read.

It didn't take long.

When he had finished, he flipped the double-sided report back and forth and looked up. "Is this it? Two pages?"

Dr Matthews gave another slow nod. "Yes, just the two pages."

"Isn't that...?"

"Brief?" interrupted Dr Matthews, picking up his own copy of the report again. "Yes, it is, Jack. Very brief."

"And...?"

"That was the first thing that struck me about it – it's far too short, and far too concise."

Bewildered, Jack looked back down at the report and quickly re-read its meagre contents. "I'm no pathologist, Doc, but..."

"The report raises more questions than answers, yes," finished Dr Matthews, a grave tone to his voice. "I agree."

"This bit here...about the external injuries." Jack tapped the photocopied sheet where a very succinct list of Stella MacIntosh's visible injuries had been noted. "She had a black eye; a split lip; a cut to the forehead; other bruising, too. Even with such limited information, that looks like..."

"An assault?"

"Well, yes. It certainly raises the question." Jack looked back up at Dr Matthews. "Would these have been recent injuries?"

Dr Matthews gave a small nod. "From the limited amount of information the report contains, I would conclude that they were quite fresh. Definitely ante-mortem, in any event. The report does not document the bruises as healing, so I would err on the side of them being current injuries. I'm no Detective, Jack..." Dr Matthews broke off and raised his eyebrows at Jack.

"It's not suicide."

"Well, I'm not sure we can leap to that conclusion, but..."

"But it's a possibility." Jack's head was filled with visions from his last hypnotherapy session. The man who had appeared in the kitchen; the man who was there when his mother died.

"It's *possible*," conceded Dr Matthews. "I certainly would not have concluded this was a definite suicide had it been one of my post mortems...and when you consider the tissue under the fingernails..."

"Whoa, where was that?" Jack re-read the report, scrutinising every word, until he found the entry, tucked away at the bottom of the page. "Tissue consistent with skin apparent underneath the deceased's fingernails on both hands." He read the sentence three times before shaking his head and letting the single sheet of paper detailing his mother's demise fall back onto the desk. "Jesus, Doc. Did none of this raise any suspicion at the time?"

"There was a brief inquest, from what I can gather. The police investigation confirmed it was a suicide by hanging, with no other party involved. There were no next of kin to raise questions or doubts. The coroner dutifully signed it off as suicide."

Jack rubbed his eyes, feeling them prickle beneath his fingers. "This tissue – found underneath her fingers. I'm assuming it was tested in some way, at the time?"

"That is more your territory, Jack. But, back in 1971 - you know as well as I do, that DNA was not a thing."

"Where would it be now?"

"The tissue?"

Jack nodded. "Yes, the tissue. Would it still be kept in storage somewhere? In some lab?" Jack could feel his mind start to whirr. "If it's still available, I want it tested. DNA can be extracted from old samples now, can't it?"

Dr Matthews nodded. "It can, yes. So long as the original sample has been kept in an appropriate environment, and hasn't been contaminated in any way."

"So, that's what we need to do." Jack rose to his feet, grabbing hold of the photocopied report. "How do I find out where the tissue might be now? If it's still available?"

"Sit down, Jack." Dr Matthew's calm tones floated across the desk, and he waved at Jack to resume his seat. "I had a feeling you were going to say that. So, I've already done some digging."

Jack felt his legs wobble and he collapsed back into his chair.

"I've found your tissue samples, Jack." He swung his computer monitor around to face the other side of the desk. "If you want to test it for DNA, it's all yours."

* * *

Time: 10.40am

Date: Tuesday 12th February 2013

Location: HMP Belmarsh, Thamesmead, South-East London

The prison officer – Warren Jamieson, according to the ID badge that nestled above an ample stomach – nodded at Jack to follow him along the narrow, windowless corridor. Jack shuddered as the echo of the reinforced door closing behind them followed in their wake. It had been a while since he had last stepped inside the unforgiving walls of Belmarsh, and it had lost none of its reputation.

As they strode further into the inner sanctum of the prison, and away from the outside world, Jack began to hear the tell-tale noises of everyday life for the incarcerated. The banging and clattering of the doors; the jangling of keys from prison officers' belts; the echoes of inmates voices bouncing off the walls, a cacophony of shouts and hollers, rising and falling like the tide. Profanities were carried along in the air as Jack followed Warren towards the secure area close to the governor's office.

"We've set aside one of the interview rooms for you. It's secure. Away from all the noise." Warren unlocked a final set of doors which swung out into yet another identical looking corridor. As they made their way along, the sound of the inmates began to fade away. The corridor was home to several offices, and Warren stopped outside a nondescript looking door marked "interview room 1".

"You get yourself settled. I'll get him brought up to you as soon as." Warren pushed open the door and then turned back the way they had just come.

Jack stepped inside interview room 1 and headed for the metal table at its centre. The table was made of what looked like heavy duty steel, and was welded tightly to the floor. Two seats, also fashioned out of metal, faced each other across the table, both also fixed to the floor with heavy-duty bolts, just to make sure.

Belmarsh had opened in 1991 and was still described as a 'new' prison – the first to be built in London since the late nineteenth century. Trying to learn from the mistakes of others, everything that could be bolted down, was – negating the possibility of something as innocuous as a chair being turned into a weapon.

Jack was still reeling from his meeting with Dr Matthews, but he pushed the thoughts about his mother's death out of his head. Now was not the time. He had just got himself seated on the uncomfortable, cold metal chair when the door opened again. Warren strode in, this time followed by a tall, lean-looking prisoner shuffling in his wake. A chain swung between them, linking Warren's beefy forearm to that of Jason Alcock.

"I can stay if you wish, Inspector," announced Warren, closing the door behind him before starting to unclasp the lock around his wrist. "But Jason here won't give you any trouble." The burly prison officer nodded to Jason Alcock, giving him a quick wink and indicated for him to sit opposite Jack in the spare seat. He leant across the table to secure the handcuff to a metal ring embedded in the table. "Regulation," he explained, nodding at the handcuff. "Although Jason here is a good lad, we still have to do things by the book."

Jack nodded. "I'm fine. You can leave."

Warren returned the nod and Jack managed to catch what he thought was a look of relief flicker across the prison officer's face. With the time approaching eleven o'clock, Jack surmised that a tea break was in order and, judging by the bulging belly fighting to remain encased in the regulation prison uniform shirt, maybe a doughnut or two.

"There'll be an officer outside in the corridor – just bang on the door when you're done." Warren departed, the door clanging shut behind him.

Jack eyed the prisoner sitting before him, taking in his rough and unshaven face, the hollow sunken cheeks and sallow skin. His closely cropped regulation prison haircut revealed a scarred scalp. Jack's eyes then flickered towards the prisoner's arms that were resting lightly on the flat metal table top. His prison issue short-sleeved blue t-shirt revealed thin, yet strong looking, sinewy arms with the tell-tale scars and track-marks that told Jack all he needed to know about this particular prisoner's past.

"How long?" Jack nodded at Jason Alcock's left forearm, the one attached to the handcuff.

"Been clean for getting on for five years now," replied Alcock, a knowing smile teasing his chapped lips. "Not much gets past you, does it?"

Jack raised his eyebrows. "That's good going – to kick the habit in prison. We all know there's as many drugs circulating inside these walls as there are outside on the streets."

"Yeah, well. Drugs got me in here, didn't they?" Alcock's expression changed, his face losing the playful smile. "I'm getting too old for all that now. I'm keeping myself clean in here – away from all the scum that deal."

"Model prisoner, I heard?" Jack held Alcock's gaze, and tried to look beyond the ex-drug addict and convicted murderer sat before him. "Not an easy thing to do in Belmarsh."

Alcock shrugged, the chains of the handcuff scraping on the metal table. "I keep my nose clean. Keep out of other people's business and expect them to do the same. People know not to mess with me."

Jack nodded. He didn't doubt it for a second. He had looked up Jason Alcock's prison record before leaving the station that morning. After the robbery and manslaughter conviction in 1982, he'd gone to juvenile detention alongside the others from the Fifteen. Alcock had then been in and out of prison for the next twenty years; mostly for violent offences and the supply of drugs. Just over five years ago, his latest sentence was handed down at the Old Bailey – this time for murder.

The facts of the case, as Jack was able to extract, were that Alcock, high on drugs, attacked a taxi driver in south-east London – hacking him to death with an axe, almost decapitating him in the process. And all for the contents of his cash box – some thirty odd pounds. With a life sentence now hanging around his neck, the transformation of Jason Alcock had been nothing short of astonishing.

The heavy drug use over the years had taken an obvious toll on his body - he looked thin and undernourished, his skin pallid, his nails stained from a co-existing nicotine addiction. But Jack could see the fire in his eyes, a hidden determination that surprised him.

"Well, I'm pleased to hear it," replied Jack, reaching into his jacket pocket to bring out his notebook. "I just have some questions for you, then I'll let you get on your way."

"It's about those Wakefield scum, isn't it?" Jason Alcock suddenly exploded into a violent cough, his chest rattling in unison with the handcuff chains.

Jack raised his eyebrows. "You've heard about them?"

Jason Alcock's coughing fit subsided and turned into a cackling laugh. "News spreads like wildfire in here. I reckon we heard about it before you did."

"So what can you tell me about them?"

This time it was Alcock's turn to raise his eyebrows. He rubbed a nicotine-stained finger along the side of his nose where a remnant of a recent wound had scabbed over. A prison altercation no doubt, surmised Jack, as he waited for a response. And one that Alcock most probably came out of on top.

"What can I tell you? Well it wasn't me, was it?" Alcock grinned, revealing an uneven set of brown stained teeth. "I think they'd have noticed if I'd nipped out."

Jack nodded, conceding the point. "I realise that. I'm wondering if you'd heard anything? Had any idea who might be behind it? You said yourself, news travels like wildfire in here." Jack let the question hang in the air. "They both worked at St Bartholomew's, didn't they? At the same time you were there?"

"You know they did – that's why you're here." Jason Alcock paused, the grin slipping from his face. He bit his lower lip, as once again his expression changed. Gone was the bravado of the convicted murderer, the top dog in his block in one of Britain's toughest jails. Right before Jack's eyes his whole demeanour changed, suddenly transforming back into the teenage foster boy that no one wanted and had kicked into the gutter. "They were animals, the pair of them. I'm glad they're dead. I actually cheered when I heard. I'm just sorry I didn't get the chance to do it myself." Alcock's voice was low and quiet, all cockiness having evaporated. "I hope they suffered."

Jack nodded, flicking to a fresh page in his notebook and making a brief note. *I hope they suffered.* The exact same words that had escaped his own brother's lips only yesterday.

"Anyone else you know of who might have felt the same? Wanted them out the way?"

"How long have you got?" grunted Alcock, shaking his head. "I should imagine everyone who ever spent any time in that place would have given their right arm to have had a crack at the Wakefields."

"I see your tattoo there." Jack inclined his head towards Alcock's right arm. "The Fifteen?"

Jason Alcock's eyes flickered towards his fading tattoo, just visible below the sleeve of his t-shirt. "We all had one. It was our mark."

"The gang?" Jack flicked open his notebook again.

Alcock gave a brief nod. "We left our mark wherever we went. Turned it into a graffiti tag. But we hid the tattoos from everyone; no one knew about them except us. It was our thing; our secret."

Jack made another note and then slipped his notebook back in his pocket. He leant forwards and slid a business card across the table. "You'll let me know if you hear of anything?"

Jason Alcock regarded the card for a few seconds before picking it up. "Of course. Reformed character me – a policeman's best friend."

A smile flickered across Jack's lips as he stood up from the uncomfortable metal seat. "I'm sure you are. Take care in here." He turned towards the closed door, ready to let Warren know that he was ready to go.

"So, how's Maccy?"

Jack stopped dead in his tracks and turned back round.

"He's your brother, right?" Jason Alcock swivelled around in his seat and held Jack in his gaze. "I recognise you from hanging around outside the school back in the day."

Jack cleared his throat. "He's doing all right, thanks for asking."

"He was a good lad, was Maccy," continued Alcock. "I'm sorry if we led him astray."

Jack shook his head and gave a small laugh. "I don't think you led him anywhere – he was big enough to make his own choices."

"But he's doing all right now?" Jason Alcock's eyes searched Jack's. "He's made better life choices than me, I hope?"

"He's getting there – still hot-headed from time to time, but he's doing all right."

Jason Alcock gave a quick nod of the head and turned back to face the metal table, pocketing Jack's business card as he did so.

Jack hesitated for a second before turning to bang on the door.

* * *

Time: 1.00pm

Date: Tuesday 12th February 2013

Location: Metropolitan Police HQ, London

"Update on Stephen Byers, just in." DC Cassidy glanced up as Jack walked into the investigation room. His journey back from Belmarsh had been a long and tedious one, and his back felt stiff. "Currently living in the north-east – a flat in central Newcastle. Released from prison on home curfew three months ago – has an electronic tag. Served two years for violent disorder and ABH. Has previously served time for assault."

"Not another one," muttered Jack. "First Alcock and now Byers – both have carried on their jailbird ways after St Bartholomew's. Seems to be a recurring theme." He sighed and slumped into one of the vacant chairs at the table. "So if he's tagged, he wouldn't have made the journey down here to commit the murders. Not without someone realising anyway."

"Seems unlikely, boss," replied DC Cassidy, getting up and fixing Jack a coffee from the hot water urn. He looked like he needed one.

As well as his back, Jack's neck ached; he rubbed it whilst gingerly stretching his head from side to side. He considered both were most probably from how he slept last night – or, indeed, hadn't slept. After Dr Matthews' late night phone call, he had lain awake for hours. The painful crick sent an electrifying twinge down between his shoulder blades, and a headache was starting to throb at his temples.

He nodded in appreciation as DC Cassidy deposited the mug of coffee in front of him. "Do we know anything about the third one? Williams?"

DS Cooper joined Jack at the table. "Better news about him, boss. Kyle Williams seems to have gone straight after being released from juvenile detention – nothing on the system of him being involved with the police or courts since the late 1980s. Currently lives on a farm, near a remote village in North Wales. Married with two kids."

"Sounds more promising," agreed Jack, sipping his coffee and still massaging his neck. "Where was he on the two murder dates?"

"Williams has spent the last eight days in hospital in Bangor." DS Cooper flipped over several pages in his notebook. "Recovering from surgery on a fractured leg and multiple fractured ribs. Seems he fell off a quad bike – was rounding up sheep on a hillside when it hit a stone or something and toppled over."

"So...neither Byers nor Williams could have travelled to carry out either murder. And Alcock has been safely tucked up in Belmarsh." Jack paused, swallowing a mouthful of coffee. "I guess we can cross all of them off the list."

"You still think it's a former resident at St Bartholomew's?" DC Cassidy tossed an open packet of chocolate digestives across the table in Jack's direction. "Someone who met the Wakefields there?"

Jack reached, gratefully, for the biscuits, noting how the newly swallowed coffee was swirling in his empty stomach. He shrugged and bit into a digestive. "Let me have the contact numbers for both Williams and Byers, I need to hear it from them myself. They might not have been able to get down here physically themselves, but they might just know who did."

DC Cassidy scribbled both numbers down onto a scrap of paper and passed it across the table.

Jack took another swig of his coffee and brought out his notebook. *I hope they suffered. It was our mark.* Jason Alcock's words echoed around his brain. The tattoo was no coincidence. And if Alcock, Byers and Williams all had alibis for the murders of both Edward and Terence Wakefield, that only left one member of the Fifteen who didn't.

Jack rubbed his temples.

His headache was getting worse.

* * *

Chapter Fourteen

Time: 1.25pm
   Date: Tuesday 12th February 2012
   Location: Metropolitan Police HQ, London

Chief Superintendent Dougie King stared out of his office window, watching as the leaden clouds above began to trickle dainty snowflakes. A few at first, bobbing about in the light, swirling wind, but within minutes the sky was thick with a blanket of snow cascading down to the ground below.

He stood, transfixed, for several minutes, watching the cars in the rear car park becoming slowly entombed in their frozen, white shrouds. As he did so, he contemplated how the drive home was now going to take longer – snow always seemed to do that – and Mrs King would be at the window, awaiting his return with a pensive look. Just then, his phone began to trill from the side of the desk.

He pulled himself out of his trance, half wondering if it was the aforementioned Mrs King asking if he was going to be leaving early, bearing in mind the deteriorating weather outside. He stepped back and lifted the receiver.

"Yes?"

"Call for you, Sir," announced Penny, his PA from the small office she inhabited in the next room. "A Dr Evelyn Riches? She says its important."

Chief Superintendent King hesitated before answering. Dr Riches? That was Jack's hypnotherapist. Why would she be calling him? All thoughts of an early afternoon drive home began to disappear.

"Put her through, Penny. Thank you." He slipped himself back into his swivel chair and waited for the call to connect.

"Chief Superintendent?" The voice that came through was calm and melodic. "It's Dr Evelyn Riches here – from St James's University."

"Hello, Dr Riches," greeted Dougie King, failing to keep the intrigue out of his tone. "What can I do for you?"

Dr Riches seemed to hesitate before replying. "I know it's a bit out of the ordinary, but I need to talk to you about something. About someone."

The Chief Superintendent drew in a slow breath, a creeping sense of unease settling in his stomach. "Yes?"

"As you may know, you most probably do, I've been seeing one of your officers for a course of hypnotherapy. A Detective Inspector MacIntosh?"

"Yes, yes," replied the Chief Superintendent, the feeling of disquiet increasing. "I'm well aware of that. What seems to be the problem?"

"Well...he's not returning any of my calls." Dr Riches hesitated once again. "I really do need to speak to him; to arrange a follow up session? We left things a little...on edge. It's nothing to worry about, but I do feel that we need to do a final session, to resolve a few issues."

Chief Superintendent King nodded to himself. Dr Riches' reassurance that all was well was not having the desired effect. His stomach churned uncomfortably. "I see. Well, I have spoken to him quite recently. He is very busy. Straight back into a double murder investigation."

"Yes, I'm sure. I just really need to speak to him."

"How did it all go, anyway?" asked the Chief Superintendent, feeling a change of subject was in order. "The therapy sessions?"

There was another pause before Dr Riches replied. "Did he not tell you when he returned to work?"

"Well...he mentioned it briefly, in passing. He said that it all went fine. That he was fine."

The pause on the other end of the line turned into silence. Chief Superintendent King found himself clutching the receiver in an ever-tightening grip. "Dr Riches? Everything did go well, didn't it? There's nothing I should know?"

Dr Riches finally broke the silence. "Sorry, yes. Well, he did make progress, yes. But there's not much else I can tell you, I'm afraid – client confidentiality, you understand." Dr Riches felt that now was not the time to mention the disturbing appearance of Jack's recovered memory, if indeed that was what it was. "He did make progress, that is very true. More than I had expected, to tell you the truth."

"So...?" A confused frown crossed Dougie King's forehead.

"So...you need to talk to him some more." Dr Riches' voice faltered a little. "Ask him about the final session. That's all I can say." She paused before continuing. "And when you do catch up with him, ask him to return my calls. Please?"

Dr Riches hung up, leaving Chief Superintendent King clutching onto an empty receiver.

Dear God, Jack, he thought to himself as he returned the phone to its cradle and sighed. What have you done now?

* * *

Time: 1.30pm

Date: Tuesday 12th February 2013

Location: Office of Dr Evelyn Riches, Psychotherapist – St James's University, London

Dr Evelyn Riches put the phone down and considered her position for a moment. Jack MacIntosh had, indeed, made progress during their ten week long course of hypnotherapy, that was true. Surprising progress, really. She smiled to herself; she had a feeling that DI Jack MacIntosh was always full of surprises.

And taking time off for himself after the course was finished had been a good idea, and one she had encouraged and endorsed. Although disappearing to a remote bed and breakfast close to the Trossachs in the dead of winter may not have been anyone else's first choice – maybe others would have thought a spa break at a luxurious country hotel more appealing – Dr Riches had recommended this particular getaway for a reason.

Jack needed time, and Jack needed space. And he would have got plenty of both at the Tannochside B&B. She was sure that Willie McArthur and his wife would have taken good care of him.

Judging by the brief chat they did have when he had returned from Scotland, and just before resuming work, the break had done him good. He sounded better in himself, more upbeat and positive. If she could have seen him she was sure that he would have looked better too; maybe lost the haunted dark circles underneath his eyes, and his vitamin D-deprived skin rejuvenated. He sounded buoyant, with tales of solitary walks amongst the heather, treks up mountain sides, and then cosy nights in by the fire with a good book. And a glass or two of malt whisky, if Dr Riches didn't know any better. She thought it unlikely that Jack MacIntosh would spend six weeks in the wilds of Scotland without partaking of a wee dram or two of the strong stuff.

She smiled again to herself and made a note in her diary to try and contact him again in a day or so. They still needed to discuss what happened at Jack's final hypnotherapy session. She might be worrying over nothing, but it needed dealing with.

And soon.

* * *

Time: 1.35pm

Date: Tuesday 12th February 2013

Location: Flat 12a, The Rivers, Riverside Estate, Newcastle

Stephen Byers hung up the phone and reached for his tobacco tin. That would teach him. He never usually answered the house phone – it was always someone trying to sell him something, or con him. He usually let it ring or disconnected it from the wall. But something made him answer it this time.

It was not a mistake he would make again.

A detective inspector from down in London somewhere. How he had got hold of his landline number, he didn't know. He never gave it out to anyone. Ever. Probably because he couldn't usually remember the sodding number himself anyway.

He cracked open the tin and pulled out a hand rolled joint. He was glad he had taken the time yesterday to roll half a dozen or so whilst numbing his brain with This Morning and Loose Women. His hand was shaking so much that it took him several attempts to light up.

The call had unnerved him.

He took in a deep drag, filling his lungs with the cannabis-fuelled smoke. He knew his probation worker, Diane, would smell it on him a mile off when he went to report in at four o'clock. She would wrinkle her nose and give him one of her disapproving looks.

But he wasn't concerned about Diane. Not right now. He needed a joint more than he needed to be in her good books.

St Bartholomew's.

As soon as the inspector on the other end of the phone had mentioned the name, Stephen Byers had frozen solid. He clamped the telephone receiver to his ear, his brain telling him to slam it down and rip the cord from the wall – but his body wouldn't obey.

Hearing that the Wakefields, both father and son, had met a sticky end was the only silver lining to the brief and mainly one-way conversation. He felt his heart leap at the news, an unaccustomed feeling of joy and relief seeping into his bloodstream almost as quickly as the cannabis was now doing.

But the happiness had been short-lived. Being unable, and a little unwilling, to assist the detective inspector much more, the conversation had been short and sweet. Well, he couldn't have been involved, could he?

Not with the bulky electronic tag around his ankle tracking his every move

No, he hadn't heard anything. And yes, he would contact the police if he did.

And no – no one knew about the tattoos. They would have been flogged within an inch of their lives if anyone at St Bartholomew's had found out.

But now, in the silence and the emptiness of his flat on the twelfth floor of the tower block close to the Tyne, Stephen Byers' mind began to whirr. Fuelled by the cannabis streaming into his bloodstream, the tremors in his hands began to increase. He had to sit on them to stop them from shaking.

The Wakefields.

Dead.

It had finally happened. He had finally done what he had promised.

Stephen Byers continued to pull deeply on his joint until he was left with the short, stubby end. Flicking the remnant into a nearby ashtray, he reached into the pocket of his tracksuit bottoms for his mobile phone.

There was a call he needed to make.

* * *

Time: 1.50pm
Date: Tuesday 12th February 2013
Location: University Hospital, Bangor, Wales

The nurse had been kind enough to bring him the ward phone, and Kyle Williams had been intrigued to find out who it was that was calling him. Maybe Sarah had lost her mobile? Or was it out of battery and she couldn't find her charger? Nobody remembered anyone's mobile number these days, did they? Apart from their own.

He had taken hold of the receiver, fully expecting Sarah to bombard him with questions as to how he was feeling, what he had had to eat today, and what progress had been made with the physiotherapists.

But it hadn't been Sarah.

And it hadn't been anyone asking about the physio sessions or the contents of his breakfast.

The conversation had only lasted a few minutes, but it had unnerved him enough that it had become noticeable.

"You all right there, Mr Williams?" The nurse who had brought him the phone peered down at him, bending over his bed to retrieve the handset. "You look a little pale." She slipped the phone into her pocket and took hold of his wrist, glancing at her fob watch with her other hand. She shook her head and tutted. "Your heart rate is a little high. Are you feeling ill, Mr Williams? Feeling nauseous or light headed?"

Kyle Williams shook his head, doing his best to ignore the distinct feeling of panic rising up inside him. "No, no...I'm good thanks. My leg hurts a little, that's all." This wasn't exactly a lie. His leg was still very sore after the surgery to insert a titanium rod and four locking screws into his shattered femur several days before. The nurse nodded and reached for his ward notes at the end of the bed.

"Well, let's see if we can't get you some additional pain relief. You're due a visit from physio later this afternoon, so you'll be needing something to help with your mobilisation." She turned on her regulation soft soled shoes and headed towards the drugs cabinet. "I'll be back in a moment, Mr Williams."

With the nurse having disappeared from sight, Kyle Williams sank back into his pillows and stared up at the ceiling.

The Wakefields were dead.

After all this time, they were dead.

A small smile crept over his lips, the pain in his leg now forgotten.

What goes around comes around, he thought to himself, casting his mind back to the last time he had seen either of them. The memories tripping through his brain made him shudder. Checking that the nurse was still out of sight and not returning with another dose of painkillers, he reached across to his bedside table and snatched up his mobile phone. He had to be quick – but what he had to say wouldn't take long.

* * *

Time: 3.30pm
Date: Tuesday 12th February 2013
Location: Isabel's Café, King's Road, London

Dominic busied himself collecting up empty glasses and plates from the newly deserted tables by the window. Humming quietly to himself, he stacked the plates on top of each other and, with the glasses clustered in his other hand, he carried them back to the kitchen.

Isabel gave him a smile as he passed by, slowly taking a sip of her camomile tea. It had been a busy day so far and her feet were aching. She leant back in the comfortable armchair and kicked off her flat-soled shoes, letting the soothing effect of the camomile wash over her. Once Dominic was safely out of earshot, she turned and faced Jack.

"I'm worried about him." She tried to force a smile to her lips.

Jack nodded and took a sip of the English Breakfast tea that he had selected from the ever-growing list chalked up on the blackboard behind the counter. He hadn't recognised anything else, and wasn't even sure you could drink half of them. He didn't need to ask who Isabel was talking about. "I know. I am too."

Isabel felt the smile slip from her face, replacing it with worry lines. "He won't talk to me anymore. I barely see him. After you left yesterday, he sat in silence – just staring out of the window. Then he got up and left without so much as a word. All I got was this."

Isabel turned the screen of her phone towards Jack, showing Mac's last message to her. "I'm sorry."

"Does he do this often? Cut himself off like this?" Isabel placed her cup down on the table, unable to disguise the faint tremor in her hands. "It's like he just wants to push everyone away from him."

Jack sighed, watching as Dominic returned to plump and rearrange the cushions on the sofas opposite. "In some ways it's just like him." Jack thought back to the hot headed teenager who kept everyone at arm's length, defying all authority and efforts to keep him on the straight and narrow, eventually leading to his own inevitable downfall. And then the hot-headed grown up – maybe slightly more willing to let people in, but still preferring a solitary existence. Not unlike Jack himself, if he were being truthful. The two brothers had more in common than Jack liked to admit.

But Isabel had been good for him – giving him a sense of purpose and direction, something he had lacked for most of his adult life. But he would always be Stuart MacIntosh, with one trigger-happy finger hovering over the self-destruct button at all times.

"How can we get through to him?" persisted Isabel, her voice shaky. "All this St Bartholomew's stuff has really affected him. While we were out in Italy he had really started to relax, really let the true man in him come out. I saw a really different side to him. But then...." Isabel broke off and reached for her tea, although she felt she needed something stronger than camomile. "When DS Carmichael came out to see us, he retreated back inside himself again. He changed, almost instantly."

"It would have dragged up a lot of unpleasant memories," replied Jack. "I don't think we can even begin to imagine what life was like for him back then. For all of them."

"But is that all it is? Memories?" Isabel's tea cup wavered again in her hand. "Because, I..." She broke off and took a large gulp of tea, trying to hide her eyes and the tears that were springing at their corners. "I overheard what you were talking about yesterday; about the Fifteen. The gang he was in. Be honest with me, Jack. Do you think he's involved with any of this?"

Jack hesitated. "At this stage, Isabel, I really don't know. I hope not." Jack placed his cup down on the coffee table and shuffled forwards in his seat. He took a deep breath. "I need to ask you where he was – at the times of the murders. I'm sorry."

Isabel nodded, no longer hiding the tears that streaked across her cheeks.

Jack brought out his notebook. "Friday 8th February – you both came back here. What time was that?"

Isabel wiped her eyes with her sleeve. "It must have been just before seven.

The café was closed and Sacha and Dominic were clearing up."

Jack nodded. "Do you remember how long he stayed?"

Isabel's shoulders heaved as a sob caught in her throat. "Not long. He said he was going to head over to yours. He just dropped off my suitcases and other bits, and pretty much headed straight out."

Jack flicked over a page in his notebook. Stu had arrived at his around eight fifteen, but before they had a chance to open a bottle of beer the call had come in from The Laurels and Jack had left. And from the looks of the uneaten Indian takeaway left on the table, Stu hadn't stuck around either.

"And what about earlier that day? Before you turned up at the café? What did you do?" Jack noted that Dr Matthews had estimated the time of death of Eddie Wakefield at between 4-5pm that day.

Isabel bit her lip as she thought back. She shook her head. "I don't know. We were in Mac's flat. I had a bath and washed my hair, while he..." Isabel broke off and swallowed. "He went out about two o'clock, saying he needed to do something. He didn't say what. He came back sometime after six."

"And the next day, Saturday the 9th? What was he doing?"

Isabel shook her head. "I have no idea. I was busy here in the café; I didn't see him at all on Saturday."

A heavy silence descended around them, the only sound being the scraping of Jack's pen as he scribbled a few notes in his notebook.

"Do you think it's him?" Isabel looked up with teary eyes. "Really?"

Jack stopped writing and shook his head. "You must know in your heart that he's not capable of something like that." Jack hoped he sounded more convincing than he felt.

"Please don't let it be him, Jack." The urgency in Isabel's voice was palpable. "Please don't let it be him." Her shoulders shuddered and fresh tears cascaded down her cheeks. "It can't be him," she whispered, her voice low. "It can't be."

* * *

Chapter Fifteen

Time: 6.30pm
  Date: Tuesday 12th February 2013
  Location: Metropolitan Police HQ, London

"What's your take on it all, Rob?" Jack eased himself down into the chair opposite DS Carmichael's increasingly cluttered desk. "I feel like I'm going round in circles."

DS Carmichael pushed a glass tumbler across the desk, and ignored Jack's half-hearted wave of protest as he filled it with a generous measure of what looked to Jack like a decent single malt. "Thanks for the details on the other boys – the rest of The Fifteen. I'll want to interview them all myself in time. But now you've traced them, you've ruled them all out for your murders? They're all clean?"

Jack nodded, taking the glass and downing a gulp immediately. The heat hit the back of his throat and he welcomed the numbness that followed. "As a whistle. Jason Alcock, who seemed like the leader of the gang, is currently in prison – and has been for the last five years. Stephen Byers has an electronic tag and lives up in the north east. Kyle Williams was in hospital recovering from surgery when both murders were committed. There's no way any of them were involved."

"I bet none of them were upset by it, though?" DS Carmichael took a sip of his own drink.

Jack shook his head. "Not in the slightest. Understandably."

DS Carmichael nodded. "So, you're back to square one?"

"I was convinced I had the answer, Rob. The killer *had* to be a member of The Fifteen. Why else would a tattoo of the number fifteen be carved into both victims? It makes no sense. Alcock confirmed it was their mark. Those were his words. And no one else knew about the tattoos. They all confirmed that. There's no other explanation – it has to be one of them. But I can't make any of it stick – they all have watertight alibis." Jack paused and downed the rest of his whisky in one. "Except..."

DS Carmichael eyed Jack across the top of his own glass. "Except what?"

"You know what I'm going to say, Rob." Jack accepted the top-up being poured into his glass and sunk another mouthful.

DS Carmichael gave a slow nod. "I do. But that doesn't make it any easier to hear."

"But I'm right, aren't I?" Jack's eyes found DS Carmichael's bird-like stare. "Aren't I?"

DS Carmichael didn't respond; instead he topped up his own glass and broke away from Jack's gaze. "There has to be another explanation, Jack."

"Does there? I've spoken to the rest of The Fifteen. They each swear blind no one else knows about the name of the gang, or the tattoos. No one but them. No one else knew, Rob. *No one.*"

Silence ensued while more whisky was drunk. It was DS Carmichael that broke the deadlock.

"Well, I guess the only question is – how well do you think you know your brother?"

* * *

Time: 4.05pm
Date: 20th April 1982
Location: West Road Recreation Ground, Christchurch

Jack ran full pelt across the grass towards the deserted playground. The rusted roundabout and climbing frames were no longer played on by smiling, happy faced children – instead they were a haven for local teenagers, huddled around in their groups as the sun set, sharing a rudimentary rolled joint, money passing from sweaty palm to sweaty palm. As he neared the entrance to the playground, he flung his school bag to the floor and leapt over the padlocked gate.

"Stu! Don't!" he yelled at the top of his lungs as he sprinted towards the abandoned swings at the far side of the playground. He could see his brother standing astride a near-motionless body lying prostrate beneath him on the muddied ground. "Stop – Stuart! Leave him alone!"

Jack's cries went unheeded. Stuart MacIntosh wasn't listening. With his sleeves rolled up above his elbows, he took a lunge at the defenceless body beneath him, his curled up fist making contact with the victim's ribs. He pummelled with his fists, one after the other, then followed up with two swift kicks to the kidneys.

Jack reached the swings to hear the sound of muffled sobs. He lunged forwards. "For God's sake, Stu. What the hell are you doing?" He made a grab for his brother's arm, but Stuart MacIntosh was stronger than he looked. He may have been two years younger than Jack, but his chest and upper body had filled out since he had been at St Bartholomew's – his arms were now wrapped in powerful, sinewy muscles. He shrugged Jack off without a thought.

"Leave me alone, Jack. This has nothing to do with you."

Jack watched, helplessly, as more punches swung through the air. He made to lunge forwards once again, determined to drag his brother away before he did any more damage – but he stopped in his tracks as the sound of sirens cut through the air.

"Stu! He's had enough now! You've made your point – let's go! The police are coming!"

This time Jack managed to grab hold of Stuart MacIntosh's arm and drag him away from the whimpering bloodied mess at their feet. They reached the padlocked gate and scrambled over the top, landing in a heap the other side. Remembering to pick up his abandoned school bag, Jack raced across the grass, following his brother towards the bank of trees and side street beyond.

They crashed out from beneath the trees and started sprinting along the pavement, not caring where they were heading so long as it was away from the ever-approaching sirens. They crossed the road and headed down a narrow alleyway between a Chinese takeaway and launderette. Reaching the end of the alleyway they stopped to catch their breath, both breathing hard. The sirens were now a mere muffled echo on the breeze.

"Jesus, Stu. What the hell was that? You want to get yourself banged up?"

"I don't care, Jack," breathed Stuart MacIntosh, wiping his bloodied knuckles on his jeans. "Just leave me alone. I don't need you anymore."

"But you could've killed him!"

"Like I said, Jack. I don't care. Leave me alone."

* * *

Time: 6.45pm
  Date: Tuesday 12th February 2013
  Location: Metropolitan Police HQ, London

"Like I said – how well do you think you know your brother?" The heady scent of whisky hung in the air. DS Carmichael had topped up their glasses some more but they were left untouched on the desk.

Jack shook his head. "Sometimes I don't think I know him at all, Rob. He's changed. Since all this St Bartholomew's business was dragged up, he's not been the same. He's withdrawn into himself. Even Isabel has noticed it. She's worried about him, I can tell."

"But he's not capable of murder, Jack. Is he?"

Jack paused just long enough to give DS Carmichael his answer. "Who knows what anyone is capable of if you push the right buttons. I'd like to say no – and in my heart I really want it to be a no – but…"

"It has to be someone else." DS Carmichael pushed himself up and out of his seat and retreated to the filing cabinets behind him. After rummaging for a few moments he returned with a folder. "More statements on the investigation at St Bartholomew's. You won't have these in the bundle I gave you earlier. Get them copied. Take them away. Whatever. The answer has to lie in there, Jack. And it has to lead you somewhere other than your brother."

* * *

Time: 8.00pm
Date: Tuesday 12th February 2013
Location: Metropolitan Police HQ, London

Jack closed the blinds, blocking out the ever-deepening night sky. The snow laden clouds that had cast their dimness across the capital all day had now slunk away, leaving a colder, crisper feel to the air in its wake. The crescent moon was visible above the rooftops, with the odd twinkling of stars high in the sky.

The hot water urn gurgled in the background as Jack and DS Cooper settled down to begin the trawl through the extra paperwork from DS Carmichael, adding it to what they already had. They would read everything again; even the statements they had already looked through. Jack had split the file evenly in three – giving a portion each to DC Cassidy and DS Cooper, and reserving a section for himself. Their remit was to scan every word, every hyphen, every full stop.

The answer was there.

They just had to find it.

DC Cassidy had announced that she needed food before commencing her stint and had slipped upstairs to the canteen, taking her paperwork with her. She intended to find a quiet corner to herself – not difficult at this time of night – where she could immerse herself in the case file whilst partaking of her favourite tuna melt panini.

"I'm really grateful to you both for staying behind and helping out tonight," Jack had said as DC Cassidy headed for the door. "You don't need to."

DC Cassidy had merely flashed him one of her smiles and waved the folder in the air as she left.

"We don't mind, boss," replied DS Cooper, getting up to make both himself and Jack a mug of coffee from the hot water urn. "And I think Amanda fancies the guy who works nights in the canteen anyway." He gave a grin as he placed the two mugs down on the table next to the paperwork. "She's happy enough, believe me."

"Well, I appreciate it anyway," mused Jack, sipping his coffee. "Whatever the motivation."

For the next half an hour, Jack and DS Cooper read in silence. The only sound came from the soft tick-tock from the wall clock, and the occasional rumble from the hot water urn. Various doors along the corridor clicked to a close, muffled footsteps passed as people packed up for the day. The sound of cars pulling out of the rear car park confirmed that the working day was drawing to a close for some.

"It makes sad reading some of this, boss." DS Cooper turned over the latest piece of paper he had been scrutinising. "Really sad."

"Indeed it does, Cooper," agreed Jack. "To think things like this were going on behind closed doors, and people turned a blind eye."

DS Cooper tapped one of the statements in front of him. "Some of the boys they've managed to trace – it's affected their whole lives. The whole experience has marked them – something they'll never be able to put behind them. It's ruined them."

Jack merely nodded, words were not required. His own bunch of statements had evoked the same feelings. Lives ruined. In some instances, lives shortened. The rate of self-harm and suicide amongst those leaving the care system was shocking.

"I can't imagine growing up in care," continued DS Cooper. "I mean, when I think of my own kids – Chloe and Thomas – it doesn't bear thinking about. I can't imagine the type of life they would have if that had happened to them."

Jack took another sip of his now-cold coffee and grimaced. "It's not the greatest start to life, Cooper, that's very true."

DS Cooper's face fell, the sudden realisation of what he had just said only just dawning on him. "Shit, boss. I completely forgot. Sorry."

"It's fine, Cooper. Really."

"I forgot you were in foster care. I'm really sorry." DS Cooper's cheeks reddened further, clashing with his ginger hair.

Jack raised a hand and smiled. "Nothing to apologise for, Cooper. Honestly." He gave the young DS a wink and returned his gaze to the paperwork. "I was one of the lucky ones. Not all foster homes were like this one. Thankfully."

DS Cooper mumbled yet another apology before hanging his head and turning his attention back to the handful of statements he had yet to process.

As Jack also resumed reading, he felt more and more privileged for the journey that he took after leaving Betty and John Garner's care. His life could not have been more different to the ones set out in black and white before him.

Different even to his own brother's.

* * *

Time: 8.35pm
Date: Tuesday 12th February 2013
Location: Metropolitan Police HQ, London – canteen

The canteen's tuna melt panini was, in DC Amanda Cassidy's opinion, to die for. It was one of the reasons she climbed the stairs up to the canteen rather than picking up a sandwich from the deli around the corner. She closed her eyes whilst she savoured her first bite. Freshly made while she waited, she saw that an extra slice of cheese had been slipped in to make it even more delicious. Andy, one of the canteen staff, had just come on duty and had tipped her a wink before adding the extra cheese.

With closely cropped blonde hair, tucked beneath a regulatory white cap, Andy McFadden was another reason she often chose to make the trip upstairs. Standing over six feet tall, with biceps that strained the stitching of the t-shirt he wore beneath his apron, DC Cassidy felt the pleasant tingle of attraction as he sauntered over to serve her. Tucking wayward strands of her jet-black hair behind her ear, she felt the heat spread across her cheeks as she caught his eye with her dark lashes.

Armed with her freshly prepared panini, and finding herself virtually alone, DC Cassidy had deposited herself in the far corner, out of sight of the three other officers sitting at one of the other tables. In her view, it was the best time to visit the canteen – the place would be deserted until later when the officers on duty would need some sustenance and sugar to keep them going through the night. Until then, it was hers.

With only the gentle hum of the kitchen, and the occasional clink of a glass or plate to keep her company, DC Cassidy took another bite of her panini and opened the folder she had brought upstairs with her. She slipped out the first bundle of paperwork containing a series of statements from now middle-aged men, each one casting their minds back to unhappier times.

After making quick work of the rest of the panini, she wiped her hands on the serviette and settled back in her seat to absorb herself in the cruel and heart-breaking world of St Bartholomew's.

* * *

Time: 9.45pm

Date: Tuesday 12th February 2013

Location: Metropolitan Police HQ, London

The door to the investigation room flew open, causing both Jack and DS Cooper to leap out of their seats. DC Cassidy burst in, her face flushed, breathing hard after sprinting down the stairs at speed.

"Jesus, Amanda," spluttered DS Cooper. He jolted the table, splashing cold coffee towards the pile of paperwork in front of him. "You nearly sent this lot flying."

"Sorry," she panted, striding over to the table, "but you need to see this."

She thrust a copy of Stuart MacIntosh's statement towards the table, waving it in front of Jack's surprised face. "It's your brother's statement," she explained. "You need to read it."

"I have read it," replied Jack. "Carmichael already gave me a copy."

"I know," continued DC Cassidy, still somewhat flushed and out of breath. "But you need to *read* it."

Still nonplussed, Jack frowned. "Why? What have I missed?"

DC Cassidy pulled a chair across to the table and sat down. "Did you read all of it? I mean, right to the end?"

Jack started to nod and opened his mouth to reply in the affirmative.

And then he stopped.

He remembered reading the statement, ripping it open almost as soon as DS Carmichael had given it to him, despite his warnings not to. But he also remembered being unable to finish it. He had read maybe two-thirds before the tears in his eyes had blurred his vision too much for him to able to carry on. And so he had stopped.

Jack felt his stomach clench. "What did I miss?" he repeated.

DC Cassidy flicked the statement to the final few pages. "There." She pointed to a paragraph on the second to last page. "At the bottom. Where he talks about the boys he shared a room with."

"The Fifteen," mused Jack, pulling the statement towards him. "We already have their details."

DC Cassidy paused before replying. "Not that one we didn't."

Jack followed her finger and felt his eyes widen as he did so. "Who the hell is Harry?"

* * *

Chapter Sixteen

Time: 8.00am

Date: Wednesday 13th February 2013

Location: HMP Belmarsh, Thamesmead, South-east London

Jack waited in the same interview room as before – settling himself down onto the same unforgiving metal chair. His journey through the various security doors was accompanied by the same clanging and buzzing sounds as each door opened and closed behind him – no one door opening at the same time as another. The laborious journey took a good fifteen minutes from start to finish.

The interview room looked the same as before, but had a new sterile odour to it. Jack breathed in, detecting the smell of pungent bleach mixed with something else he couldn't quite define. As he glanced down, he could still see the wet streak marks on the tiled floor at his feet – evidence of a recent clean.

Jack gave an involuntary shudder – he didn't quite wish to think about what may have gone on inside these stark walls that would require the floors to be bleached clean. The sound of the door opening prevented the invasive and somewhat unsavoury thoughts from entering his head any further, and Jack watched as Warren entered the room, closely followed by a shuffling Jason Alcock. The familiar chain leading from Warren's wrist to the prisoner's jangled noisily as the door was closed behind them and Alcock made his way over towards the table. As before, the chain was unclasped from the prison officer's wrist and snapped into place on the metal ring securely embedded into the table.

"I'll be out in the corridor," confirmed Warren, turning to leave. "Give the door a bang when you're done."

When they were alone, Jason Alcock slipped into the seat opposite Jack and smiled. Jack noticed a missing tooth that hadn't been apparent yesterday. In addition, there was a fresh cut above his right eyebrow that had been steri-stripped shut, a swelling to his upper lip and a painful looking purple bruise below the right eye. From the state of him, Jack was fairly sure Jason Alcock had been involved in a fight. You didn't need to be a detective to work that one out. And with the addition of purple coloured abrasions across the knuckles on Alcock's right hand, some of which had broken the skin and looked to have recently bled, it looked as though he had given as good as he got.

"Bit of trouble?" Jack nodded at Alcock's injuries, and received a smirk in reply.

"Nothing I couldn't handle. You should see the other guy."

"I thought you were keeping your nose clean," remarked Jack. "Being the model prisoner?"

"Just because I get into a fight doesn't mean it was me who started it. Some blokes in here just want to try their luck."

Jack shrugged. Fair point. He knew from experience that fights could erupt inside a prison over the most minor of indiscretions – sometimes it could be just a look that sparks the fire. "Well, it looks like they picked the wrong guy to pick a fight with this time."

"I'm pretty sure he won't try it again – a few nights in the hospital wing should make sure of that." Jason Alcock managed another smile, although wincing at the swelling to his lip. "I'm also sure that you didn't come all this way to check up on my welfare – as touched as I am. What is it that you actually want, Inspector? I'm missing my breakfast for this."

For all his faults, and judging by the list of previous convictions and violence on his police record Jack was convinced he had plenty of those, Jack couldn't help beginning to like Jason Alcock.

"Sharp man, Alcock. I need to ask you about Harry."

"Harry?" Alcock's eyebrows raised, threatening to dislodge the steri-strips. "Harry who?"

"That's the thing – we don't know. His surname, that is." Jack paused and held Alcock's bruised and battered gaze in his. "But he shared a room with you, back at St Bartholomew's. Room fifteen."

Jason Alcock frowned. "No he didn't. Who told you that?"

Jack hesitated. "A boy from St Bartholomew's. They said someone called Harry joined you in room fifteen." Jack watched Alcock's frown deepen. "Did he join your gang? Did he become a member of The Fifteen?"

Jason Alcock shook his head slowly and raised his hand to touch his cut lip. The handcuff chain clinked over the surface of the table as he winced with pain. "Nah – they're mistaken, mate. No Harry shared our room."

"Really? You're saying they're wrong?" Jack's voice failed to hide the irritation that was creeping in. "Come on – this is a murder investigation. Every second you stay silent tells me you're hiding something, Alcock. You don't want to get caught up in a conspiracy to murder, not when you're trying to sort yourself out in here." Jack nodded at the walls surrounding them. "Wouldn't do your prison record any good, would it?"

"I'm telling you – I never knew anyone called Harry, and no one else shared our room." Jason Alcock fixed Jack with a hardened stare. "I swear."

Jack looked deep into Jason Alcock's eyes. The hardened criminal maintained eye contact and didn't flinch or blink once. Jack began to feel the unwelcome gnawing sensation in the pit of his stomach once again– if he wasn't very much mistaken, it looked like Jason Alcock was telling the truth.

"You really have never heard of someone called Harry at St Bartholomew's?" Jack softened his tone. "No one at all?"

Jason Alcock shook his head. "Honestly, no. No lad called Harry. It's the God's honest truth."

"And no one else was a member of The Fifteen?"

Another shake of the head. "Just the four of us. Cross my heart. Who said there was someone else?"

Jack pushed himself up out of his chair and sighed. "It doesn't matter now. Thanks anyway. You'd best get off for your breakfast." He made his way over to the door and gave it a few quick raps. While waiting for Warren to unlock it, he turned round and gave Jason Alcock one last look.

"Keep your nose clean in here. No more scrapes."

* * *

Time: 9.45am
Date: Wednesday 13th February 2013

Location: Metropolitan Police HQ, London

"The files we have for St Bartholomew's go back to the beginning of the 1960s." DS Cooper brought up the file on the whiteboard. "But I'm guessing we don't want to go back that far."

Jack shook his head. "No. Stu went there in 1977 – in his statement he says this 'Harry' joined them some time later. Let's try 1978 to 1982. Can you print the records off from that thing?" Jack motioned towards the whiteboard. DS Cooper returned the gesture with a smirk and a nod.

"Already on it, boss," he replied. Jack's displeasure and, at times, downright hatred for all things technical was well known throughout the department, and even the building. Still preferring his trusty cork pin-board to the new technology, Jack would often remind people how it helped solve the Peter Holloway case last summer if he saw them raise so much as an eyebrow when he got out the drawing pins.

DS Cooper leant back to scoop up the paperwork that was being spat out of the printer behind them. "How shall we do this? Divvy it up three ways?" He flapped the thick bundle of paperwork in the air. "Do a couple of years' worth each?"

Jack nodded and took a wad of sheets from DS Cooper's outstretched hand. Not for the first time, he wondered if they were wasting their time. Jason Alcock had been pretty convincing. Maybe this 'Harry' was a red herring.

So far Stu was the only one who had mentioned him, and that worried Jack. "After this, see if you can catch up with Byers and Williams again – see what they remember about our friend 'Harry'."

DC Cassidy nodded. "Will do." She reached across the table and took her share of paperwork.

"We all know what we're doing?" Jack settled down into one of the vacant chairs. "Anyone with the name Harry, or possibly Harold, said to be a resident of St Bartholomew's. I'm not sure how good their registration and document keeping was – I suspect it's a bit haphazard. I don't think the management was all that great." Jack thought back to his visit to see Albert Dawson, making a mental note to pay the old man another visit.

DC Cassidy nodded and slipped into a seat next to Jack, already starting to spread out the individual pieces of A4 paper in front of her. "My guess is it'll be a bit of a jumble."

"You're not wrong," muttered DS Cooper, from the other side of the table. "None of it looks like it's in alphabetical or even chronological order. And I've got medical notes here jumbled in amongst registration details of the boys that were taken in. It's a mess."

"And remember we don't have a surname yet, either." Jack started studying the first page of his bundle. "So we'll just have to focus on the christian name for now."

"Don't forget to look for Henry, too," added DC Cassidy, using a well-manicured fingernail to track down the names on her first sheet. "Just like Prince Harry. His real name was Henry."

"Why is Harry short for Henry?" questioned DS Cooper, frowning. "I've never understood that."

"Now is not the time," interrupted Jack, tapping the papers in front of him. "We've a lot to get through." He paused before adding, "plus I have no idea."

* * *

Time: 10.45am

Date: Wednesday 13th February 2013

Location: Metropolitan Police HQ, London

"I've got two, boss," said DC Cassidy, waving a sheet of paper in Jack's direction. "One is a Harry Miller; one is a Harry Chamberlain."

"I haven't got anyone called Harry." DS Cooper nodded at his own pile of papers. "But I do have a Henry."

Jack nodded. "OK. Follow them up. Get dates of birth, dates they attended St Bartholomew's – anything you can to figure out who they are and where they might be now. Addresses. Phone numbers. Anything."

"Boss." DC Cassidy made to get up and fix both herself and DS Cooper a drink. "Coffee?" She glanced back over her shoulder at Jack, who had now risen from his chair and was heading towards the door.

He shook his head. "No, not for me, thanks. There's something I need to do."

Jack left the investigation room and headed back to his office. His own list had drawn a blank as to the identity of the missing 'Harry' – but he also had something else on his mind.

The scarf.

He still couldn't get out of his mind the vision of the Swap Shop scarf and its appearance at Edward Wakefield's murder scene.

When he had first seen it, his stomach had clenched so tightly he had felt faint. And the feeling had not left him. Stu had been very off hand and dismissive when he was asked about the scarf at the café on Monday, and with two unidentified DNA profiles within its fibres, Jack felt the investigation was taking an alarming turn. If Stu's DNA was on the scarf...he shuddered and forced the thought from his head. Jack knew he shouldn't hide his brother's links to the scarf from his team, or from the Chief Superintendent, but just thinking about it made him feel sick.

He closed his office door, firmly, behind him. His desk was a mess, but he dismissed it as a minor inconvenience. He woke up his computer monitor and sat down. The monitor was still showing the image of the plastic evidence bag containing the Swap Shop scarf. Before heading over to Belmarsh earlier that morning, Jack had pulled up the image once again, a niggling sensation gnawing at the back of his mind that there was something about it he was missing.

And it hadn't taken him long to spot it.

Clicking on the image once again, Jack enlarged the picture so that it filled the screen. The multi-coloured stripes were clear to see through the plastic bag, and the logo printed across the middle. But what had made Jack one-hundred-percent sure that the scarf belonged to his brother stared out at him from one of the corners.

* * *

Time: 12.05pm

Date: Monday 28th September 1981

Location: West Road Comprehensive School, Christchurch

There weren't many perks to being in Year 4 at West Road Comprehensive School – but one of them was being allowed out of the school grounds at lunchtime. Jack pulled his rucksack high up onto his back and headed off in the direction of the local parade of shops, just around the corner on Tennyson Road. The shops did a roaring trade at lunchtime from the Year 4 and Year 5 pupils – the queue outside the fish and chip shop could snake all the way along the path and past the newsagents; even round the next corner on some days.

Jack quickened his step as he glanced at his watch. He just wanted a portion of chips, and didn't fancy having to queue for most of his lunch break to get it. He had got changed after PE as quickly as he could, and left the changing rooms before any of his classmates had finished in the showers. His hair was still wet and his school shirt clung to the damp skin on his back.

As he rounded the corner, he relaxed when he saw no huddle of uniforms outside the door to the fish and chip shop; just one Year 5 boy about to step inside. Jack reached into his pocket and closed his hand around the bunch of loose change Mary, his foster mother, had given him earlier that morning.

As he approached the parade of shops, with the smell of chip fat and frying fish wafting over in the air, his attention was drawn to a group of boys crossing the road and heading in his direction.

Jack's heart sank.

"All right, Jack – get us some chips." Stuart MacIntosh broke away from the other three teenage boys and headed towards Jack. "Go on, I'm starving."

Jack flashed a look at the gang of youths, recognising them as the usual bunch his brother hung around with, minus their trademark motorbikes. Today they seemed to be on foot.

"You should be in school, Stu," was all Jack could find to say, continuing to walk towards the parade of shops.

"I'm not well – Matron phoned in this morning." Stuart MacIntosh matched Jack's stride. "Go on, I'm really hungry. Just a small portion of chips."

"You look fine to me," replied Jack, casting a quick glance up at his brother as they arrived outside the chip shop. "You should be in school," he repeated.

Stuart MacIntosh shrugged. "I feel better now. Anyway, come on, Jack – you must have loads of pocket money. Just buy us a bag of chips. Go on, please!"

Jack sighed, watching the other members of the gang hovering by the roadside, pulling out packets of cigarettes from their pockets and sharing them around. He shook his head. "All right. Wait here."

"Cheers, bruv," grinned Stuart MacIntosh, as he turned around and jogged back to his friends, holding out his hand for a cigarette.

It took Jack less than five minutes to order and pay for his chips. He put a generous helping of salt and vinegar on both portions, and wrapped them back up to keep in the heat. Stepping back outside, Jack noticed that Stuart and his gang were still there, laughing and joking raucously about something, disturbing the otherwise quiet stillness in the street.

As Jack came into view, Stuart MacIntosh whipped his head around and grinned. "Here he comes!" He held his hand out as Jack approached, and accepted the bag of chips with a glint in his eye. "Thanks, bruv!" Just as Jack turned to go, Stuart grabbed hold of his arm. "Look what that crazy arsehole did to my scarf!" He pointed to a cigarette-butt-shaped burn hole at the end of his Swap Shop scarf, the edges tinged in a now singed, burnt-brown colour. "It's gone clean through, the moron!"

Stuart MacIntosh directed his last statement to the broad shouldered youth Jack knew to be called Jason.

Jason Alcock lifted his head and brandished the culprit between his nail-bitten fingers, showing the glowing ember of his stubby cigarette. "Sorry, Maccy lad," he laughed, taking another drag. "Come on, give us one of those chips."

With that, Stuart MacIntosh turned away from Jack and began passing around the bag of chips, not giving Jack so much as a backward glance. Jack sighed and began heading back towards school, clutching his bag of chips but no longer having the appetite to eat them.

* * *

Time: 11.00am

Date: Wednesday 13th February 2013

Location: Metropolitan Police HQ, London

Jack shut the image of the Swap Shop scarf down, complete with the cigarette burn in the corner, and switched off the monitor. He needed to speak to Stu. And, it was becoming increasingly clear, he also needed his DNA – neither of which was going to be easy.

His eyes came to rest on his notepad where there was a scribbled contact number for Jenny Davies, and next to it was the printed copy of the post mortem report for Stella MacIntosh. Without pausing in case he changed his mind, Jack picked up the phone and dialled.

"Jenny, hi. It's DI Jack MacIntosh here."

"Inspector," greeted Jennifer Davies on the other end of the line. "How can I help you?"

"Tissue samples from underneath a set of fingernails." Jack saw no reason not to get straight to the point. "I need them rushed through. It's urgent."

There was a pause on the other end of the phone while Jack could hear some staccato tapping of a keyboard. It was several seconds before Jennifer's gentle Welsh lilt filled his ears.

"I've already processed all your outstanding requests, Inspector. The results were sent through just this morning." Some more tapping of the keyboard. "And I don't have any other outstanding tests results for you – everything has been analysed and reported on."

Jack gave a brief shake of his head. "No, this isn't in relation to the Wakefields." Jack paused, not quite sure how to phrase his request. "This one is something different – it's personal."

Jack then heard Jenny sigh. "Inspector, we are really snowed under. If you were to send in your sample request, in the usual fashion..."

"I know, I know," interrupted Jack. "I realise how busy you all are, and I really appreciate all you've done to fast track the samples for our current investigation. And I know DS Cooper is, too." Jack paused again – he knew Jenny had a soft spot for his detective sergeant, and believed a bit of name dropping couldn't hurt. "I'm sure I heard him say that he was going to pop over sometime soon – to thank you personally."

Jenny hesitated on the other end of the line, and Jack could almost hear her brain weighing up the proposition. He held his breath and waited.

"OK, Inspector." There was the hint of a smile seeping into Jenny's soft tones. "Tell me what you have and I'll get it processed as a priority."

* * *

Time: 11.30am

Date: Wednesday 13th February 2013

Location: Metropolitan Police HQ, London

"Nothing, boss," announced DC Cassidy, as Jack re-entered the investigation room. "My two can't possibly be our guy."

Jack sat down next to DC Cassidy, trying to push the thoughts of both the tissue from his mother's fingernails and the Swap Shop scarf out of his mind. "How so?"

DC Cassidy tapped the paper in front of her. "I have a Harry Miller – date of birth February 1975. He came to St Bartholomew's in 1979 at the age of four. He would have been too young to have been our Harry."

"OK, the other?"

"Harry Chamberlain. Right age group – born in September 1970. Started at St Bartholomew's in 1977 aged seven. But he died in 1979, aged nine. Measles."

Jack nodded. "OK, anything from you, Cooper?" He looked over at DS Cooper who was stacking up his St Bartholomew's paperwork.

"Nothing here either, boss." He shook his head. "My Henry is a Henry Cooper, no less. I kid you not. Joined St Bartholomew's in 1982 aged twelve. So he would have been too late to have been a part of The Fifteen. In any event, he is also dead – died in Afghanistan in 2009."

Jack sighed. "Well, at least we can rule them out. Thanks, good work. How did you get on with Byers and Williams?"

DS Cooper again shook his head. "Byers says he doesn't know anyone called Harry. Adamant that no one else shared their room."

"Kyle Williams was the same," added DC Cassidy, lowering her eyes to the handwritten notes she had taken. "Said they never shared a room with anyone else; it was always just the four of them. And he never knew a Harry."

Jack massaged his temples, feeling another headache coming on. According to Stu, Harry existed and shared their room. According to the rest of The Fifteen, there was no such person.

Someone was lying.

It was just a question of who.

"Let's move on. Where are we on the forensics? Jenny says she uploaded the rest of the results this morning?"

DS Cooper clicked the whiteboard into action and located the file with the forensics reports. "Everything is back from both murder scenes. Nothing much of use to us. We just have the two outstanding unidentified male DNA profiles from the scarf at Eddie Wakefield's crime scene. One of the profiles is interesting though."

Jack raised his eyebrows. "How so?"

"Well, it's also been found at Terence Wakefield's house. On a light switch."

"So, one of our unknown males had his DNA at both crime scenes," commented DC Cassidy. "I reckon that's our guy."

Jack nodded, ignoring the continued churning sensation in his stomach. "Anything further on the witness statements at The Laurels? And what came of the house-to-house enquiries in Terence Wakefield's street?"

DC Cassidy took over control of the mouse and brought up the evidence log on screen. "All statements are now in. As we thought, no one at the nursing home appears to have seen anything out of the ordinary on the day Eddie Wakefield was murdered. Everyone on duty that day has been re-interviewed and all the CCTV has been reviewed. But as we know, there are two exits from the building that are not covered by CCTV and it would be quite easy to slip in and out without raising suspicion."

Jack nodded. "The faulty door close to Edward Wakefield's room is my guess. Can we make sure all employees are interviewed – not just those on duty that day. Including those who have left in the last twelve months. And let's have another look at that visitor log. Someone knew about the exits that don't have CCTV."

DC Cassidy nodded and added several notes to her notebook. "The house-to-house of Terence Wakefield's neighbours hasn't thrown up too much either. No one seems to know too much about him. He kept himself to himself – rarely seen outside except when he popped to the local shop for his booze and fags once his benefit payments were in. An occasional trip to the bookies next door to the shop – but he certainly wasn't a regular. I got the impression no one was all that sad to hear of his demise."

Jack nodded. "OK, thanks. And we know he didn't make that many trips to see his father in the nursing home either."

"There was one neighbour, though, who may have seen something interesting." DC Cassidy tapped the mouse and brought up a witness statement belonging to Sylvia Brennan. "She lives across the street from Terence Wakefield, almost directly opposite. By all accounts she's the typical neighbourhood busybody who sits behind her net curtains all day, quietly watching the comings and goings of the street."

Jack's ears pricked up and he motioned for DC Cassidy to continue. A curtain twitching busybody might be just what they needed.

"She saw a man call at Terence's house at the approximate time we believe he was murdered. The time of death, according to Dr Matthews, wasn't long before when we know the police liaison officer called just after 3pm."

"Description?" Jack knew it was a longshot but he asked the question anyway.

DC Cassidy gave an apologetic shrug. "She only saw him from behind, as he was knocking at the door. She's certain it was male. Average height. Average build. Wearing a long coat and woollen hat. All black."

"Mr Average," mused Jack, sighing. "Nothing else? She didn't see him from the front when he left?"

DC Cassidy shook her head. "No. She says she went through to the kitchen after Terence had let the man in – she had a cake in the oven and the timer was going off. By the time she came back, the man must have already left because the next thing she reports seeing is the police liaison officer drawing up outside."

"OK, thanks. Well, it's a sighting at least." Jack suddenly paused. "You said that this neighbour saw Terence let the man in. Did she actually say that?"

DC Cassidy scrolled back through the witness statement on screen to the final section. "Yes, here it is. It says right there. 'I saw Terence open his front door. I could see it was him and he was still dressed in his pyjamas even though it was gone half past two in the afternoon. He stood back and let the other man inside.'"

Jack slowly nodded to himself. "Terence knew his killer."

* * *

Time: 2.30pm
  Date: Friday 9th February 2013
  Location: 5 Charlotte Street, Finsbury

He rapped loudly on the front door, noticing the peeling paint on the door frame and missing door number. A faint outline of the number five had bleached into the woodwork, the brass number plate itself long since gone and forgotten.

The frosted glass panel gave nothing away as to what lay on the other side of the door – but he could guess. He had been in these types of houses before. The unkempt tiny front gardens, if you could call them that, with grass and weeds growing rampantly to knee high; the odd rusty bicycle or tin bath lying forgotten underneath the window, an occasional discarded mattress lying on its side.

Terence Wakefield's home was no different. It didn't yet have the mattress, but it did have a rusting bicycle, minus one wheel, and several tins of abandoned paint stacked in one corner. The grass was, indeed, knee high, and weeds crawled unabated through the cracks in the crazy paving of the short path that led to the front door.

Come on, he breathed, silently to himself. Open the door.

The journey over had been uneventful. He had used three different disguises along the way, just to make sure. The street where Terence Wakefield lived was typically quiet; rows of Victorian terraced houses squashed together either side of the road, with tiny, square front gardens giving the allure of Victorian wealth and decadence, but in reality were just another space within which to discard unwanted items. Squinting along the street, he guessed that the vast majority of inhabitants were elderly. There were no cars parked illegally on the double yellow lines, and no visible comings and goings from within any of the narrow houses. Life would revolve around daytime TV and afternoon naps, not commuter timetables. Despite their age, most of the houses were well-kept, with freshly painted window frames and front doors.

Terence Wakefield's house stood out like a sore thumb.

As he strode purposefully along the deserted road towards number five, he had noticed a twitching net curtain from opposite. A sly look to the side had revealed a neat, gravelled front garden with two pot plants either side of a gleaming UPVC front door. The one front window showed a set of crisp net curtains draped across. As he looked, he noticed a slight movement at the side; too far away to make out anything more than a figure hovering by the curtain. He had instinctively dipped his head lower and pulled down his woollen hat more firmly.

As he neared Terence Wakefield's front gate, he had snatched another furtive look across the road – this time he could see a pale face at the corner of the window, the net curtain hitched to the side. He saw short white hair, and a pair of spectacles perched on top of a thin nose.

A busybody neighbour, he had thought to himself. He turned away and pulled up the collar of his long coat, walking steadily up to the front door of number five. His clothing would give nothing away about his size or form, and he was confident that his facial features were hidden.

Rap rap rap.

He knocked once again, louder this time – feeling the intense stare of the busybody across the street boring into the back of his neck. He resisted the urge to turn around for another look.

Raising his hand for a third time, he noticed movement behind the frosted glass.

Someone was home.

The door creaked open and, for the first time in over thirty years, he locked eyes with the man he knew to be Terence Wakefield.

"Terence Wakefield?" he enquired, feigning a smile. "Terry?"

The man before him had aged – and not in a fine-wine kind of way, either. He was dressed in a greying vest, displaying evidence of several days' worth of tea, coffee and other, possibly worse, stains, one on top of the other. His baggy pyjama bottoms were held together at the waist with a piece of grubby string. He shuffled along as though he were a man in his eighties or nineties, with his hair unkempt and plastered to his scalp. Several days' worth of stubble graced his unwashed chin.

A pair of bloodshot eyes peered out from underneath heavy eyelids, and a frown crossed the man's forehead as he tried to place his visitor. His mouth opened, revealing cracked and broken teeth – the stale smell of yesterday's vodka seeping out of the pores on his sallow skin.

"Yes?"

"Can we go inside?" He maintained his smile, holding his breath against the musty aroma that had followed Terence to the door.

Terence Wakefield stepped back to let the man inside, and instantly the frown on his brow turned into a look of recognition.

"Oh, it's...it's you..."

* * *

Time: 11.55am

Date: Wednesday 13th February 2013

Location: Metropolitan Police HQ, London

"Stu?" Jack had been surprised that his call had been answered, fully preparing himself for the empty sound of non-stop ringing and then the click of the voicemail service. "It's me."

"What can I do for you, Jack?" His brother's voice sounded faint and far away.

"I wanted to check you were OK," replied Jack, "after our chat at Isabel's.

I know it's not easy talking about this stuff."

"I'm OK, Jack." Mac paused. "What do you really want?"

"Look, meet me for a pint. I've got a few hours to kill. The pub across the road from the station." Jack glanced at his watch. "It's nearly lunchtime."

There was silence on the other end of the phone, with just the faint sound of breathing.

"My treat," added Jack.

"All right, I'll be twenty minutes."

If Jack had been surprised that his call had been answered, he was even more surprised that Stu had accepted his lunchtime invitation.

Now he just needed not to ruin it.

* * *

Chapter Seventeen

Time: 12.30pm

Date: Wednesday 13th February 2013

Location: Duke of Wellington Public House, London

Jack brought two pints of Guinness over to the rickety table and placed them down on two crusted and stained beer mats. "They didn't have any dry roasted peanuts – just salted." He dropped a packet into the centre of the table.

Mac wrinkled his nose. "I guess they'll have to do." He picked up his pint and took a sip. "This is an unexpected pleasure, Jack. What do you want?"

Jack took the seat opposite, a small bar stool, and feigned surprise. "Why do I have to want something? Can't I just invite my brother out for a lunchtime drink?"

Mac gave a rueful smile. "You know as well as I do that you don't do this, Jack. Not unless you want something."

Jack returned the smile and picked up his own pint glass. After taking a sip, he nodded at the laminated bar menu sitting on the table. "Fancy a bite to eat while we're here? They do a good ploughman's or their toasted sandwiches are decent, too."

Mac eyed Jack over the top of his Guinness and narrowed his eyes. "Food as well as a drink. What is it that you want, Jack? Just spit it out. You're no good at this."

Jack sighed and nodded. "OK, so maybe there is something I need from you – but I also wanted to have a drink with my brother. Is that allowed? We haven't seen much of each other since you got back from Italy."

Mac shrugged and continued to sip his drink. "That's because you're always working." Mac cast his eyes over to the window by their side, nodding in the direction of the Metropolitan Police HQ across the road.

"Maybe," Jack conceded, shifting uncomfortably on his wooden stool. "But this is nice, isn't it? You and me? A couple of pints?"

Mac spluttered into his Guinness, sending foam across the table. "You really are no good at this, Jack! Jesus, I thought all you coppers had interview skills. Just tell me what you want and we can then enjoy our drinks."

"The Harry you mentioned in your statement to Rob...DS Carmichael." Jack took a sip of his Guinness. "I'm having trouble tracking him down. You don't have a surname?"

Mac shook his head. "It was a long time ago, Jack."

"Nothing else you can tell me about him?"

Mac took a long mouthful of his drink and again shook his head. "Nope. Didn't know him that well to be honest."

"But he shared your room? With the others?"

Mac fixed Jack with a darkening look. "Look, what is this, Jack? I told your mate Carmichael all I remembered. Can't we just leave it at that?"

Jack detected the barriers once again and decided it was time to retreat, turning his attention back to his drink.

"Is that what you asked me here for? Just to ask about a lad I haven't seen for thirty years?" Mac prodded the packet of peanuts with his pint glass. "We could have done this over the phone."

"No," replied Jack. "No it's not. I've had a letter." Jack put his pint glass down and shifted closer to the table. "Social services got in touch with me. They're relocating some of their offices and apparently they have some boxes in storage that they can no longer hold onto."

"Boxes?" Mac frowned. "What boxes?"

Jack shrugged. "I'm not sure. They just said they had boxes that belonged to us – boxes from the Old Mill Road flat."

"Old Mill Road?" Mac's frown deepened. "Blimey, that's going back a bit. What could they possibly have of ours from there?"

"I've no idea – but they're quite keen to get rid of them." Jack paused and swallowed another mouthful of Guinness. "I've arranged for the boxes to be sent to me. I thought we could go through them together."

"I guess so," replied Mac, slowly, ripping open the packet of peanuts and throwing a few into his mouth. "If you want."

"I'll let you know when they arrive. We'll arrange a time for you to come over – bring Isabel, if you like. Make an evening of it. It's your birthday in a couple of days."

Mac tossed some more nuts into his mouth and washed them down with some of his Guinness. "Next thing, you'll be offering to cook."

"I wouldn't go that far," grinned Jack. "I might stretch to a takeaway, though."

The two brothers continued sipping their drinks in silence for a while, with Mac emptying out the last of the nuts onto the laminated bar menu. After a few minutes, he broke the deadlock.

"What was the real reason you asked me here?" Mac wiped the froth from his top lip and eyed his brother. "I know you, Jack MacIntosh. This isn't about some boxes or a takeaway. Or even Harry."

Jack hesitated before giving a conciliatory nod. There was nothing else for it – he would have to tell the truth. "OK, maybe there was something else, as well as the boxes. But don't freak out."

Mac's gaze narrowed. "Freak out about what?"

"It's all just routine."

"If it's all just routine, why would I freak out?" Mac's voice now had a hardened edge to it. "*What* is all routine, Jack?"

Jack shook his head, already knowing how the rest of the conversation was going to pan out. He knew his brother too well. The hot-headedness was returning in spades. "Just hear me out."

"I'm all ears, Jack."

The barriers were well and truly up now and Jack knew it, but he had no option but to press on. "It's this investigation – into the murders of the

Wakefields. Edward and Terence."

"You've already asked me about them."

Jack pressed on. "I've managed to trace all the boys in The Fifteen, Stu. Jason, Stephen and Kyle. None of them remember a Harry."

"Well, they're lying then."

"Why would they lie?"

"I have no idea." Mac drained the rest of his glass, not taking his cold, steely eyes from Jack as he did so. "What's it got to do with me, anyway?"

Jack knew he was just going to have to come out and say it, although he already knew what the reaction would be. His brother was nothing if not predictable.

"I need DNA samples from all of you. All of The Fifteen."

The statement hung silently in the air between them. The pub was relatively quiet for a Wednesday lunchtime – with just the occasional 'ping' from the fruit machine in the corner.

"DNA?" Mac eventually replied. "Why's that?"

"To rule you all out of the investigation, that's why," replied Jack, pushing his half-finished pint away from him. "I already have samples from the other three; I just need one from you now." Jack hoped his tone didn't give away his first lie of the day. Whilst the DNA of Jason Alcock and Stephen Byers would be in the system somewhere, with their frequenting of the criminal justice system, he didn't have any DNA for Kyle Williams; and he didn't intend to obtain any.

Mac stared into his now empty pint glass, his face frozen, showing no emotion. Jack eyed him, warily, from across the table, trying to predict his brother's next move. He opened his mouth to speak again, to break the awkward silence, but Mac beat him to it.

"You brought me here to ask for my DNA?" The edge to Mac's voice was harsh and frosty, mirroring the weather outside.

"No, not just that...and it's just routine anyway. Stu..."

"Routine, my arse." Mac stood up, scraping his bar stool forcibly across the tiled floor. "I'm leaving."

"Look, Stu...it's just to rule you out of the investigation, that's all. Along with the others. If you've got nothing to hide…"

Mac shot Jack a fierce look. "Don't give me that one, Jack. I'm not some kid you've dragged in off the street. I know what you're doing. You suspect me. Admit it. You all do. I'm not giving you anything that I don't have to."

With that, Mac grabbed his leather jacket from the seat of the bar stool and barged past Jack, striding towards the door. "Leave me alone, Jack," was his parting shot before pulling open the heavy wooden door and disappearing out into the chill.

Jack remained seated and held his head in his hands. That went well, he thought to himself. He knew it had been a bit of a long shot, appealing to his brother's better nature, but he hadn't quite expected him to react like that. He needed that DNA to take him out of the suspect pool. Stuart couldn't be involved − he just couldn't be.

Jack stirred as a member of the bar staff approached him. "Excuse me? Are these finished with?" The young waitress was pointing at Mac's empty glass and Jack's half-finished one. He nodded, waving the glasses away. He had no appetite to finish his own Guinness anymore, and the peanuts would stick in his throat. As he watched the young girl place the glasses onto her tray, his gaze rested on Mac's empty pint glass.

And an idea formed in his mind.

* * *

Time: 3.15pm
Date: Wednesday 13th February 2013
Location: Metropolitan Police HQ, London

Chief Superintendent Dougie King gestured for Jack to sit down. "Nice to see you, Jack. I've been meaning to catch up with you." His conversation with Dr Riches yesterday was still weighing heavily on his mind.

Jack eased himself into one of the vacant visitors' chairs, a chair he was fairly familiar with. He liked the Chief Superintendent; respected him. Respect that he felt sure was mirrored back at him in the other direction. Which was good, considering what he was about to say.

"How's the Wakefield murder investigation going?" Dougie King squeezed his generous frame into his swivel chair and beamed at Jack from across the desk. "Any news?"

Jack gave a non-committal shrug. "Enquiries are continuing, Sir. It's quite a complex investigation. Forensics are in – not really giving us many leads. It's thrown up two DNA profiles that are not on the database."

"So what can I do for you? Something in relation to the investigation?"

"In a way." Jack paused. He knew he was going to test the Chief Superintendent's loyalty and support to its maximum, but he felt he had nowhere left to turn. "I have a hypothetical situation that I need to discuss with you."

"Hypothetical?" Chief Superintendent King's eyes widened and his eyebrows hopped up a notch. "In what sense?"

"Well." Jack took in a deep breath and focused on the top of Dougie King's wiry, close-cropped Afro hair, trying his best to avoid the penetrating look that he knew his senior officer would be sending in his direction. "If the only way you could get a DNA sample to rule someone out of an investigation was to obtain it illegally – would you do it?"

Chief Superintendent Dougie King's eyes widened even further and he let out a long sigh. "Jack. Jack. What are you getting yourself into?"

"It's purely hypothetical, Sir," repeated Jack, still avoiding the Chief Superintendent's gaze. "I'm just interested in what you would do."

"So…you want to rule someone out by swabbing them for DNA, but the only sample you can get is not going to be legal." Chief Superintendent King leant forwards, resting his elbows on his desk. "*Hypothetically* speaking."

Jack nodded. "That's about the size of it, Sir."

"I suppose there's no point in me asking why it can't be done legally?" Dougie King raised his bushy eyebrows again. "You don't want to arrest this person, do it by the book?"

"Hypothetically, that may not be possible. Or desirable. So…if a sample was to be obtained by other means, would you do it?" Jack finally let his gaze meet the dark eyes of his senior officer. "*Hypothetically.*"

Dougie King held onto Jack's gaze for several seconds before replying. "*Hypothetically*, Jack, I would tread very carefully. Any such evidence, as you know, would be inadmissible..."

"But if it was just to rule them out?"

"But what if it rules them *in*, Jack...?" The rest of the Chief Superintendent's sentence was left unfinished. He leant back in his chair and sighed, his voice taking on a sombre tone. "Be careful, Jack. That's all I can say. Be careful. I give you a lot of leeway in general, to do things your own way, to follow your own instincts – instincts that are, admittedly, usually correct. I do that because you're my best DI. But even I have my limits."

"Understood," replied Jack, getting to his feet, and making his way towards the door. As he made his way out into the corridor beyond, the Chief Superintendent's soft tones followed in his wake.

"*Hypothetically*, Jack, we never had this conversation."

* * *

Time: 5.00pm
　Date: Wednesday 13th February 2013
　Location: Kettle's Yard Mews, London

The boxes had arrived earlier that day. Mrs Constantine from the flat below had kindly taken them in to prevent a 'we tried to deliver your parcel' card being thrust through his letterbox. The two boxes now stood on Jack's coffee table, with just a short covering letter from the Department of Social Services confirming that, due to another relocation of their storage facilities, they no longer had the capacity to keep personal items.

Jack had been unaware that any such personal items existed.

Until now.

He stood staring at the boxes for some minutes. The first few years of his life had been packed up into two cardboard boxes – two surprisingly small cardboard boxes. Taking a pair of scissors, he sliced through the parcel tape and unfolded the top edges of the first box. Unsure quite what he would uncover, he got himself a bottle of Budweiser from the fridge and downed several gulps before continuing.

The first items he brought out of the box were some tattered books. Most of them he remembered, as they had been stacked on the bookshelf in the bedroom he shared with Stuart. There was a copy of Fantastic Mr Fox in very good condition, plus Frog and Toad Are Friends and The Tiger Who Came to Tea. Jack found himself smiling as he remembered their mother reading The Tiger Who Came to Tea to both him and Stuart before tucking them up in bed.

Next came various battered Topsy and Tim books and a few of Enid Blyton's Noddy adventures. There were a few hardbacks too – picture books on cars and aeroplanes, plus several on animals.

There were a few books that he didn't recognise, which he guessed were his mother's; books she must have kept in her bedroom. At the bottom of the box, Jack found some wooden toy cars, a bag of dominoes and a pack of dog-eared playing cards. In addition, there were two wooden puzzles, undoubtedly with pieces missing. Underneath the books and toys, at the very bottom, were several sheets of yellowed paper. Jack carefully pulled them out, the paper so aged that it felt as though it may disintegrate underneath his touch. He caught his breath when he saw what they were.

The first was a painting he had done for their last Christmas at the flat. It was of a Christmas tree, with splodges that he presumed were presents, plus a large red blob in the sky which he assumed had to be Father Christmas. He held the painting, gingerly, in his hand. He remembered it being pinned up in the kitchen, above the worktop where the biscuit tin used to be. Every time he slipped a digestive from the tin, he would see his Christmas painting.

One of the other sheets of paper was a scribbled drawing by Stuart – a mass of colourful swirls and lines. Jack had no idea what it was meant to be, but their mother had kept it.

The final sheet of paper brought a lump to Jack's throat. It was something he vividly remembered doing on a rainy day when they were all stuck inside the flat and unable to go to the park. He held the aged paper in his hand and cast his eyes over the handprints that decorated the page. There were three sets of handprints, varying in size. Starting on the left were the smallest prints – in a vivid blue. Those had to be Stuart's, they were so tiny. In the middle were Jack's slightly bigger hands, in a deep scarlet red paint. Then the third set - the one that caused the lump in his throat to thicken. It was the largest set of handprints of the three; large, yet delicate at the same time. Prints that belonged to his mother. In a pale purple coloured paint, the circular palm and long, spider-like fingers reached out to Jack from the right hand side of the page.

He placed his own hand over the top, mirroring his mother's. The touch of a dead woman's fingers, he mused, taking another mouthful of beer and removing his hand.

He placed the paintings back inside the box, together with the books, toys and puzzles. Ancient 1960s and 1970s memorabilia – probably worth a fortune today if they hadn't been so damaged by two energetic boys. He then reached for the second box, and again snipped away the parcel tape and opened the flaps.

Reaching inside, he could immediately see that this box contained entirely different mementos. There were no books or toys, no puzzles or games. No pictures painted by their tiny hands. No handprints bringing back long-forgotten memories.

Instead, the second box appeared to contain nothing but photographs.

Jack frowned as he brought a handful of the photographs out, and swigged another mouthful of beer. He couldn't remember there being any photographs in the flat, certainly none in frames or on the shelves. He remembered their mother had a cheap camera that she would sometimes take to the park, or on days out to the beach – but Jack had never seen any of the photographs themselves. He, himself, only had the one photograph left of their mother, which currently sat in a frame on his bedside table.

The largest photograph was in a thick, wooden frame, showing Stella

MacIntosh with her two sons. Both Jack and Stuart were sitting on her lap, one knee each, beaming out towards the camera. In another slightly smaller photograph, it was just Jack and Stuart on their own, playing with what looked like a large cardboard box. Jack smiled as he remembered his brother's obsession with cars, and how their mother would make one from an empty Fairy Liquid cardboard box.

The next handful of photographs were loose inside the box and appeared to be a collection of pictures of Stella MacIntosh on her own. Mostly in black and white, with only some in colour, the photographs mainly depicted her in a variety of provocative poses, stretched out on her bed or laughing towards the camera.

Jack let the photographs drop from his hands, back into the box. He rooted around in the bottom of the box for whatever might be left and found a small trinket box containing a few necklaces and rings, a bracelet that Jack had never seen her wear, and a silver compact mirror. He placed the trinket box back inside the box and began to stack the various photographs back on top. As he did so, one last picture fell from the pile and caught his eye.

This one was of Stella and the boys at the local playground that was opposite the Old Mill Road flat. Jack remembered how he used to love the roundabout, spinning round and round until he felt dizzy, screaming at his mother to make it go faster.

In this photograph, Stella was standing in front of the roundabout, hugging each of her boys close to her with one arm around each of them. The day looked to be hot and sunny; Jack and Stuart were each dressed in shorts and t-shirts, and Stella had a long, floaty dress on, with a flower in her hair. Her smile was radiant.

Jack guessed that it must have been sometime in the previous summer of 1970. But it wasn't the sunshine or the style of dress that had caught his eye.

It was the shadow.

The sun was behind whoever had been taking the photograph, and it caused a shadow to be cast across the baked grass by the side of the roundabout.

The shadow of a man.

Jack dropped the picture as if it had scalded his fingers. He quickly rummaged back through the box and drew out a selection of the other photographs. Photographs of Stella and her boys; photographs of Stella on her own.

There was one question and one question only that was forming on Jack's lips.

Who was behind the camera?

* * *

Chapter Eighteen

Time: 9.15am
Date: Thursday 14th February 2013
Location: Metropolitan Police HQ, London

Jack leant back in his chair and groaned. The day had only just begun but he already felt exhausted. He had tossed and turned most of the night, with images of the man behind the camera flooding his brain. He couldn't help thinking that he could be the man he had seen at the end of his last hypnotherapy session; his recovered memory, if that was what it was.

And his disastrous meeting with Stu in the pub had also played on his mind. All in all, sleep had evaded him.

He again ignored the bundle of telephone messages on his desk, guessing that at least one would be from Dr Riches. He didn't feel like he could face her right now.

Moving the stack of messages to one side, he noted the day's early-morning post sitting on top of his in-tray. He picked up the bundle, bound by an elastic band, and flicked through the contents. Several circulars went straight into the bin, unopened. There was a copy of the latest police federation magazine which he slid back into the in-tray to look at another time. Some other random pieces of junk mail went the same way as the circulars.

The last item of post piqued Jack's interest. It was a plain white post card, without picture or image. Just a plain white card with a space for a written message on one side. He flipped the card over, noting that it had no postmark or stamp.

He frowned as he looked at the handwritten message in the centre.

Daniel Hopkins

14th March 1982

St Bartholomew's

An innocent man is in prison

That was it; nothing more, nothing less. The writing was in block capitals, made with a black biro pen. Jack immediately dropped the card to his desk, and reached into his desk drawer for a spare evidence bag. It was probably no use, having gone through several pairs of hands already before reaching Jack's desk, but he slid the card inside the bag using a small pair of tweezers he also found languishing in the drawer.

Frowning, he thought back to the investigation so far, but the name Daniel Hopkins meant nothing to him.

Jack reached for his desk phone and jabbed the internal number for the investigation room where he had left DS Cooper and DC Cassidy trawling through the visitor log for the Laurels. It was DS Cooper who answered.

"Cooper? I need you to check something out for me. Run the name Daniel Hopkins and the date 14th March 1982 through the system. Find out anything you can."

He replaced the receiver and leant back in his chair, turning the plastic evidence bag over in his hands. For the moment, he pushed the man behind the camera out of his mind and concentrated on a new name.

Daniel Hopkins.

* * *

Time: 10.00am

Date: Thursday 14th February 2013

Location: Metropolitan Police HQ, London

It had taken DS Cooper less than thirty minutes to arrive, breathless, at Jack's door, confirming that Daniel Hopkins had been a former resident at St Bartholomew's.

"According to the records, he arrived at St Bartholomew's in September 1980 when he was nine years old." DS Cooper perched on the edge of Jack's cluttered desk. "He died on 14th March 1982, aged eleven, having disappeared from the home. He was found a few days later in local woodland."

Jack glanced at the printout DS Cooper handed him. Running his eyes down the scant details, his eyes focused on the words at the bottom.

Strangled.

Evidence of sexual assault.

"See if you can get hold of the case file – get it emailed over and printed out. I want to see anything to do with the investigation into his murder."

"You think this could be linked to the Wakefields investigation, boss?"

"I don't know, Cooper." Jack turned the postcard over in his hands. "But for some reason the name St Bartholomew's seems to be everywhere I turn."

With somebody, somewhere, thinking it was important enough to send an anonymous note, Jack wrote the name Daniel Hopkins on his notepad, followed by a question mark.

Just who were you Daniel Hopkins?

* * *

Time: 1.30pm

Date: Sunday 14th March 1982

Location: St Bartholomew's Home for Boys, Christchurch

Danny Hopkins gritted his teeth and hauled the large bag of compost out of the greenhouse and towards the vegetable plot. His skinny arms quivered under the strain. The compost bag was almost as big as he was, and the effort to move it was making him stumble. In the end he dragged it, two-handed, across the grass.

"Hopkins!" A booming voice bellowed across the garden. Danny flinched and turned to see Edward Wakefield striding towards him. "Mind you don't split that bag, boy!" The caretaker thundered towards him and Danny shrank back into the shadows of the greenhouse.

Edward Wakefield picked up the compost bag with one hand and deposited it at the side of the vegetable garden. "There. Now, get to work. I want to see that compost spread evenly across this whole plot."

Danny stepped out of the shadows, but wasn't quick enough to escape the quick slap to the side of his head from the caretaker's shovel-like hand. "That's for slacking. Now, off you go!"

Danny stumbled over towards the vegetable plot, his right ear stinging like crazy. He felt the warm trickle of blood start to make its journey down the side of his neck. Brushing it away, he picked up a spade and began to dig into the compost bag.

"And don't forget tonight, lad." Edward Wakefield bore down on Danny's small frame from behind, but he kept his voice low so no one else could hear. "Same time. Same place. Don't let me down."

Danny nodded. He wouldn't let Edward Wakefield down. *Nobody* let Edward Wakefield down. Not if they valued the use of their legs and didn't want to be eating through a straw for the next fortnight. He felt a sickness start to spread within him as soon as he saw the burly caretaker stride away in the direction of the main building. He hated the parties that the Wakefields had in the disused part of the home. Once a hospital wing, it had been closed down once the new Matron's extension had been built at the rear.

Nobody used the hospital wing anymore.

Nobody except Edward Wakefield.

Danny shuddered in the early Spring sunshine. At a little over four feet six inches, he was small for his eleven years. And he was weak, too. He was told that he had had rheumatic fever as a baby, although he didn't remember. His elfin face gave him a delicate appearance.

He continued digging, ignoring the painful blisters that were screaming from the palms of his hands. Suddenly, feeling a sharp pain in his chest, he bent over his spade and began to cough violently. His chest wheezed as his lungs fought to suck in more and more air. Gasping, he reached into his pocket for his inhaler, his body shuddering as he placed it into his mouth and pulled the medication into his airways.

The coughing eventually subsided, and he slipped the inhaler back inside his pocket, noting that it was virtually empty. Making a mental note to go and see the Matron later, he resumed his digging.

* * *

Time: 12.15pm
 Date: Thursday 14th February 2013
 Location: Metropolitan Police HQ, London

The evidence had landed on his desk at a little after midday. Jack had left DS Cooper and DC Cassidy in the investigation room with the instruction that he was in his office if they should need him. Judging by the waves of dismissal from both of them, needed he was not.

And that suited Jack just fine. He settled down at his desk and made a space – moving memos, messages and urgent case reviews into his in-tray. He noticed, not for the first time, that the in-tray was far more well populated than the out-tray.

The Daniel Hopkins murder case notes were contained in two thin folders. The first folder, when opened, contained the bundle of witness statements used at trial and a full transcript of the trial itself. It was barely half full.

The second folder was so light, Jack initially thought it was empty. But peering inside he surmised that this must be the evidence bundle, such as it was. The folder contained a small bunch of photographs and some laboratory reports, with an evidence log sheet tucked in behind.

That was it.

Jack sighed and took the bundle of witness statements out of the first folder and settled back to read.

* * *

Time: 2.15pm

Date: Thursday 14th February 2013

Location: Metropolitan Police HQ, London

The witness statements had taken him a little over two hours to read. Not because they were particularly long, or because there were that many of them – in fact, there were only five statements in the folder as a whole – but because Jack had read them over and over, countless times each, making notes as he went.

A murder investigation with only five witness statements had set off the first sense of disquiet within Jack. But that was not all that was wrong. The statements themselves were short; *very* short. Concise was probably the term that would have been used. But to Jack, they were just short. Woefully short.

The statement of the manager Albert Dawson merely confirmed that Daniel Hopkins had arrived at St Bartholomew's on 5th September 1980. Very little was said about his short life at the foster home, other than he had gone missing on the evening of 14th March 1982 – with his body found several days later in a wooded area not far from the home. Albert Dawson confirmed that he did not hear or see anything untoward on the night of Daniel's disappearance.

Another short statement from the Matron at St Bartholomew's, Nora Sparrow, confirmed that she had seen Daniel Hopkins at approximately 6.30pm on the day he disappeared, as she issued him with a replacement inhaler for his asthma. A photocopy of the medical log showed that the inhaler had been issued to Danny at 6.35pm. As far as she knew, he was heading back to his room after having already eaten his supper. She also confirmed that she did not hear or see anything untoward on the night of the boy's disappearance.

The next two witness statements piqued Jack's curiosity. Edward and Terence Wakefield both signed statements to say that Danny had helped in the gardens during the afternoon of the day he disappeared, but that neither of them heard or saw anything untoward on the night Daniel disappeared.

Jack let the statements fall back onto his desk and reached for his, now cold, cup of coffee.

Everyone interviewed at St Bartholomew's apparently heard nothing and saw nothing.

Jack's experience and intuition told him that that was highly unlikely.

The final statement in the folder caused Jack the most disquiet. A confession statement. It was the shortest statement of the bundle, and at barely more than one side of A4 paper, a man called Adrian McLeish had confessed to the murder of Daniel Hopkins and sealed his own fate.

* * *

. Time: 6.30pm

Date: Sunday 14th March 1982

Location: St Bartholomew's Home for Boys, Christchurch

The Matron's office was part of the new-build extension at the rear of the home. Built in 1977, the year of the Queen's Silver Jubilee, it was aptly named the Elizabeth Building in her honour. Although Danny wasn't quite sure why the Queen would be honoured to have such an ugly red-bricked square building named after her.

He approached the main door and pressed the buzzer. The Elizabeth Building was always locked, due to it containing all manner of drugs and medicaments to keep the foster home boys happy and healthy.

Well, maybe not happy.

And most of the time not so healthy, either.

Danny's ear still stung from the wallop he had received from Edward Wakefield earlier that afternoon. The blood had dried up and he had managed to wash the stains out of his top; more or less. All that was left was a small, healing cut which would eventually scab over.

He pressed the buzzer for a second time before the door was finally opened. He pushed his way inside and heard the door click shut behind him. Matron Nora Sparrow was as old as the hills. All the boys at St Bartholomew's thought she was at least a hundred years old, but in reality she was probably no more than sixty. She looked older, though – much older. Her face was a mismatch of crazy paving style crevasses, with a bony beak-like nose in the centre of two pin-prick eyes. She wore a pair of prescription-strength glasses which perched on the end of her bird-like nose. Sparrow by name, sparrow by nature.

Nora Sparrow was less than five feet tall and maybe only an inch or two taller than Danny. She seemed to shrink as each year passed by.

"Daniel, have you come for your inhaler?" She peered out from behind her office door at the end of the small reception area.

He nodded and walked towards her, passing three other doors that remained closed. One was an examination room, the other two had beds for when boys were deemed too sick to return to the main home and needed to remain under the Matron's watchful eye.

"Well, come on in." She gestured for Danny to follow her back into her office. As he walked in, she was already rummaging inside a drugs cabinet that ran along the back wall. Danny watched as she selected a small box from the top shelf. "Same one as last time, Daniel." She turned and handed him a small inhaler for his recently diagnosed asthma. "Same instructions as before. You're happy with how to use it?"

Danny nodded. "Yes, thank you, Matron." He took the inhaler and slipped it into his pocket.

Nora Sparrow locked up the drugs cabinet and moved closer to Danny, about to show him out of her office. As she did so, she noticed the cut behind his right ear. There was still a smear of dried blood on his ear lobe.

"That looks sore, Daniel. And recent. How did you cut yourself like that?"

Danny's hand went instinctively up to his right ear. He avoided the Matron's gaze. "Oh, I walked into the greenhouse door earlier. While I was working in the garden."

Nora Sparrow nodded, slowly, and took a further step forwards to take a closer look. "I can clean that up for you, if you want? Give it a dressing?" She went to reach out towards Danny's ear, but he quickly stepped backwards.

"No, honestly. It's fine. It's just a small cut. Doesn't even hurt. I should be more careful and look where I'm going." With that, Danny turned and bolted from the room.

Nora Sparrow followed him out into the reception area and watched as he pressed the release button for the door and tumbled outside, sprinting for the sanctity of the main building. After he had gone, she returned to her office to update Danny's medical records log.

Walked into a greenhouse door.

Nora Sparrow tutted under her breath. From her experience in treating the boys of St Bartholomew's over the last thirty-five years, there were a fair number of them that seemed clumsy enough to do just that.

Regularly.

She shook her head and reached for the medical records log.

* * *

Time: 2.30pm
Date: Thursday 14th February 2013

Location: Metropolitan Police HQ, London

Jack read Adrian McLeish's brief statement three times, and added yet more notes to his ever-growing list. McLeish was a frequent visitor to St Bartholomew's – helping out in the greenhouses as part of a day release programme. According to his statement, he had 'special educational needs', but this was not elaborated upon any further.

In less than one hundred and fifty words, Adrian McLeish, with a shaky signature at the bottom of the page, had signed away his freedom.

The second folder of evidence threw up more questions than answers. With just the one bunch of photographs, the evidence appeared scanty at best. Looking through the pictures, Jack saw that the vast majority were of the young boy's clothing, with just a few depicting the crime scene.

The photographs taken were not as detailed nor of the quality that would be taken now, but Jack lined them up on his desk anyway. The first few were crime scene photographs, showing Daniel Hopkins' lifeless body in situ – clumsily hidden beneath a pile of twigs and leaves in a nearby wood. Once the body had been removed from the scene, a series of photographs were taken of his clothing.

A pair of blue jeans, worn at the knees and splattered with dried mud.

A yellow short-sleeved t-shirt with a small rip at one shoulder.

A pair of white trainers with green stripes at the sides – the word 'Dunlop' on a tag at the heel.

There was an evidence log detailing the evidence taken – and where it was currently located. Jack made a small, final note at the end of his list of actions – 'evidence in storage'.

He underlined it.

Twice.

Jack spent the rest of the afternoon checking up on the current state of play with both Wakefield investigations. He read the statement of Sylvia Brennan and re-read those from the staff at The Laurels.

At a little after four o'clock, DC Cassidy knocked at the door. "Thought you might need a refill." She stepped into Jack's office, brandishing a mug of steaming hot coffee, freshly brewed.

Jack nodded his appreciation. "Thanks, you're a mind reader. This one's gone stone cold."

DC Cassidy swapped the mugs and let her gaze fall on the two folders still at the centre of Jack's desk. "Are they the case notes from that poor little boy's murder?"

Jack continued to nod. "Yes. Such as they are."

DC Cassidy peered inside one of the folders and wrinkled her nose. "Seems a little thin on the ground. But he confessed, didn't he? The guy that was convicted?"

Jack reached forwards and picked up Adrian McLeish's confession statement once again, passing it over to DC Cassidy. "He did, indeed. But he later retracted it – once he actually got access to some legal advice. He pleaded not guilty at the trial."

DC Cassidy quickly cast her eyes over the statement. "Not much to it, is there?"

Jack shook his head. "It's shocking as far as a confession goes. It's all pre-PACE. No interview tapes. No videos. No interview transcripts. We don't know what the hell was said to him when he was interviewed to get that confession out of him."

DC Cassidy dropped the statement back on Jack's desk. "I can't imagine how you would conduct an investigation or interview without PACE. How could you ever be sure about what was said? It would be the police's word against the suspect's."

Jack smiled ruefully and gave a small laugh. "Police officers never lie, Amanda, didn't you know? If a police officer says someone is guilty, then they clearly are. It's an open and shut case."

DC Cassidy laughed and turned back towards the door, taking the cold coffee with her. "Me and Chris are just finishing up – we've been searching for Harrys and Henrys in The Laurels visitor books. So far no joy, it's like looking for a needle in a haystack. Do you need us for anything else?"

Jack flicked open the second folder and pulled out the evidence log. "I need the physical evidence on Daniel Hopkins sent off to the lab. The young boy's clothing. Get it sent over by courier. Today." Jack handed the evidence log across to DC Cassidy. "Get Cooper to ring Jenny and warn her it's coming; she's got a soft spot for him. Tell her it's urgent. Then you two head home. Or to the pub. Or wherever it is you youngsters go."

DC Cassidy smiled and headed for the door.

"Oh, and first thing in the morning, find out all you can on Adrian McLeish."

DC Cassidy nodded and shut the door behind her, leaving Jack alone with his thoughts. Glancing at his watch, and realising he didn't really have anything to go home for, he picked up the transcript of the trial of *R v McLeish* once again and started to read.

* * *

Time: 7.00pm
Date: Thursday 14th February 2013
Location: Metropolitan Police HQ, London

Jack put the transcript down. It hadn't made for happy reading. Adrian McLeish clearly had a learning disability, and under today's rules he would have had his police interview undertaken with an appropriate adult in attendance – but there was no such protection in the early 1980s.

His trial had been brutal. The prosecutor had torn him to shreds in the witness box. The Judge had allowed the confession to be admitted as evidence, dismissing the half-hearted appeals by the defence, so it was put to the jury as evidence of his guilt.

Adrian McLeish had faced an uphill struggle to convince the jury of his innocence.

Not surprisingly, he had failed.

The jury took less than an hour to reach a unanimous verdict. Guilty.

At no time during the trial did the fact that the defendant had a learning disability and a mental age of eight raise any sorts of alarm bells.

Feeling his stomach starting to growl, Jack slotted the Daniel Hopkins case notes back inside their respective folders. As he reached for his jacket, he quickly tapped out an email to DS Carmichael.

'Re: Operation Evergreen. Take a look at Daniel Hopkins – strangled and sexually assaulted. St Bartholomew's March 1982. Case notes in my office.'

Snapping off the overhead lights, Jack slipped his phone into his pocket. He noticed there had been nothing from Stu. He had sent him a brief message, apologising for the scene in the pub, but it had elicited no response. With Daniel Hopkins now playing on his mind, Jack had no energy left to deal with his brother.

* * *

Chapter Nineteen

Time: 9.30am
  Date: Friday 15th February 2013
  Location: Metropolitan Police HQ, London

DC Cassidy brought the front page of the Christchurch Evening News for Monday 15th March 1982 up onto the whiteboard screen. The headline stood out in bold, two inch sized letters.

FEARS GROW FOR MISSING BOY

'An eleven-year-old boy from St Bartholomew's Home for Boys has been reported missing. Last seen at approximately 6.30pm yesterday. The boy is described as being small for his age – at four feet six inches - with light brown hair. Daniel Hopkins has lived at St Bartholomew's since September 1980 and manager Albert Dawson says that it is most out of character for him to have disappeared. Anyone with any information is urged to contact the local police.'

The newspaper article was short and to the point. A tiny black and white headshot of Daniel Hopkins was nestled in the corner. DC Cassidy closed the article down and brought up another, from the same newspaper, dated four days later.

BODY FOUND IN SEARCH FOR MISSING BOY

'A body has been found in woodland close to St Bartholomew's Home for Boys. A police spokesperson has confirmed that the body was found by a member of the public early this morning. No formal identification has been made. A search has been underway for missing eleven-year-old Daniel Hopkins since last Sunday. No formal statement has been forthcoming from management at St Bartholomew's Home for Boys. The area remains sealed off as investigations continue.'

DC Cassidy closed the article and brought up the next, dated 20th March 1982

BODY IDENTIFIED AS MISSING FOSTER HOME BOY DANIEL HOPKINS

'Police today released the formal identification of the body found in woodland yesterday, confirming it as that of missing eleven-year-old Daniel Hopkins. A murder investigation has been launched. The manager at St Bartholomew's Home for Boys, Albert Dawson, refused to make a formal statement, other than asking for privacy at this 'incredibly sad time'. A number of flowers have been laid at the woodland site by members of the public, but the area remains sealed off.'

The next newspaper article DC Cassidy could find was eight days later, on 28th March 1982.

DANIEL HOPKINS MURDER – LOCAL MAN ARRESTED

'A local man has been arrested by police in a dawn raid at his house in a village on the outskirts of Christchurch. The twenty-three-year-old is said to have been a frequent visitor to St Bartholomew's Home for Boys, but it is as yet unclear if he knew the victim personally. A police spokesperson confirmed that a twenty-three-year old man had been arrested on suspicion of murder and was currently being held at Christchurch Central Police Station.'

"And that's it?" Jack raised his eyebrows at the whiteboard screen.

"Pretty much," confirmed DC Cassidy, clicking the mouse to bring up one final newspaper article. "Just one more entry on 29th March when Adrian McLeish was charged." The headline filled the screen:

DANIEL HOPKINS MURDER – MAN CHARGED

'Local man, Adrian McLeish, aged twenty-three, has been charged with the murder of eleven-year-old Daniel Hopkins. He appeared at Christchurch Magistrates Court early this morning and was remanded in custody. The manager of St Bartholomew's Home for Boys, Albert Dawson, thanked the police for their thorough investigation and again requested privacy so the home could grieve for the loss of one of their own.'

"Thorough investigation, my arse," muttered Jack. "Nothing else after that?"

DC Cassidy shook her head. "Not really, guv. Nothing until the trial – and even then it was a tiny paragraph, not even front page. The paper spent most of its time focusing on the Falklands War which had just broken out. Adrian McLeish seems to have been forgotten."

Jack nodded. "OK, so what about after the trial? I understand that his mother was quite vocal in her opinions that her son was innocent."

"Yes, she was – but it wasn't really covered in the local newspapers. I guess they felt that they had their man. The only articles I could find appeared in newspapers close to where Mrs McLeish now lives in Stirling, Scotland. It seems that after the trial she and her husband moved back over the border to be closer to family."

"I don't blame her," replied Jack. "It can't have been very pleasant living in the area after her son was convicted."

DC Cassidy brought up another newspaper article, this time from the Stirling Daily Herald. "Most of the articles I could find on the case are written by the same reporter Angus McIntyre."

"Anything you think is relevant?" Jack squinted at the whiteboard.

"Not a great deal. In the months that followed the trial, a lot of calls for a re-trial, suggesting that Adrian didn't get a fair trial because of his learning difficulties. But the arguments seemed to peter out after a while, and he again seems to have been forgotten." DC Cassidy enlarged the newspaper article on the screen. "The only significant step forward was in 1990." A front page headline from the same Stirling Daily Herald filled the screen.

DANIEL HOPKINS MURDER – APPEAL DISMISSED

'An appeal against conviction for murder lodged by Adrian McLeish – originally from Stirling – has been dismissed by the Court of Appeal in London. McLeish was convicted in 1982 of the murder of eleven-year-old Daniel Hopkins. Mr McLeish's mother, Isla McLeish, said she was deeply disappointed with the decision. Lawyers for Adrian McLeish confirmed that they would be working on a fresh appeal, citing that their client's interrogation by officers breached the new Police and Criminal Evidence Act, and that 'no stone would be left unturned' in their pursuit to overturn this miscarriage of justice.'

"As Adrian McLeish is still languishing in prison, I'm guessing they didn't turn over many more stones – no further appeal?" Jack reached for the now cold mug of coffee in front of him.

DC Cassidy shook her head. "No, nothing more. Everything seems to have just stopped." She closed the newspaper article on the whiteboard. "Mrs McLeish's husband, Archie, died in 1991. Maybe she felt she couldn't carry on fighting alone to clear his name?"

"Well, if the PACE argument didn't swing it for the Court of Appeal back in 1990, then they'll need some fresh evidence."

"Do you think he did it?"

"Whether he did or not, it doesn't look like he had the fairest of trials." Jack rubbed his eyes. "Another job for the lab. See if you can pull McLeish's DNA off the database and ask Jenny to compare it to the clothing she has for Danny."

"Sure," nodded DC Cassidy. "You think it's connected to the Wakefields' murders?"

Jack shrugged. "I honestly have no idea, but let's do it anyway."

"I'll get Chris to ring Jenny. She'll put a rush on it if he asks her nicely." DC Cassidy gave Jack a wink and got to her feet.

Jack smiled. "Good idea. Then, if you could get all those newspaper articles printed out and file a report on the system. Everything needs to be there in black and white before anyone will even think about opening this can of worms again." He shrugged back into his jacket and followed DC Cassidy towards the door, "In the meantime, I'm heading off to see our lovely Albert Dawson again."

* * *

Time: 11.30pm
   Date: Friday 15th February 2013
   Location: 3 Wagtail Drive, West Hampstead, London

Mandy opened the front door and smiled. "Inspector, how nice to see you again. Come on in." She stepped back to allow Jack space to enter the hallway of the neat bungalow.

Nothing much had changed since his last visit. The bungalow smelt of polish, and also had the aroma of recent vacuuming. Mandy motioned for Jack to follow her through to the back bedroom, where he found Albert Dawson in his usual position – propped up in bed, surrounded by medical equipment and other paraphernalia.

Jack had wondered why Albert had chosen to be cared for in his own home, and not a nursing home. But when he entered the bedroom, and again saw the floor to ceiling windows looking out onto the neat, well-kept garden, and noticed the weak sunlight dancing off the freshly swept patio slabs, with the faint sound of music playing on the radio wafting in from the kitchen, Jack considered that maybe the old man had got it right.

"Albert," announced Mandy, leading Jack into the bedroom, her voice raised a notch to penetrate Albert's ears. "You've got a visitor. It's that nice policeman again. You remember?" She went over to Albert and plumped up his pillows behind his head, helping to lift his slight frame into a more upright position. "I'll go and make you both a nice cup of tea."

With that, Mandy turned and side-stepped out of the cramped room, humming to herself as she made her way back to the kitchen.

Jack quietly eyed the old man as he shuffled over to the one and only chair by the window. A quick glance outside showed a gentle dusting of snow on top of the bird table, and a grey squirrel hanging upside down from the nut feeder. Another one bounded across the grass.

"I see your squirrels are out in force." Jack turned back towards Albert Dawson, but received no response. He perched himself on the vacant chair, moving packets of sterile syringes to the floor. He leant forwards, leaning his arms on the edge of the bed. "Now, we both know that you can hear me perfectly well, Albert, and that you can understand everything I'm saying." Jack paused, listening for Mandy's return with the tea. He could still hear the kettle boiling, so he pressed on. "So, let's stop playing games. Firstly, who was Harry?"

Albert Dawson remained motionless, his expression fixed and vacant.

Jack tried again. "I'm told he shared a room with the boys I mentioned last time– room fifteen?"

Still there was no response from the old man. Jack decided to try a different tactic.

"OK. How about you tell me about Daniel Hopkins instead, then?"

This time Jack noticed a faint flicker of what he thought was recognition cross the old man's sunken face. He looked older today, even though it had only been four days since Jack was last here. Older. Thinner. Weaker. Mandy would have you believe he wasn't the full ticket, and lapsed in and out of lucidity – but Jack knew better. He was no doctor, but in his opinion Albert Dawson was as sharp as a pin. And, up to now, had been pulling the wool over everyone's eyes.

Except Jack's.

He had seen enough people across the table in interview rooms to know when someone was lying.

"I'm going to ask you again, Albert. What can you tell me about Daniel Hopkins?"

Another flicker crossed Albert's translucent skin. His rheumy blue eyes fluttered, and for a split second he caught Jack's gaze.

"See. I know you can hear me."

Albert Dawson's breathing seemed to quicken; his shallow breaths coming in shorter, sharper rhythm. His narrow chest, swamped in a light blue hospital style pyjama top, rose and fell with increasing frequency.

"Why don't you just tell me about how Daniel Hopkins died?" pressed Jack, still with one eye on the door. "I'm sure you know. I'm sure you know *exactly* what happened to him."

More shallow breaths. More flickering of the eyelids.

Jack noticed that the sound of the boiling kettle had now ceased, and the unmistakeable clink of mugs and spoons was coming towards them. Mandy's frame appeared in the doorway, with a tray laden with two mugs and a plate of shortbread fingers.

"Let's see now." She balanced the tray on the end of the bed. "One for you, Inspector." She passed a mug across to Jack, who accepted it with a smile. "Help yourself to the shortbread. And this one is for you, Albert. I'll just put your thickener in. I've added cold water so it's not too hot for you." She placed Albert's tea on the sideboard and went through the process of scooping thickening powder into the mug and stirring it vigorously. As she did so, she glanced over her shoulder. "So, what have you two been talking about? Albert? I hope you've been making the Inspector feel welcome." She gave a wink in Jack's direction and continued to stir Albert's tea. "I'm not sure he understands much, but you never know..."

Jack smiled again and took a sip of his tea. I'm sure the wily old dog understands perfectly, he thought to himself, wincing as the hot tea hit his throat.

"Albert?" Mandy turned around with his thickened tea and frowned. "Are you feeling all right, Albert? You look a little flushed."

She put the mug down on his bedside table and felt his forehead. Frowning again, she took his limp wrist in her hand and took his pulse, staring at her fob watch as she did so.

"Hmmm, your pulse is a little high, Albert. Are you feeling unwell?" Mandy gently slipped an arm behind Albert's shoulders and helped to prop him further up in bed. She brought the mug of cooled tea to his lips. "Maybe a nice cup of tea will sort you out. And then I'll get you some more painkillers. Are you in pain, Albert?"

Albert Dawson gave a grunting noise in between sips of tea. Jack watched silently as Mandy let the old man take a few more sips before resting his head back on his pillow and reaching for a bottle by his bedside.

"I'll just give him another dose," she explained, waggling the bottle in Jack's direction. "His MS can give him lots of pain sometimes. This will make him more comfortable." She pulled the correct dose into a fresh, sterile syringe and then administered it through the tube that led to his stomach. "But it does tend to make him quite sleepy – so if you need to talk to him, I'd make it quick."

Jack nodded, sipping more of his tea. He had already got the answers he had wanted from Albert Dawson – albeit without the old man uttering a word. The look on his face when Jack had mentioned the name Daniel Hopkins had been enough.

"We were just talking about a young boy that used to live at the foster home Albert worked at – back in the 1970s and early 1980s. Young lad by the name of Daniel Hopkins. Danny to his friends." Jack paused, watching Albert Dawson's frail body beneath the thin blanket. Another flicker crossed his face; another tremble in the fingers knotted in his lap. "I think Albert, here, used to know him quite well."

"Oh, that's nice," said Mandy, clearing up the packaging from the syringe and putting the medicine bottle back on the bedside table. "I'll just tidy these away and leave you two to it." She collected Albert's half-drunk mug of tea and padded back out to the hallway, heading for the kitchen.

"So - Daniel Hopkins, Albert." Jack bent closer towards Albert Dawson. "I know he was killed at St Bartholomew's. And I'm pretty sure the wrong person has been convicted of his murder. We have DNA these days, Albert. And soon enough we'll have the results; even after all this time. And another thing I know..." Jack paused, making sure he had Albert's full attention. He moved to the end of the bed, placing his empty mug on the sideboard, and leant in as close as he could to look directly into the man's watery eyes. "You know who really killed him." Jack maintained eye contact for several seconds before stepping away towards the door.

He was done with Albert Dawson.

As he reached the threshold of the bedroom door, Albert's voice carried towards him, clear and strong, belying the feeble and weakened appearance of his exterior.

"Prove it."

Jack froze in his tracks and turned around to see the old man following him with his taunting gaze.

"Prove it," he repeated, the pale skin on his face breaking out into a toothless grin.

* * *

Time: 2.15pm
Date: Friday 15th February 2013
Location: Belgrave Square Gardens, London

He had managed to slip into the private Belgrave Square gardens without raising so much as an eyebrow, holding the gate open for a young mother struggling with a pushchair and following in her wake. The day was crisp and clear, with a light dusting of overnight snow still clinging to the frozen ground.

The gardens were almost deserted and he chose a secluded bench beneath a tree. Unfolding a copy of yesterday's Evening Standard, he noticed very little was being said about Edward and Terence Wakefield; only a small piece at the bottom of page five. Smiling to himself, he sipped at his takeaway coffee cup.

The truth would eventually come out and everyone would know what the Wakefields had done. Their name would be front page news on every national newspaper in the land.

But not yet.

Not until the final piece of justice had been served.

Tell no one.

Trust no one.

Hadn't that been their motto?

The woman that he had followed into the gardens was approaching the bench, her toddler asleep in the pushchair. He exchanged a polite smile and glanced down at the slumbering child, wrapped up in a padded jacket and trousers, with a fleece blanket tucked around his sides. The child's face was tinged pink from the cold, but his expression was one of peace and contentment. He was safe and protected.

Just as he should be.

He felt the familiar flicker of hatred start to rise within him, and pushed himself up off the bench. Glancing at his watch, he made his way towards one of the gates.

It was time to start his final preparations.

* * *

Time: 2.15pm

Date: Friday 15th February 2013

Location: Isabel's Café, King's Road, London

"You just missed him." Isabel set the two teas down on the table. "Literally. He left about half an hour ago. Took his coffee with him."

Jack picked up one of the mugs. "No problem, it was you I came to see anyway. How was he, by the way?"

Isabel sat down opposite Jack and gave a small shrug. "He was OK. Better, I think. He looked a little bit more like his old self."

Jack took a sip of his tea. It tasted better than the mug he had at Albert Dawson's. "I messaged him yesterday – we had a bit of a falling out. I wanted to make it up to him later, buy him a few beers for his birthday."

Isabel smiled. "Try him again. Like I said – he seems better. Like a weight has been lifted from his shoulders. He didn't stay long – just enough time to devour some cake." Isabel nodded towards the remnants of a chocolate birthday cake she had stayed up half the night to bake.

"Good." Jack took another gulp of tea. "So, show me the fortune cookie. Sorry I haven't got around to it sooner, but things are really manic at work at the moment."

Isabel reached into the pocket of her cardigan and brought out the small slip of paper.

'The best way to get rid of an enemy is to make them a friend'. Jack gazed down at the words and slowly shook his head. "I'm still not convinced."

Isabel gave a weak smile. "I know. I feel a bit silly now. It just spooked me, that's all. I keep feeling he's going to pop up again when I least expect it."

Jack handed the paper back. "I wouldn't worry about it. Honestly. But if you want, I'm still happy to come along to your themed evening tomorrow. If it'll put your mind at rest..."

"Oh, it would, Jack," beamed Isabel. "It really would. Thank you, so much"

Jack saw the smile on Isabel's face but it didn't mask the dark circles still present beneath her eyes. "Is Stu coming?"

Isabel gave a small laugh. "I've asked him, Jack. But you know what he's like."

Jack nodded. He certainly did. "Well, I'll see you tomorrow." Glancing at his watch, he downed the rest of his tea and reached for his jacket. "Sorry, I have to get back."

"Please take some cake for the team." Isabel quickly got up and cut three thick slices of cake and wrapped them each in a serviette. She placed them in a paper bag and handed them to Jack at the door. "It needs eating up."

Jack smiled.

He knew someone who wouldn't say no to a piece of Isabel's chocolate cake.

* * *

Time: 3.45pm
Date: Friday 15th February 2013
Location: Metropolitan Police HQ, London

DS Cooper bit hungrily into the thick slice of cake, a smear of chocolate frosting covering his lips.

DC Cassidy threw him another serviette. "You are such an animal. I don't know what Jenny sees in you!"

DS Cooper continued munching, a smile adding to the icing on his lips.

"Speaking of Jenny – what did she say about the extra samples of Daniel Hopkins' clothing? And running the McLeish DNA?" Jack slipped off his jacket and sat down at the investigation table. "I know I've asked a lot of the lab recently."

DS Cooper wiped his mouth and swallowed the remains of the cake. "She was fine about it, boss. She's got her team making the Danny Hopkins' samples a priority, and she's running McLeish's DNA as we speak."

"That's good. I don't suppose the visitor log book from The Laurels has shown anything up?"

DC Cassidy shook her head. "We've looked for all Harrys and Henrys going back to November last year, but there's nothing. We could ask to look at the dates further back?"

"Maybe." Jack pulled out his notebook. "My trip to see Albert Dawson was interesting. He definitely knows what happened to Daniel Hopkins, basically taunted me to prove it. I expect Rob will want to pay him a visit in due course."

"So what's next?" DC Cassidy started brushing cake crumbs from the table. "Shall I get onto The Laurels and get the visitor log books from before November?"

Jack nodded. "OK, do that. But then it's home time. It's Friday night - you must have somewhere else you'd rather be. Take an early one, both of you."

While DC Cassidy rang through to The Laurels, Jack stepped out into the corridor. There was one thing he needed to do.

The phone went unanswered as expected, and Jack left a brief voice message.

"Stu. It's me. Come over tonight; the boxes have arrived. And I need to apologise...again."

* * *

Time: 7.00pm
  Date: Friday 15th February 2013
  Location: Kettle's Yard Mews, London

Jack pulled two bottles of Budweiser out of the fridge and snapped off the lids. "Thanks for coming over, Stu. As I said, I need to apologise."

Mac took hold of the bottle and gave a shrug. "No need. You were just doing your job."

"Yeah, but asking my brother for a DNA swab." Jack gave an apologetic smile. "It wasn't very tactful. I'm sorry."

Mac gave another shrug and went to sit down on the sofa. "Leave it, Jack. I needn't have gone off on one. It just reminded me of being inside. Just leave it, yeah?

Jack nodded and joined him on the sofa. "Happy Birthday, anyway." The two of them clinked bottles.

"So, these are the boxes?" Mac tipped his beer bottle towards the two cardboard boxes sitting on the coffee table.

"They are," confirmed Jack. "But let's eat first, though. Have a couple of beers. This stuff can wait a bit longer."

Mac nodded in agreement and took another long pull on his beer, watching as Jack headed back to the kitchen to bring through a couple of plates and cutlery, plus the takeaway bag from the Chinese along the street.

"I wasn't sure what to get; Chinese or Indian. But they're still doing a special menu for Chinese New Year, so I plumped for that." Jack placed the plates and cutlery down onto the coffee table, moving the boxes onto the floor. He unloaded the bag, bringing out eight foil cartons plus a small bag of prawn crackers.

"Jesus, Jack, how many people are you feeding?" Mac's eyes lit up as he saw and smelt the food, his stomach reminding him that he hadn't eaten anything since breakfast.

Jack shrugged. "I just ordered one of their set menus – a New Year Special." He ripped off the lids to both the special fried rice and mushroom rice – then did the same to the rest of the cartons, until all eight were on display.

"I can always have some more tomorrow," he conceded.

"And the day after," added Mac, already diving in and spooning a generous pile of rice onto his plate, followed by a serving of Kung Pao chicken. "I do love a Chinese, though. Isabel doesn't really like it much, she prefers Indian."

For the next few minutes, silence prevailed in the flat as they loaded up their plates and began to eat. Mac shovelled food into his mouth like he hadn't eaten in a fortnight, and Jack hid a smile behind his fork. He always remembered Stu being a bit of a gannet when they were younger, hardly pausing for breath in-between mouthfuls.

"You remember Betty Garner's shepherd's pie?" Jack felt himself start to laugh as he recalled the memory. "You were only small but you could eat platefuls of that stuff!"

Mac echoed Jack's laughter and almost choked on his chicken. He reached for a swig from his beer bottle. "God yes, Betty's shepherd's pie! That was amazing! I loved it. And her sausages and mash."

Jack found himself smiling at the memory, too. "Those were the days eh?"

They each piled a second plate with more food, and lapsed back into silence. Jack finally put his second plate down, feeling bloated and unable to eat any more. Mac continued to shovel the last of his plateful into his mouth, barely coming up for air.

"I remember Betty used to say you had hollow legs," remarked Jack. "She could never understand where you put all your food."

Mac laughed and swallowed at the same time. "I liked Betty."

Jack nodded in agreement. "Give me your plate and I'll get rid of these cartons. Then we'll go through the boxes. It won't take long – there's not much inside."

"You've already had a look?" Mac handed over his plate.

"Just a brief one." Jack took the remains of the takeaway back to the kitchen, stowing the uneaten food away in the fridge for tomorrow. He stacked the dirty dishes in the sink, and grabbed two more beers before returning to the sofa. He handed Mac his third bottle. "You're getting the tube home tonight, right? You didn't bring your bike?"

Mac nodded. "Yep, left the bike at home. Don't sweat, brother."

Jack sat back down and sipped on his own beer. "You want to do this?" He nodded at the boxes on the floor.

Mac paused but gave a quick nod. "Let's do it."

Jack made space on the coffee table for both boxes and opened the flaps to the first one. This was the one he already knew contained the books and toys that he remembered from their bedroom at the Old Mill Road flat, but he wondered if they would spike any memories in his brother.

Mac peered inside and immediately a broad grin crossed his face. "Hey, I remember these." He pulled out the wooden toy cars and spun their wheels. "And these!" He reached in again and brought out a handful of Topsy and Tim books. "I'm sure Mum used to read these to us at bedtime. Did she, Jack?"

Jack nodded. "I'm pretty sure she did, Stu." He sat back and watched as his brother was transported back in time, amazed at how many childhood memories had seeped into the brain of a two-year-old.

"I'm not sure I remember these, though, Jack?" Mac pulled out the dominos and wooden puzzles. "I didn't know we had dominoes."

Jack continued to watch in silence as Mac rummaged amongst the rest of the box's sparse contents. Finally, he plucked out the paintings from the bottom.

"Do you remember those?" Jack tapped the painting he had done of the Christmas tree, and Mac's colourful, scribbled pattern. "I'm sure Mum had them pinned up in the kitchen, above the biscuit tin?"

Mac gave a non-committal shrug. "I'm not sure, Jack. But I do remember doing this one!" He held up the painting of the three pairs of handprints – his own, Jack's and their mother's. He ran a finger over the bumpy paint. "I remember getting all messy with the paint and Mum plonking us both in the bath afterwards!" He smiled as the memory sharpened. "I'm sure we did our feet, too. Was there not one with our footprints in there?" Mac peered back inside the box.

"I didn't see one," replied Jack. "But I'm glad you remember. That was a fun day."

Jack himself remembered how their mother had covered the whole of the kitchen floor with newspaper, and then tipped thick paint onto three plates – red, blue and purple. Rolling up their sleeves, she had then shown her two boys how to press their hands into the paint and then press them down onto the blank paper. Looking at the painting in Mac's hand, he could almost feel the paint squishing in between his fingers, and hear the squeals of delight coming from both of their small mouths.

Jack took a mouthful of beer and pulled the second box towards them. "This one just has photos. I don't really remember any of them. Mum must have kept them in her bedroom." He pulled out a handful of the photographs, handing Mac the largest one in a wooden frame first. He placed the rest down on the table. "I don't remember her having any photos out at all."

Mac shook his head, gazing intently at the framed picture. "No, me neither." He then reached for the others, spending a few minutes leafing through the black and white pictures, then those in colour, while Jack stayed quiet.

"You can take some, if you like." Jack nodded at the photos in Mac's hand. "I know you don't really have any of Mum."

Mac placed the bundle of photographs back down on the table and nodded, slowly, to himself. "Maybe," he muttered, "maybe." As he let go of the photographs, his eyes fell onto the corner of a leaflet that was obscured by one of the boxes. He pulled it out and squinted at the title. "What's this? He turned the leaflet over in his hands, and then looked up, expectantly, at Jack.

"Ah, that'll be Dr Riches." Jack took another slug of his beer. "She gave me a bundle of the things after my last session – she's quite big on leaflets."

Mac lowered his eyes once more to the leaflet in his hands. 'The Unseen Victims of Suicide'. After a few seconds, he cleared his throat. "Did she love us?" His voice was quiet and flat. "Mum? Did she love us?"

Jack opened his mouth but found himself closing it again; he wasn't quite sure what to say. He finally managed to loosen the words that had been sticking in his throat. "I'm sure she did, Stu. I'm sure she did."

"But not enough to stay with us."

"I don't think it was that black and white, Stu." Jack picked up the remaining photographs and began returning them to the box. "I don't think what happened to her meant that she didn't love us, or want to be with us."

Jack couldn't bring himself to say the word 'suicide'. His finger lingered on the photograph in the park – and the shadow of the mysterious man who was holding the camera.

"Do you ever remember there being a man in the flat?" Jack cast a sideways glance at his brother who he noticed had returned the leaflet to the table and was finishing off his beer.

"A man?" Mac swallowed and turned to look at Jack. "What do you mean 'a man'?"

"A man," repeated Jack, simply. "Do you remember Mum ever having any friends over in the flat? Any male friends?"

Mac shook his head, draining his beer bottle. "No. I don't remember any man. But I don't really remember much about that flat. Why, do you?"

Jack shrugged. "I'm not sure. I just wondered."

The rest of the evening passed with a few more beers being opened, and the finishing off of the bag of prawn crackers. They scrolled through the sports channel but couldn't find much worth watching. By the time Mac decided it was time he was leaving, Jack was already yawning.

"Safe journey." Jack held the door open as Mac shrugged himself into his jacket and pulled on a pair of leather gloves. He wrapped a scarf around his neck and pulled a woollen beanie hat down low over his eyes, ready to face the short walk to the tube. The temperature outside had fallen to below zero, and, according to the weatherman on the ten o'clock news, it was going to fall even more.

"See you, Jack." Mac raised a hand as he left, jogging down the communal stairs. "Thanks for the food."

Jack lingered in the doorway, watching his brother disappear out of sight before stepping back into the warmth of his flat. He closed the door and turned towards the kitchen, snapping on the kettle as he passed. He eyed the sink full of plates and cutlery, deciding that the washing up could wait until tomorrow. As it always could.

Before he could talk himself out of it, he returned to the front door and the suit jacket which was hanging on the back, and reached into its inside pocket. He brought out several clear, plastic evidence bags that he had brought home with him, and a pair of thin, latex gloves.

"Sorry, bro'," he muttered to himself, as he snapped on the gloves and then returned to the sink. Standing next to the draining board were the bottles of beer they had been drinking from all evening. Jack had made sure his were kept separate from his brother's. He paused, momentarily, before sighing and depositing a beer bottle in each bag. "Sorry," he repeated, as he sealed each one.

Jack turned away leaving the sealed bags on the draining board, ready to take into work in the morning. But, for now, he needed some sleep.

"Be careful, Jack." Chief Superintendent Dougie King's voice echoed inside Jack's head as he padded towards his bedroom. "Be careful."

* * *

Chapter Twenty

Time: 8.45am

Date: Saturday 16th February 2013

Location: Metropolitan Police HQ, London

Jack tucked the plastic evidence bags underneath his desk. He had lain awake most of the night wondering if he was doing the right thing. He could see Chief Superintendent King's disapproving stare boring into him, so he pushed the bags further out of sight with his foot. If he did this, he would be crossing a line. Not that he hadn't crossed lines before, on many an occasion, but this one...this one could well and truly trip him up and there would be no way back. He pushed the thought from his mind.

It was Saturday and technically the team were meant to be having a day off, but a murder investigation – now a double murder investigation – had no respect for personal lives. He knew that if he went down to the investigation room he would find both DS Cooper and DC Cassidy already hard at work. They would put the hours in until the job was done.

As if on cue, the door to Jack's office creaked open and DC Cassidy popped her head inside.

"We thought you might be here, guv." She pushed open the door and ushered DS Cooper in ahead of her. He was carrying a cardboard tray laden with takeaway coffee cups and several greaseproof paper bags.

"Picked these up on my way in, boss." DS Cooper deposited the cardboard tray on his own desk, and handed Jack one of the taller cups together with a paper bag that looked and smelt like it contained a bacon and egg sandwich. "Normal coffee, just milk and no fuss." He winked at Jack as he passed DC Cassidy her much smaller espresso cup.

"You know me well, Cooper," replied Jack, moving a pile of paperwork out of the way so DC Cassidy could perch on the end of his desk. "You're both in early."

DS Cooper slipped behind his desk and switched on his computer monitor. "I got a call early this morning from Jenny. She and her team worked through the night on the Danny Hopkins clothing samples."

Jack raised his eyebrows and took a sip of his coffee. "Through the night? What did you have to do to make that happen ...or do I not want to know?"

DS Cooper's cheeks reddened as he hid a sheepish look behind his computer.

"You *definitely* don't want to know, guv." DC Cassidy sipped at her tiny espresso cup and flashed a teasing smile towards him. "But if it helps us get results..."

DS Cooper cleared his throat. "Jenny ran Adrian McLeish's DNA profile against the samples from Danny Hopkins' t-shirt and jeans. No matches."

"No matches? Nothing?" Jack's eyes widened. He took a bite out of his egg and bacon sandwich. "She's sure?"

DS Cooper nodded. "There are quite a few potential samples on the clothing, apparently. Blood and semen. Other stains too. But she says none of them belong to Adrian McLeish."

Jack felt his head begin to spin, but before he had a chance to say anything else, DS Cooper continued.

"But that's not all, boss. She ran the DNA we have for both Edward and Terence Wakefield against the samples too. And guess what?" DS Cooper's eyes sparkled as he looked over his monitor towards Jack, unable to hide the grin forming on his lips.

Jack's eyes widened even further. "The Wakefields? You're kidding me?"

DS Cooper shook his head, enthusiastically. "No, boss. Straight up. She said that both Edward and Terence Wakefield's DNA showed up multiple times on both the t-shirt and the jeans." The printer in the corner of the office began to churn out paper. "I've printed the report out for you."

DC Cassidy hopped off Jack's desk and retrieved the paperwork. "What do you think it means for our investigation, guv?" Handing the report to Jack, she drained her espresso cup and dropped it into the bin. "Evidence of both of our murder victims on that poor little boy's body."

Jack shook his head, quickly scanning the report. "I'm not sure, but make sure you pass this onto DS Carmichael. He'll need to know about the links to the Wakefields."

"Jenny's running some more tests," added DS Cooper. "She said that it looked like several other DNA profiles are present, plus other fibres that they'll try and analyse today."

Jack leant back in his chair, taking another bite of his sandwich. More DNA profiles. He quickly glanced back down at the plastic evidence bags he knew were safely tucked away underneath his desk. Why does everything always come down to DNA? He pulled his gaze away from the bags. "OK, so we wait to hear back from the lab. For whatever reason, the Danny Hopkins case is linked to our double murder – it has to be. My little chat with Albert Dawson yesterday pretty much said so."

Jack paused, drumming his fingers on his desk as his mind flicked through the possibilities. How could the deaths of the Wakefields be linked to a murder thirty years ago? Revenge? If so, who by? From what he had read in the case notes, Daniel Hopkins had no family to speak of. No next of kin. Apart from the other boys at the foster home, who had possibly taken on the role of his family, he had no one. He was completely alone.

Jack looked up. "Amanda. How do you feel about a trip to Scotland?"

* * *

Time: 10.15am
   Date: Saturday 16th February 2013

Location: Metropolitan Police HQ, London

Chief Superintendent King raised his eyebrows at Jack from across the other side of his desk. "Scotland?"

Jack nodded. "I know it sounds like a long shot, but I just know that this young lad's murder is connected in some way to our investigation. I just don't know how yet."

Jack had outlined the forensic results from Daniel Hopkins' clothing, and how the samples had failed to reveal any sign of Adrian McLeish's DNA, the man currently languishing at Her Majesty's pleasure.

"It can't be just a coincidence, Sir. There has to be a link. Both of my murder victims' DNA is on that poor lad's clothing."

Chief Superintendent King nodded, slowly, leaning forwards with his elbows on his desk, resting his chin in his hands. "I see. Are you saying that the person who killed this young boy might not be Adrian McLeish?" He lowered his eyes to the brief report Jack had brought with him. "You think it was someone else? The same person who killed your two murder victims?"

Jack shrugged and shook his head. "Of that, I'm not sure. But my gut tells me they are connected. One way or another."

Chief Superintendent King brought his gaze up to meet Jack's and sighed. Jack MacIntosh. A maverick who overstepped the mark and rubbed people up the wrong way without even trying. Bending the rules, if not breaking them on occasion. But he was Jack MacIntosh. And Jack MacIntosh got results.

If Jack MacIntosh's gut was telling him something, Chief Superintendent King knew it was time to listen.

He gave a slow nod.

"OK. You've got your trip to Scotland."

* * *

Time: 1.45pm
   Date: Saturday 16th February 2013
   Location: Metropolitan Police HQ, London

Jack pushed his chair away from his desk and regarded the plastic evidence bags still languishing by his feet. Unconsciously, he started to reach towards them. It would be so easy to get an answer, once and for all. To rid himself of the unease, the doubt, the uncertainty...the suspicion. To rule him out once and for all, and then concentrate on finding the real killer of Edward and Terence Wakefield.

But he couldn't shut out the words of Chief Superintendent King echoing inside his head, on a constant, never-ending, merry-go-round.

"What if it rules them *in*, Jack?"

Jack's thoughts were interrupted by the chirping of his phone. Reaching into the pocket of his jacket, he saw that it was Isabel.

"Hi, Isabel. What can I do for you?"

"Just a call to ask what time you're coming tonight?"

Jack let a frown hover across his brow. "Tonight?"

"You've forgotten already, haven't you?" Isabel's voice was tinged with disappointment. "About my Italian evening tonight?"

"No – no, of course I haven't forgotten," replied Jack, slapping himself on the forehead. "Caught me on the hop, that's all. I'll be there."

"OK, well if you're sure. It's starting at six-thirty. But if you want to get here earlier..."

"I'll be there by six, I promise," reassured Jack. "Save me a good table."

Jack ended the call and slipped his phone back in his jacket pocket. He could do without a night out at the café, but he had promised. Part of him wondered if Stu would put in an appearance, but that would be anyone's guess right now. He had seemed all right last night, but... doubt still tugged at the back of Jack's mind.

Jack looked back down at the plastic evidence bags by his feet. Taking a deep breath, he reached for his desk phone and dialled an internal number.

"Hi – it's me. I need a favour."

* * *

Time: 5.45pm
  Date: Saturday 16th February 2013
  Location: Isabel's Café, King's Road, London

Jack took a seat at the far corner of the café, facing out towards the front door. From there he would be able to see anyone and everyone as they arrived. It was early, and there was only a handful of people milling about inside, deciding on their choice of coffee and where to sit.

Jack nursed his own coffee – a new Italian blend that Isabel had bought in especially for the evening's event. He sipped at it – it was strong and somewhat bitter. He dumped a spoonful of sugar in and gave it a stir.

Isabel was behind the counter and flashed Jack an appreciative glance as she busied herself lining up various delicacies in the display case. He saw from her expression that she was still worried about Kreshniov. Although Jack doubted it, what if he did show up? Jack was not quite sure what he would do, and took another mouthful of now-sweetened bitter coffee as he contemplated his choices. He could arrest him – there was at least enough grounds for the theft of Isabel's inheritance money, and committing murder within the walls of the Metropolitan Police, that was for sure.

Over the next hour, the café began to fill up. Jack watched the tables being laid with red, white and green tablecloths and plates of Italian antipasti were circulated to entice the visitors. For a flat fee, coffee and selected snacks were provided all evening, and from the ringing of the till it already looked as though Isabel was doing a roaring trade.

Nursing his third coffee, now getting used to the harsher taste so that it no longer needed the extra sugar, Jack surveyed the room once more. His detective instinct dismissed the female visitors in the café – Kreshniov was good at disguises, but even he wouldn't be able to pull that one off.

The rest he also dismissed. They all had the wrong stature, the wrong shape of the head, the wrong hands. A master of disguise he may well be, but Jack was sure that, so far, Kreshniov had not graced Isabel with his presence.

Sacha and Dominic were also in attendance, and as the evening progressed, Jack watched as Sacha moved with grace and efficiency through the café, delivering fresh coffee and replenishing the snacks on each table. Dominic, Jack was sure, would be hard at work in the kitchen, keeping the ovens stocked and loading and unloading the dishwasher.

The only person who was missing was Mac.

Jack shook his head and sipped his fifth coffee. He had messaged his brother several times to remind him of Isabel's theme night, and that he ought to put in an appearance. In typical Stuart MacIntosh style, the messages had gone unanswered.

Jack picked at some green olives and mozzarella. His brother was old enough to look after himself. And at this precise moment in time, Jack had a double murder investigation that was stalling, and he didn't have time for the childish ways of his younger brother. And if he was brutally honest, he didn't really have time for the hunt for the elusive Kreshniov either, although he was loathed to tell Isabel that. In his view, Kreshniov was long gone. After his brief reappearance last summer, Jack was sure that the Russian had gone to ground.

But Isabel had been insistent, and Jack had relented. An evening in the café wasn't so bad – it wasn't as though Jack had any other pressing engagements on a Saturday night, as depressing as that sounded. If he wasn't here, he would most likely still be at work, or at home with a takeaway and a couple of cans of beer – or something stronger. Instead he was enjoying a nice evening, sampling some quality coffee and food.

Jack glanced at his watch. He had been lost in his own thoughts for the last twenty minutes. He quickly glanced around the café, which was noticeably busier than when he had last looked. His heart began to pump a little faster, and not just because of the caffeine from five coffees. Sleeping on the job, MacIntosh, he chided himself.

He swept the room once again. Who had arrived in the last twenty minutes that he didn't recognise? He scoured the tables and was satisfied that he could recognise everyone who was seated. He then turned his attention to those standing in the middle of the floor, perusing the coffee menus and chatting amongst themselves. Most of them seemed young; too young to be Kreshniov, even with his skills at disguise.

Scanning the café further, Jack noticed a man standing at the counter with his back to the room. He seemed to be counting out some money, facing Sacha behind the till. Where was Isabel? Jack hurriedly glanced around but couldn't see her. His heart rate quickened even more as his gaze retuned to the lone gentleman still standing at the counter. There was something about his posture that tweaked something in Jack's memory. The way the shoulders sloped. The way he gestured with his hands. His wavy, light brown hair brushed the top of his collar, and when he glanced to the side, his profile told Jack that he was wearing some wire-rimmed spectacles.

Jack got to his feet, jostling the table as he did so. Some of his coffee spilt onto the saucer and began to soak into the thin, Italian-style biscuit that was lying there. More coffee had landed on the tablecloth, and Jack went to mop up the mess with a serviette as he squeezed himself out from behind the table.

Another glance towards the counter told him that the man was edging away. Jack threw down the soggy serviette and tried to slip past the group of latecomers who had congregated in the middle of the café. As he did so, one of them stepped sideways, right in the middle of Jack's path, blocking his view of the counter. Jack collided with the man's back.

"Oh, sorry, mate, didn't see you there," apologised the burly man, turning round to see Jack behind him. He tried to move out of the way, but as he did so, several others in the group filled the gap, themselves stepping out of the way of a customer threading their way back to their table armed with coffees and snacks. Jack cursed under his breath as he tried to peer past them; but all he could see was a wall of bodies between himself and the counter.

More prolific apologising followed, until eventually Jack was able to slip past and head towards Sacha at the till. He quickly swept the room – where had the man gone? He couldn't see anyone who looked like the rather vague description he had in his head of the man at the counter.

"The customer that was just here," asked Jack, somewhat breathlessly, switching his attention back to Sacha. "Where did he go?"

Sacha looked up from the till where she had been depositing some coins, her face pink and flushed. "What customer?"

"The one that was just here. About so-high. Wore glasses?" Jack held a hand out to just above his own head.

Sacha shrugged and shut the till. "Everyone's just a blur tonight, Jack. We're so busy." She stopped to brush a strand of hair from her glowing forehead. "We're rushed off our feet. I don't remember him, sorry."

"What did he buy?" Jack persisted, turning to scan the room once again.

"Erm..." Sacha frowned and looked down at the till roll. "Looks like a coffee – to takeaway."

To takeaway.

"Oh yes, I remember now – a takeaway coffee, and he left a large donation in Isabel's charity box, too." Sacha nodded at the Macmillan Cancer Support charity box that sat by the side of the till.

Sticking out of the top of the box was what looked like a piece of card with several notes wrapped inside. Ever the detective, even when off duty, Jack picked up the cake tongs by the display cabinet and slowly pulled the card out of the slot and let it fall to the counter. Teasing the card open, he counted out five ten pound notes. With the card fully unfolded, he took in a sharp breath.

* * *

Time: 8.15pm

Date: Saturday 16th February 2013

Location: Isabel's Café, King's Road, London

Jack shot out onto the pavement outside the café, swivelling his head from side to side. A cold, February night on the King's Road, the place was almost deserted. As far as he could see, the street was empty, except for one intrepid and dedicated jogger who was heading towards Jack, running in the direction of Sloane Square.

Jack looked beyond the jogger, seeing a lone black cab in the distance, its red brake light snapping on as it slowed down and turned, disappearing out of sight. Could the man have hailed a taxi in the time it had taken Jack to realise he was missing? Had the taxi been waiting for him outside? How long had he been gone? Ten, twenty seconds? Longer? Jack looked in the other direction and saw nothing; the road stretched away into the distance, empty and deserted.

He thought back to the piece of card he had pulled out of the charity box, causing his stomach to clench.

A post card with no writing. Just a picture on the front.

A picture of Liberec, Czech Republic.

An old haunt of Boris Kreshniov's.

Jack pulled out his phone and dialled. He wasn't surprised when the call went straight to voicemail.

"Stu? Where are you?" Jack paused, although he wasn't sure why. It wasn't as if his brother was going to suddenly pick up the phone and talk to him. "You should have been here tonight. At Isabel's. Something's happened. Call me."

* * *

Chapter Twenty-One

Time: 7.50am
Date: Sunday 17th February 2013
Location: London City Airport, London

Jack fastened his seatbelt and gripped the arm rests by his side with both hands. Flying wasn't his favourite pastime – if he'd had his way, this little sojourn up to Scotland would have been aboard a train on the East Coast mainline, where he could sit back and relax, watching the world go by outside his window.

Granted, he could watch the world go by looking out of the tiny, matchbox-sized window by his side, but cruising at thirty-odd thousand feet above the ground wasn't his idea of relaxation. He closed his eyes as he felt the aircraft change direction and taxi to the top of the runway, bumping and scraping over the tarmac as it did so.

No, the Chief Superintendent had been quite clear – "take a cheap flight out of City Airport, up and down in a day." So here he was, heart rate elevated and beads of perspiration starting to spring up on his brow.

Jack heard a not-so-well disguised snigger by his side. He opened one eye and peered sideways.

"Something amusing you, DC Cassidy?" He forced his face to remain deadpan, hiding the emerging smile that he could feel twitch at the corners of his mouth. Another snigger, even less well hidden than the first one, erupted from behind a strategically placed hand.

"Not at all, boss," she replied, failing to stop her own smile from breaking out. "It's just that you don't seem all that comfortable. Is flying not your thing?". DC Cassidy cocked her head to one side, clearly enjoying Jack's disquiet.

"I think that's abundantly clear, DC Cassidy," remarked Jack, fighting back the urge to laugh. "Flying is definitely not 'my thing'. We'll make a detective out of you yet."

"You'll be fine once we're up in the air." DC Cassidy gave Jack's hand a comforting tap as the plane's engines suddenly roared and the aircraft began to hurtle at full speed down the uneven runway.

Jack gripped the arm rest even tighter, and closed his other eye. If he had had his eyes open, he would have seen his knuckles turning whiter as his grip increased. At least the sound of the plane's engines drowned out any remaining sniggering from beside him.

The 7.40am flight from London City Airport to Edinburgh had taken off just ten minutes late, and began climbing higher and higher through the dense cloud cover above the City of London, jumping and jolting as it battered its way through to the clearer skies above.

Jack's stomach flipped as he felt the aircraft cabin shudder and drop slightly, his hands squeezing the life out of the arm rests even more tightly than before, if that were even possible.

"It's just an air pocket," explained DC Cassidy, "it'll level out soon." The snigger was now absent from her voice. "And we won't be up here very long anyway. The flight is really short."

Jack gradually opened his eyes and tentatively released his vice-like grip on the arm rests. He nodded his appreciation at DC Cassidy. It was true. The flight time was a little over an hour, something that Jack was increasingly thankful for.

"Not even enough time to get a decent drink, really," continued DC Cassidy, unfastening her seatbelt and craning her neck behind her for any sign of the cabin crew. "We might manage a cup of tea, but I was hoping for a bacon roll as I've not had breakfast yet."

The mention of food made Jack's stomach flip once more. His seatbelt remained securely fastened despite the light above his head now going 'green' to indicate that movement around the cabin was now permitted. Jack wasn't going anywhere until his feet were safely back down on terra firma. Moving he was not.

"You came up this way not so long ago, didn't you, boss?" DC Cassidy turned herself back to face Jack, giving up on trying to locate someone to get her a cup of tea. "That was in Scotland, wasn't it?"

Jack nodded and found his voice. "Indeed it was. I stayed in a small bed and breakfast place not too far from the prison we're going to today, actually. Not that you'd have known it – I was in the middle of nowhere and had no idea there was a prison anywhere nearby."

HMP Lochside was merely three miles from the Tannochside B&B and how Jack had managed not to run into it on one of his many rambles he couldn't fathom. From the map and its website, the low security prison appeared to be tucked away behind a range of hills, disappearing inconspicuously into the landscape.

"What on earth did you find to do in the middle of nowhere for six weeks?" continued DC Cassidy. "I wouldn't have lasted six days! I would have been bored out of my brain."

Jack gave a small laugh, his anxiety levels dropping as the aircraft had finally levelled out. "Believe me, I was never bored. I spent a lot of time walking, climbing a few mountains – well, I called them mountains, but apparently they were hills. The scenery was stunning. I even got into a bit of photography while I was there." Jack smiled to himself at the memories. "And I was generally just alone. It was exactly what I needed."

DC Cassidy didn't look too convinced. "But there were shops, right?"

Jack shook his head, still smiling. "Not the types of shops you mean, Amanda. There was a small village about a mile or so away – it had a convenience store, if you could call it that. Bread, milk, eggs, newspapers. That kind of thing."

"It was worth it, though?" DC Cassidy's face took on a more serious expression, her tone low and sincere. "You know...after...your sessions?"

"After my therapy, you mean?" Jack laughed again. "It's no secret, Amanda. People know I had a course of therapy. And yes, it was worth it. The solitude afterwards was just what I needed."

"And the therapy?" DC Cassidy raised her eyebrows, questioningly. "That was worth it, too?"

Jack paused, trying his best to keep the smile plastered to his face. He had practiced this look many times before – and he felt that he had it down to a fine art now. He nodded. "Yes, it was worth it, too. It worked a treat. You could say that I'm cured."

Jack was surprised at just how easily the lies tripped from his tongue. It was almost second nature. He didn't even have to think about it anymore. And for a split second, he could almost believe it to be true himself.

"Anyway, less about me." Jack swiftly changed the topic of conversation. "Let's talk about you."

"Me?"

"Yes, you. And your plans for promotion. You're Sergeant material, you know that. You should apply." Jack forgot about the bumpiness of the flight and fixed DC Cassidy in his gaze. "I mean it. You should do it."

DC Cassidy's cheeks coloured slightly and she lowered her eyes to her lap. "Maybe."

"Maybe? Why just maybe?" Jack frowned. "You've got it in you, for definite. You'd pass it easily. Why not go for promotion?"

"You'll think I'm daft." DC Cassidy's cheeks darkened further.

"Why would I think you're daft?" Jack shook his head. "You've a good brain in there – you're a great detective."

DC Cassidy paused and then gave a small shrug. "Because – well, if I got promotion to a DS then I might not be on your team anymore; maybe not even at the same station. They might move me somewhere else. I like working with you and Chris. We make a good partnership. I..." She broke off and gave another shrug. "I'm not sure I'd like working in another team as much as I like this one."

Jack's smile broadened. "Well, that's good to know. I think we make a great team, too. But just because you get promoted to a DS doesn't mean you'd instantly get assigned elsewhere. You're a great detective, Amanda, and my team needs great detectives. DS or no DS. You put that application in. That's an order."

DC Cassidy returned the smile and gave a small nod. "Boss."

The rest of the flight passed without incident, and Jack even managed to remove his grip from the arm rests completely and look out of the window. DC Cassidy secured them two scalding hot, tasteless cups of tea and then slipped some earphones into her ears to listen to some music. As he watched the clouds below, Jack also succeeded in pushing the thought of Kreshniov's possible reappearance to one side, and even the image of the Swap Shop Scarf slipped towards the back of his mind. Today was about Danny.

A short while later, the tasteless tea drunk and forgotten, Jack felt his stomach lurch as the aircraft appeared to lose height and the sound of the engines lessened. A look of alarm crossed his face.

"Ladies and gentlemen," announced the Captain over the tannoy. "We are now beginning our descent into Edinburgh. Please fasten your seatbelts."

* * *

Time: 8.30am

Date: Sunday 17th February 2013

Location: 3 Wagtail Drive, West Hampstead, London

He had watched her routine from across the road at various times over the last few days. The night carer left at 7am on the dot, and Mandy O'Sullivan from the Chiltern Care Company took over. She would arrive at 6.50am, parking her small Fiat Punto on the road outside number 3 Wagtail Drive. With a brief handover, sometimes conducted on the front doorstep, the night carer would leave and Mandy would step inside.

He brought up the small, pocket-sized binoculars to his eyes and watched through Albert Dawson's front window. Mandy could be seen flitting in and out of the front room from time to time, dusting and tidying here and there, but her main focus was usually at the back of the bungalow.

He had secured a spot in Albert Dawson's garden shed, and made sure he slipped into it before 8.30am when Mandy would draw back the curtains in the old man's room to allow him to gaze out into the garden.

So, it was there that he now settled down, watching through his binoculars as Albert Dawson received the first of his daily doses of medications. He adjusted the focus to bring Mandy into view, watching as she fussed around Albert's bedside, plumping his pillows and adjusting his sheets. She was extremely attentive to her elderly patient, of that he could not fault her. He could see her chatting away as she bustled around his bed space, although she rarely got anything back in response. How anyone could be that cheerful when surrounded by catheter bags full of urine and incontinence pads full of much worse, he could not fathom. Turning the man onto his side so that she could apply the moisture barrier cream to his bottom; changing the daily dressings on his weeping pressure sores; mopping up the vomit from his pyjamas and bedding when he couldn't tolerate his feed.

Mandy was a saint.

Which made what he was about to do prick at his conscience.

Poor Mandy would suffer; but the man she was tending to would suffer the most.

After the morning medication routine had been completed, Mandy would spend time in the kitchen, washing and sterilising. She would sometimes open the kitchen window for some fresh air, and he would hear her dulcet tones floating across the garden as she sang along to the radio. Katherine Jenkins she was not, but she could hold a tune better than most people.

Albert Dawson slept a lot. He had started to keep a diary during his days in the shed, and Albert was nothing if not predictable. He would nap at regular intervals throughout the day, but his longest sleep of the day would usually come just after lunchtime – between two and four o'clock in the afternoon.

It was during that time, he had noted with increased curiosity, that Mandy would often slip out of the bungalow and hurry down to the shops around the corner. He had followed her on a couple of occasions, noting her regular purchase of a gossip magazine, several chocolate bars and a scratch card from the newsagents. She then liked to have a few minutes chatting with the person behind the till, before making her way back to the bungalow. She was never gone for very long – he had timed her and worked out she spent on average twenty-four minutes away from Albert Dawson.

Twenty-four minutes.

That was more than enough time for what he had planned for the old man.

* * *

Time: 12.15pm

Date: Sunday 17th February 2013

Location: HMP Lochside, Scotland

The prison was set some five hundred metres back from the nearest road – and even that was only a private access road, itself some three miles from the nearest form of habitation. If you didn't know it was there, HMP Lochside was invisible.

Travelling along the access road in their Ford Focus estate hire car, DC Cassidy clung onto the door handle as they bounced in and out of yet another pothole.

"Jeez, doesn't look like this road sees much traffic," she commented, as Jack weaved around a particularly deep looking hole in the centre of the track.

It was a single carriageway road, but they weren't in any danger of meeting anything coming from the opposite direction. The scenery on either side was dense woodland, and the track stretched away into the distance and over the horizon. The only movement they saw was a herd of deer hovering by the edge of a clump of trees, warily eyeing the newcomers as they passed by.

"Nice setting though," added Jack, gazing out through the windscreen.

"Damn site better than Holloway or the Scrubs."

DC Cassidy nodded in agreement and lowered her eyes to the folder sitting on her lap. She flicked it open and re-read the sparse details.

"Adrian McLeish – born in June 1958. Makes him almost fifty-five. Convicted in 1982 of the murder of Daniel Hopkins, aged eleven. Jailed for life. Hasn't made parole due to his inability to accept his guilt and refusal to participate in any offender rehabilitation programmes." DC Cassidy paused and looked up from the folder. "Can they do that? Refuse him parole just because he maintains his innocence?"

"They can't really refuse parole just on that basis – but it makes the job of the Probation Service a damn site harder," replied Jack, cresting the horizon to enable them to see HMP Lochside in the distance. "I would suggest it's more due to the fact that he's not cooperating on any rehabilitation programmes - that'll be the real sticking point. I mean – you're a convicted child killer but you won't take part in any programmes to satisfy the authorities that you won't re-offend? It would be a brave probation officer who signed off that parole release, wouldn't you think?"

"I guess," replied DC Cassidy. "Now you put it like that." She looked up at the impressive façade that was getting closer by the second. "He's spent the last twelve years of his sentence here. Moved due to his family living nearby in Stirling."

They approached the outer security gate, manned by two bored looking security guards who ticked them off on their visitors' log and waved them through the gate. A more thorough security check was made at the second gate, where they were stopped by two further security guards, and an Alsatian dog sniffed inside and outside the car. One of the guards, an officer that wouldn't have looked out of place in the Royal Marines, took a long handled mirror and proceeded to check the underside of the car.

"Can't be too careful these days," explained the muscled security guard, catching the intrigued look on DC Cassidy's face. "Not with everything that's going on in the world. We might be stuck out in the middle of nowhere, but everyone's a target."

The second security check passed, they continued their journey along a short track into a small parking area and then headed across to the main entrance. More security checks and they were at last admitted inside the prison.

Although the building had looked relatively old from the outside, on the inside it was all modern sliding security doors with electronic keypads, and CCTV cameras at every turn. Jack and DC Cassidy were taken along a main corridor that was wide and airy, through three more sets of electronic security doors, and further into the depths of the prison itself. There was a calm feeling all around them, and it was surprisingly quiet. Jack compared it to the bangs and clatters of his trip to Belmarsh to see Jason Alcock. An entirely different world. An entirely different planet almost.

They were introduced to the Governor – Deborah Levy – who shook both their hands, vigorously, leaving Jack with no doubt as to who was in charge.

"The majority of the inmates are at exercise at the moment," Ms Levy explained. "Hence it's quite quiet. But it is a relatively calm place for the majority of the time. We pride ourselves in running a harmonious environment, where the inmates respect one another." She smiled and gestured for both Jack and DC Cassidy to take a seat in the visitors' chairs opposite her desk.

Jack nodded as he sat. Harmony and respect. A somewhat elusive combination in most of the prisons Jack had visited in his career. "Thank you for seeing us," he added.

"We generally house prisoners who are coming up for parole. Many go out on day-release into the community to prepare them for the outside world. We don't see an awful lot of trouble here. Coffee?" Ms Levy nodded towards a coffee percolator on an adjacent desk.

Jack shook his head. "No, thank you, Ms Levy. We're fine. We don't want to take up too much of your day."

"So, I gather you would like to speak with Adrian McLeish?" Ms Levy addressed the question towards Jack, but cast a smile in DC Cassidy's direction. "May I ask why?"

"His name has come up in an ongoing investigation," explained Jack, keeping to the rehearsed and practiced speech he and DC Cassidy had prepared earlier. "We're investigating a double murder and we would just like to ask him a few routine questions. If you don't mind."

"Of course," replied Ms Levy, rising to her feet. "Not a problem. I'll get one of the officers to take you along to the visitors' room to see him. He's waiting for you." She gestured for Jack and DC Cassidy to follow her.

"Isn't he outside on exercise with the others?" enquired DC Cassidy, as they exited the room and followed Ms Levy along the corridor.

The Governor was well-dressed in a tailored grey pin-stripe suit - tapered trousers and a beige shirt beneath a close-fitting jacket. Her hair was scraped up from her face and fixed into a high bun atop a well-made up face with high cheekbones. The sound of her high-heeled boots echoed along the deserted corridor.

"Adrian doesn't generally mix with the other inmates – he has his own exercise times, away from other prisoners." Ms Levy stopped at a security door and used the electronic keypad to unlock it. The door slid open and Ms Levy led Jack and DC Cassidy through. "It's for his own safety as much as his own choice."

"I thought you said this was a calm prison – that you don't get a lot of trouble?" Jack raised an eyebrow at DC Cassidy. "Why would he be in danger?"

"Oh, I wouldn't go so far as to call it danger," replied Ms Levy, the electronic door sliding shut behind them. "Adrian struggles with social situations and finds it difficult to interact with others. Other inmates can sometimes misunderstand him and his gestures, and that in turn can lead to friction. We found that letting him have his own space is the best way of dealing with it." She paused and flashed another smile at Jack. "We're lucky that we have the space here to accommodate him."

They carried on along the corridor and approached a further set of doors; this time they were manned by a stout-looking prison officer holding a clipboard.

"I shall now leave you in the capable hands of Gary, here." Ms Levy nodded and smiled at her visitors once more. "I'll see you before you leave." With that, she turned on her heels and tapped her way back along the corridor, disappearing out of sight.

The prison officer known as Gary grinned broadly at Jack and DC Cassidy, clearly pleased to see some visitors. He brandished the clipboard, pulling out a pen from his top pocket. "Greetings, both of you," he said, in a broad Glaswegian accent. "If I can get yous both to sign your names here, I can get you through the door."

Jack took the clipboard and pen, scribbling a signature next to both of their names which were already printed, together with the date and time.

"Perfect." Gary began unlocking the door and then ushered both Jack and DC Cassidy through. "It's the first door on your right, just there. Go right in – he's waiting for you." Gary nodded at the door in front of them, and re-secured the door behind them. "I'll just be out here."

Jack was the first to step into the visitors' room and see Adrian McLeish for the first time.

And he wasn't at all what he expected.

* * *

Time: 1.00pm
Date: Sunday 17th February 2013
Location: HMP Lochside, Scotland

Adrian McLeish sat behind a Formica table, dressed in a plain white t-shirt and blue jeans. Although almost fifty-five, his appearance had a baby-faced quality to it – a moon-shaped face with full lips and a child-like smile. His cornflower blue eyes twinkled at Jack and DC Cassidy as they took their seats opposite him.

"Hello, Adrian. My name is Jack MacIntosh. I'm a police officer with the Metropolitan Police in London." Jack tried a smile of his own. "And this here is my colleague – Amanda Cassidy. She's with the Metropolitan Police, too."

"Hello, I'm Adrian." Adrian McLeish's smile broadened even further. "London! I'm going to go to London – my mum is going to take me. We're going to have tea and cake and go to the zoo!" He paused, his sparkling eyes darting from Jack to DC Cassidy and back again. "They told me I had visitors! I don't get many visitors!"

Adrian McLeish was almost bouncing out of his seat with excitement.

"Do you know why we're here, Adrian? Can I call you Adrian?" asked Jack, pulling the folder that DC Cassidy had brought in from the car across the table and opening it up.

Adrian McLeish nodded his head, energetically. "My name is Adrian – my friends call me Ade. My friend Toby calls me Ade. He comes to see me. You can call me Ade, too."

"OK, Adrian – Ade – I'm going to ask you a few questions from quite a long time ago." Jack paused and tried to hold Adrian McLeish's gaze in his own. "But if you can't remember, or you don't want to answer, then you don't have to. Is that OK?"

Adrian McLeish carried on nodding, rocking back and forth in his chair like an excited schoolboy.

"Ade, do you remember a place called St Bartholomew's Home for Boys?"

* * *

Chapter Twenty-Two

Time: 1.15pm
   Date: Sunday 17th February 2013
   Location: HMP Lochside, Scotland

"I didn't go there that day," replied Adrian McLeish, the twinkle vanishing from his eyes. "I told the policeman that. I didn't go there. Not that day."

Jack nodded. "I'm sure you did tell the policeman that." He looked down at the brief confession statement that was slotted inside the folder. There was no mention of Adrian McLeish denying being at St Bartholomew's on the day of Danny's murder; in fact, quite the opposite. "But I think they must have written it down wrong. Why do you think they were saying that you *did* go there? Why did they say that, Ade, when you told them that you didn't?"

Adrian McLeish frowned a little, his wide forehead wrinkling with thought. "Because they don't like me. None of them like me. They all think I'm stupid." Adrian paused and looked down at the table. "That bad man. He didn't like me at all."

"What bad man?" Jack raised his eyebrows and glanced sideways at DC Cassidy.

"The one in charge. The one that used to tell me what to do in the garden." Adrian McLeish's eyes remained cloudy. "He didn't like me at all. He used to hit me when no one else was looking." Adrian began rubbing at his forearms.

263

"He was a very bad man."

Jack pulled out a photograph of both Edward and Terence Wakefield, along with one of Albert Dawson. He knew that technically any identification wouldn't be valid, but he had a hunch which one Adrian McLeish would be picking, no matter how many photographs he showed him. "Can you see the bad man in one of these photographs, Adrian?"

Adrian McLeish leant closer towards the table, studying the pictures for several seconds. Then he raised his hand and stabbed a finger at the photograph of Edward Wakefield.

"That's the bad man," he confirmed, nodding his head. "He was a very bad man."

Jack slipped the photographs back inside the folder. "Did you know Daniel Hopkins?"

Adrian McLeish was silent for a moment and then nodded his head, slowly. "Danny. Yes, Danny. He died."

"Did you know him before the police came to see you? Had you spoken to him before at the home?"

Adrian shook his head, vigorously. "The bad man would keep me away from the other boys. He said that I would scare them."

"OK. So – on the day that Danny died – at your trial you said that you were home alone, that your mum had gone to stay with your grandmother overnight because she was ill? Is that right?"

Adrian McLeish nodded, the light returning to his eyes. "Granny wasn't well. I liked Granny. She always gave me pocket money to buy toffees."

Jack returned to the folder and brought out Adrian McLeish's confession statement. "The thing is, Adrian – Ade – when you spoke to the policeman you agreed that you *had* killed Danny and that you *had* gone to St Bartholomew's that night. And the policeman wrote it all down on this piece of paper." Jack turned the statement around to face Adrian across the table. "And then you signed it. Do you know why you did that?"

Adrian McLeish flicked his eyes towards the statement and he began to shift, nervously, in his chair. "Because he told me to."

"Who told you to?"

"The policeman. He told me that if I said I did it, then I could go home."

Jack nodded. "But he didn't let you go home, did he?"

Adrian McLeish's eyes began to well up, tears sprouting at their corners, and his bottom lip began to quiver.

"It's OK," soothed DC Cassidy, reaching across the table and placing a comforting hand on Adrian's forearm. "We're here to help you."

"I know you didn't kill Danny Hopkins, Adrian," agreed Jack, placing the confession back in the folder. "And as soon as we find out who did, we'll help you get out of here."

Adrian McLeish's moonlike face lit up, his eyes shining, not just from the tears but from added happiness. "And I can go home?"

Jack nodded. "In time, yes, you can go home. We just have to catch the really bad man who did this, first." Jack let his eyes fall on the photographs of Edward and Terence Wakefield before he closed the folder. "One more thing, Adrian. Ade. At your trial – the policeman said that your sweatshirt was with Danny when they found him. Do you know how it got there?"

Adrian McLeish shook his head again. "I don't know. The policeman asked me again and again. It got very confusing. It was a hot day and I took it off. I don't remember anymore."

Jack indicated to DC Cassidy that they were done.

"We're going to call in on your mum before we go back to London, Ade," added DC Cassidy, following Jack's lead and standing up. "Does she come and visit you here often?"

Adrian McLeish nodded, happily. "Every two weeks. On a Saturday. She brings me cake."

"Well, we'll remind her to bring one with her next time she visits, is that OK, Ade?"

Adrian McLeish looked up, his cheeks shiny with wet tears, and beamed. "Dundee cake. Tell her Dundee cake. It's my favourite!"

* * *

Time: 2.34pm
   Date: Sunday 17th February 2013
   Location: 3 Wagtail Drive, West Hampstead, London

Mandy left the bungalow at precisely 2.34pm. Just as he had expected her to. He waited until she had walked to the end of the road and turned out of the quiet cul-de-sac, disappearing out of sight. He quickly and quietly slipped out of his car, having taken the opportunity to vacate the shed when Mandy was setting up Albert's feed and had her back turned towards the garden. He jogged across the road towards number three. He'd already assessed that the best point of entry would be from the rear — those floor to ceiling patio windows would be a breeze to break into. He walked up the garden path without even looking over his shoulder, and followed it around to the back garden.

He looked at his watch. 2.36pm.

The quickest Mandy had ever been was nineteen minutes, so he still had plenty of time. He cornered the side of the bungalow and edged across the patio, taking a quick peek through the window to see Albert Dawson lying flat on his back, eyes closed and mouth open.

Fast asleep.

As expected.

He reached into his pocket and pulled out a multi-purpose tool. With gloved hands, he got to work on the patio door lock. It would be a simple job; there was only one central lock and no bolts. He worked quickly and silently, and within two minutes the lock gave a satisfying click.

Taking hold of the handle at the side, he gently slid the door open, hearing only a faint gliding noise as he did so. Albert Dawson remained asleep, unaware of his intruder.

2.39pm

Once the patio door had slid back sufficiently, he slipped noiselessly inside the bungalow, one soft boot hitting Albert Dawson's plush carpet, followed by the other. The room was cramped, without much space to manoeuvre. He stepped around the one chair that was by the side of the bed and approached

CHAPTER TWENTY-TWO

Albert's bedside. Still the old man snored on.

2.40pm

Slipping the multi-tool back into his pocket, he exchanged it for some-thing sharper. The knife gleamed in the low-lying sunlight that had followed him into the room. He leant closer to the sleeping Albert Dawson and stood studying his face for a while. He hadn't laid eyes on the man for some thirty years – and standing there, watching the man breathe contentedly, stirred unwanted and unbidden emotions from within.

The Wakefields had been bad.

But Albert Dawson had been worse.

He allowed Eddie Wakefield to run the foster home as his own personal playground; facilitating the abuse of numerous boys supposedly under his care, turning a blind eye to the cruelty being inflicted.

No – Albert Dawson was worse. Much worse.

And Albert Dawson needed to pay.

2.43pm

He held the knife less than an inch from the old man's nose, and began to roughly shake him awake. It would have been easy to cut the man's throat as he lay sleeping, quickly and quietly ending his life. But Albert Dawson didn't deserve an easy end to his life. He needed to face the end, and see it coming.

He shook the old man's shoulders and Albert Dawson began to splutter as he was roused from his deep sleep. His watery blue eyes fluttered open, and a frown crossed his already deeply-lined forehead. He began to make a gurgling sound, disgruntled at being disturbed.

For a moment, the expression on Albert Dawson's face was one of confusion.

Then, it turned to one of fear.

* * *

Time: 2.35pm
   Date: Sunday 17th February 2013
   Location: HMP Lochside, Scotland

"So how did that sweatshirt end up with Danny Hopkins' body? That's the only thing that links him to the murder." DC Cassidy resumed clutching at the dashboard as they made their way, bumpily, back towards the main road. "We now know his DNA isn't there."

"That and his so-called confession," agreed Jack, taking the Ford Focus around a particularly deep-looking pot hole.

"That confession isn't worth the paper it's written on," commented DC Cassidy, pulling the sun visor down as the low lying sun sent bright shears of sunlight directly into their faces. "It should never have been allowed."

Jack nodded, slowing down as they passed another herd of deer watching them from the treeline to their left. "In today's world, yes – but things were very different back then. The police force and the legal system was an entirely different machine."

Jack steadily steered the car past the deer, HMP Lochside disappearing into the distance behind them. After another mile and a half, they came to the junction with the main A84. He swung the car left, in the direction of Stirling. It would only be about half an hour's drive to Mrs McLeish's house.

"What will you do? About Adrian?" DC Cassidy relaxed back in her seat, no longer needing to brace herself against a pot-hole strewn road. The A84 looked like it had recently been resurfaced. "We're both convinced he didn't kill Danny Hopkins, correct? You think it was the Wakefields?"

Jack gave a slow nod. "But what I think doesn't really matter. I'll hand it over. Technically it's a closed case – so I'll let someone else take the bold decision to re-open it. It'll probably go before the Criminal Cases Review Commission."

The rest of the drive passed by in comfortable silence. DC Cassidy fiddled with the radio, finding a local radio station playing what sounded like a medley of Scottish folk music. Initially, she had turned her nose up and gone to switch it over, but Jack swiped her hand away and proceeded to drum

268

his fingers on the steering wheel along with the music while the countryside swept by outside.

Neither of them had thought far enough ahead to have brought any food with them, and by the time they drew up outside the home of Mrs Isla McLeish, both of their stomachs were grumbling loudly.

Number twelve was a neat-looking chalet-style bungalow, set back from the road. Jack looked along the street at a number of identical looking bungalows, the only difference being perhaps the colour of the front door, or the curtains hanging in the windows. Each had a square, pocket-sized front garden laid to lawn, edged by a white picket fence.

DC Cassidy led the way up the garden path, and gave the front door a quick tap. Almost immediately, the door was pulled open and a smiling face greeted them. "Lovely to meet you both," spoke Mrs McLeish, her soft Edinburgh lilt spilling from her mouth. "Do come in." She stepped backwards to allow Jack and DC Cassidy room to cross the threshold.

Mrs McLeish was a small woman; tiny, in fact. Jack estimated she could be no more than four foot ten in her stockinged feet. She had a slender face, with a delicate nose, but she had the same cornflower blue eyes as her son. He glanced down and saw that she was wearing a pair of floral slippers, encasing tiny, pixie-like feet. She was small-boned, and had a crisp white apron tied around her narrow waist.

The smell of fresh baking wafted through from the kitchen beyond, and DC Cassidy's eyes shone as the aroma hit her nostrils. Her stomach grumbled in anticipation. "Something smells nice, Mrs McLeish," she said, stepping further into the hallway towards the enticing scent. "Have you been baking?"

Mrs McLeish smiled and shuffled in her slippers along the narrow corridor, waving at Jack and DC Cassidy to follow. "Please come through. And call me Isla." She led them into a small living room, the floral theme from her slippers continuing in the drapes that hung from the curtain poles and the upholstery on the two-seater sofa and single high backed armchair. "Please, take a seat. I'll be away and bring us in some tea. You'll take some tea, won't you?"

Both Jack and DC Cassidy nodded. "That would be really kind, Mrs McLeish...Isla," replied Jack, correcting himself and taking a seat in the armchair. "If it's no trouble."

"Ach, away with you," flapped Mrs McLeish, turning in her slippers and making her way back towards the kitchen. "There's no trouble in a pot of tea."

The kettle must have been freshly boiled before Jack and DC Cassidy had arrived as, within a few moments, Mrs McLeish bustled back with a tray laden down with a china teapot and three cups with saucers, along with a separate milk jug and sugar bowl. As soon as she placed the tea down on the coffee table she hurried back to the kitchen to bring in two further plates piled high with what must have been her morning's baking.

"You'll have some cake with your tea?" said Mrs McLeish, placing the plates next to the tray. "I'm sure you must both be hungry. Please, help yourselves."

"Oh my, Isla," grinned DC Cassidy, her eyes widening at the treats on display. She had seated herself on the sofa, and leant forwards to breathe in the aroma. "Did you make all of this yourself?"

Mrs McLeish nodded, her blue eyes shining whilst her cheeks pinked. "Ach, it was nothing." She perched herself next to DC Cassidy on the sofa and tucked a strand of grey, wispy hair behind her ear. "Just a few bits and pieces. I always do my baking on a Sunday. Adrian likes his Dundee cake, as he probably told you."

"Indeed he did," nodded DC Cassidy, reaching forwards to pick up a freshly baked wedge of Dundee cake. "I said we would remind you to bring one to him on your next visit."

Mrs McLeish chuckled to herself and began pouring the tea. The smile on her face didn't quite reach her eyes this time. "I haven't forgotten to bring him his cake in thirty years. A fresh Dundee cake, every fortnight."

"It must be hard for you, Isla." Jack glanced around the small living room, noting how every available surface was adorned with framed family photographs. There were some older ones; black and white pictures of a toothless, grinning baby, and others of a toddler sitting on various family members' laps. Others were in colour, all depicting a young man beaming out at the camera. Jack recognised the wide lipped smile, and the innocent cornflower blue eyes twinkling out of a round, moon shaped face. He noticed there were no recent pictures.

"Yes, indeed." Mrs McLeish cleared her throat, gently, and passed one of the teacups to DC Cassidy. "Adrian's father – my husband Archie – he passed away some years ago now."

"You don't have any other children?" DC Cassidy balanced her teacup on her knee and bit into the rich fruit cake.

Mrs McLeish shook her head. "No. We always thought we would have more. Always intended to have more. Archie wanted a house full. But..." She paused, standing up to pass another teacup to Jack. "Well, Adrian was such a special little boy. We knew that from the moment he was born. He took a lot of looking after in the early days – I don't think I would have been able to cope with another child." She sat back down next to DC Cassidy and sipped her own tea. "And then Archie became ill...so, another child was not really on the cards."

DC Cassidy nodded, licking the cake crumbs from her fingers. "Well, he's a very special young man. We had a very pleasant conversation with him earlier today."

"Which is really the purpose of our visit, Mrs McLeish." Jack took a drink from his tea cup and placed it back down on the coffee table. "I'm sorry if we're dragging unpleasant memories back up again, but can you tell us anything else about the day of Daniel Hopkins' disappearance? We note from the trial transcript that you weren't at home that night?"

Mrs McLeish continued sipping her tea, her composure steady. The only clue as to the painful nature of the memories now being resurrected was a cloudiness in her eyes, and a sombre tone that entered her voice.

"That's true, I wasn't, Inspector. And I have to live with that for the rest of my life. If I had been there..." She broke off and blinked away the moisture from her eyes. "Things could have been so very different."

Jack nodded. "You stated that you were at your mother's house that night – attending to her as she was unwell?"

"Yes," confirmed Mrs McLeish, dabbing at her eyes with a cotton handkerchief. "She had had a fall. She wasn't in the best of health anyway, so I went to stay with her overnight."

"Was that something you did regularly? Leaving Adrian home alone overnight?" Jack picked his cup up once more and drained the rest of his tea. He eyed DC Cassidy reaching for a piece of freshly baked golden shortbread.

Mrs McLeish gave a small nod. "Like I told the officers at the time. Adrian was perfectly capable of being left alone for short periods; he was more than capable of looking after himself. Archie – my husband – was working away on the oil rigs, so it was often just me and Adrian by ourselves. I'd been to my mother's overnight before. Adrian is fine and perfectly safe on his own so long as he can keep to his routines."

"And there would have been no way, in your opinion, that he could have left the house and got himself over to Bartholomew's?"

Mrs McLeish shook her head quite forcefully. "No. Not at all. There is no way Adrian would have done anything that wasn't part of his routine." She paused and drank from her tea cup. "It was a Sunday. I left him watching his favourite TV programme. He would then have heated up his dinner at 6.30pm – I left him a chicken and mushroom pie, as he always had chicken and mushroom pie on a Sunday. After dinner he would read two of his favourite comics and then change into his pyjamas. He would be in bed by 9.30pm. He was as regular as clockwork."

"And there is no way that he would have left the house?"

Mrs McLeish continued to shake her head. "No, never. He couldn't have found his way to St Bartholomew's anyway – he would have to have taken two buses."

"That crossed my mind when I was reading the witness statements," agreed Jack. "Your house was some distance from St Bartholomew's."

Mrs McLeish nodded. "We were about twelve miles outside Christchurch at the time – in a small village. It would have taken two buses to get him even close to that foster home, and even then they didn't run on a Sunday."

"So how did he normally get to St Bartholomew's?" asked DC Cassidy, washing down her piece of shortbread with another cup of tea. "On the days that he went to do his voluntary work?"

"The charity that organised the work – they ran a minibus," replied Mrs McLeish. "They would come to pick him up and then bring him home at the end of the day. He would never have known how to get there himself."

"From looking at the evidence, Mrs McLeish, the case seems to have been decided on Adrian's confession and his sweatshirt that was found with Danny's body." Jack paused. "And the fact that no one can corroborate his whereabouts that night."

"That confession was beaten out of him." Mrs McLeish wiped away a tear that had formed in the corner of her eye. "They told him he could go home if he signed it. He has the mental age of a child of eight, Inspector. He will do exactly as you tell him to."

Jack nodded, and gave what he hoped was a sympathetic smile. "I'm sorry. Police procedures were very different at that time – and juries were often swayed by even the flimsiest of evidence if it was backed up by a confession."

"What about the sweatshirt, Isla?" added DC Cassidy. "A lot hinged on the fact that it was found with Danny. Adrian confirmed it was his."

Mrs McLeish sighed. "Yes, it was his. You could tell from the photographs – I had sewn a patch onto the elbow. And in any event, his name was on the label."

"But you have no idea how it happened to be found with Danny?" DC Cassidy felt the woman shudder next to her on the sofa.

"No." Mrs McLeish's voice was barely a whisper. "Adrian didn't come home with it one day. I don't remember when exactly. I asked him what he had done with it, but he couldn't remember."

* * *

Time: 1.30pm
Date: Saturday March 6th 1982
Location: St Bartholomew's Home for Boys, Christchurch

Adrian McLeish liked working in the greenhouses. In the summer he liked watering the vegetables and picking the tomatoes off the tomato plants when they were bright red and juicy. He was good at tomato picking - he knew not to pick them when they were small and green, because they wouldn't taste very nice. The bad man had told him that. He also liked putting the tiny little seeds into the earth and watching them grow.

But there was one thing that he didn't like about working in the green-houses; they were so very very hot.

Although it was only early March, the sun was out and, with no clouds in the sky, the heat was baking down onto the glass frames of the main greenhouse where Adrian was doing his first batch of watering. He could feel the sweat running down his face and dripping off his chin. He rubbed his saturated brow with the sleeve of his sweatshirt and carried on watering. The sound of the water made him feel very thirsty, and made him feel even hotter.

The greenhouse was full of lettuces, cucumbers, peas and beans, carefully nurtured and protected from the cold, frosty nights. Adrian's job was to carefully water each and every plant; row after row after row.

When he had finished watering the final row of lettuces, he put the watering can down and pulled his sweatshirt up and over his head. He had a t-shirt on underneath so he was sure it would be all right. If he had only been wearing a vest, his mum would have told him off.

Adrian felt instantly cooler, and picked up the watering can once more. He folded the sweatshirt up and placed it on a wooden potting bench by the door, so that he would remember to pick it up when he went home. After watering the lettuces, his next job was the peas. He went to the tap and filled the watering can up to the brim and headed over to where the plants were spaced out in neat lines.

He didn't really like peas. They were green, and Adrian didn't really like green things.

He liked red things. Like red tomatoes.

Adrian couldn't wait for the summer when the greenhouse would be full of tomato plants, climbing steadily towards the glass ceiling, giving off that lovely tomato-scent. He smiled to himself as he started watering the soil around the peas. He couldn't wait to have the job of picking the ripest and juiciest tomatoes.

Red and shiny.

Not green.

Definitely not green.

* * *

Time: 2.43pm

Date: Sunday 17th February 2013

Location: Fraser's Newsagents, West Hampstead, London

Mandy O'Sullivan lingered by the confectionery counter, unable to make up her mind. She had already chosen a copy of Look magazine, as it had an article on Tom Daley's new TV show 'Splash!'. She had enjoyed watching the slightly mediocre Saturday night show, which had just finished its first series, even if it was mostly just to see Tom in his skimpy swimming trunks. The magazine also had a Downton Abbey special, another one of her guilty pleasures.

She hovered over the chocolate bars, unsure which one she should pick. She fancied a nice cup of tea when she got back – Albert would be dead to the world for at least another hour. She could catch up on all the celebrity gossip and have a quick chocolate fix at the same time. Unable to decide, and conscious of the time, she plumped for a large bar of Cadbury's Dairy Milk and a packet of Maltesers.

Already looking forward to putting her feet up, Mandy headed towards the till, pulling her purse from her bag. She glanced at the scratch cards but resolved to be good; she spent far too much money on them, mostly for little excitement or reward. No, she would do a couple of lucky dips on

Saturday instead.

Smiling at Barbara, the middle-aged shop assistant behind the till, Mandy placed her purchases on the counter.

"Hello, Mandy," greeted Barbara, scanning the barcodes on the magazine and chocolate bars. "How's Albert today?"

"He's doing well, thank you, Barbara." Mandy began rummaging in her purse for some loose change. "I'll be glad when the weather picks up, though. It looks like we're in for some more sleet or snow soon. I can't wait for Spring, to be able to open the windows for him."

Barbara nodded, her large hooped earrings clinking as she did so. "It has certainly been a cold one lately. That's £3.25."

Mandy counted out the coins and passed them across to Barbara's outstretched hand. "There you go." She scooped up her magazine and slipped the chocolate into her shoulder bag. "How's your husband these days?"

"Oh, he's much better now, thank you. We were all concerned for a while, thinking it might be something serious. Well you do, don't you? All the articles they have in these magazines, and in the newspapers."

"So, it wasn't cancer in the end?" Mandy leant up against the counter.

Barbara shook her head, her earrings swinging back and forth. "No. Turned out he had haemorrhoids! That's what all the bleeding was. But I'm glad he went to have it checked out. You can't be too careful, these days, can you?"

"Absolutely," agreed Mandy. "You read about it all the time, don't you? People ignoring the signs until it's too late." Mandy glanced down at her magazine, where she seemed to get most of her information from these days. "I was only reading about something the other day..."

Barbara glanced up as a customer entered the shop and headed straight towards the till. "I'd better crack on, Mandy."

Mandy took a look at her watch and nodded. "Yes, I'd better get back. I don't like leaving Albert on his own for too long. Although what he could get up to in my absence I'll never know!"

"See you tomorrow, Mandy. Take care."

Mandy tucked her magazine under her arm and headed back in the direction of Wagtail Drive, already looking forward to a fresh pot of tea and a bit of Tom Daley.

* * *

Time: 2.46pm
 Date: Sunday 17th February 2013
 Location: 3 Wagtail Drive, West Hampstead, London

The knife slid cleanly through the old man's wasted thigh. Years confined to bed with MS had caused whatever muscles he had to fade away.

But he could still feel pain.

The knife cut, jaggedly, deep into the flesh; blood seeped out and dripped onto the incontinence sheets below. Albert Dawson began to wriggle, but his frail frame was no match for the muscular arm that was pinning him down.

The old man tried to speak, gasping for breath – but the pressure of the arm across his chest made his lungs struggle to inflate. His face contorted in pain and shock.

2.47pm.

The knife continued its journey, carving haphazardly into the man's wizened skin. Only when he was happy with the result did he turn his attention to the old man's face and finally speak.

"This is from us," he murmured, staring deeply into Albert Dawson's rheumy eyes. "This is from the Fifteen. And from Danny."

He dangled the bloodied blade in front of Albert Dawson's face, watching as the old man's eyes widened to the extent that his eyeballs might pop out of their sockets. Fear penetrated every pore of his being, and he began to shake, violently beneath his flimsy pyjamas.

Smiling to himself, he let the blade linger for a few more seconds, delighting in the horror crossing the old man's face as he contemplated his own death. Chuckling, he snapped the blade shut and returned it to his pocket.

That would be too easy. Too clean. Too humane. He needed to see Albert Dawson suffer – just as so many boys had suffered under his care. How Danny had suffered.

He momentarily felt a pang of sorrow for Mandy. She would most likely lose her job – leaving a patient in her care was most probably in breach of her employment terms. She was a kind and caring person, good at her job. It was unfortunate that she would end up suffering as well as Albert.

He shook thoughts of Mandy from his head and turned his attention back to the old man cowering in front of him. With a gloved hand, he reached up and smothered Albert Dawson's face, pressing down on his nose and mouth.

The old man began to struggle, trying to move his head from side to side to dislodge the gloved hand – but any efforts he made would be futile. And Albert Dawson knew that. His eyes showed that he knew that.

A second gloved hand held the old man's head steady, while the first continued to press down harder and harder on his nose and mouth.

Albert continued to struggle for breath, but he was weak. His lungs screamed out for oxygen, but none was going to come in time to save him. His struggles became less and less, the muted murmurings from his mouth fainter and fainter, until he stopped moving altogether. His chest rose and fell for the final time, devoid of oxygen and now devoid of life.

2.50pm

* * *

Time: 4.15pm
  Date: Sunday 17th February 2013
  Location: 12 Heatherbank Drive, Stirling

There was silence for a few moments. Jack indicated to DC Cassidy that it was maybe time for them to leave. "Thank you for seeing us, Mrs McLeish," he said, getting to his feet. "We'll leave you to get on. We've a plane to catch." He glanced at his watch – their flight was at 6.15pm. They would have to get a move on.

"What happens now?" Mrs McLeish stood up, her eyes searching Jack's. "You do believe me, don't you? That my Adrian didn't kill that poor, wee boy?"

Jack nodded. "I don't believe he did, Mrs McLeish. Isla. And we'll do whatever we can to put things right."

"He would never have touched a hair on that wee bairn's head, and that's the truth." Mrs McLeish followed Jack and DC Cassidy out into the hallway, as they headed for the front door. "He's a gentle giant, is my Adrian. He wouldn't hurt a fly."

* * *

Time: 7.45pm
　Date: Sunday 17th February 2013
　Location: City Airport, London

Jack turned up the collar of his coat as he stepped out of the terminal building into a wall of sleet. The forecast had predicted a warm front crossing the south-east overnight, but to Jack it didn't feel very warm. The freezing rain stung his cheeks as he followed DC Cassidy in the direction of the taxi rank. As he jogged towards the road, he felt his mobile begin to vibrate in his pocket.

DC Cassidy had already managed to bag a taxi and was standing on the pavement, hopping from foot to foot, gesturing for Jack to hurry up. Leaving his phone to ring through to voicemail, Jack turned his face into the wind and quickened his step.

Once inside, he slammed the door shut and collapsed onto the leather seat.

"Welcome back to England," laughed DC Cassidy, shaking the frozen rain from her hair. "Scotland's weather was better than this!"

Jack smiled, brushing the sleet from his coat and peering out of the misted up windows. "And it's not often we can say that." London looked dark and drab. And cold. It was at times like this that he missed his fireside whisky with Willie McArthur.

As the taxi made its way back towards the station, Jack fished out his phone and noticed that, while they were in the air, DS Cooper had messaged him twice and had now also left a voicemail. Jack read the latest text message first, the words sending a shiver down his spine that had nothing to do with the freezing wet weather outside.

Albert Dawson was dead.

* * *

Time: 9.00pm
Date: Sunday 17th February 2013
Location: 3 Wagtail Drive, West Hampstead, London

The sleet had eased off but it had already soaked through to Jack's shirt beneath his coat. It stuck, uncomfortably to his back as he stepped out of the taxi. It was only a short walk up the neatly kept garden path to number three. The front door was already open, a uniformed PC on the doorstep with the crime scene attendance log.

Jack nodded in greeting, flashing his warrant card.

"Dr Matthews is waiting for you inside, Sir," responded the PC, nodding over his shoulder.

Jack stepped into the hallway and collected a set of protective clothing. Easing himself into the white protective suit, and slipping on some overshoes, he headed further into the bungalow towards where he knew Albert Dawson's bedroom could be found.

The area outside the bedroom was full of bodies, but Jack could already see the unmistakeable tall stature of the police pathologist, a clear head and shoulders above everyone else. Dr Matthews caught Jack's eye and nodded.

"Jack." Dr Matthews stepped away from the pack and headed in Jack's direction.

"Doc," greeted Jack, letting his eyes wander past the balding pathologist towards Albert's room. "What can you tell me?"

"Elderly gentleman, bed bound from MS. Found by his carer, Mandy O'Sullivan, at approximately three o'clock this afternoon."

Jack instinctively looked towards the doors leading to the kitchen and front room.

Dr Matthews shook his head. "She's been taken away by one of your officers, Jack. No sense in her hanging around here. She was in no fit state to remain at the scene; she was in quite a state of shock. I believe she's being interviewed as we speak."

Jack nodded and made a mental note to call and see if Mandy was still at the station. The taxi had dropped DC Cassidy off en route, Jack wanting her to start compiling a brief report on their trip to see Adrian McLeish. "Anything else?"

"I've not been here long myself, Jack. I've only had a cursory look at the body so far. There's not a lot of room in there."

Jack remembered the cramped bedroom on his previous two visits.

"Unofficially, it looks like asphyxiation, once again," continued Dr Matthews. "Similar to Mr Wakefield, Senior."

"And..?" Jack didn't need to ask.

Dr Matthews nodded. "Yes, Jack. The number fifteen on the right upper thigh."

"Does anyone know how the killer got in?"

"I gather it is believed to be through the rear bedroom patio door. It was found to be open when his body was discovered."

"Time of death?"

"I can be quite confident on this one, Jack. The carer said that she left the bungalow at a little after two thirty, and Mr Dawson was alive and well. She discovered him on her return at around three o'clock."

Jack mentally began to join the dots. The killer had been watching, and waiting. Biding his time. "Thanks, Doc. I'll come by when you do the post mortem. I'd like to be present for this one."

"Of course, Jack. I'll let you know when he's going to be on the table."

Jack made to step past Dr Matthews and head towards Albert Dawson's bedroom. Just as he did so, he felt a light touch to his shoulder.

"Have you done anything about your mother's post mortem?" Dr Matthews kept his voice low, ensuring that no one else was in ear shot. "And the samples for DNA?"

Jack paused at the threshold to the bedroom. Slowly, he nodded. "I've arranged for the samples to be analysed. I guess we'll see what happens after that." Jack flashed a grateful look at the pathologist. "Thanks for your help with it, Doc. I appreciate it."

Dr Matthews returned the nod and held up his hands. "I hardly did anything, Jack. I just hope you get the answers you're looking for."

With that, he turned and began heading towards the front door.

Jack watched him go.

The answers I'm looking for.

Right now, Jack wasn't quite sure what those answers might be.

* * *

Chapter Twenty-Three

Time: 8.45am

Date: Monday 18th February 2013

Location: Westminster Mortuary, London

The mortuary was just as cold as he remembered. But Jack was greeted warmly as he stepped into the reception area. Nicola Warner, mortuary receptionist, nodded at him and smiled.

"He's waiting for you." She waved towards the corridor that Jack knew led to the post mortem rooms. "Go straight through."

"Thanks." Jack headed towards the room that housed the protective clothing, picking up a rubber apron and a pair of what could only be described as wellington boots. Suitably clothed, he headed out towards the swing doors that led to Dr Matthews' main examination room. It had been a while since he had last attended a post mortem, although he knew that he should probably attend more often than he did. DS Cooper was always eager and Jack was more than happy to allow the young sergeant to extend and add to his knowledge.

But this one – this one Jack needed to see for himself.

"Good to see you, Jack." Dr Matthews was already gowned up and ready to start. His mortuary technician had wheeled in Albert Dawson, and the elderly former St Bartholomew's manager had been laid out on the steel examination table, silently awaiting the first incision.

"Morning, Doc." Jack sidled in and glanced at the frail looking body. In much the same way as Edward Wakefield, Albert's body seemed to have shrunk into itself, nothing more than skin and bone.

As always, Dr Matthews switched on his voice recorder and then angled the overhead lights ready to begin. Jack watched as the pathologist proceeded to select a sharp, yet delicate-looking, scalpel and made his first cut. A 'Y' shape incision, leading from the shoulders to the breastbone, and then down across the abdomen towards the pubic bone. Soon Albert Dawson's skin and subcutaneous tissue was opened up to reveal what lay beneath.

Jack didn't care to think how many times Dr Matthews had performed this same procedure; how many bodies he had sliced open; how many hearts he had held in his hands; how many times he had been present during a person's final journey, most of whose exit from this world had been traumatic and painful. The sound of snapping bone brought Jack out of his daydream, the rib cutter grabbing his attention and sending a shiver down his spine.

Dr Matthews proceeded to meticulously explore the body of Albert Dawson, his long fingers teasing and caressing the scalpel with the same grace as a fine artist. Organs were examined and weighed, notes were written, photographs were taken. Much of it passed Jack by in a blur; he was watching but he wasn't really seeing. His eyes kept being drawn to the old man's right upper thigh where the unmistakeable carving could be seen. Dr Matthews looked up and caught Jack's eye.

"We have the same again, Jack."

Jack watched as Dr Matthews explored the tattooed wound and took several close-up photographs. He then let his eyes track up the pale and emaciated body, coming to rest on Albert's gnarled and liver-spotted hands. Jack watched as Dr Matthews examined the hands, turning each one over and teasing out any material that had embedded itself underneath the fingernails.

He couldn't help it, but he instantly thought of his mother. Had this been what her post mortem had looked like? Had she had her chest and abdomen exposed, her ribs cut away from her breastbone, her skull sliced open to reveal her brain? Had her heart, stomach, liver, lungs and kidneys all been removed from her body and weighed?

He shuddered and swallowed back the hint of bile that had risen unbidden into his throat. The body lying on the steel table before him was no longer Albert Dawson. Instead, he saw his mother – he saw Stella MacIntosh. With her head turned to the side, looking towards him, she flashed him one of her wide smiles; smiles that caused her dimples to pop up, one on each cheek. Her eyes sparkled and shone as Jack held her in his gaze. She raised an arm and beckoned Jack towards her.

Jack felt himself sway and grabbed hold of the metal counter behind him.

"You all right there, Jack?" Dr Matthews paused, scalpel in hand, glancing at Jack with concerned eyes. "You need to step out for a minute? I'm about to open the stomach. It's not the most pleasant part."

Jack shook his head – both in answer to Dr Matthews' question, and also to rid himself of the vision of his mother swimming before him. Dr Riches would have a field day, he thought to himself, keeping a steadying hand on the metal counter behind him. Seeing his dead mother on a post mortem room table...she would lock him up and throw away the key.

He watched as Dr Matthews delved inside Albert Dawson and proceeded to remove his stomach.

* * *

Time: 10.45am
Date: Monday 18th February 2013
Location: Westminster Mortuary, London

After last night's wave of sleet and freshening winds, Jack had been grateful when the day had dawned bright and clear. Cold, but clear. He stepped out of the mortuary, noticing the slight increase in temperature as he did so. The sun hung low in the sky, casting its weak rays down to the cold and wet pavement below. He coughed and blew his nose in an attempt to dislodge the heady concoction of aromas that clung to his nostrils and airways. He would be smelling death for the rest of the day.

Pulling out his phone, he switched it back on and checked for any messages. He was expecting DC Cassidy to have news of her interview with Mandy O'Sullivan and he had left DS Cooper chasing up the house-to-house enquiries along Wagtail Drive, which should have got underway early that morning. In addition, DS Cooper was going to check if there were any CCTV or private cameras in the vicinity – an affluent area in West Hampstead, Jack was pretty sure there would be some.

As he scrolled through, the phone burst into life. It was DS Carmichael calling and Jack immediately hit the 'accept' button.

"Rob?"

"Hi, Jack. Glad I caught you. Is this a good time?"

"As good as any, Rob. I'm just out of the mortuary. What's up?"

"Just reminding you about later." DS Carmichael paused and Jack knew that he would be grinning at the other end of the phone. "I'm not going on my own, Jack. My mum would kill me."

Jack stifled a laugh. "I'll be there, Rob. What time are we leaving?"

"About two-thirty? I'll drive."

Jack nodded. "I'm on my way back to the station now. Catch you later."

"Before you go, Jack. That favour you asked for." DS Carmichael paused. "You still want me to do it?"

Jack came to a halt in the middle of the mortuary car park, a chill flickering through his veins. Suddenly the smell of death intensified in his nostrils. The bottles. He had asked DS Carmichael to send them anonymously to the lab for him, but now he wondered if that was a good idea. Torn between wanting to know, and not wanting to know, Jack shook his head.

"No, don't worry, Rob. I'll leave it for now. Thanks."

Pushing the thought of the beer bottles currently languishing underneath his desk out of his mind, Jack slipped the phone back in his pocket and glanced down at the clothes he was wearing. Frowning, he headed towards his car, deciding that he needed to stop off at the flat before heading back to work. He needed a shower and a change. He smelt of death.

And Mrs Tindleman would not appreciate that.

* * *

Time: 11.00am
   Date: Monday 18th February 2013
   Location: Hampstead Heath, London

They had been there all through the night, and into the morning too. He had watched from the corner of the street, masked behind a low wall and lamp post. He had now got so used to seeing the macabre pantomime, he could predict who the next actors on stage would be.

The police had been the first to attend, securing the scene, then the ambulance service had arrived – although Albert Dawson was clearly beyond any form of medical help by that point in time. The balding pathologist had taken a while to arrive. It was dark before his Volvo pulled up outside the police cordon. He stayed only briefly – but his main part in the show would come later.

The police were present throughout the night; a large van arriving with all sorts of lights and equipment. Under the cover of darkness, he had seen Albert Dawson leave his home for the very last time – wheeled out on a hospital-like stretcher and into the back of the waiting black 'Private Ambulance'.

As morning broke, he watched as several groups of police officers worked their way along Wagtail Drive, knocking at each door, presumably to ask if the residents had noticed anything unusual or out of place.

But he had been careful. He didn't think he had been seen, but if he had, he didn't think he was conspicuous enough to have registered in anyone's memory for long. But, in essence, it didn't really matter anymore.

The end was coming.

He had left mid-morning and made his way over to Hampstead Heath. The grass underfoot was wet and muddy in places, but the air was crisp and dry. He again had found a quiet spot, away from the dog walkers and joggers and sat for a while, lost in his own thoughts.

It was over.

It was finally over.

He had accomplished what he had set out to do.

Exactly as he had promised, all those years ago.

Did he feel relief now? Sorrow?

To be honest, he felt neither.

But he hadn't done this for himself. He didn't matter. He hadn't mattered for a long time.

He had done it for Danny.

Reaching into his pocket, he pulled out a battered black and white photograph, worn and frayed around the edges.

Danny.

The boy's face was unmistakeable. He looked so pure. So innocent. So young.

And that had been why he did what he did.

For Danny.

"I'm just sorry it took me so long," he murmured, staring down at the photograph in his hands. As he stared into Danny's innocent eyes, he remembered the last time he saw him.

* * *

Time: 11.00pm

Date: Sunday 14th March 1982

Location: St Bartholomew's Home for Boys, Christchurch

The corridor outside room number seven was empty. Danny's footsteps made no sound as he padded along the stone tiles – the only light coming from a small window up high, casting eerie moonlight across his path.

He carried on past the doors to rooms eight and nine, envying the sleeping and slumbering bodies that would be behind each one; those inside finally able to put the toils of the day behind them and escape into the relative comfort and safety of sleep. At least until the sun came up.

There would be no such respite tonight for Danny.

He stealthily made his way down the stone steps to the ground floor; everywhere was still and quiet, not a sound to be heard. Notwithstanding the quietness, he tiptoed as silently as he could across the flagstones to the rear of the entrance hall, and to the door that led to the scullery and kitchen beyond. He knew from his previous nocturnal trips, that he would be able to slip unseen out of the back door.

Entering the scullery, Danny quickly headed towards the adjoining door that led to the kitchen. A hive of activity during the day, the place was frozen in time during the hours of darkness. The only sound was the rhythmic humming coming from the fridges and freezers at the far end, and a dripping tap at the huge Butler sink by the window. Rows upon rows of stainless steel pots and pans lined the shelving that hugged each wall. He hurried past and headed for the back door. With the cast iron key still in the lock, it was easy to unlock and slip unnoticed outside.

The air was frigid in the rear courtyard, and Danny wheezed as he took in a deep breath. His chest still hurt from a recent chest infection, and his asthma was always made worse by the cold. Curling his fingers around the inhaler in his pocket, he made his way across the deserted courtyard towards the disused part of the home.

The hospital wing.

The imposing building rose up, menacingly, from the ground and Danny's heart began to thud faster inside his chest. From the outside it looked frightening enough – with its barred windows and grotesquely contorted stone gargoyles above the main entrance – but it was what lay beyond the Victorian stone walls that scared Danny the most.

* * *

Time: 11.00pm

Date: Sunday 14th March 1982

Location: St Bartholomew's Home for Boys, Christchurch

He had guessed that Danny would leave his room about now, and he had been right. Waiting in the darkness of the shadows at the end of the corridor, he saw the door to room seven open soundlessly, and the figure of a boy emerge.

Danny carefully closed the door behind him and quietly padded along the corridor towards the stairs. He didn't notice the shrouded figure silently watching his every move.

Once Danny was out of sight and heading down the stone steps, he quickly jogged from his hiding place and followed on behind as closely as he dared. He was confident Danny was unaware of his presence; his own footsteps were as silent as the night.

Once on the ground floor, he quickly scanned the deserted entrance hall to see Danny creeping towards the rear of the building, heading in the direction of the scullery. He had never been quite sure where Danny disappeared to at night, but now it was all starting to make sense. He followed as closely as he could and entered the scullery, just in time to see Danny's small figure disappear through the connecting door to the kitchen. He's heading for the back door, he thought to himself as he silently quickened his step.

Upon entering the kitchen, he hung back in case the moonlight from the clear night outside illuminated his presence. Through the large window above the Butler sink, he saw the crescent moon casting a pale white light across the room, making the rows of pots and pans opposite gleam and glisten.

He heard Danny turn the cast iron key in the lock, the faintest click echoing through the night air. There was a scraping sound as Danny pulled the door towards him and disappeared outside. Satisfied Danny was out of sight, he hurried through the kitchen and hovered by the open back door.

Danny had his back to him and had only taken a couple of tentative steps towards the abandoned brick building opposite.

That must be it, he mused. That must be where he goes.

The old hospital wing.

He watched as Danny took another couple of steps forwards. Satisfied that Danny was caught up in his own thoughts, he slipped quietly through the open doorway and into the shadows that hugged the rear porch. The air was cold; really cold. He held his breath as much as he could, not wanting Danny to spy the frozen plumes escape his mouth as he hid from sight.

It seemed like forever, but it was only a few more seconds before Danny moved towards the entrance to the hospital wing.

He remained lurking in the shadows, watching as the door was opened from the inside and Danny disappeared. He shivered, not just because of the cold but because of what potential horrors were going on behind the decrepit walls in front of him.

His body started to ache with the cold and he pulled the Swap Shop scarf more tightly around his neck before stepping out of the shadows.

* * *

Time: 11.10pm

Date: Sunday 14th March 1982

Location: St Bartholomew's Home for Boys, Christchurch

He found his way into the old hospital wing surprisingly easily. Although the front door was locked and only able to be opened from the inside, old buildings such as these had numerous other ways to break in. He had skirted around the outside and noted several windows on the ground floor that were insecure.

He chose one around the back, out of sight of the entrance, and was happy that he would be able to enter unseen. What he was going to do when he got in, he wasn't quite sure. But he needed to know what was happening inside the building – and what was happening to Danny. Whatever it was, it was unlikely to be very pleasant.

He made quick work of the window pane – it was already loose in its rotting frame – and it easily slid out without splintering. The frame itself almost disintegrated at his touch, so within seconds he had a gaping hole within which he could drag himself inside.

Landing softly on the other side, he held his breath. He was fairly certain his entrance had not made a sound, but you could never tell. He waited, motionless, by the empty window for a minute or two, but heard nothing.

Glancing around, he turned full circle to get his bearings. Having never been inside the old hospital wing, he wasn't sure where he was. The room he had landed in was bare, save for a solitary light bulb hanging from the ceiling. There was no furniture at all, and nothing to give a clue as to what was here before the hospital wing's demise.

He shivered again and started to move towards the door; the only door and therefore the only means of escape. He padded silently over and placed an ear to the cold surface of the wood. He wrinkled his nose; it smelt musty and old. Shivering again, he pulled the scarf ever tighter around his neck and tucked the ends inside his jacket.

There appeared to be silence on the other side of the door, so he decided to take a gamble. If it was the wrong choice, he might just have enough time to hurtle back through the room and dive out of the window before getting caught.

He tried the handle of the door and felt the door give a gentle click. He tentatively pulled it towards him and felt the door move; thankfully it gave no sound, not even a squeak. As he had expected, and hoped, the corridor on the other side was empty. It was a wide space, its walls flanked with rows of metal framed hospital beds stacked one of top of the other. Everything appeared to be abandoned and deserted.

Quickly looking left and right, he made the decision to turn right and head down to where he thought he could hear faint voices. His heart was hammering inside his chest and the palms of his hands were thick with sweat.

What was he doing here?

What was he hoping to find?

More shivers engulfed him and he quickened his step. He would just have a quick look to see what was going on, but then he would leave as quickly as he had arrived. The place was giving him the creeps. He would then tell the others what he had seen, and they could decide together what to do next.

The others.

His heart gathered so much pace it threatened to explode inside his chest. It crossed his mind that he hadn't told any of the others where he was going. Hadn't filled them in on his suspicions. Why hadn't he done that? They could have come with him, or at least provided some backup as look-outs.

But he hadn't told a soul.

He shook his head. Now was not the time to question his decisions; now was not the time for doubts. He was here. Alone. And Danny needed him.

He moved closer to a door at the far end of the corridor, feeling he could definitely hear voices coming from behind it, getting louder the nearer he got. There were several voices, more than one anyway, and laughing; lots of laughing. And also what sounded like jeering, and some kind of tinny music was playing in the background. He stood there, rooted to the spot, straining to hear what the voices were saying, but the sound was too muffled. As he stepped closer, the door began to open.

Heart racing, he leapt to the side where there was a tall stack of metal chairs, and hid himself behind their tangled frames. He clamped a hand across his mouth to stop himself from uttering a sound, and hoped that his heartbeat didn't sound as loud on the outside as it did pumping inside his chest. The door was pulled open and the noise of the voices and merriment beyond intensified.

A figure staggered out into the corridor. A portly gentleman dressed in a suit, but looking rather the worse for wear. Peering out from behind the chairs as much as he dared, he saw that the man's suit jacket had been discarded and his shirt tails were untucked. In one hand he carried a bottle of wine, from which he took an occasional swig while tottering unsteadily out into the corridor. In his other hand he pulled a much smaller figure in his wake.

He craned his neck to see past the chairs.

But he already knew exactly who it was.

The figure was Danny.

* * *

Time: 11.20pm

Date: Sunday 14th March 1982

Location: St Bartholomew's Home for Boys, Christchurch

Not knowing what else to do, he waited in the shadows, nervously biting his lower lip. The man had continued along the corridor, drunkenly staggering from side to side, and entered a room next to a stack of discarded hospital beds. Danny's tiny frame was pulled in behind him, and the door slammed shut.

His head began to throb. He didn't know what to do next. Should he go? Should he stay? There was still the sound of laughter coming from the room nearest to him, the one Danny had emerged from in the clutches of the drunken man. Laughter and more jeering could be heard, and someone had turned up the volume of the tinny music.

As he listened, there was one voice that could be heard over and above everything else.

The booming voice of Edward Wakefield.

He felt his whole body start to shake, now more with fear than from the cold. The minutes ticked by and with every second that passed he felt that fear rising. He should never have come alone. He should really never have come alone.

After what seemed like a lifetime, the door next to the stacked hospital beds opened and the portly gentleman staggered back out. He was no longer carrying the bottle in his hand, and he was no longer dragging Danny in his wake. The man's face was as white as a sheet, matching his ice-white hair. His alcohol reddened cheeks were now pale and ghost-like. The man stumbled forwards, bouncing off the walls as he tripped over his own feet. He appeared to have lost the use of his legs, using the walls to support him as he lurched in the direction of the voices and laughter.

Shrinking back against the wall behind the metal chairs, he watched as the man grabbed hold of the door handle and yanked it open.

"Eddie!" the man yelled, managing to slur even one simple word. "Eddie!" He stumbled inside the room and let the door crash shut behind him.

With the man gone, he peered out from behind the chairs, straining his ears to hear what was being said behind the closed door – but all he could hear was his own pounding heart. He glanced along the corridor towards the room the man had staggered out from, and noticed that the door was open wide.

Where was Danny?

He waited, hearing only muffled sounds coming from behind the closed door, although someone appeared to have turned the music off. He looked again along the corridor, but still no Danny emerged.

Fear coursed through him like a torrent and he sprang to his feet. He needed to find Danny and get him out of this place. He would drag him back through the window himself if he had to. His legs felt like jelly but he ran as fast as he could towards the open door, praying that the drunken man wasn't going to come back to finish what he had started.

He reached the doorway and peered inside, expecting to see Danny huddled and frightened in the corner.

But instead he saw a nightmare.

* * *

Time: 11.50pm
Date: Sunday 14th March 1982
Location: St Bartholomew's Home for Boys, Christchurch

As his wide-eyed gaze came to rest on the lifeless figure lying on the battered and stained mattress, he felt his legs collapse from beneath him. The room swayed in and out of focus, and he felt bile rise up from within.

He didn't need anyone to tell him that Danny was dead.

Staggering backwards, he felt for the door frame to steady himself. Turning to the side, he vomited on the floor by his feet, coughing and choking as he emptied his stomach. He scrunched his eyes shut as he felt burning tears begin to erupt.

He looked back towards the crumpled body lying in the centre of the mattress. Danny's eyes were open but were staring, lifelessly, towards the ceiling. A trickle of blood snaked out of the corner of his mouth. His clothes had been removed, discarded in a pile next to him; the wine bottle that he had seen the man swig from was lying, emptily, on its side.

Just at that moment, a familiar booming voice echoed along the corridor.

"You just stay right there, boy. Don't you dare move a muscle. *Don't even breathe*"

* * *

Chapter Twenty-Four

Time: 3.00pm
  Date: Monday 18th February 2013
  Location: 7 Palace Mews Road, London

"I'm so glad you could come." Mrs Tindleman's beaming smile reached her eyes, causing them to shimmer and sparkle. "Come in, come in. Don't let all the heat out." She moved back to let Jack and DS Carmichael step into the warm hallway. The short walk from the car to the front door had been enough to let the cold air seep quickly into their bones.

"Nice of you to invite me," replied Jack, hoping he sounded sincere as he hovered just inside the door. He heard the sound of voices and laughter coming from further inside, and felt the familiar feeling of awkwardness start to wash over him. Social gatherings were not his forte.

Admittedly, many things were not Jack MacIntosh's forte, but an after-noon spent with people he had never met before, especially in the middle of a murder investigation, came very high up on the list.

"It's the least I could do," stated Mrs Tindleman, reaching out to take Jack's coat as he shrugged himself out of it. "And I'm sure it's what Charles would have wanted." She disappeared in the direction of the kitchen. "Go on through. I'll be with you in a moment."

DS Carmichael took his own jacket off and hung it up on one of the pegs behind the front door. He leant in, close to Jack's ear. "You'll be fine. Stick with me. Backs against the wall at all times." Jack's face deepened into a frown, and DS Carmichael tapped the side of his nose. "I've a feeling she's got ulterior motives – asking us both here. She'll be wanting to pair us both off, you mark my words. She does it all the time." He gave Jack a conspiratorial wink. "As I said, backs to the wall."

Jack followed DS Carmichael towards where the laughter and chatter was coming from. They both entered the front room and Jack instantly recognised it from his previous visits. He watched as Mrs Tindleman, entering from the kitchen, grabbed hold of her son's arm and pulled him towards her for a quick peck on the cheek.

Jack smiled. The house that had once been full of sorrow and sadness, devoid of all feeling except grief following the death of Charles Tindleman, was now warm and homely.

"Most of you have met my son before," announced Mrs Tindleman, still hanging onto DS Carmichael's arm. "But this here is his colleague, Detective Inspector Jack MacIntosh." She stepped back and swept her arm towards Jack in a flourish, as if announcing the arrival of royalty.

Jack instantly felt his cheeks redden beneath his stubble. It was now that he wished he had taken the extra time and had a shave. He had managed to pull out a freshly dry-cleaned suit from the back of his wardrobe, and thanks to his six-week excursion to the Scottish countryside, with all its fresh air and hill-walking, he found that he slipped into it a treat and almost looked quite dapper. But he could have done with a shave. He rubbed a hand, self-consciously, across the prickles gracing his chin. At least the smell of death should, hopefully, have been washed away. He surreptitiously gave himself a sniff.

"Honestly, just Jack is fine." He managed to make his mouth work, feeling how dry it had become all of a sudden. He tried a smile, feeling ten pairs of eyes, some behind spectacles, boring into him as he edged into the room.

"Well, I don't know about you, Jack," announced DS Carmichael, gently releasing himself from his mother's clutches. "But I need a drink. Ladies, please excuse us." He stepped back and took Jack by the elbow, steering him in the direction and safety of the kitchen.

Once inside, and the door shut behind them, DS Carmichael broke out into a broad grin. "That was painful, eh?" He laughed as he wrenched open the large refrigerator. "What do you fancy? There are some beers in here, plus I'm sure there'll be some gin around somewhere. Wine?"

"Anything," replied Jack, leaning up against the worktop by the sink. "So long as it contains alcohol I really don't care. I don't think I can go back in there without it."

DS Carmichael laughed again, pulling two bottles of beer from the fridge and snapping off the tops. "I think you'll find we'll be quite safe. I'm guessing everyone in there is either a member of the WI, or goes to one of mum's evening classes. I forget what she does now. Knitting maybe? Or crochet? I'm not even sure I know the difference..."

A knitting group or the WI. Jack grimaced and took the beer offered by DS Carmichael, instantly taking a large gulp. As far as social gatherings went, it wouldn't have been his first choice.

"There is one good thing to come out of it though," said DS Carmichael, nodding towards the front room, where they could hear several bouts of laughter and the pop of a prosecco bottle.

"And what's that?" enquired Jack, downing more beer.

"I think we're safe on the match-making front. Everyone out there is somewhere north of sixty."

Jack laughed into his beer and followed DS Carmichael back towards the living room, where they were greeted by a wall of merriment, with Mrs Tindleman busy pouring out what looked like their fourth bottle of prosecco.

"Would either of you two boys like some bubbly?" asked Mrs Tindleman, waving the empty bottle. "I've plenty more where this came from!"

DS Carmichael held up his beer bottle. "We're good, thanks, Mum."

"Well, now that we all have our glasses full, it's time we toasted my new venture." Mrs Tindleman put the empty prosecco bottle down next to three others and raised her glass, her small frame tottering slightly as she did so.

"Yes, what is this all about? Drinking in the afternoon? I'm intrigued." DS Carmichael edged further into the room, glancing around at the bank of mostly grey-haired women perched on the sofa and armchairs, others resting against the window ledge. All had their drinks in their hands, their eyes sparkling in the same way as the prosecco in the glasses they held aloft. "And why are *we* here?" As much as he loved and adored the way his mother had dragged herself out of the depths of despair following the sudden death of her husband almost five years ago, he couldn't see himself, or Jack for that matter, joining the ranks of the WI. His baking skills were definitely not up to scratch, and from the various evenings he had spent at Jack's bachelor flat, he was sure the detective inspector lurking behind him was equally devoid of knowing how to prevent a soggy bottom.

"You're both here because I have some exciting news to tell you all – something that I'm sure you will feel is close to your own hearts, as well as mine." Mrs Tindleman took another fortifying sip of bubbles. "As you know, this year would have been myself and Charles' fortieth wedding anniversary." She glanced over at the mantelpiece where a silver-framed photograph of Charles was still standing proudly in the centre, amongst an array of other family pictures.

Jack followed Mrs Tindleman's gaze and looked at the familiar photograph of Charles Tindleman with his arm around a young Robert Carmichael – a proud father with his son on police graduation day.

"Charles left a sum of money in his will to be donated to a charity of my choice," continued Mrs Tindleman, turning back and smiling at the expectant faces of her guests. "Until recently, I couldn't make up my mind what charity to give the donation to, there are so many that would be worthy. I invested the money in a high interest account while I decided." She paused and took another sip of prosecco. "Most of you in this room know that Charles and I couldn't have our own children – we married young and knew early on that having our own children wouldn't be possible. But then how delighted we were when Robert, here, came into our lives." Mrs Tindleman looked up, her eyes glistening at the corners with unbidden tears. "He brought us sunshine and happiness when we had only known of dark clouds and despair. That little boy allowed us to live again, and to look forward to a future filled with love and, well...now he's all grown up, I'm ever hopeful of some grandchildren!" She broke off and smiled, warmly, at

DS Carmichael, whose own cheeks were now starting to burn. "But I digress! Today I am pleased to announce that I have decided what to do with Charles' charity money. I have set up a Trust – the Tindleman Trust – to support disadvantaged children, foster families and prospective adoptive parents. I'm hoping it will provide help and advice for anyone going through the fostering and adoption process, for both adults and children alike. There will be a hub where people can meet, exchange ideas, or just talk. And for the children, a much needed programme of days out, clubs and activities, to help them adjust to their new surroundings and their new families – and, well, to help them become *children* once again."

Her speech over, Mrs Tindleman looked around the room, smiling at each of the faces that had been hanging onto her every word. The tears that had threatened to spring from her eyes were now trickling down her flushed cheeks. Silence lay heavily in the pot-pourri scented air, the only sound coming from the gentle tick-tock of the mantelpiece clock. It was as though everyone in the room had been holding their breath; no sound escaped their mouths, not even a blink crossed their eyes.

After what seemed like an eternity, one sound broke the stillness.

DS Carmichael stepped forwards and started clapping – slowly, at first - a broad grin breaking out on his face. After a few moments, he was joined by Jack, inching out from where he had been languishing by the kitchen door. He stepped forwards, standing next to his sergeant, shoulder to shoulder, and began to clap.

Very soon the ripple effect circulated the small living room, and before long the whole huddle of knitting enthusiasts and WI members had placed their glasses of prosecco down and were clapping along. Mrs Tindleman's tears were not the only ones being shed.

DS Carmichael went and enveloped his mother in a warm embrace, almost engulfing her tiny frame. He kissed the top of her head and squeezed her, tightly.

"You're amazing," he said, simply. "Just amazing."

Once the clapping had petered out, DS Carmichael slipped back into the kitchen and brought out two more bottles of prosecco, popping the corks to much jubilation. With everyone's glasses refreshed, he stood in the centre of the room and made a toast.

"To my Mum. This is the most kind-hearted and generous thing that anyone could do – but nothing surprises me about that. You are the single-most loving and caring person I have ever met. You took me in when no one else would. I will never, *ever*, be able to repay you for the hope and trust that you put in me. I know for a fact that I would not be the man I am today without the start that you gave me. And, Dad, too – of course. He would be so proud of you today."

DS Carmichael broke off, his own eyes misting up and his voice beginning to crack. He raised his beer bottle in the air. "To Mum and Dad – and the new Tindleman Trust."

Jack raised his own bottle and surreptitiously wiped the moisture from his eyes. Swallowing a large mouthful of beer, he caught the gaze of Mrs Tindleman as she turned to wipe her eyes on a cotton handkerchief. For a few seconds, as everyone gave another ripple of applause, and murmurings of support and appreciation filled the air, their eyes connected across the room. Jack gave another nod and raised his beer bottle in her direction; no words were needed.

The rest of the afternoon passed in an unexpectedly pleasant way. Jack found that the knitting circle were a fantastically crazy bunch of old ladies who liked nothing more than a chat and a giggle, and they had an extraordinarily sharp sense of humour. And there was also more to the WI brigade than an ability to bake a good scone or knowing the entire words to Jerusalem.

One particular lady from the WI seemed to take quite a shine to Jack and insisted that he sit down next to her, so he squeezed himself on the edge of the already overpopulated sofa. He turned towards DS Carmichael and mouthed the word 'help' several times before the detective sergeant put him out of his misery and dragged a floral footstool over to join them.

"So, how are you getting on with our Detective Inspector, here?" joked DS Carmichael, his dark eyes sparkling.

"Ooh, he's just lovely," crooned Edna Johnson, an octogenarian with the brightest blue eyes Jack had ever seen. Her thinning grey hair was tucked up high on her head in a tiny bun, and she smelt, not unpleasantly, of lavender. "Just lovely." Edna placed a gnarled hand on top of Jack's knee and gave it a squeeze; in the other, she held a delicate cup of Earl Grey tea. Jack found himself smiling back at her, a look of bewilderment in his eyes.

"I can't understand why some lovely young lady hasn't snapped him up," she continued, giving another squeeze of his knee.

"No, quite," agreed DS Carmichael, his grin widening.

"And the same goes for you, young man," continued Edna, turning her attention away from Jack. "It's about time you settled down and gave your mother some lovely grandchildren."

It was now Jack's turn to grin, reaching forwards and placing his empty beer bottle on the coffee table. "Quite right, Edna," he smiled, delighting in it being DS Carmichael's turn to squirm in his seat.

"You young men, these days," she chattered. "You need to find yourselves some decent women, that's what you need to do."

Jack smothered a laugh with the back of his hand.

"I keep saying the same thing, Edna, but does he listen to me?" Mrs Tindleman joined Edna on the sofa just as one of the other WI ladies got up to replenish the plates of scones and Victoria sponge cake that were quickly being demolished. "I was having the same conversation with my friend, Jeanie, at the library only last week." She looked up and winked at her son, taking another sip of her prosecco. "She's waiting for grandchildren, too."

"It took my Johnny far too long to furnish me with mine," added Edna, "but he got there in the end. There's five of them now, and even two great grandchildren."

"Five grandchildren, and two great grandchildren? That's wonderful, Edna," gushed Mrs Tindleman, casting a teasing glance in DS Carmichael's direction. "You're so lucky!" She paused and sipped once again from her glass. "But I thought your son's name was Timothy? Not Johnny?"

Edna sipped her Earl Grey tea, and nodded. "Yes, yes, he is. That's what we christened him – but everyone calls him Johnny. It started at school, I think, as one of those nicknames. And then it just seemed to stick."

"Johnny Johnson," mused DS Carmichael. "When I was at high school I got called Tinders. Tinders Tindleman." He made a face. "I hated it."

Jack had just picked up a fresh bottle of beer from the coffee table when he stopped, the bottle frozen at his lips.

Johnny.

Johnny Johnson.

"Edna – you're amazing." He took a gulp from the bottle then turned and planted a kiss on the old woman's powdered cheek, getting a nostril full of lavender as he did so. "I love you." Pushing himself up from the sofa he turned towards Mrs Tindleman, a bemused expression on her face that matched that on Edna's. "I'm sorry, Mrs Tindleman, but I have to go."

With that, he strode over to the kitchen where his coat had been draped over one of the breakfast stools, and fished his phone out of his pocket. Stabbing the screen, he wrestled himself into his coat and prayed that there was someone still there. It was answered on the third ring.

"Cooper? Good, you're still there. I need your help." Jack made his way along the hallway towards the front door. "I need you to come and pick me up. Now."

"On my way, boss," replied DS Cooper. "What's up?"

Jack paused, feeling his heartbeat increasing as the adrenaline kicked in. "It's Harry. I know how we can find him."

* * *

Chapter Twenty-five

Time: 5.30pm

Date: Monday 18th February 2013

Location: Metropolitan Police HQ, London

"It's his bloody surname." Jack burst into the investigation room. "We should be looking for a Harrison. Where are those lists from St Bartholomew's?"

DC Cassidy quickly sprang to her feet. "Nice suit, guv. Very smart! You scrub up well!" She quickly gathered the paperwork together and passed it over. "While you've been out, I've typed up the interview with Mandy O'Sullivan, poor woman was distraught. And Chris has accessed the CCTV on the road leading to Wagtail Drive. The house-to-house has also confirmed several residents have private cameras. Chris was about to follow that up when you called. Where is he anyway?"

Jack loosened his tie and took hold of the papers. "He's gone up to the office. He had a message from Jenny."

DC Cassidy gave a grin. "I think she's quite smitten with our Chris. And he goes a bit pink when you mention her name!"

"Enough teasing," smiled Jack. "We've got work to do." He looked down at the paperwork from St Bartholomew's. "I can't believe we didn't think of this."

"Are we still going for the same time frame, guv?" DC Cassidy turned over the first page of her pile. "1978 onwards?"

Jack nodded. "I think so. 1978 through to 1982. Check how many boys have the surname Harrison."

Just then, Jack's mobile began to ring. "Speak of the devil." Jack brought the phone to his ear. "Cooper, what's up?"

* * *

Time: 5.40pm
Date: Monday 18th February 2013
Location: Forest Road Cemetery, Nr Christchurch

The grave had been quite hard to spot, tucked away at the back of the cemetery where the ground was more uneven. The grass was longer here, rising up in unruly tufts like a bad hairstyle, and twigs littered the ground from the overhanging trees above.

Mac picked his way through the rows of headstones, noting that very few had flowers compared with the rest of the cemetery. Those that did have flowers, their blooms had wilted and died many months before, and now their brittle remains were left scattered above ground, mirroring the skeletons that lay beneath them.

It had taken Mac a while to track down this particular cemetery, but when he finally did he had felt compelled to come. Trawling through the online archives for the Christchurch Evening News, he had found a tiny section, only one paragraph and twenty words long, detailing that the funeral was to take place on 2nd April 1982 at the Forest Road Cemetery.

He turned the collar of his leather jacket up, feeling the biting chill of the stiff breeze on his neck. There was a moisture on the breeze too; soon there would be sleet hammering down from the oppressive looking clouds above – and maybe snow to follow.

Mac's eyes searched the headstones in the gathering dark until he found the one that was the purpose of his visit. Looking over his shoulder to see if anyone had followed him – why they would, he had no idea – he trudged through the stumpy grass to the grave at the end of the back row. Its position gave the impression it had been squeezed into this unloved part of the cemetery; a small space for a small person.

Daniel Hopkins' headstone was small and nondescript, having been weathered over the years to a depressing grey. Mac had to bend down to make out the inscription.

DANIEL HOPKINS

20th February 1971 – 14th March 1982

REST IN PEACE

That was all the headstone revealed about the inhabitant below ground. There was no 'loving son', or 'will be missed'. No poem or other words of love and emotion. It was as if Daniel Hopkins had mattered as much in death as he seemed to have done during his short life.

Mac swallowed past the lump that had formed in his throat, and knelt down on the sodden grass, instantly feeling the damp soak into his jeans. He brushed the stray twigs and leaves from the top of the grave and using a bottle of water he had brought with him, he washed away the smattering of pigeon droppings that were the only decoration on the headstone.

Daniel Hopkins had been laid to rest at the age of eleven; he had not been given the chance to see what life had in store for him, what paths he would choose, whose lives he could touch. All of that had been taken away from him the moment the doors of St Bartholomew's Home for Boys had closed behind him.

Mac brushed the weathered grains of grit from the headstone and let his fingers linger over the grooves of the inscription – DANIEL HOPKINS.

"Sorry, mate," was all he could muster. "I'm really sorry."

* * *

Time: 5.45pm

Date: Monday 18th February 2013

Location: Metropolitan Police HQ, London

"What have you got for me, Cooper?" Jack entered the office that he shared with DS Cooper and noticed the young detective sergeant staring intently at his computer screen. "I've got Amanda searching back through the records of St Bartholomew's again, searching for Harrisons."

DS Cooper flicked his gaze up to meet Jack's. "Good shout. I don't know how we didn't think of that before."

Jack was about to reply when he noticed the expression on DS Cooper's face. His eyes were bright and shiny, and his mouth was twitching into a smile.

"Go on then, spit it out." Jack pulled up a chair to join DS Cooper at his desk and noted that the laboratory reports for Daniel Hopkins were loaded up onto his computer screen. "Are those more results for the Danny Hopkins case?"

DS Cooper nodded and clicked on one of the entries. "Jenny sent some more results through – this time from fibres found on the boy's t-shirt." The laboratory report filled the screen, with a few close-up photographs of several red and green looking strands of woollen-type fibres at the bottom of the page.

"And?" Jack leant in closer towards the screen. "From his t-shirt, you say? Do they have any idea what type of fibres?"

DS Cooper hesitated. "They do, as a matter of fact. Or at least they have a pretty good idea." He clicked on one of the photographs to enlarge it so that it filled the screen. "And it links straight back to our Eddie Wakefield murder scene."

Jack felt his stomach flip.

DS Cooper continued, his voice hitching up a notch. "These fibres here...found on little Danny Hopkins' t-shirt...match other fibres already on the system."

"Match? As in...?" Jack raised his eyebrows.

"As in highly likely they are from the same source." DS Cooper broke out into a broad grin. "And you'll never guess where they're from."

Jack rubbed his eyes. "Put me out of my misery, Cooper. It's been a long day."

DS Cooper paused and clicked the mouse to minimise the image of the red and green fibres. He then pulled up a different image; an image that, to Jack, needed no explanation.

An image that Jack instantly recognised.

The Swap Shop scarf.

"It's great news, isn't it?" DS Cooper continued to beam. "Fibres from this scarf have been found on Danny Hopkins' t-shirt. You said the cases were linked, and you were right. It's mad, isn't it?"

Jack swallowed past the lump in his throat. It was certainly that, all right. "How sure are they?" he asked, steadying his voice as best he could. "That they're from the same source?"

DS Cooper gave a small shrug. "About as sure as they can be. Nothing is 100%, but they seem pretty confident."

Jack cleared his throat and patted DS Cooper on the shoulder. "Good work. Let me know if anything else comes in." With that, Jack pushed himself up out of his chair and left the office.

He needed some air.

He needed to breathe.

And, more than anything, he needed to speak to his brother.

* * *

Time: 6.00pm
Date: Monday 18th February 2013
Location: Metropolitan Police HQ, London

Jack stood in the car park outside the rear entrance, slipping between two unmarked police cars. He shivered – both from the cold and also from the call he was about to make. He was alone in the car park, save for two hardy smokers jumping from foot to foot in the far corner, pulling quickly on their cigarettes before their disappearance was noted inside. The PCs had their backs towards Jack and took no notice of him.

The air was crisp and cold, with just the hint of oncoming snowfall in the air. The sky itself was dark and clear. The ground beneath Jack's feet was already frozen with early evening frost, with a thick layer of ice likely before sunrise. But Jack's mind wasn't truly on the weather. He pulled DC Cassidy's phone out of his pocket and tapped in his brother's number. He hadn't replied to any of Jack's calls from Saturday night, and appeared once again to be avoiding all contact. So another tactic was required.

The phone rang for several seconds before the call was answered.

"Yup?" Mac sounded breathless.

"Can you talk? It's me." Jack hadn't quite planned what he was going to say, not believing that his brother would answer the phone to an unknown number. He hurriedly tried to scramble his thoughts together inside his head.

"Jack." Mac's voice was flat, devoid of any emotion. "You got a new phone or something?"

Jack's mouth went dry, unsure of how he was going to keep the conversation going. "No, my battery's flat and I forgot to bring my charger into work." It was such a pathetic excuse and Jack knew that his brother would see right through it.

"What can I do for you?" Mac's voice was hesitant, and Jack thought he could hear traffic in the background. "I've not got long."

Jack opened his mouth to speak but found that no words were forming.

"Jack? You still there?"

"Yeah, yeah I'm still here. The line went a bit crackly, that's all." Jack hoped the lie might buy him some more time.

"Well I need to get going soon. I know I didn't get back to you about Saturday...Isabel's Italian evening...I just, well, I just couldn't face it."

"Your scarf." Jack got straight to the point.

CHAPTER TWENTY-FIVE

"My what?"

"Your scarf – the Swap Shop one."

Mac paused on the other end of the phone. "Again? What about it? I thought we went over this before. I've not got time for this, Jack."

"Do you remember a young lad from St Bartholomew's – murdered back in 1982?" Silence filled Jack's ears. Now it was his turn to wonder if his brother had disappeared. "You still there, Stu? Lad by the name of Daniel Hopkins?"

"What about him?" The edginess to Mac's voice intensified.

"So you do remember him? Danny?" Jack paused. "You remember what happened to him?"

A small sigh escaped Mac's lips. "Of course I remember what happened to him. It's not something you forget in a hurry, is it?"

"Granted." Jack bit his lip. It wasn't going to be easy, saying what he needed to say – so he may as well just come out with it. "Fibres from your scarf have been found on his clothing."

"You what?"

Jack thought he could hear a gasp from the other end of the phone. "Fibres from your scarf, the Swap Shop one," repeated Jack, more forcefully this time, "have been found on Daniel Hopkins' clothing." He paused. "Your scarf was found at the scene of Eddie Wakefield's murder. I know it's yours as it has the cigarette burn in the corner. The fibres on Danny have been tested and they come from your scarf. I want to know how they got there."

Jack's eyes fell on the two uniformed PCs jogging back across the car park towards the rear entrance. They both caught Jack's eye and nodded in acknowledgement, but quickly hurried inside out of the ever-increasing cold, their cigarette break over. Jack pressed the phone to his ear as two ambulances rushed past the car park entrance, the sound of their piercing sirens filling the night air. "Stu? Can you still hear me? I also need to know where you were yesterday afternoon – Albert Dawson has been found dead."

There was continued silence on the other end of the phone, and Jack swapped the handset to his other ear, turning away as a fire engine and two police patrol motorbikes now screeched past in pursuit of the ambulances.

"Stu?"

In the silence that followed the sirens, Jack heard the very sound that he didn't want to hear.

His brother had hung up.

* * *

Time: 6.15pm
Date: Monday 18th February 2013
Location: Forest Road Cemetery, Nr Christchurch

Mac left the cemetery under the cover of darkness and headed for his motorbike which he had left in a small layby at the entrance. The temperature had dropped as soon as the sun had disappeared, and Mac turned his head away from the strengthening breeze.

The call from Jack had irritated him.

"That bloody scarf," he muttered, reaching for his crash helmet and swinging his leg across the motorbike seat.

Just as he was about to start the engine, his phone beeped with an incoming message.

It was short and to the point.

"Come now."

* * *

Chapter Twenty-Six

Time: 6.50pm
 Date: Monday 18th February 2013
 Location: St Bartholomew's Home for Boys, Christchurch.

He paused at the rusting gate and stood looking at the building that had been the source of so many of his nightmares. How could an inanimate object such as it was, in effect just a collection of bricks and mortar, provoke such deeply set emotions of hatred and fear? When you looked at it, that was all it was – bricks and mortar.

But St Bartholomew's was far more than that.

It may be made of bricks, but it was held together by more than just mortar- cruelty was its chosen binding.

He stood for some time before pushing the gate. It swung open on its one remaining hinge, the metal scraping noisily on the concrete path beneath. He stepped forwards, heaving two heavy rucksacks up onto his shoulders, and started his final journey towards the imposing Victorian façade.

The path was still overgrown with weeds and thistles; the cold weather failing to halt their growth. He kicked away a stray beer can and crushed another underfoot, as he picked his way in between the piles of discarded rubbish. Several blackened areas suggested previous visitors had celebrated with nocturnal bonfires; abandoned bottles of cheap cider and rusted cans littered the way towards the front entrance.

He remembered the first time he had stepped through the cavernous front door – he remembered it as if it were yesterday. It marked the day that plotted the end of his life as he knew it – life transformed into something wholly different from the moment he crossed the threshold.

He flicked on the torch he carried in his gloved hand and climbed the crumbling steps. The door itself was gaping open; it didn't look like it had been closed in decades. The hinges were rusted and rotten; the wooden panels broken and splintered. Ivy and other invasive weeds suffocated the walls, pointing to the way inside.

Aiming the torch into the dark space beyond the door, he poked his head inside. The air smelt damp and musty. Pushing himself further through the gap, he noticed piles of bricks and concrete scattered across the floor of what had once been the entrance hall. The upper floors and roof had caved in at various sections, leaving the building nothing but an empty shell. He gazed upwards, looking directly through a wide open space, seeing the stars twinkling above in the clear night sky.

The stairs had collapsed, wooden bannisters splintered and wrecked. He picked his way further inside, in-between the rubble, and headed towards the rear – an unseen force pulling him where he knew he needed to go.

Before it could all be over.

* * *

Time: 7.00pm
Date: Monday 18th February 2013
Location: Kettle's Yard Mews, London

Jack tried the number again but it went, predictably, straight to voicemail. He let the phone slip from his fingers and clatter onto the coffee table.

Where are you, Stu?

Jack ran a hand through his hair and rubbed his eyes. This was not the time to go AWOL – if he didn't catch up with his brother soon, someone else most definitely would. Finding the same fibres from the Swap Shop scarf on Danny Hopkins' body couldn't be kept from the investigation team any longer. And it was only a matter of time before Jack would have to disclose his brother's links to both the scarf and the tattoo. He couldn't keep it under wraps for much longer; the ice he was skating on was beginning to crack.

Snatching up his phone once more, he stabbed again at his brother's number, getting the same predictable voicemail message.

Before he was able to leave yet another message, there was a rapid banging on his door. It sounded both urgent and frantic. Jack leapt to his feet and wrenched the door open, hoping and praying that maybe it would be his errant brother.

It wasn't.

"Jack!" Isabel practically fell across the threshold and collapsed into Jack's arms. "Oh, Jack!"

"Isabel?" Jack quickly slipped his arms under Isabel's shoulders and guided her into the flat. "Here, sit down. You're freezing."

Isabel was shaking, uncontrollably; her pale skin felt ice-cold to the touch.

"I...I ran all the way f...from the t...tube." Her words came out in gasps, in between bouts of shivering and shaking that wracked her body. "The c...communal door downstairs - the l...lock is broken. I...I came straight up."

Jack nodded and led her towards the sofa, her eyes wide and frightened.

"What is it? What's happened?" Jack prized Isabel's fingers from his arm and sat down next to her. "I've been trying to get hold of Stu, but he's not answering."

"Y...you won't...you won't get hold of him," cried Isabel. Her face now awash with tears. "He's gone."

"Gone?" Jack frowned, his mind beginning to race. "What do you mean gone?"

Isabel's shoulders trembled again and she wrapped her frozen arms around herself. "He left me a note. He's gone."

"OK, let's back up." Jack reached for his phone again. "I'll call him..."

"He won't answer, Jack. He's *gone*." Isabel steadied her voice and rummaged in one of her pockets. "He left me this." She held out a folded piece of paper.

Jack took the note, instantly recognising his brother's scrawl. He began to read with an ever-growing feeling of disquiet. It didn't take long. He flipped it over to see if there was anything else on the reverse. There wasn't. He flipped it back and read it again.

"You see, he's gone," repeated Isabel, her voice quiet. Tears continued to stream down her cheeks. "He's leaving me. He's *left* me." More sobs wracked her slight frame and she rubbed at her cheeks with the sleeve of her jumper.

Jack felt her shudder next to him. He looked once more at the note and shook his head. "No...no he's not."

Isabel looked up, confusion now mixed in with her pain. "But it says...he says he's gone. He's left."

Jack continued to shake his head, and pushed himself off the sofa. He went to grab his jacket from the back of the door. "No...no he doesn't. Look, here." Jack held the note up. "At the bottom. 'I have to go'. That's what he says. 'I'm sorry. I have to go back'."

"B...back where?" Isabel wiped her eyes. "Where's he going?"

Jack knew there could only be one place.

* * *

Time: 7.05pm

Date: Monday 18th February 2013

Location: St Bartholomew's Home for Boys, Christchurch

The scullery and kitchen appeared to have survived better than the rest of the building. The walls were still intact, as was the roof; the decay that had engulfed the rest of the home had yet to reach this far. He walked through the adjoining door into the kitchen, the same way he had done that fateful night. The night Danny Hopkins had lost his life.

It had been a clear night, just like tonight, he mused, as he stepped into the kitchen. He remembered the thin crescent moon had been out, casting its pale, eerie glow, illuminating the path as he followed Danny through to the abandoned hospital wing.

Shivering now, not just because of the chill air seeping in through the broken kitchen window, he headed towards the back door. The door was more or less intact, but the wood had warped with age and the seasons, so he had to pull it violently before it gave way. It scraped, noisily, across the flagstones below.

Stepping out into the rear courtyard, he held his breath. He had been right to come back. He *needed* to come back and face up to what had happened all those years ago – and what had happened since. It was only fitting - this was where it had all started, so this was where it would finally end.

He might have got his revenge on those truly responsible for Danny's death – the Wakefields would breathe no more, and Albert Dawson's miserable life had been snuffed out, too. But even that wasn't enough.

The building itself was evil.

The hospital wing was even more decayed than it had been during his time at St Bartholomew's. The ancient brickwork had been badly weathered, the stone gargoyles above the entrance were chipped and disintegrated, until they represented nothing more than a concrete shell. The windows were all broken – their metal bars and glass long gone; their frames reduced to splinters and dust.

Yes, he had been right to come back.

One last time.

* * *

Time: 7.15pm

Date: Monday 18th February 2013

Location: St Bartholomew's Home for Boys, Christchurch

Mac stood at the entrance to St Bartholomew's Home for Boys and gritted his teeth. He had vowed never to set foot in the place again after his last visit with Jack some nine months ago. That visit was meant to have put all the ghosts from this particular part of his past to rest.

The rusting gate had already been pushed open, and he walked straight through and along the weed strewn path up towards the front door. He noticed the place had attracted yet more fly-tipping; more discarded empty bottles and cans, black bin bags full of rubbish.

He arrived at the steps to the main entrance and noted the door, such as it was, was wide open. Mac could see inside with the light of the moon overhead, but he wished he had had the foresight to bring a torch. Taking a deep breath, he once again stepped over the threshold, pushing past the ivy and other weeds climbing up the brickwork, and entered St Bartholomew's.

It looked much the same as it had last summer; maybe a fresh pile of rubble where yet another section of the roof had fallen in. But most of the interior of the entrance hall was in the same decrepit and decaying state that he remembered. He picked his way past the piles of collapsed brickwork and headed towards the scullery.

If he was anywhere, this would be where he was, Mac was certain.

The scullery had been largely untouched by the collapse of the rest of the building, and Mac quickly jogged through and entered the kitchen. It was bare now, save for the large wooden table in the centre – even the large Butler sink had been stripped. All the shelving, that had once groaned under the weight of pots and pans, now lay empty and full of dust.

Mac headed towards the back door which was wide open.

He was here.

* * *

Time: 7.25pm
    Date: Monday 18th February 2013

Location: St Bartholomew's Home for Boys, Christchurch

He found the same window as he had that fateful night thirty years ago. It wasn't hard to remember; the memory of that night had never been far from his thoughts. The window frame had disintegrated completely to leave nothing but a gaping hole amongst crumbling brickwork. Without hesitation, he threw both rucksacks in first and then pulled himself through the hole, landing softly on the inside.

Nothing had changed.

Even though *everything* had changed after that night.

The room was still bare; just an empty shell. Picking up both bags, he walked towards the corridor, no longer needing to creep or hold his breath as he had done before, no longer fearful of being discovered. There would be nobody here this time. There would be no laughter, no singing, no soft tinny music coming from the radio grating on his ears.

The corridor looked the same, albeit smaller than he remembered. It was still lined with abandoned metal hospital beds, and towering stacks of unwanted chairs. The only addition had been mounds of hospital mattresses and other bedding that were now piled high at the end of the corridor. The place smelt damp and musty, but the building appeared to have survived in much better shape than the rest of the home. It still had a roof, at least.

All the ground floor windows were smashed, letting in the elements from outside – the cold, the wind, the rain, the sleet – but the hospital wing itself remained standing firm, refusing to succumb to the decay that had set in elsewhere.

He made his way past the stacked hospital beds. He knew where he had to go before all of this could be over, once and for all. Edward and Terence Wakefield had deserved to die for what they had done within these walls; and Albert Dawson deserved to suffer the same fate. Between them they had ruined countless lives behind the disguise of providing care and comfort to those less fortunate.

But what happened now was up to him.

And there was only one choice he had left.

* * *

Time: 7.30pm
 Date: Monday 18th February 2013
 Location: St Bartholomew's Home for Boys, Christchurch

Mac stood in the rear courtyard, staring up at the old hospital wing. He shivered, both due to the bitterness of the wind but also because of the imposing structure towering over him. His gut told him he was in the right place. It couldn't be anywhere else.

"Come now," the message had said.

He crunched across the gravel and approached the main door. Despite decades of neglect and decay, the thick, oak panelled door seemed to be standing firm. He pushed a shoulder against it, but it wouldn't give an inch.

Mac swept his eyes along the outside wall, noting the lower windows were all broken, their frames splintered. Not one single pane of glass was intact. He edged along the perimeter of the building and rounded the corner – yet more rows of smashed windows and rotten frames faced him along the rear. Choosing one that had no jagged pieces of glass in the corners to snag him, Mac heaved himself up and swung his legs round, finally jumping into the abandoned hospital building.

* * *

Chapter Twenty-Seven

Time: 7.45pm

Date: Monday 18th February 2013

Location: M3 motorway

The journey was meant to take approximately two hours, but Jack didn't have two hours. He had activated the blue lights on his dashboard and floored the Ford Mondeo, taking it to speeds that it hadn't experienced in many years. Isabel clung to the dashboard, her knuckles white, but she was otherwise silent.

Jack checked in with the local station, and they confirmed that back-up would be meeting him on scene. He estimated that he would be there in another forty-five minutes, so long as the Mondeo held up. Late at night, the road was quiet, so he pushed the speedometer past 100mph. He glanced sideways to see Isabel's ashen face, her eyes staring wildly out of the windscreen ahead. She didn't let go of the dashboard.

"Don't worry" he murmured, his eyes now fixed on the road ahead. "I've done advanced driving training – we'll be fine."

Isabel nodded, but maintained her claw-like grip.

* * *

Time: 7.45pm

Date: Monday 18th February 2013

Location: St Bartholomew's Home for Boys, Christchurch

Hesitating in the doorway, the room looked almost the same as he remembered - even the mattress was still there in the centre. They hadn't even had the decency to remove it. It made him shudder to even look at it. Pinching his eyes between his thumb and forefinger, he tried to rid himself of the vision of Danny Hopkins' broken body lying there...just lying there...pale and limp.

His feet had rooted to the spot the last time he was here, just as they were now. He forced his legs to move forward, edging around the mattress, keeping his distance, not wanting to touch it.

Just like he had before.

Danny's face had been ghost-white. His eyes stared, emptily, towards the dirty ceiling, where nothing but a single lightbulb covered in cobwebs was hanging. The lightbulb was now long gone, but he could still see the lifeless eyes of his friend, despite the darkness that had followed him into the room.

He tore his gaze away from the dirty, stinking mattress – certain he could still see Danny's blood or worse stained on its surface – and took in the rest of the room. It, too, had piles of musty bedding rolled up at the back, stacked one on top of the other. He considered that they could come in useful and went to drag a bundle out towards the corridor.

Now it was time to end things.

Once and for all.

* * *

Time: 7.45pm

Date: Monday 18th February 2013

Location: St Bartholomew's Home for Boys, Christchurch

Mac landed, softly, in a room that looked like it might have been some sort of office when the hospital wing had been open. Maybe it had been a doctor's office, he mused, taking in the shelving that wrapped around the walls, and the dusty tomes that still lay lop-sided and abandoned in amongst piles of yellowing paper.

What had once possibly been a desk lay in pieces, discarded by the door – a pile of broken and splintered wood, coated by a thick layer of dust and dirt. He stood, lingering by the window, unsure of his bearings. But he was sure he was in the right place.

He would be here.

Somewhere.

Just as Mac was about to move, there was a loud bang – the sound of a door slamming or something hard crashing to the floor. It made his fast-beating heart thump even more wildly inside his chest. More thudding and scraping noises followed, metal on metal, slicing through the air and causing him to shiver as his hairs stood on end.

His legs felt heavy, his muscles devoid of strength. He thought about what Jack would do.

Jack.

It was now that he wondered if he should have told Jack where he was going. Maybe his brother could have helped him? Good old Jack. Dependable Jack. Good-in-a-crisis Jack.

But, no – he had followed his usual hot-headed response to a problem, and decided he could handle things by himself.

He was on his own, whether he liked it or not.

He only hoped Isabel was all right. He hadn't meant to hurt her, but he knew that he had. The stirrings inside his head, the memories flooding his brain, the nightmares he had shut away for so long – she shouldn't have to cope with that. Nobody should. He thought he had managed to bury St Bartholomew's, locking it away, out of sight.

But he had been wrong.

The banging and clattering was getting louder and more intense, before it ceased just as quickly as it had started – a surreal silence then filled the air. Mac was still rooted to the spot by the window.

He was definitely here.

Willing his legs to move, Mac crossed the room and headed out of the solitary door next to the mangled desk. Peering out, he saw a short corridor that ended in a ninety-degree bend. The noises had been coming from that direction, so Mac edged along the wall and poked his head around the corner.

For a moment, he was unsure what he was seeing.

Hospital beds lay tipped onto their sides, stacked haphazardly one on top of the other. Together with the metal chairs, they lay strewn across the corridor from one side to the other, creating a metal mountain. In between the assortment of beds and chairs, random bundles of what looked like bed linen had been stuffed into various gaps and crevices.

Mac edged closer, stumbling over a discarded chair. He pulled himself up and over the first metal barricade, scrambling over the bare metal legs of a hospital bed and dropping down the other side. More beds and chairs were scattered along the length and breadth of the corridor, and he picked his way in between them. He headed towards one of the doorways where he thought he could hear movement.

Movement and something else.

What was it?

He paused and sniffed the air.

It smelt like petrol.

* * *

Time: 8.05pm
Date: Monday 18th February 2013
Location: Ringwood, Hampshire

"I'm about thirty minutes away, at a guess," said Jack, swinging the Mondeo onto the A338 at 60mph. The roads were still deserted, not a bad thing as he careered onto the opposite carriageway. Isabel's fingers were still clamped, tightly, to the dashboard. "Any news on the local units?"

"They're about to arrive on scene in ten minutes, and will await your instructions, boss," replied DS Cooper, his voice crackling through the hands-free set. "They say they would have got there sooner, but there's been an incident in Poole and they were diverted."

Jack nodded, his eyes still fixed intently on the road ahead as he swung around a tight bend. The tyres of the Mondeo rumbled across the cat's eyes as he took the bend wide to maintain his speed. "OK, Cooper. I'll let you know when we get there."

Jack ended the call and stamped down hard on the accelerator, a look of determination on his face.

"How does it feel?" Isabel glanced sideways at Jack. "Being back here?"

Jack managed to shrug and shake his head at the same time. "I haven't been back this way much, that's true. I don't tend to think too much about my time here, to be honest."

"But the past has a way of catching up with you doesn't it?" Isabel's face was still ashen and drawn, the glow from the street lights as they passed gave her a haunted look.

"I guess you know all about that." Jack tried a smile as he eased the car down to 40mph, pulling onto a smaller road not far from St Bartholomew's. "I know it won't mean much to you right now, but I really don't think you have anything to worry about from Kreshniov. I don't pretend to know what game he's playing, but...I really don't think he means you any harm." The road stretched out into the night and Jack pushed the Mondeo back up towards 60mph, isolated houses flashing past them in a blur. "He's had plenty of opportunity to harm you if that was his aim. I don't know, he's just..." Jack's voice petered out. Who was he trying to kid? He could no more get inside Boris Kreshniov's head than he could his own brother's.

"And what about Mac?" Isabel asked the question Jack had been fearing for the whole duration of the journey. "What's going on with him? It's like...one minute he's the Mac I know, and the next..." Isabel gave a shrug, her shoulders starting to tremble with a fresh bout of tears. "I just don't think I know him anymore. And what is he doing all the way out here?"

Jack swung the car onto a single lane track nestled in-between deserted fields and hedgerows. He had no answers and didn't try to make any up. The silence was interrupted by the hands free phone chirping with an incoming call.

"Guv?" DC Cassidy sounded breathless. "You need to hear this."

Jack turned up the volume and slowed the Mondeo. "Go on."

"Toby Harrison." DC Cassidy paused. "That's him. That's our Harry."

Jack's eyes widened. "Toby Harrison? You're sure?"

"Positive. We found him on the St Bartholomew's admission records, out of sequence. Everything fits. Arrived in 1981 aged twelve. Left when the home closed; when he was aged sixteen." DC Cassidy paused and Jack could hear the rustling of paper and muted voices in the background. "We're trying to trace him now – he doesn't appear to have a police record, though."

"Good work." Jack's heart thudded faster in his chest as he swung the Mondeo around a blind bend in the single lane track. Stu had been right all along. A mixture of relief and guilt washed over him. He hadn't been lying about Harry. Jack should have trusted him.

"That's not all, guv." DC Cassidy's voice crackled back onto the line. "I got The Laurels to send over the rest of their visitor log books for the last twelve months. Toby Harrison visited his grandfather once a month, without fail. Ernest Harrison – room E18."

Jack let the information sink in while he squinted through the darkness ahead. Room E18 was right next door to Edward Wakefield. And within spitting distance of the faulty fire exit door. "Great work, Amanda. Both of you. Let me know the minute you manage to trace him."

Jack cut the call.

They were nearly there.

* * *

CHAPTER TWENTY-SEVEN

Time: 8.05pm

Date: Monday 18th February 2013

Location: St Bartholomew's Home for Boys, Christchurch

Mac stared, open-mouthed, at the huddled figure crouching before a stained and dirty mattress. The whole place reeked of petrol.

"Harry – what in God's name are you doing?" Mac stepped into the room, holding one hand over his nose and mouth to ward off the fumes. His eyes quickly darted around the windowless space. He noted the floor was drenched, as was the mattress. Three discarded petrol cans lay on their sides.

Toby Harrison looked up and smiled.

"Mac! Maccy-boy, you made it!" His dark eyes danced, wildly, as if fuelled by something akin to the petrol sloshing around their feet.

"*What* are you doing?" repeated Mac, fear and horror sweeping his body.

"I'm ridding this place of evil. Danny should never have had to come here...the things they did to him." Toby's voice cracked. "Do you know what they did to him in this place?" His eyes bore deeply into Mac's, tunnelling ferociously until Mac had to look away. "Do you?"

Mac nodded. "Yes, I know. You told me, remember?"

"I saw what they did to him. I *saw* it, Maccy!" Toby gestured to the room around them. "It was in here, you know. In this very room." He pushed himself to his feet. "On this very mattress. This is where they snuffed him out. They didn't even have the decency to get rid of it." Toby kicked at the mattress with a dirty boot. "They just let him die right here, then picked him up and dumped him in the woods. *They made me watch.*"

Toby's voice caught in his throat. "I stood in those woods while they buried him beneath leaves and twigs like he was nothing more than an animal..."

* * *

Time: 1.45am

Date: Monday 15th March 1982

Location: St Bartholomew's Home for Boys, Christchurch

"Stand there and don't move!" Edward Wakefield's menacing tone cut through the otherwise stillness of the cold night air.

Toby Harrison's legs trembled. He felt sick, but had already vomited up the entire contents of his stomach and there was nothing left except acid. He choked back the acrid taste and wiped his mouth on his sleeve.

"I don't even want to hear you breathe." Edward Wakefield glared at Toby before turning his attention to the other two figures standing behind him. Terence Wakefield's pasty face had a thin sheen of perspiration, giving him a wax-like appearance in the moonlight. His father had told him to carry Danny Hopkins' limp body over his shoulder and trek the one and a half miles to the fringes of the woodland that skirted the grounds of St Bartholomew's.

And Terence always did what his father told him.

"Start digging." Edward Wakefield thrust a rusty spade towards his son. "We don't have all night." He knew that the woods were a haven for dog walkers – early morning dog walkers – some even setting out before the sun was up.

Toby Harrison watched as Terence Wakefield began to shovel earth from beneath a wide-bodied tree. The ground was frozen and hard. It had been an exceptionally dry winter with not a drop of rain, freezing or otherwise, gracing the landscape for weeks. The sheen of perspiration on Terence's brow now turned into droplets of sweat.

All the while, Danny Hopkins lay lifeless on the cold ground at Edward Wakefield's feet. The man barely gave the boy a second look.

Toby felt himself sway as the nausea rose up once again inside him and he turned away, unable to look at poor Danny's broken body. Instead he started to whimper.

"I thought I told you to keep quiet!" Edward Wakefield's thunderous voice spat towards Toby, making him flinch. Within seconds, Edward Wakefield was at his side, grabbing hold of both of his arms in his vice-like grip. "Shut up! Stop snivelling!"

Toby then felt himself propelled forwards so that his face was mere inches from Danny's still form.

"Unless you want to end up like your friend here, keep quiet! I don't want to hear another sound."

With a final thrust of Toby's head towards the ground, Edward Wakefield turned away to oversee the digging of the makeshift grave. The other figure, hanging back in the shadow of the trees, Toby recognised as the portly gentleman who had dragged Danny to his death in the hospital wing. He, too, looked somewhat shell-shocked, his face white and blotchy. Saying nothing, he merely twisted what looked like a jumper or sweatshirt in his hands, wringing it like it was a damp tea towel.

Toby staggered backwards and leant up against a nearby tree trunk, his legs quivering like unset jelly. He wiped his eyes on the Swap Shop scarf that hung loosely round his neck.

"It's no good, the ground's too hard." Terence Wakefield flung the spade onto the ground with a thud.

Cuffing his son around the ear, Edward Wakefield grabbed the spade and began stabbing at the frozen earth. "You're useless. Bloody useless!" With a final smack around the head, he sent Terence flying onto his knees.

Grunting with effort, Edward Wakefield put all his weight behind the spade, forcing it, time after time, into the ground. After a minute of frenzied digging, he threw the spade angrily onto the hardened ground, blood dripping from his hands.

"Just drag him over!" he yelled, kicking at the ground with his boot. "Cover him up! Now!"

Terence scrambled to his feet, cowering beneath his father's imposing shadow.

"Put his clothes back on first." Edward Wakefield threw Danny's clothes at his son. "You. Help him." He glared at Toby, his eyes bulging with anger. "NOW!"

Toby staggered away from the sanctity of the tree, tears cascading down his cheeks. He watched in horror as Terence Wakefield proceeded to pull Danny's underwear and jeans back over his limp legs. His tiny body flopped like a rag doll, rigor mortis not yet setting in. Terence wiped his brow as more droplets of sweat dripped down onto Danny's jeans.

"I said help him!" Edward Wakefield picked up Danny's t-shirt and thrust it towards Toby's quivering form.

Toby took the t-shirt in his trembling hands and tried to place it over his friend's head. The tears in his eyes made everything around him blurry. As he leant in closer, the Swap Shop scarf fell forward onto Danny's body.

"For God's sake, hurry up! The pair of you are useless!" Edward Wakefield bent down, pushing Toby out of the way, and began pulling Danny's yellow t-shirt over his head, forcing his arms through the sleeves. Blood from his blistered hands smeared across the bottom hem. He wiped the rest on Danny's jeans and looked up. "You see this here?" He nodded down at Danny's body. "You breathe a word of this to anyone – ever – and you'll end up just like him. Understand?!"

Toby nodded, ashen-faced.

"I said, *DO YOU UNDERSTAND*?!" Edward Wakefield's voice echoed around the woodland. His eyes bulged and spit flew from his mouth as he shouted across the top of Danny's body.

"Y...yes." Toby's voice shuddered. "I...I understand."

"You tell *NO ONE*. You hear?" Edward Wakefield pushed himself to his feet and glared across at Toby. "You tell *NO ONE*. You trust *NO ONE*." Wrenching the Swap Shop scarf from on top of Danny's chest, he flung it towards Toby with a venomous look.

Toby nodded, and watched as Edward and Terence Wakefield slung Danny's body into the shallow grave and began dragging leaves, twigs and branches across to cover his pale body. Before Danny was completely covered the portly gentleman, who had been hovering in the shadows, stepped forwards and handed Edward the sweatshirt he had been holding so tightly. The name on the label was clearly visible – 'Adrian McLeish' – and Edward tossed it in beside Danny's partially covered body.

After a few minutes, with Danny's body covered by enough twigs, leaves, branches and chilled earth, Edward Wakefield grabbed hold of Toby's arm and dragged him out of the trees, back in the direction of St Bartholomew's. He leant in close to Toby's ear.

"You tell no one."

* * *

Time: 8.05pm
Date: Monday 18th February 2013
Location: St Bartholomew's Home for Boys, Christchurch

"They made me watch."

Mac nodded, still staring horror-struck at the petrol-soaked mattress. "Yes, I know," he whispered, his own voice cracking. "But you know what would have happened if we had told anyone...they were evil, Harry. Remember what they said. *Tell no one. Trust no one.* They were evil."

Toby nodded, slowly, then threw his head back and began to laugh, manically. "Yes, yes they were! And now they are all dead!" The glint had returned to his eyes. "I told you I would make them pay! And I did. And so now you know why this place can't be left standing. This is the final part of the plan, Mac. Very soon it will all be over – all the pain and suffering will be gone and we can all rest in peace." He paused and looked back towards Mac, who was still hovering in the doorway. "I'm actually quite glad someone else is here with me, at the end."

Mac frowned. "The end?" He watched as Toby brought a box of matches out of his pocket and deftly lit one. He let the flame flicker, teasingly, in front of him before he tossed it down on to the petrol-soaked mattress.

Mac stood back, horrified, and screamed. "Jesus, Harry! What are you doing?!" He leapt to the side, and it was then that he noticed he was standing in a puddle of petrol, and the liquid had soaked into the bottom hem of his jeans, almost up to his ankles.

Toby sprang out of the way of the fire that quickly erupted and engulfed the mattress. His eyes danced wildly in the flames as he lit two more matches, tossing them both into the far corners of the room and watching the pools of petrol ignite.

Mac stumbled backwards out into the corridor, already feeling the searing heat. "Harry...!" he spluttered, the heat catching at the back of his throat. "Stop..."

Toby sprinted out of the room that had once seen the dying breath of Danny Hopkins, and flung two more lit matches into the doorway. He pushed past Mac, knocking him sideways, and ran towards the tangle of beds, chairs and bedding strewn across the corridor. Mac tripped over an abandoned chair, landing on his hands and knees. He could only watch, helplessly, as Toby threw more lit matches towards the makeshift barricade. Flames roared up, eagerly consuming their liquid feast, spreading rapidly from one side of the corridor to the other.

Mac scrambled to his feet, conscious that his hands were now soaked in petrol. He could do nothing but watch as Toby ran, manically, up and down the corridor, throwing matches towards bundles of petrol-soaked bedding, laughing hysterically as the fire raged around them. Within seconds, the whole corridor was alight – a searing wall of flames beating down on them.

Mac searched frantically for a means of escape – but all he could see was fire, and all he could feel was intense heat starting to prickle at his skin.

He looked down and saw that the petrol had soaked up to his knees.

* * *

Time: 8.45pm

Date: Monday 18th February 2013

Location: St Bartholomew's Home for Boys, Christchurch

As Jack neared the farm track that would lead them up to St Bartholomew's, he noticed blue flashing lights in the distance ahead. Good. The local unit must have arrived, he thought, glancing at the dashboard clock. The last fifteen miles had taken him longer than he had hoped. He floored the Mondeo and drove as fast as the rutted track would allow towards the top of the hill, and swung in behind two marked police cars, their doors open and lights flashing.

It wasn't until Jack flung his own door open and stepped outside that he could smell the burning.

And then he saw the flames.

"What the...?" Jack ran towards the rusted gate, but was faced with two uniformed officers blocking his path.

"We can't let you go in, Sir," said one of the officers, holding up both of his hands to bar Jack's progress. Nodding his head over his shoulder, he continued. "Looks like the place has been alight for a while – we've called for the fire brigade and they'll be here in minutes. But until then, we can't allow you inside the grounds."

Jack stared, open mouthed, at the imposing Victorian building looming up into the dark sky above; flames stabbing high above what was left of the roof.

"Where...?"

"Looks like it's at the rear, Sir," answered the officer, still standing his ground at the rusty gate. "The old hospital wing out the back is our guess. It's the only part of the original building that's been left standing."

Jack felt his knees shake and gripped hold of the wire fence that encased the grounds to steady himself.

"But my brother..." He cast a glance over his shoulder towards where he saw Mac's motorbike parked in the mud next to a dark coloured Vauxhall.

Unmistakeable.

His brother was here.

"My brother," continued Jack, his throat closing in on him. "My brother – he must be in there." He made another attempt to move forwards, but was held back by the same officer.

"Jack?" The voice was faint, but floated through the air like the flames dancing before them. "Jack?"

Isabel came into focus, edging around the front of the Mondeo, and stumbling over the uneven ground. Jack turned to see her gazing skywards at the raging inferno in front of them, the light of the flames reflected back in her glassy eyes. Her face drained of even more colour, if that were possible, and her bottom lip began to tremble. "Jack?" she repeated, lurching forwards and grabbing hold of his arm. "What...?"

Jack pulled her in close and turned her away from the flames. The heat of the fire was palpable on their skin, even from this distance, and just as he pulled her in even closer, an enormous explosion ripped high up into the night sky.

* * *

Chapter Twenty-Eight

Time: 9.05pm
  Date: Monday 18th February 2013
  Location: St Bartholomew's Home for Boys, Christchurch

Jack and Isabel watched, helplessly, as the fire crews broke down the wire fencing to gain access to the burning building. Fiery-orange flames shot high into the sky, casting pieces of burning debris down around them like hot rain.

Three fire engines drove as far as they could around the side of the main building and were now directing huge jets of water towards the inferno. The two police officers who had been standing guard at the gate had now disappeared and Jack took the opportunity to disentangle himself from Isabel and rush through the cordon. He ran towards the chaotic scene at the rear of the home, managing to get as far as the doorway to the Elizabeth Building before his progress was halted by the fire crew.

"We can't have you back here, mate," shouted one firefighter, attempting to herd Jack backwards. "It's not safe. That structure could go at any minute."

The noise from the raging fire and the engines pouring water on the flames made communication almost impossible without shouting. Jack held his hands up and took several steps backwards, not once taking his eyes off the scene of devastation playing out before him. The heat was intense, and was already making his skin prickle and his eyes water.

"My...my brother...," replied Jack, straining to be heard above the chaos. "He's in there..."

The firefighter shook his head, lifting the protective visor of his helmet. "You still can't be here," he replied, his voice roaring above the noise. "You need to step back."

Jack stumbled backwards, watching the flames pouring out of each and every window. The roof had been breached and was now also ablaze. He nodded, and retreated further back towards the shadows and away from the intense heat, the firefighter turning his attention back to the job in hand. Jack watched a dozen firefighters scattering around the blazing building, aiming giant powerful hoses to disgorge torrents of water directly into the open windows and up onto the burning roof. The whole building was awash with flames, and all Jack could do was look on.

Even in the shadows, the heat was still growing in intensity, but Jack felt his feet were fused to the spot. He couldn't move, even if he wanted to. The air was now filling with smoke and Jack brought an arm up to over his nose and mouth, the soot tickling the back of his throat. He could hear the garbled shouts and commands wafting over the smoke-filled air, as firefighters coordinated their efforts to control the blaze.

A team of six firefighters rushed past Jack, dressed in full protective gear and breathing equipment, heading for the back of the burning hospital wing. He felt his legs start to give way and forced himself to retreat, stumbling over his own feet as he did so.

Isabel.

He needed to get back to Isabel.

* * *

Time: 9.10pm
 Date: Monday 18th February 2013
 Location: St Bartholomew's Home for Boys, Christchurch

Alan Barnes, Station Manager for Southern Fire Brigade, had been a firefighter for twenty years. In all that time, he had never seen anything like this.

Ever.

The inferno was raging out of control, taking no notice of the powerful water jets pummelling the flames. Whatever had started the fire was clearly not running out of fuel anytime soon; if anything, it appeared to be accelerating. It was very quickly turning into a fruitless exercise, and he knew it. Despite that, he rubbed the soot and sweat away from his brow and pulled on his breathing apparatus, and followed his team of six to the rear of the building.

After arriving on the scene, he had been given reports that one person was inside – apparently the brother of the detective inspector he had seen hovering, ashen-faced, at the entrance. If the initial survey of the scene had been correct, gaining control of this fire was likely to be futile – it would very quickly turn into one of containment and then a recovery exercise.

He shook his head as he rounded the corner towards the rear of the building. "No one can survive this," he murmured to himself, his voice muffled beneath his breathing apparatus. "No one." As he approached his team, his earpiece crackled into life.

"Way in located. I repeat, way in located."

The rear of the hospital wing had been protected from the main body of the fire; the heat was noticeably decreased and only some of the upper windows were showing signs of fire activity, flames licking at the rotten window frames. His team were centred around a rear lower-ground window, at present untouched by fire.

"Update," commanded Alan Barnes, reaching the window where four firefighters remained, two having entered the burning building. "Update your positions."

Several seconds passed before his earpiece crackled once more.

"Not good, sir," came the reply. "Body located. Male. Deceased."

* * *

Time: 9.20pm
  Date: Monday 18th February 2013
  Location: St Bartholomew's Home for Boys, Christchurch

Two more fire crews and an ambulance had now joined the throng, their blue lights blinking and strobing across the burning shell of St Bartholomew's. Isabel clung to Jack inside the Mondeo, her whole body quivering. He reached into the back seat and pulled across a discarded jumper, wrapping it around her shoulders in a fruitless attempt to warm her up. Although the night was cold, he knew her shivers were not due to the icy temperatures, and no amount of extra clothing was likely to help.

His own body shook, and he gripped the steering wheel for stability while gazing out of the windscreen towards what now looked like a war-zone. Flames had now spread across to the main building and were making short work of the already decayed structure. Fire licked, greedily, through the open windows and across the collapsed rooftop.

More firefighters were now appearing around the front of the home, retreating from the rear hospital wing. One firefighter, perhaps the one in charge mused Jack, was waving his crew back towards the comparative safety of the entrance, his arms gesticulating back towards the gravel drive.

They were pulling back.

The structure was no longer safe.

Jack felt his stomach clench.

He felt sick. So very, very sick.

The firefighter he had seen rounding up the crew continued past the Mondeo and jogged towards the flattened perimeter fence and the waiting ambulance. After a few words, the paramedics got back into their vehicle and the firefighter waved the ambulance through, heading towards the hospital wing.

They didn't seem to be in a rush.

CHAPTER TWENTY-EIGHT

They had turned off their flashing blue lights.

Jack watched the firefighter turn towards the Mondeo, and for a moment their eyes met.

The expression on the firefighter's face told Jack all he needed to know.

* * *

Time: 9.25pm

Date: Monday 18th February 2013

Location: St Bartholomew's Home for Boys, Christchurch

Jack persuaded Isabel to remain in the Mondeo while he slipped out and made his way across the weed-strewn front entrance and around to the rear. He rounded the corner and saw the ambulance parked up between two fire engines, its rear doors wide open, a waiting stretcher on the ground.

The firefighter Jack had seen earlier was waiting by the side of the ambulance, apparently listening to communications via his earpiece. Jack caught the firefighter's eye once again, and found the burly, six-foot man striding towards him, a grave expression on his face.

"You can't be here," the firefighter announced, gesticulating back towards the fire still raging out of control behind them. "This structure is about to collapse at any moment." He paused and held out a gloved hand. "I'm Alan Barnes – Station Manager."

Jack hesitated a moment before taking hold of the proffered hand. He noticed the grave look on the firefighter's face had now softened, and was replaced with one of sadness and compassion.

Why is he looking at me like that? thought Jack, as the two of them slowly shook hands. "I'm DI Jack MacIntosh," he replied. "I'm...my brother..."

Alan Barnes nodded. "I know." He looked over his shoulder at the waiting ambulance crew. "If you want to be here you'll need to wear this." In his other hand he carried a spare helmet with protective visor, and held it out for Jack. "And stay back. This place could go at any time."

Jack nodded and pulled the helmet onto his head.

Alan Barnes turned away and walked back towards the waiting paramedics. Jack saw that water was still being thundered into any visible openings from the high pressure hoses, but the fire still seemed to be raging out of control. He again felt the heat start to singe his skin. Looking past the ambulance and fire engines, Jack saw two figures emerging from around the corner of the hospital wing, carrying what at first looked like a charred and blackened sack between them. As they got closer, Jack saw that it wasn't a sack at all – it was a body.

The firefighters approached the ambulance, their faces beneath their breathing apparatus looked grim. Jack watched as they carefully lay down their cargo on the waiting stretcher and then stepped back. Jack found himself walking forwards. He wanted to see, yet he didn't want to see. He wanted to know, but he really didn't want to know.

Jack had been in the police force a long time, and attended enough accident scenes to know that when paramedics didn't rush to approach a body on their stretcher it was because there was nothing they could do. He coughed to clear his throat of the smoke that was irritating him, and strode more quickly towards the ambulance.

He caught the eye of Station Manager Alan Barnes, who for one moment held up a hand to indicate Jack needed to stay back – but then relented and nodded to Jack to approach the stretcher. Despite the chaos still raging around them, the air around the ambulance was still and almost serene. It felt to Jack as though he had stepped into a bubble, cut off from the world outside, where nothing and no-one could touch him. It was a place just for him; and for Stu. One last time together.

He forced his eyes towards the stretcher and clenched his fists, pressing his nails into his palms to try and feel some sort of pain – anything to take away the rising feeling of panic surging inside him. The body was blackened and burned. Any exposed skin and tissue peeled away from the underlying bone; the body's fat had melted to feed the flames. Whatever clothing Stu had been wearing had been burnt clean away.

Jack brought a hand to his mouth, forcing the bile back down. The face was unrecognisable; the fire had ravaged every facial feature to leave only charred bone behind.

"I'm sorry." Alan Barnes appeared at Jack's side, and placed a gloved hand on his shoulder.

Jack nodded, but couldn't drag his eyes away from the charred remains. He wanted to stay inside his bubble for just a bit longer. As he took in the scorched body once again, he noticed that one side was less damaged than the other, as if it had had some sort of protection. Maybe Stu had been lying on his side, protecting that part from the flames. Although not much was left, an area of the right upper arm was exposed and still had a covering of skin.

Jack blinked and peered more closely.

The smell of burning flesh hit the back of his throat and he began to gag.

Holding a hand up to his nose, he took another step towards the stretcher.

* * *

Chapter Twenty-Nine

Time: 9.35pm

Date: Monday 18th February 2013

Location: St Bartholomew's Home for Boys, Christchurch

"It's not him." Jack stumbled back from the stretcher, his eyes wide. "I tell you, it's not him."

A frown crossed Alan Barnes' blackened forehead. "But you said...?"

"Yes, I *know* what I said," replied Jack, his voice catching in his throat. "I thought he was alone...but this...this isn't him." He paused and nodded towards the unidentified body. "Stu has a tattoo – on his right upper arm. It's not there. It's not him."

Both Alan Barnes and Jack looked past the ambulance and back to the raging fire still consuming the hospital wing.

"Shit," replied Alan Barnes, pulling his protective helmet back on. "He's still in there."

Jack was manhandled out of the way and told in no uncertain terms to stay back and don't try to go inside. Jack watched as Alan Barnes ran back towards the rear of the burning building, shouting instructions as he went, and grabbing his breathing apparatus. Looking up at the flames still spewing out of each and every crevice in the disintegrating building, Jack shuddered. Going inside was not something he was planning to do. Instead he followed the Station Manager around to the rear of the hospital wing, his heart thumping inside his chest.

Stuart was still inside.

Jack watched as Alan Barnes coordinated his team at the same window they had entered through previously. More flames were now pulsating through the upper windows, smoke billowing out to create a dusty fog all around them. Jack put a hand to his mouth to stifle the cough at the back of his throat, feeling his eyes start to water.

"Two minutes!" commanded Alan Barnes, shouting to be heard above the noise of the fire. "That's all we have. Then I want you all back out. No arguments. And switch your comms on."

Two firefighters, breathing apparatus in place, immediately dragged themselves into the open window, disappearing into the smoky blackness beyond. Alan Barnes looked across at Jack and held his gaze for a second before pulling himself into the blackened hole and out of sight.

* * *

Time: 9.40pm

Date: Monday 18th February 2013

Location: St Bartholomew's Home for Boy's, Christchurch

The corridor was so thick with smoke that Alan Barnes couldn't see more than a foot in front of him. He could see and feel the fire still raging across what looked like some sort of homemade barrier of now twisted and melted metal. The flames were not abating, despite the torrents of water flooding into the building. The blaze was still consuming everything in its hungry rampage.

They inched forwards along the corridor, the wall of ferocious heat hitting them squarely with every step they took.

"The other one was found just here." The firefighter at the head of the small group indicated to the base of the burning barricade of twisted metal hospital beds and chairs. "Looks like he tried to climb through it."

Alan Barnes nodded beneath his visor and edged forwards. Peering through the flames he could just about make out entrances to two or maybe three more rooms; each one was thick with fire, flames raging around the doors. The heat was immense and the air was toxic. What oxygen there was, was being devoured, greedily, by the encroaching flames. Even if they managed to find a way through the burning barricade, there was no way anyone could be found alive beyond. And if they managed to get through, they may very well not get back again, protective equipment or no protective equipment.

"Hold up," he commanded, his voice crackling through everyone's earpiece. "We're not going to get through that." He shook his head. "Everyone retreat."

* * *

Time: 9.43pm
Date: Monday 18th February 2013
Location: St Bartholomew's Home for Boys, Christchurch

Jack saw the firefighters jumping down from the window, one by one, empty handed. They hadn't been gone long, but every second had felt like an hour. As the final firefighters retreated and passed him by, the knot in his stomach tightened as the sudden realisation hit him.

Stuart was still in there. And Stuart was dead.

Visions now flashed through his mind in a cascade of memories - his mischievous smirk; his laughter; his smile; his infuriating energy.

All gone.

Snuffed out.

Just as his knees began to buckle, he saw the same two paramedics from earlier hurtle around the corner, one carrying a spinal board, the other shouldering a cumbersome medical bag. Shouts followed from all directions, but before Jack could regain his balance, Alan Barnes' head appeared in the window. He had something draped over his shoulder.

Laying the spinal board down onto the rough ground, the two paramedics scrambled into positon – one took the feet, the other took the shoulders, of what Jack could now see was another charred body.

* * *

Chapter Thirty

Time: 10.45pm

Date: Monday 18th February 2013

Location: The Forest District Hospital, Nr Christchurch

The A&E Consultant leant forwards, forearms resting on the cluttered desk. "He will need to be transferred as soon as he is stable." Dr Shah's expression was grave. "He needs a specialist burns unit."

Jack nodded. "We'll follow in the car." His voice sounded cracked and hollow; his throat sore from breathing in so much smoke. He turned towards Isabel. She still clung to his arm, unable to let go. "Won't we?"

Isabel gave a nod. "Will he...?" Her voice trembled. "Will he be...?" She couldn't find the strength to finish the sentence, shuddering as yet more tears slid down her already saturated cheeks. Her grip on Jack's arm tightened.

Dr Shah gave a sympathetic smile. Jack watched as the Consultant's deep brown gaze seemed to follow the tears escaping Isabel's reddened eyes. A gaze that must have looked upon many a distraught relative or loved one, and had to deliver equally horrifying news, time and time again. Jack felt himself shudder.

"It's too early to say," replied Dr Shah, the tone of his voice soothing and comforting. "Mr MacIntosh has suffered 45% burns, mostly third-degree. I won't lie to you – third degree burns to that extent are often fatal." He paused to let the horrifying news sink in. "But the paramedics did an excellent job at the scene. Getting fluids into him quickly is of paramount importance. Dehydration is a big factor in burn survival. We will be stabilising him here, and then he will be transferred to London. He will need quite extensive skin grafting." Dr Shah hesitated, shifting his gaze to Jack. "He has a long road ahead of him if he is going to survive – he is at risk of sepsis, septic shock, organ failure and not to mention any wound infections post skin grafting."

Jack nodded his thanks, the doctor's words washing over him.

"Can...can I see him?" Isabel looked up, her wide eyes brimming with yet more unshed tears. "Before...before he goes?"

Dr Shah nodded. "Of course. I'll take you through now."

Jack and Isabel were led through the A&E Department towards the treatment rooms at the far end. The journey was short. They snaked past the queue at the reception desk and in between the plastic chairs of people waiting to be triaged. They were taken through a set of double swing doors that bore the name 'RESUS' and were confronted with a scene straight out of a medical TV drama.

Mac was lying in a hospital bed, head against the wall, surrounded by banks of monitors and screens. A hand flew up to Isabel's mouth and Jack felt her swaying by his side. Mac was surrounded by four doctors, all in blue scrubs, each focused intently on their patient; none of them seemed to notice that they had two additional observers. Bags of fluid were hanging by Mac's bedside, and several lines were leading into his veins. His charred clothing, what had been left of it, lay discarded in a heap on the floor where it had been cut from his body.

Dr Shah gestured that Jack and Isabel could approach the bed. "We've sedated him, and are giving more IV fluids. Thankfully, he doesn't have much in the way of damage to the lungs, and his airway is more or less clear. He is breathing on his own, which is a good sign. The worst burns are to his arms, legs and torso."

Isabel took a hesitant step forwards. One of the attending doctors stepped to the side and gave her an encouraging smile.

"Is he...?" Isabel took in Mac's stricken body and felt her heart heave. "Is he in pain?" Her voice was no more than a whisper.

The doctor at her side shook her head. "No, he won't be in any pain right now. He's had some strong painkillers, but...often when burns are quite deep, such as these, the nerve endings are damaged so he won't be feeling pain in the usual sense."

Isabel nodded and swallowed back her tears. Stepping forwards, she placed a trembling hand on a heavily bandaged arm. Jack hovered in the background, watching as Isabel tenderly covered Mac's hand with her own. He could see that his brother's face appeared to have escaped the worst of the flames – some singeing to the hairline, some scorch marks to the cheeks and chin – with sterile surgical gauze only placed across his forehead. The rest of his body was covered – and for that, Jack was thankful. He had seen many burn victims before, and the sight was anything but pleasant. The monitor at Mac's bedside, recording his vital signs, was beeping rhythmically and reassuringly.

"We'll be moving your brother as soon as the transport has been arranged," spoke Dr Shah, who remained at Jack's shoulder. "He'll be comfortable enough for the journey. The doctor at the other end will reassess him and take you through the next steps of his treatment."

"You mentioned skin grafts?"

Dr Shah nodded. "Yes. They could be quite extensive. The plastic surgeons will explain what that entails."

Jack managed a faint smile to acknowledge this thanks. "Is he...can he talk? Can he hear us?"

"He has been lightly sedated, but it is very likely he can still hear you." Dr Shah motioned for Jack to step forwards. "By all means try."

Jack hesitated for a moment, listening to the steady beat of the monitors, before stepping closer to Mac's bedside. Isabel still had hold of one of his bandaged hands, still tenderly stroking its surface. With two of the attending doctors making way for him, Jack bent his head closer to Mac's pillow – the unique aroma of charred human skin was more intense the closer he got. He wrinkled his nose.

"Stu?" Jack's voice was barely audible above the beeps from the monitors.

"Stu?" He raised his voice, and leant in a little closer. "Can you hear me, Stu?"

Jack paused, watching his brother's face for any signs of recognition, any clue that he was still conscious. To begin with there was nothing and Jack was about to turn away when he saw a momentary flutter of his eyelids.

"Stu?" Jack leant closer. "You can hear me, can't you?"

Both Mac's eyelids fluttered once again, slowly opening into the barest of slits. At the same time, his lips began to twitch.

"Stu...it's really important. If you can hear me – I need you to tell me who else was with you tonight." Jack paused, watching for any further movement. The seconds ticked by agonisingly slowly. "I need a name, Stu."

No sound came from Mac's lips, but his eyelids opened another fraction.

"It's important, Stu," persisted Jack. "Just nod your head if it's who I think it is." Jack caught Isabel's gaze across the bed before turning his attention back to Mac. "It was Harry, wasn't it? At the foster home tonight? It was Toby Harrison, wasn't it?"

The question hung in the sterile air for what seemed like eternity. The monitor recording Mac's heart rate began to beep faster, attracting a concerned look from one of the attending doctors. Jack continued to study his brother's face, watching as his eyes fluttered open and he stared directly out towards the ceiling.

"It was Harry, wasn't it?" Jack repeated, keeping his voice low and steady. "Toby Harrison."

In between the beeps from the rapidly beating heart rate monitor, Mac slowly began to nod his head.

* * *

Time: 2.40am
Date: Tuesday 19th February 2013
Location: The Forest District Hospital, Nr Christchurch

Jack stepped outside the entrance to the A&E Department and, not for the first time that night, wished he still smoked. Despite the chill, several slipper-clad patients sat on a low wall beneath a 'this is a no smoking site' sign, pulling greedily on their cigarettes. Their hospital gowns flapped around their bare, exposed legs, their IV drip stands motionless by their sides.

In two minds whether to go over and see if anyone would offer him a cigarette, Jack instead turned away and drifted towards a set of concrete benches. He rubbed his eyes, his fingers and hands still embedded with the aroma of smoke and charred flesh. As he made to sit down, he noticed a figure leaning up against a lamp post by the ambulance bay. Sensing his presence, the figure looked up and the two men locked eyes.

Station Manager Alan Barnes acknowledged Jack with a nod of the head. "Need a caffeine hit?" He raised his takeaway coffee cup. "There's a machine, just inside the door."

Jack shook his head. "No, thanks. I'm fine."

Alan Barnes took a sip of the coffee, closing his eyes as he did so. Jack noticed the firefighter's face was still smudged with soot, black streaks across his forehead and cheeks. He was still dressed in his firefighting gear, although minus the breathing equipment. The smell of smoke still lingered.

"He OK?" Alan Barnes opened his eyes and turned towards Jack. "Your brother?"

Jack hesitated and gave a shrug. "So far. They're moving him soon, to a specialist burns unit in London. Once they can find a bed."

Alan Barnes nodded, gravely. He had seen the extensive burns on Stuart MacIntosh's body as he dragged him out of the burning building.

"Thanks for getting him out." It sounded lame, but it was all Jack could think to say.

Alan Barnes, predictably, brushed aside the compliment. "Part of the job, mate. I hope he makes it."

Jack shuddered. The thought that Stu might not pull through caused a chill to ripple through his body.

"He almost got out, you know." Alan Barnes stepped over towards the concrete benches and sat down next to Jack. "I found him close to the back of the building. He'd managed to crawl through the barricade and looks like he found an old WC. I nearly missed him, the smoke was so thick." Alan Barnes paused. "He'd turned all the taps on, and looks like he tried to douse himself in water. I reckon that might have bought him some time."

Jack felt his heart squeeze.

Alan Barnes continued. "It was one of the worst scenes I've been to in a long time." He gave Jack a faint smile. "I really hope he makes it." With exhaustion seeping from every pore, the firefighter stood up and tossed his coffee cup into the bin. "I've a couple of lads in getting checked over for smoke inhalation. I'd better go see how they're doing. I'll see you."

Jack nodded as Alan Barnes turned away and headed back to the front entrance. As he did so, Jack saw Isabel's tiny frame waving at him.

* * *

Time: 7.05am
Date: Tuesday 19th February 2013
Location: The Forest District Hospital, Nr Christchurch

The drive to the West London Acute Burns Unit would take a good couple of hours, with the ambulance carrying Mac being blue-lighted all the way. Jack had informed the travelling paramedics that they would meet them at the other end, and nodded as the emergency vehicle's doors were closed. He had his own blue lights in the Mondeo, but felt that maybe he and Isabel would prefer a less frantic journey back to London.

As they crossed the car park in the breaking dawn light, Jack's mobile began to vibrate in his pocket. He stifled a yawn as he pulled it out, expecting it to be DS Cooper requesting an update, but instead it was an unknown number. Hesitating momentarily, wondering whether to answer it or not, Jack hit the 'accept' button.

"Yes?" Jack unlocked the Mondeo and motioned for Isabel to get inside, out of the chill early morning air. She balanced the cardboard tray of takeaway coffee on the roof before opening the passenger door.

"DI MacIntosh?" The voice was faint, and Jack had to place his fingers over his opposite ear to cut out the noise of the departing ambulance. Faint, but vaguely familiar.

"Yes? Speaking."

"It's Jennifer – Jenny Davies. From the lab."

It was then that Jack was able to place the faint Welsh lilt from the other end of the phone. "Ah, Jenny. What can I do for you?" He glanced at his watch, noting the time.

Jenny Davies paused, and Jack took the opportunity to open the Mondeo's driver's door and slip inside out of the icy wind that was whipping across the car park. He took hold of the hot coffee Isabel passed towards him and took a sip.

"It's that DNA sample you asked me to work on – the one from 1971? Stella MacIntosh?" continued Jenny. "The tissue under the victim's fingernails?"

Jack froze with the coffee cup underneath his nose, the steam from the scalding liquid billowing out in front of him. With everything that had been happening, he had pushed that particular DNA request to the back of his cluttered mind. "You have a result?"

Another slight pause. "I do...of sorts," replied Jenny, her voice faltering slightly. "It's a little strange though, I'll tell you that."

Jack's chest tightened. "Strange in what way?" He recognised the familiar feeling of disquiet in the pit of his stomach.

"Well...we've managed to isolate a decent DNA strand from the sample..."

"You have DNA?" interrupted Jack, his eyes widening. "You managed to get DNA from the tissue sample?" His hand holding the coffee cup began to tremble, slightly. "I thought it might have been a long shot – the sample was so old."

"No, the sample was in good order. Kept in ideal conditions – it was as good as the day it was obtained."

The day of my mother's post mortem, thought Jack. "Go on."

"Well, as I said, we got a good DNA sample. I ran it through the system overnight. You said it was urgent, so…"

"And?" Jack almost didn't want to ask.

"We got a hit."

Jack almost dropped the coffee cup into his lap. "You did what?"

"A hit," replied Jenny, the hint of a smile entering her voice. "We got a hit."

"Well, that's…that's just amazing." Relief and disbelief in equal measures washed over Jack, the implications already running through his head at a hundred miles an hour. A hit meant a name. And a name could mean an address. And an address meant they could trace him.

It was then that he stopped, and reality returned. Jenny had mentioned something was strange. Trepidation began to creep in, displacing the elation that had been prematurely flooding in.

"You mentioned that something was strange?"

Jenny hesitated once more. "Yes…well, I'm not sure I'm the best person to explain. You should call Chris…DS Cooper. He didn't want to bother you in the early hours of the morning, not with what has happened, but…" She cleared her throat. "You need to call him."

* * *

Chapter Thirty-One

Time: 10.35am

Date: Tuesday 19th February 2013

Location: West London Acute Burns Unit, London

The Adult Acute Burns Unit was a new, state of the art facility; a stone's throw from St James's University and only a few minutes from the Metropolitan Police HQ. It rose four storeys high, with a smoked-glass frontage housing one main entrance with a motion-sensitive door. A small private road along one side led to the emergency ambulance drop off point at the rear.

Upon arrival, Jack and Isabel had been shown to the second floor, and the well-equipped private room that would become Mac's home for the foreseeable future. He had already been wheeled in on his hospital bed and was already hooked up to a number of IV drips and monitors.

All floors and surfaces were spotless; the whole building had a not-unpleasant aroma of cleaning materials mixed with fresh bed linen. Jack had decided to leave Isabel alone inside the room; she had barely left Mac's side from the moment they had arrived. She sat on the lone visitor's chair, one hand gently draped over his bandaged arm. The plastic surgeon had already been to assess, and had outlined a very detailed initial plan for the next few days.

Jack closed the door to Mac's room behind him and went in search of a quiet spot. Wandering along an empty corridor, he spied an open space next to some lifts with a variety of sofas and chairs arranged around a low table.

A large window looked out onto a quiet courtyard area with raised beds that would be full of colour in summer, surrounded by wooden picnic-style benches. Next to the lifts was a vending machine, and Jack punched the button for a black coffee, perching on the arm of a sofa while the machine spat out the hot liquid. Taking the plastic cup gingerly in his hands, already feeling the heat searing his fingers, he settled into a chair in the corner by the window. Placing the hot cup on the window sill next to a few potted plants, he pulled out his phone.

All the way back to London he had been mulling over the information Jenny had passed on, turning the words over and over inside his head, feeling them toss and turn as they approached London.

A DNA hit.

They had a DNA hit; that had been clear. But what hadn't been quite so clear was why Jenny felt it was strange. Throughout the entire journey, Jack had felt himself swinging between feelings of elation and trepidation – elated that he might at last find out the truth behind his mother's death, after all this time, but also disquiet that something was clearly not right with the result.

"Cooper?" Jack held his phone in one hand whilst taking hold of the plastic coffee cup again and taking a tentative sip. It was scalding hot still. He almost chuckled to himself at the irony of a vending machine spitting out burning hot coffee, capable of searing the skin, or worse, in an acute burns unit. He swallowed his amusement along with the boiling liquid. "Jenny rang me. From the lab. She reckons I need to speak to you."

DS Cooper had answered the phone almost on the first ring, giving Jack the impression he had been waiting for the call. "Yes, boss. Jenny worked on your sample all night."

"So she said," replied Jack, blowing across the surface of the coffee. "She mentioned you got a hit."

"We did – remarkably quickly, as it goes." DS Cooper's voice rose a notch. "These things can take days sometimes, but we got a hit after only a few hours." DS Cooper paused. "I saw the name on the sample, boss. Stella MacIntosh. I've kept everything off the system, you know...so no one else knows."

"I'm grateful for your discretion, Cooper." Jack cleared his throat. "So, what can you tell me?" He tried another sip of the black coffee, desperate for the caffeine hit. His head was fogging over now he had stopped driving, and exhaustion from the night's events was beginning to return. "Jenny said something about it was strange?"

DS Cooper could be heard rummaging amongst paperwork in the background. "Well, yes. It was. Strange, I mean." He paused, and Jack heard more rustling of paper. "So, the DNA result got a hit – a James Quinn. Running his name through the database showed us that his DNA was taken back in 1998, after a series of burglaries. He served three and a half years, released at the back end of 2001."

"OK." Jack sipped more coffee, frowning as his head continued to thump. "Anything else?"

DS Cooper continued. "Well, we couldn't find anything else on the system for him until he was declared deceased in 2002."

"Deceased?" Jack swallowed a mouthful of hot coffee too quickly, wincing as it scalded its way down to his stomach. His heart sank. "So, he's dead then?"

"Well, this is the strange part." DS Cooper rustled more paperwork. "Obviously, his fingerprints were on the system too, taken at the same time as the DNA. And these have been flagged up as being present at the scene of several more burglaries in 2005 through to 2010. Fingerprint analysis at the time said that the match was in the region of 99%."

Jack put the plastic cup of coffee back down onto the window sill, massaging his tired eyes. "Run that by me again, Cooper? I'm not sure I follow…"

"James Quinn is recorded as having died in 2002– but his fingerprints have shown up at several crime scenes since then." DS Cooper hesitated. "But that's not possible, is it, boss?"

"No," mused Jack, his mind starting to race. "A 99% match, you say?"

"Reports at the time say it was conclusive in their eyes," replied DS Cooper. "And that's not all."

"You have more?" Jack's heart was thudding inside his chest, any feelings of exhaustion starting to be swept aside.

"The MO for the burglaries in 2005 to 2010 match those that James Quinn was convicted of in 1998. He had a very distinctive method of committing his crimes. And..." DS Cooper paused only briefly, excitement entering his voice. "In the final burglary, in 2010, the home owner was present. It was a horrific ordeal by all accounts – he tied her up and gagged her. But she remembered a startling amount of detail about her attacker. She said that, and I quote - 'he told me that the police would never find him. He told me that he was already dead.'"

"Jesus," muttered Jack, swigging back the rest of the coffee. "What did the investigation team say at the time about the fingerprints of a dead person turning up at their crime scene?"

"They called it an anomaly, boss. The cases remain unsolved."

"An anomaly, my arse," retorted Jack, rising to his feet and dropping the empty coffee cup into a bin. "He's played us – he's played us all. Get me all you can on James Quinn and how he was meant to have died. I'm coming right over."

* * *

Time: 4.00pm
Date: Tuesday 19th February 2013
Location: Metropolitan Police HQ, London

Isabel had been happy enough to stay by Mac's bedside and would update Jack if there was any change. The plastic surgeons were pleased enough with his condition, and were planning on going ahead with the skin grafting as per the treatment plan. Jack had smiled gratefully, nodded towards his brother's semi-conscious face, and then darted back to the station as fast as he could.

He still had all the reports from last night to file, and that would have to take precedence over the mystery concerning James Quinn. For the time being, at least. By the time he started uploading his reports, various interim details were flooding onto the system from the scene of crime officers at St Bartholomew's. They had seized the Vauxhall car parked at the entrance next to Mac's motorbike; a quick DVLA search confirming that it was registered to a Tobias Arthur Harrison – current address in Maidstone. Inside, they had found a mobile phone, a change of clothing, and four handwritten letters, all removed for further analysis. Initial reports also confirmed that the interior of the vehicle smelt strongly of petrol.

A CCTV camera had picked up Toby Harrison's car stopping at a petrol station just outside of Maidenhead, and he could be seen filling various petrol canisters at the pumps.

"What I can't work out is why Stu was there." Jack filed his last report and sighed. Tiredness was again encroaching on him and he rubbed his eyes. He had sunk two strong coffees as soon as he had got back to the station, courtesy of DC Cassidy, but the caffeine had yet to take effect. "Or even if this Toby Harrison character really meant to burn himself down along with the foster home."

DS Cooper clicked the whiteboard screen. "Crime scene reports say there was enough petrol inside to incinerate the place ten times over. The fire service will do their own investigation, but I can't see it being anything other than intentional. And as for Toby Harrison..." DS Cooper brought up four thumbnail photographs onto the screen. "These have just been uploaded. The handwritten letters found in the car. One is addressed to whom we assume is his wife – someone called Cassie – and two are addressed to what is believed to be his children."

Jack raised his eyebrows. "What do they say?"

"They pretty much give concrete proof as to his intentions – he wasn't planning on coming out of there alive, that's for sure."

Jack frowned again. "But why was Stu there? I can't get anything out of him at the moment, he's too sedated, but..." Jack shrugged and shook his head. "I don't understand that piece of the puzzle."

DC Cassidy had been quietly looking through her notebook. She leant across the investigation room table and took control of the mouse. "I've been looking into the mobile phone data that's been analysed already." She clicked the screen. "An initial crude look at Toby Harrison's phone showed that he had been in touch with all four members of the Fifteen over the last twelve months or so."

"The lying gits," commented Jack. "They swore blind they never knew anyone called Harry, or whoever he was meant to be."

"It looks like there were several phone conversations between them all, but most of the communication was by text message. The most recent messages to each of the Fifteen basically requested that they deny all knowledge of him."

"Which they did," grunted Jack, tiredness affecting his mood. "And Stu, too?"

DC Cassidy nodded. "Looks like he was sent the same messages as the others, yes, but..." She paused and bit her lip.

"But what?"

"The last couple of messages on the phone were to your brother, asking to meet. One said 'meet me tonight – you know where.' The last one said 'come now'."

"St Bartholomew's," murmured Jack, nodding slowly. "But why? I still don't know why. Why was Stu singled out?"

DS Cooper took the mouse and clicked back to the thumbnail pictures of the letters found in Toby Harrison's car. "That might be answered by the content of one of the letters – the one addressed to Cassie." DS Cooper double-clicked on the image of one of the letters and the screen was filled with a page of scrawling handwriting. "He mentions that he has carried around a horrific secret all these years – he goes on to mention Danny Hopkins, so we are pretty confident that's what he's referring to. He goes on to say that he's had to live with the knowledge that an innocent man is in prison for a crime committed by others. He then goes on to name them – Edward and Terence Wakefield, and a person he had never seen before. He gives an account of witnessing the murder of Danny Hopkins – or at least the immediate aftermath – and how Eddie Wakefield threatened to do the same to him if he breathed a word to anyone."

"And Stu?" pressed Jack. "Does he mention my brother?"

"Not in so many words," replied DS Cooper. "But he finishes the letter by saying that he only confided in one other person about the events of Danny Hopkins' murder. Someone he trusted. And together they had to bear the guilt and horror of the true knowledge of what went on that night."

"Stu," breathed Jack, nodding to himself. "He must have told Stu."

* * *

Time: 3.30pm

Date: Monday 15th March 1982

Location: St Bartholomew's Home for Boys, Christchurch

Toby Harrison pushed his wheelbarrow towards the compost heap. His arms ached and the sun was hurting his eyes. The Matron had phoned the school to say that he wouldn't be attending that day, and probably not for the rest of the week, either. A regular occurrence by the look of his attendance record, but the school appeared unconcerned. They were used to receiving calls about the boys from St Bartholomew's being unwell.

And it was true. He was unwell. The bruises on his shins and his back were testament to that.

He tipped the weeds onto the compost pile and wiped his brow with the back of a dirty hand. He preferred it here anyway; away from the jeering looks and cat calls that he was subjected to most days. Boys from foster homes, and especially St Bartholomew's, made you an easy target. You were fair game for every bully this side of the New Forest.

Toby turned the wheelbarrow around and headed back to the vegetable patch. He still had two rows of carrots, turnips and sprouts to work through, and he didn't want to get on the wrong side of Edward Wakefield. Not today. Not after last night.

Glancing up through the sunlight, he saw a familiar figure running towards him.

"Quick, the greenhouse!" Mac grabbed hold of Toby's arm and dragged him across to the door of the nearest greenhouse, pushing him inside.

"Jesus, Mac, what are you doing?" Toby hurriedly looked around outside for any sign of either Wakefield. "I'll get whipped again if I don't finish this weeding."

"Never mind that. I managed to nick these from the kitchen!" Mac laughed and threw a cold sausage roll at Toby. "Quick, eat it before they realise it's missing!"

Toby hesitated, his stomach growling but feeling no appetite even for his favourite sausage roll.

"Come on, Harry." Mac spoke with his mouth full. "What's up?"

"I need to tell you something." Toby nibbled at the corner of his sausage roll. "About last night."

Toby took the next five minutes to relay the horrors that he had witnessed the night before, and to tell Mac that their friend Danny Hopkins was dead. The look on Mac's face mirrored Toby's – all colour draining from his cheeks, a feeling of sickness quickly spreading through his insides.

"We can't tell anyone, Mac. Nobody." Toby's eyes were wide and panic-stricken. "They said they would do the same to me, and to anyone I told. And they mean it."

Mac found himself nodding, his face white. He now very much regretted the sausage roll.

Toby grabbed his friend by the arm. "You tell no one. You trust no one. Only me. Got it?"

Mac nodded, silently, no words able to get past the lump in his throat.

Toby pushed his uneaten sausage roll into his pocket. He would throw it in a bin when nobody was looking. "Oh, and here – take your scarf back." He leant across to the potting bench and grabbed Mac's Swap Shop scarf. Handing it back to him, he locked eyes with his friend. "Remember, Mac. Tell no one. Trust no one."

* * *

Time: 4.20pm
  Date: Tuesday 19th March 2013
  Location: Metropolitan Police HQ, London

"Imagine having that on your conscience," murmured DC Cassidy, her eyes watering. "It doesn't bear thinking about."

"The last letter is one addressed to the police," added DS Cooper. "It's basically a full confession of his part in the murders of Eddie and Terence Wakefield, and Albert Dawson. Explaining how and why he did it. There was a photograph attached, too."

DS Cooper clicked on a black and white image which then filled the screen. "We think that's Danny there at the front. And with him is Toby Harrison. Otherwise known as 'Harry'."

Jack peered at the picture, his eyes scanning the group of young boys huddled together on the steps to St Bartholomew's. None wore smiles. Their faces were flat and devoid of emotion. Jack's eyes came to rest on each face; faces that were now all too familiar to him.

Jason Alcock. Stephen Byers, Kyle Williams. And Stuart MacIntosh. All standing side by side on the top step.

And at their feet, with an arm draped over the shoulder of the tiny frame of Daniel Hopkins, was Toby Harrison. Jack looked into the eyes of 'Harry' and felt that all too familiar tug of recognition.

* * *

Time: 10.30am
  Date: 22nd November 1982
  Location: Bournemouth Crown Court

Jack heard the aged wooden seat creak beneath him as he strained to see past the head of the newspaper reporter seated in front of him. The sound was amplified by the muted hush that had descended, curtain-like, over courtroom number one.

"All rise." The Court Usher's clipped tone cut through the stillness, and Jack found himself rising to his feet alongside his foster mother, Mary. He glanced sideways, finding her kind and concerned face turned towards him. She had quietly suggested that maybe Jack would rather not attend the sentencing hearing, attending the trial only a few weeks ago had been traumatising enough. But Jack had been determined to go – he owed it to Stuart to see it through to the end. And he needed Stuart to finally look at him, one last time.

And so, dutifully, Mary stood by his side – supporting the foster son that had captured her heart.

Jack managed what he hoped was a smile in return.

He felt sick, really sick. He couldn't stomach any breakfast that morning and had been up as soon as the sun began to break through on the horizon. The smell of brewing coffee and pastries that had hit his nostrils from the court canteen on their way in had merely brought bile up into his throat.

As they stood, he felt his legs trembling beneath his coarse flannel school trousers; if it hadn't been for Mary's soft, yet talon-like, grip on his hand, he was sure that his knees would buckle and he would have ended up on the cold, stone floor beneath.

Jack's attention was drawn to a movement from the right side of the courtroom. Four heads appeared, procession-like, rising up from the bowels of the court just beneath the dock. The first head had very closely cropped fair hair, and Jack knew that it belonged to Jason Alcock. The leader of the gang, his face bore a defiant expression and what looked like a fresh bruise with dark purple edges just below his left eye.

Behind him came the dark curls that belonged to Kyle Williams. No look of defiance graced his face – Jack could only see fear and dread etched onto his drawn features. Wild eyed, he glanced around the courtroom, desperately searching for a friendly face.

Next in the solemn procession came Stephen Byers. With a tall, sinewy frame, he towered over both boys before him. Jack noticed that his face, too, sported a fresh lump beneath one eye – mirroring that of his co-defendant – a lump so fresh that it was forcing his left eye closed. He stood stock-still, staring ahead without any expression on his face; looking straight out across the sea of bobbing wigs before them, hands behind his back as if on military inspection.

Jack craned his neck to get a clearer view of the fourth defendant. As during every day of the trial some three or so weeks earlier, Stuart MacIntosh brought up the rear and stared resolutely at his shoes. Jack willed him to look up, to catch his eye, even just for a fleeting glimpse; just so that he could tell his brother that everything would be all right.

Jack had no idea if things would be all right – he suspected that they wouldn't but he needed his baby brother to look at him. Just once. Even if just for a second.

But Stuart MacIntosh remained with his head lowered, and his face hidden.

Whilst the defendants were filing into the dock, flanked by two security guards, His Honour Judge Trowbridge shuffled in from his private chambers and sat down behind his raised bench with an audible sigh.

Jack felt his foster mother's hand tighten its grip, squeezing reassuringly as they resumed their seats.

"In the matter of Regina versus Alcock, Byers, Williams and MacIntosh, court is now in session. Will the defendants please remain standing." The Court Usher turned towards His Honour Judge Trowbridge and passed him a thin, manila folder.

The judge leant forwards in his seat and cleared his throat, the fleshy jowls that flanked his face wobbled in time with his movements. A pair of pale blue, watery eyes peered out from behind a pair of wire-framed spectacles, and lowered their gaze to the paperwork in front of him. Opening the folder and pausing only to turn over the first page, he raised his gaze to address the dock.

"You each stand before me, convicted of the offence of robbery – contrary to Section 8 of the Theft Act 1968. One of you, Jason Alcock, have also been convicted on manslaughter, contrary to common law."

His Honour Judge Trowbridge paused, allowing the gravity of the situation to sink in. The court room remained in total silence as he turned his head and nodded at one of the wigged barristers on the benches before him.

"Mr Harcourt? I trust you wish to outline the facts of the case."

Jack listened as the prosecution barrister, a tall, thin man dressed in black robes, proceeded to inform the court how the defendants had meticulously planned the robbery; how they brought weapons, such as baseballs bats and knives, to the scene, and how they had terrorised the shopkeeper, leading to him suffering a heart attack from which he later died.

Jack tuned out the barrister's dull tones and fixed his eyes on Stuart, noticing how he still refused to look up, still staring intently at the courtroom floor. Jack's mouth felt dry and his heart continued to bang, painfully, inside his chest. He gripped Mary's hand a little tighter.

With the prosecution barrister concluding his outline of the facts, each defence barrister got to their feet to offer mitigation for their clients. The courtroom heard how each defendant came from the local foster home, with no mother or father figure in their lives. Mention was made of a failing education system that allowed them to skip classes and then slip through the cracks and be forgotten. A lack of discipline and moral guidance was blamed.

His Honour Judge Trowbridge looked unimpressed. He nodded as the last defence barrister took their seat. The row of reporters sat in front of Jack had their pens hovering above their notepads – those that frequented courtroom number one already knew that His Honour Judge Trowbridge did not suffer fools and was renowned for his less than lenient sentences.

You could hear a pin drop before the judge cleared his throat and began.

"This is one of the most disturbing cases that has ever had the misfortune to grace my courtroom. On 10th May this year you each took the decision to travel to the Wellington Stores in Christchurch with the sole intention of committing the crime of robbery. You took an empty holdall bag with you, to fill up with your stolen wares. This was not a spur of the moment decision. This crime was planned in advance and each of you knew your involvement.

You took baseball bats and knives with you, subjecting the shopkeeper to an unprecedented level of violence and intimidation. Mr McCormack was so terrified that he later collapsed with a heart attack. A subsequent cardiac arrest and he was unable to be resuscitated."

His Honour Judge Trowbridge paused and looked back up at the dock. Both Jason Alcock and Stephen Byers continued to stand up straight, hands behind their backs, their stony stares fixed on the wall opposite. No emotion crossed their features. Whether they were listening to anything being said within the courtroom's walls was unclear, their expressions gave nothing away. The smaller stature of Kyle Williams stood between them, his eyes flicked nervously between his barrister before him and the public gallery.

Jack noticed that the smaller boy appeared to be trembling.

Gripping his foster mother's hand even more tightly, Jack leant forwards and focused on his brother's motionless form on the far side of the dock. During the whole of the prosecution's speech, and his own defence barrister's mitigation on his behalf, he refused to look up or even acknowledge where he was.

As throughout the trial, Stuart MacIntosh's gaze remained fixed on the floor at his feet.

"I have in my possession a probation service report on each of you. And whilst I will take into consideration the mitigation afforded to you on your behalf by your legal representation today, including your backgrounds and your young ages, this in no way exonerates any of you from responsibility for your own actions. Each of you had the opportunity to turn back, but you did not." The judge paused again, glancing back down to the wigged heads on the benches that were hanging onto his every word. "As I am sure that you will already have been advised by your legal teams, I have no option but to impose a substantial custodial sentence on each of you."

Jack's heart was thumping inside his chest. His stomach clenched tighter and tighter, the overwhelming feeling of nausea once again welling up inside.

Look up, Stu. Look up.

"Jason Alcock," continued the judge. "You alone have been convicted of the offence of manslaughter. For this I sentence you to eight years' imprisonment. For the offence of robbery, I sentence you to a further eight years' imprisonment – to run concurrently."

The hushed silence of the courtroom deepened. Those that had been fidgeting in the public gallery, sat stock-still, frozen in time. The reporters' pens hovered silently over their notepads, not making a sound. Breaths were held. If it had been possible, hearts would have stopped beating.

"Kyle Williams," His Honour Judge Trowbridge continued. "You have been convicted of the offence of robbery. I take into account that this is your first offence and your previous good character. I sentence you to six years' imprisonment."

The trembling that Jack had seen in Kyle Williams' legs increased, and his tear-rimmed eyes widened in shock. Jack watched as he grabbed the wooden railing in front to steady himself.

"Stephen Byers."

Jack watched as the tallest defendant straightened his posture, pinning back his shoulders and puffing out his chest. He set his cold, steely eyes dead ahead, defiantly sticking out his chin towards the judge. Stephen Byers knew what was coming. It was hardly going to be a surprise.

"You have been convicted of the offence of robbery. I sentence you to eight years' imprisonment."

Jack saw a brief movement to his left, at the end of the public gallery seating area. He glanced sideways to lock eyes with a dark haired boy about his own age who was struggling to stand up, being restrained by a large, burly man at his side. The boy wriggled and tried to pull his arms free from the vice-like grip around his shoulders, the sound of their scuffling drawing the attention and a disapproving look from the court usher.

"Stuart MacIntosh." Jack's head whipped back round to face His Honour Judge Trowbridge, all thoughts of the boy thrashing around in the public gallery evaporating in an instant. His heart felt like it was about to leap out of his mouth. The judge's words echoed in his ears and he again tightened his grip on his foster mother's hand.

"You have been convicted of the offence of robbery. I sentence you to eight years' imprisonment."

Jack again strained to see his brother's face. At the mention of eight years, Jack briefly saw the mop of hair rise slightly – eyes peering out from beneath the unruly fringe. He gasped as he saw the deep cut to Stuart's lower lip and the surrounding crusted blood.

Jack couldn't be quite sure, but for a brief moment he thought he saw his brother's eyes flicker towards his own. Just for a split second. But then, as brief as the glimpse had been, if it had even been there, it was gone.

"Take them down," bellowed the judge, already gathering up his paperwork and glancing at the clock.

The Court Usher nodded towards the security guards in the dock, and the four defendants turned to walk in single file back the way they had come – back down to the depths of the cells beneath. Jack slid closer to the edge of his seat, still straining for one more sighting of his brother before he disappeared from view.

"Tell them!"

The shout rang out across the quiet courtroom, causing people to jump in their seats and whip their heads around to the cause of the outburst. "Just tell them!"

Jack turned his head towards the commotion, watching as the young lad he had seen earlier leapt out of his seat in the public gallery and hurtled down the three steps towards the floor of the courtroom. The man who had been at his side and tried to restrain him, merely grabbed at thin air as the boy evaded his clutches.

Several of the barristers jumped to their feet, their wigs dislodged by their sudden movement. They quickly whipped their black gowns around them, as if they offered some form of protection, seeking to distance themselves from the intruder. Heads turned towards two thick-set security guards who sprang across the courtroom from their positions at the door, both lunging towards the slightly-framed boy who was making a dash towards the dock.

For that was where he was headed.

The dock.

Jack continued to watch open mouthed and speechless, as he saw the boy engulfed by both security guards, iron-like grips locked around his shoulders forcing him to the floor. His legs buckled and he hit the stone floor with a thud.

His Honour Judge Trowbridge was whisked away from the commotion by the Court Usher, hurriedly disappearing back through the internal door that led to his chambers. His sentencing duties complete, he was not keen to hang around and witness the aftermath it had caused.

The pandemonium was over in a matter of seconds, and calm was restored to court room number one. Not one of the four defendants had so much as blinked an eye as they continued their procession down into the cells and out of sight.

"Tell them!" The boy's words were muffled now, as he lay beneath the heavy-set security guards, face down on the cold floor. "Tell them what they did!"

The reporters that had been sitting on the benches in front of the public gallery had already whipped out their notebooks and begun to scribble an extra few paragraphs to their otherwise mundane reporting of the sentencing in court number one. The unexpected excitement would liven up their afternoon submissions to their editors and maybe earn them a printable piece on page four or five instead of languishing at the bottom of page fifteen underneath a piece on a missing tortoise.

"Come on, Jack," murmured Mary, guiding Jack out of the public gallery and towards the exit. "I think we've seen enough for today."

Jack shuffled to the end of the row of seating and followed his foster mother towards the door. As he did so, he cast a brief look back over his shoulder, watching as the wide-eyed and distraught boy was unceremoniously dragged to his feet.

For a split second the two boys' eyes met.

* * *

Time: 4.40pm
   Date: Tuesday 19th February 2013
   Location: Metropolitan Police HQ, London

It had been Toby Harrison, 'Harry', that Jack had seen all those years ago. The young boy who had created such a commotion at the sentencing hearing that he had to be restrained by security guards.

Jack would recognise those eyes anywhere. He looked back at the black and white photograph, where Toby Harrison's arm was draped across the shoulders of Daniel Hopkins.

What had he been shouting in the courtroom? Tell them? Although he could never be sure, Jack had a feeling that he knew what the young Toby had meant by his outburst.

Tell them.

Jack sighed and rubbed his eyes. "Good work, both of you. We got there in the end." He rose to his feet and stretched, hearing his back click. "I'm going to step outside for some air."

"And Adrian McLeish? What happens now with the Daniel Hopkins case?" DC Cassidy looked up as Jack made his way towards the door.

"Technically not our case, but I'll make sure everything finds its way to the right people." Jack flashed DC Cassidy a smile. "Don't worry. With Toby Harrison's confession and the evidence that he discloses about the Wakefields' role in Danny's death, plus the DNA evidence, he'll not spend a day longer in prison than he needs to. I'll make sure of it." Jack stepped out into the corridor, slipping on his jacket. "And while I'm gone, just find out where we are on notifying Mrs Harrison – we'll need to get a family liaison officer out there if it hasn't yet been organised. Have a chat with the local force."

"Will do, boss," replied DC Cassidy, reaching for her notebook and jumping to her feet to follow Jack out into the corridor. "Just one more thing, remember when we went to see Adrian McLeish?"

Jack nodded.

"Well, I phoned the prison for their visitor log books – guess whose name crops up as Adrian's only other visitor apart from his mother?"

"Toby Harrison," breathed Jack, nodding as he remembered Adrian McLeish's excited tones.

'*My name is Adrian – my friends call me Ade. My friend Toby calls me Ade. He comes to see me.*'

"Good work. See - you need to apply for that promotion." Jack gave DC Cassidy a wink. "And the two of you take a break. Go home if you need to. You look like you've been up all night like me. We can catch up again tomorrow." Jack turned and headed towards the stairs. It was true, he needed some fresh air – but in reality there was someone he needed to see.

* * *

Chapter Thirty-Two

Time: 6.45pm

Date: Tuesday 19th February 2013

Location: HMP Belmarsh, Thamesmead, South-east London

Interview room one looked and smelt the same. The air had the aroma of another dousing with industrial strength disinfectant, causing the back of Jack's throat to begin to itch. But it was marginally better than the smell of death from the mortuary.

Jack had barely had a chance to sit down when the door sprang open. Warren Jamieson led Jason Alcock over to the metal table, giving Jack a sly glance as he did so.

"This is getting to be a bit of a habit," grinned Alcock, waiting while Warren unclasped his chain and clipped it back onto the metal ring embedded in the table. "I'm seeing more of you than I do my own cell mate!"

Jack nodded his thanks to Warren, who retreated without a word to the corridor outside.

"To what do I owe this pleasure, then?" Jason Alcock slipped into the metal chair opposite Jack. "Not that I'm complaining. It gets me out of my cell. It's nice to see someone else's face for a change."

Jack noticed that Alcock's face had healed since the last time he had visited. The cut above his eyebrow had now formed a hard, crusty scab, and the purple bruising to his cheeks had now yellowed. But the gap in his teeth remained. "You keeping well?" Jack nodded towards Alcock's face. "No more scuffles?"

Jason Alcock grinned again, the gap between his teeth visible. "You know me, Inspector. Model prisoner, that's me."

Jack felt a smile ghost his lips. "Well, I'm glad to hear it."

For a few seconds the two men sat across from each other in silence. The only sound was a faint clunking from a hot water pipe somewhere, and the clinking of Alcock's handcuff chain.

It was Jack who spoke first. "Thanks for the note."

Jason Alcock's eyebrows hitched up a notch. "Note?" He feigned surprise, but the smile plastered to his lips gave him away. "What note?"

"The note. The postcard." Jack brought the simple white card out of his pocket and placed it on the metal table. "It was most kind of you."

Alcock held up his hands in mock surrender, the handcuff chain scraping across the table. "I don't know what you're talking about, mate."

Jack's lips twitched. "I know it was you."

"You know what was me?" Jason Alcock's eyes glinted.

Jack tapped the postcard. "Tipping me off about Danny Hopkins."

"Danny who?" Alcock raised his eyebrows again and tried to suppress his grin.

"You'd never make a poker player, Alcock. It's written all over your face."

Jason Alcock shook his head. "How did you know it was me?"

"I'm a detective. It's what I do. You got your mate Warren out there to hand deliver it." Jack paused and gave Alcock a wink. "We have CCTV on our entrances. He wasn't hard to spot." Jack slipped the postcard back inside his pocket. "But I mean it, thank you. It means a lot to the chap who's been in prison all this time; and to his family."

A cloud crossed Jason Alcock's face. "Well, no one should be banged up for something they didn't do. I'm in here because I'm guilty. It's my fault, so I can live with that. But to be in prison for something you didn't do..." Alcock shook his head. "Nah, it didn't sit right with me."

"Did you know what Toby Harrison was planning?" Jack fixed his eyes on Alcock from across the table. "That he was going after the Wakefields, to get his revenge? Revenge for Danny?"

Jason Alcock held Jack's gaze and didn't blink. "Do I need my solicitor present for this little visit?"

Jack felt the smile return to his lips and shook his head. "No, no solicitor. I'm just interested."

Alcock sighed. "Well then, no. None of us knew. I mean, I knew he was around. He messaged all of us a few times, but he never said nothing. Nothing about the Wakefields. He just wanted us to deny we ever knew a Harry."

"Which you did."

Jason Alcock smiled. "Well, technically I didn't know anyone called Harry. His name was Toby." His grin widened and he gave Jack a shrug. "Telling the truth, me."

Jack shook his head. "It's fine, I get it. Was he a member of the Fifteen? Toby?"

"Nah. The Fifteen was just us four. That was the God's honest truth. He would hang around with us sometimes, but he was never one of The Fifteen. Not really. He thought he was, but he wasn't."

"But he shared your room? Room fifteen?"

"Towards the end, yes. It wasn't long before we all got banged up. He was so excited when Wakefield had slung him in our room, but it didn't last long. Within a month or so, we were gone."

* * *

Time: 9.30pm
   Date: 10th May 1982
   Location: St Bartholomew's Home for Boys, Christchurch

Toby Harrison sat on the mattress and looked around the bare walls of room fifteen. He had been so excited when Edward Wakefield had dragged him up the stairs by the collar of his t-shirt and thrown him inside. It had been the happiest day of his life. Even when the snarled threat of "tell no one" was barked in his ear, it didn't dampen his spirits. He was with his friends. He was with The Fifteen.

But now he was alone.

He stared vacantly at the damp walls and shivered. The mattress they had all shared was now empty and cold. Pulling the thin, moth-eaten blanket around his shoulders he curled up and lay down on his side.

His friends were gone. And they wouldn't be coming back. Edward Wakefield had said as much, laughing gleefully as he relayed how they had all been arrested and were looking at long stretches behind bars. They were unlikely to get bail, so they wouldn't be coming home; not for a long time. Maybe not ever.

Turning over, Toby pulled the blanket closer around him. As he did so, he felt something beneath him. He wriggled and managed to pull it out.

A smile crossed his lips, despite his sadness.

Mac's Swap Shop scarf.

Toby wrapped it around his neck.

He would look after it for him.

He wouldn't let it out of his sight.

* * *

Time: 7.15pm

Date: Tuesday 19th February 2013

Location: HMP Belmarsh, Thamesmead, South-east London

Jack pushed himself up from the metal chair, feeling how his legs had gone numb in just half an hour sitting on the cold, hard surface. "You take care now." He held out his hand across the table. "You need anything; you know where I am."

Jason Alcock hesitated, then slowly extended his arm and shook Jack's hand. "You too, Inspector."

Jack nodded and made his way towards the door. He was about to rap on the door to get Warren's attention, when he heard the clinking of handcuff chains as Jason Alcock turned round in his seat.

"How's Maccy?" Jack turned to see Jason Alcock's pensive face. "I heard there was a fire. Last night. Back at the foster home."

Jack felt a lump form in his throat as the events of last night washed over him. He was in desperate need of some sleep; his body ached and his eyes were red and sore. He could also still smell the faint aroma of smoke. He didn't bother to ask how Alcock knew what had happened at St Bartholomew's. As he said, news travelled like wildfire within these thick walls.

"He's doing OK." Jack tried a smile. "Stable, I think is the term they use. Sedated, for now."

Jason Alcock nodded, any cockiness evaporating. "Well, you pass on my good wishes. He was always a good lad was Maccy. What happened was insane."

Jack nodded once again and turned back towards the door, giving it three sharp raps to get Warren's attention.

"Indeed it was."

* * *

Time: 8.15pm
  Date: Tuesday 19th February 2013
  Location: Metropolitan Police HQ, London

Jack sat down and accepted the mug of strong coffee. He needed it. He felt like he had been hit by a train, exhaustion taking over.

"You look like shit, Jack." Chief Superintendent King raised his eyebrows while he took a sip of his own coffee. "And I mean it."

Jack gave a rueful smile. "I feel like shit, Sir."

"Your brother?"

Jack sipped the scalding coffee. "Stable. But critical. They're not sure if they can save one of his legs; the burns are so extensive." Jack's voice cracked and he took another drink.

"You need time off? You can take as long as you want, you know that."

Jack shook his head. "I've only just come back, Sir."

"That makes no difference with me." Chief Superintendent King held Jack's gaze. "Take whatever time you need."

Jack gave another shake of the head. "I'll carry on, Sir. I need the distraction."

"Well, if you're sure."

"I am sure, Sir. I'm fine."

"Speaking of fine." Chief Superintendent King put down his mug and began rummaging amongst the paperwork on his desk. "Dr Riches would like to catch up with you. I have her number here although I'm sure she's left you many messages." He retrieved a post-it note with the hypnotherapist's number scrawled across the middle.

"One or two, Sir." Jack accepted the post-it note and slipped it in his pocket.

"Do I need to be worried, Jack?" Chief Superintendent King sighed. "About you? About Dr Riches? She seemed a little agitated."

"Nothing to worry about, Sir," replied Jack, taking another sip of coffee, desperate for the caffeine to hit. "I'll ring her – I promise."

They sat in companionable silence for a few minutes, sipping their coffees and listening to the soft ticking from the wall clock behind the Chief Superintendent's desk. As Jack drained his mug and made to get up from his chair, Chief Superintendent King caught his eye.

"And that other issue, Jack? Do I need to be worried about that too?"

"What other issue would that be, Sir?"

"Your *hypothetical* problem. Has it been resolved?" Chief Superintendent King raised his eyebrows again.

Jack carried on standing up from his chair. He flashed a reassuring look across the table. "Hypothetically, Sir, the problem went way."

"Really?" A look of relief flashed across the Chief Superintendent's face. "So I have no cause to be concerned?"

"Not about that, Sir, no. As I say, the problem hypothetically disappeared. Forget I ever mentioned it."

Chief Superintendent King nodded. "Get yourself off home, Jack. As I said, you look done in."

Jack nodded and headed for the door. "I will. Soon. I have one or two things I need to tie up in the office first."

Once he was alone, Chief Superintendent King relaxed back in his swivel chair and sighed.

At least that was one less thing to worry about. *Hypothetically.*

Until the next time.

And with Jack MacIntosh, there would always be a next time.

* * *

Time: 9.15pm

Date: Tuesday 19th February 2013

Location: Metropolitan Police HQ, London

Jack looked at his computer screen and rubbed his eyes. The caffeine in the Chief Superintendent's coffee hadn't had the desired effect. He needed sleep, and he needed it soon. But one name kept circulating around inside his brain.

James Quinn.

Was he the man? Was he the man in the photograph?

Jack picked up the black and white photograph from his desk and looked into his mother's eyes. She beamed out towards the camera, her face alive with happiness, holding onto her two boys in front of the roundabout on a scorching summer's day. The shadow to the side then drew Jack's gaze. It seemed to be the only thing he could think about now; the dark outline of the muscular figure invaded his every waking moment and haunted him in his dreams.

James Quinn.

Jack tore his eyes away from the picture and looked across the office towards DS Cooper.

"Cooper? You don't have a home to go to?"

DS Cooper smiled, sheepishly. "I'm meeting Jenny after she finishes work."

Jack gave him a smile and a wink. "I see. Well, while you're still here, remind me what we've got on James Quinn?"

DS Cooper rummaged amongst his paperwork and pulled out a notepad. "He apparently fell overboard from a cross channel ferry in March 2002. No body was ever found. His next of kin had a declaration of death issued in 2009 – saying that he died at sea."

"Hmmm," murmured Jack, drumming his fingers on the black and white photograph. "Find out all you can on him – last known address, description if possible, employment details, friends and family, even his bloody shoe size. And search for any other burglaries or crimes that fit his MO."

"On it, boss," nodded DS Cooper, tilting his computer monitor towards him.

Jack returned his gaze to the photograph.

I'll find you, James Quinn.

No matter how long it takes, I'll find you.

* * *

Chapter Thirty-Three

Time: 3.30pm
  Date: Monday 4th March 2013
  Location: West London Acute Burns Unit, London

Jack jogged up the steps of the Adult Acute Burns Unit and entered through the sliding doors into the foyer. He decided to take the stairs – he had been sitting around all day and needed to stretch his legs.

Arriving on the second floor, Jack headed along the corridor, passed the potted plants and vending machine, and walked towards the far end. Halfway along the corridor, he noticed that the door to his brother's room was opening and a familiar figure stepped out.

Although the figure never turned around, and walked away from Jack in the direction of the lifts, he felt he knew exactly who his brother's visitor had been. Frowning slightly, he arrived at Stu's door and walked in to find his brother sat up in bed, with Isabel at his side.

"Hey, bro." Mac lifted a bandaged hand. "Pull up a chair."

Jack dragged a wooden chair across to Mac's bedside and took in his brother's appearance. He had improved beyond belief since being admitted almost two weeks ago. With the first skin graft having already taken place, he was making steady progress. He was still weak, but the doctors were cautiously optimistic, although they stressed that there was still a long road ahead.

"How are you doing?" Jack nodded at the bandages on both Mac's arms, and the IV drips of painkillers and antibiotics still hooked up. He leant across and glanced at the medical notes at the foot of the bed, but their contents meant nothing to him.

"All good. Still painful, but the morphine helps." Mac managed a smile. His face had more or less healed, with just a few red patches across his forehead. His eyebrows and eyelashes were beginning to grow back. "Physio were pleased with me this morning. I can almost walk in a straight line now, with some help."

Jack knew that the real damage caused by the fire lay underneath his brother's hospital bed covers. The first skin grafts had been performed on his legs, which had been the most badly affected by the inferno. The first of several that were planned. The grafts appeared to be taking; the doctors still used phrases such as 'satisfactory progress' and 'as expected' – however, the word 'amputation' had still been used on occasion. If the grafts didn't take, then that was still a possibility. Jack shuddered at the thought. "That's good, Stu. That's really good. But how are *you*?" Flashing a quick look across at Isabel, he turned his gaze back to his brother. "I'm pretty sure I just saw Dr Riches leaving here just now."

Jack caught the look that Mac and Isabel exchanged. "Come on, what's going on? Why was she here?"

"Jack, I..." Isabel started to speak, but Mac raised a hand to cut her off.

"It's OK, I need to be honest...with both of you." He reached for the glass of water by his bedside and took a mouthful. "It's time."

"Time for what?" Jack frowned, concern seeping into his voice. "Do I need to...?"

Mac held up his hand again. "Please, Jack. Just listen. Let me tell you in my own words. I haven't been completely honest with either of you. But after what happened..." He broke off and took another sip of water. "Dr Riches was here just now. And she was visiting me."

Jack pulled his chair closer, eyes widening.

"I've been seeing her for some therapy; since we got back from Italy." Mac looked between Jack and Isabel. "It's where I've been when you couldn't get hold of me." He paused and shook his head. "I'm sorry, I should've said something."

Jack exhaled and felt the tension leave his body. "Therapy? But that's good, Stu. You shouldn't have felt like you needed to hide it, especially from me."

Mac nodded. "I know. But this St Bartholomew's thing really started messing with my head. And with Toby too...I know I should've said something, but you know me. I like to make things harder for myself...and others." He managed a weak grin. "I know she helped you, Jack, so I gave her a call."

"She did," acknowledged Jack. "And is it helping? The therapy?"

Mac hesitated for a second and then nodded. "I think so. It's early days but...she listens."

Jack nodded. "Well, that's good. I'm pleased." As in most hospitals, the temperature in the room felt warm, so Jack slipped off his coat and loosened his tie.

"Hey, what are you so dressed up for today?" Mac nodded his head towards Jack's suit and tie and his freshly shaven chin. "You look smart for a change, bro!"

Jack glanced down at his best suit. He had even polished his shoes. "It was the first day of the Peter Holloway trial today. I've spent the best part of the day at the Old Bailey." Jack looked up and noticed the shadow that had crossed Isabel's face. "I wanted to tell you in person. I would've called, but..." He tried a reassuring smile. "Holloway changed his plea. Guilty to all charges. There won't be a trial. You won't have to give evidence. It's over."

Isabel's bottom lip began to quiver. "R...really?" She choked back the tears that were springing up in the corners of her eyes. "It's really over?"

Jack nodded. "Completely. He'll be back for sentencing in a few weeks, but by the look on the judge's face he won't be seeing daylight for the rest of his natural life."

Isabel bowed her head and let the tears trickle down her cheeks.

"Look, I'll leave you two to it." Jack got up and slipped his coat back on. "I really need to get out of this suit."

With a wave and a promise to call back later in the week, Jack left the room and headed for the stairs. As he did so, he pulled out his phone and dialled the number he had been avoiding for far too long. It was answered almost immediately.

"It's Jack MacIntosh. Returning your call." Jack paused. "Well, returning lots of your calls."

"Detective Inspector MacIntosh," replied Dr Evelyn Riches, her voice light and welcoming. "How good to hear from you. I've been expecting your call."

* * *

Chapter Thirty-Four

Time: 1.30pm
  Date: Sunday 5th May 2013
  Location: Albury, Surrey

The cherry blossom was out in abundance, lining the roadside with perfect buds of pale pink. The warm Spring sunshine and light breeze had made the journey extremely pleasant.

Boris Kreshniov smiled to himself as he swung the hire car he had just picked up into the village of Albury; a quiet, idyllic picture-postcard village nestled in the sleepy Surrey countryside.

A village he already knew very well.

He smiled again as he began to recognise the houses as he passed by, keeping well below the regulatory 30mph. He noticed the small shop and post office, the quaint country pub; the place hadn't really changed at all since he was last here. No sprawling green belt developments providing starter homes or affordable housing – the village boundaries looked just as they had done before, remaining intact and keeping the hungry planners at bay.

He nodded, satisfyingly, to himself.

Good.

He didn't like change.

He wanted things to be just like they were before.

A few hundred metres into the village, he turned down a small single track road that nestled alongside the chocolate-box church – aptly named Church Lane. Passing by the small, well-cared-for cemetery and vicarage, the car approached the end of the lane and stopped outside a beautifully maintained detached house, set back from the road amongst mature trees and gardens.

The Glade.

Isabel Faraday's childhood home.

Opening the door to step outside onto the narrow path, Boris Kreshniov looked towards the front gate which nestled into a perfectly trimmed hedge. To the side, an estate agent's board had been hammered into the ground.

SOLD

Boris Kreshniov smiled once again.

Home.

* * *

Message from the author.

Thank you for reading and I hope you enjoyed The Fifteen!

As an independently published author I am really grateful to receive reviews. Just visit the Amazon book page and click on 'write a customer review'.

To stay in touch and find out about more Detective Inspector Jack MacIntosh publications, please visit:

www.facebook.com/michellekiddauthor

www.michellekiddauthor.com – where you can sign up for my newsletter

@AuthorKidd (Twitter)

@michellekiddauthor (Instagram)

email me at michelle@michellekiddauthor.com

Acknowledgement

A huge thank you to my advance readers - Sarah Bezant, Sara Taylor, Ian White, Phil Burridge, Agnieszka Andrzejak, Peter Woods - this book would not have been possible without your help! Much love and thanks to you all!

Printed in Poland
by Amazon Fulfillment
Poland Sp. z o.o., Wrocław

64561361R00233